WILD HUNGER

Other novels by Chloe Neill

The Heirs of Chicagoland Novels

WILD HUNGER

WICKED HOUR

SHADOWED STEEL

SILVERSPELL
(An Heirs of Chicagoland Novella)

DEVOURING DARKNESS

The Captain Kit Brightling Novels

THE BRIGHT AND BREAKING SEA

A SWIFT AND SAVAGE TIDE

The Chicagoland Vampires Novels

SOME GIRLS BITE

FRIDAY NIGHT BITES

TWICE BITTEN

HARD BITTEN

DRINK DEEP

BITING COLD

HOUSE RULES

BITING BAD

WILD THINGS

BLOOD GAMES

DARK DEBT

MIDNIGHT MARKED

BLADE BOUND

HIGH STAKES
novella in *Kicking It*

HOWLING FOR YOU
(A Chicagoland Vampires Novella)

LUCKY BREAK
(A Chicagoland Vampires Novella)

PHANTOM KISS
(A Chicagoland Vampires Novella)

SLAYING IT
(A Chicagoland Vampires Novella)

The Devil's Isle Novels

THE VEIL

THE SIGHT

THE HUNT

THE BEYOND

The Dark Elite Novels

FIRESPELL

HEXBOUND

CHARMFALL

COLD CURSES

An Heirs of Chicagoland Novel

CHLOE NEILL

BERKLEY
New York

BERKLEY
An imprint of Penguin Random House LLC
penguinrandomhouse.com

Copyright © 2023 by Chloe Neill
Excerpt from *The Bright and Breaking Sea* copyright © 2020 by Chloe Neill
Penguin Random House supports copyright. Copyright fuels creativity,
encourages diverse voices, promotes free speech, and creates a vibrant culture.
Thank you for buying an authorized edition of this book and for complying with
copyright laws by not reproducing, scanning, or distributing any part of it in
any form without permission. You are supporting writers and allowing
Penguin Random House to continue to publish books for every reader.

BERKLEY and the BERKLEY & B colophon are registered trademarks of
Penguin Random House LLC.

Library of Congress Cataloging-in-Publication Data

Names: Neill, Chloe, author.
Title: Cold curses / Chloe Neill.
Description: First edition. | New York : Berkley, 2023. | Series: An Heirs
of Chicagoland novel ; 5
Identifiers: LCCN 2023016613 (print) | LCCN 2023016614 (ebook) |
ISBN 9780593549827 (trade paperback) | ISBN 9780593549834 (ebook)
Subjects: LCSH: Vampires--Fiction. | Shapeshifting--Fiction. |
Magic--Fiction. | Chicago (Ill.)--Fiction. | LCGFT: Vampire fiction. |
Paranormal fiction. | Novels.
Classification: LCC PS3614.E4432 C65 2023 (print) |
LCC PS3614.E4432 (ebook) | DDC 813/.6--dc23/eng/20230410
LC record available at https://lccn.loc.gov/2023016613
LC ebook record available at https://lccn.loc.gov/2023016614

First Edition: November 2023

Printed in the United States of America
1st Printing

I have no words;
My voice is in my sword

—William Shakespeare, *Macbeth*

COLD
CURSES

ONE

A claw swept across my face, and I felt the hot breath of hell. The monster had arrived.

I shook myself awake and stared into the eyes of my One True Enemy, who sat on my chest like a succubus. Sleek and black and glaring at me with unabashed loathing.

"*Rawr*," she said.

"What?" I asked, trying to make sense of my surroundings. "And why?"

"That, Elisa, is a cat," said the wickedly gorgeous shapeshifter currently in human form beside me. Connor Keene's hair was dark and wavy, his body toned and muscles taut. One strong arm was slung over his eyes, and a smile curved his very kissable mouth. "I'm surprised you didn't know that."

He might have been my future husband, but I gave him a look nearly as gnarly as the one I'd given the cat. "Why," I began again, with admirable patience, "is it *this* cat and why is it in this house?"

"Nothing to do with me," he said. And gave Eleanor of Aquitaine an arch look. "Cat, why are you here?"

Eleanor of Aquitaine (not Eleanor or Elle, unless you wanted scratching) belonged to, or owned, Lulu Bell, my roommate and sorcerer. But we weren't in the loft Lulu and I shared; we were in Connor's town house. Only Connor "lived" in the town house, but we'd all taken up at least temporary residence there recently. Me, because he was my future husband. Lulu, because she was my bestie and I wanted her safe. Alexei Breckenridge, because he was Connor's best friend and Lulu's (boyfriend? friend? friend with benefits?) something or other. He'd stayed over at the town house during Chicago's most recent supernatural disturbance and hadn't yet left.

And now, apparently, we'd added the damned cat.

At my apparently rude question, said cat jumped off the bed and slunk into the bathroom.

"Demon visitation complete," I said. At least until she made it into the closet and began running through our clothes like they were a joint car wash and scratching pad.

I glanced at Connor. "How are you feeling?"

He rolled his shoulder, testing. "A little sore, but I'll manage." Connor was the son of the North American Central Pack's current Apex, Gabriel Keene. Connor had already taken down three challengers in his effort to ascend to Apex when his dad retired. And they kept coming.

"Nothing tonight, right?"

"Nothing tonight," he said. "You?"

"Depends on the actual demons," I said.

I was a vampire born into Chicago's Cadogan House and an associate Ombudsman, one of Chicago's human-supernatural liaisons. Less than a week ago, we'd sealed away Andaras (aka Rose, aka Eglantine, aka "Rosantine"), the first demon to enter Chicago in two hundred years. While she was no longer a problem, she'd triggered two of the wards in the city's Victorian-era magical defense system. We were still trying to get the apparently single-use wards online again, and keep the city from being overrun by demons walking through the literal gap in our defenses. A few demons had made it through already; we were battling them as we found them now and sprinkling copious amounts of salt—a new addition to the Ombud operating procedure—across Chicago. We hadn't had a night off since we'd brought the House back, and we were basically on call until the problem was resolved.

In addition to their penchant for troublemaking and violence, Rosantine had temporarily sent Cadogan House and its inhabitants—including my, Lulu's, and Connor's parents—into another dimension. Did not enjoy; did not wish to repeat.

Connor pulled me against him, enveloped me in warmth and magic and . . . him. "Just give me one minute," he said. "And then you can yell at the cat."

I snorted. "One minute," I said, and smoothed a hand over his chest. He made a satisfied sigh and closed his eyes. There were shadows beneath them—faint, dark crescents brought on by too much magic and too much physical exertion.

"I know you don't *want* to stop until you've claimed the throne," I said. "But if you *need* to stop before you can do that, it's fine. We will find a different way to be."

He was quiet for a moment, then smoothed a hand over my long, wavy hair. "A different way?"

"Well, we could join the circus. You could be the strong man in those little glittery shorts. I'll do the trapeze. We'll live out of an RV and eat take-out Chinese."

"That's quite a plan."

"Maybe better as a backup situation. In the meantime, continue kicking their asses."

"That's the plan," he said, and kissed my forehead.

The bedroom door, already cracked, was pushed open fully by the sorceress who stepped into the doorway. Her gaze searched the room, but she ignored us—entwined as we were.

"Your minute is up," I said.

"Her Highness is in the bathroom," Connor announced. "Elisa scared her off."

"*Lulu*," I said—a question, a declaration, and a curse in two syllables.

"She was getting lonely," Lulu said, moving into the room. There was a lot of feisty spirit in that petite frame, and an apparent skill at old magic—the bloody, potentially evil kind. But the paint-spattered white coveralls, rolled up at arms and ankles, mitigated the effect. She was an artist first, a sorceress second. And until a week ago, a completely nonpracticing one. Demons had changed everything.

Lulu was currently working on a mural in Hyde Park, not far from Cadogan House.

I narrowed my gaze as she strode to the bathroom, where something made a clunking sound. "What did she destroy?" I called out.

Lulu emerged, the cat sitting queenlike in her arms. "Here, or there?" she asked with a smile.

My stare didn't change. "What did she pee on at the loft?"

"Let's just say, if pee was gold, we'd both be rich. And I hope you didn't like those pink sneakers."

"You're both very entertaining," Connor said, rolling over to reveal the smooth curves of muscle across his back. "But maybe you could entertain somewhere else?"

With impeccable timing, Alexei stepped into the room, bagel in hand. Silently, he looked at us, then at Lulu and the cat, then chewed. Like Connor, Alexei was tall and strong, with pale skin and dark blond hair. Alexei didn't talk much; he was a man of quiet loyalty who said much with his piercing hazel eyes. And knew how to back up a friend.

"And you brought her here why?" I asked.

"We can't leave her alone at the loft forever," Lulu said. "And with the demons out there, who knows how long we'll be camped out here."

"I'll deal with the demons," I said. "And your parents are working on repairing the broken wards." Lulu's parents were powerful sorcerers.

"I know. I was just saying. Nobody expects it to be immediate. Freaking demons."

"Freaking demons," Connor and Alexei muttered in unison.

Lulu stroked Eleanor of Aquitaine, who purred beneath her paint-stained fingers. While that cat wanted nothing to do with me, she plainly loved Lulu. And it wasn't my style to break up a family.

Resigned, I sighed and looked at Connor. "Your house, your rules."

"I don't have a problem with it," he said, voice muffled from the pillow. "She actually likes me."

And that stung a little. "She can stay," I told Lulu. "Just keep her out of this room. And any other room in which I might make an appearance."

"That's most of the house." Lulu's voice was flat.

"Is it?" I asked as innocently as I could manage.

My screen buzzed, and I plucked the thin rectangle of glass from the side table.

"Work," I said, and even the cat went silent. Work rarely delivered good news an hour before I made it into the office.

"Elisa," I answered. "And you're on speaker with a demon cat and the sups who enable it." This was not the time for video.

"Roger" was the caller's response. Roger Yuen was the Ombudsman and my boss. "I'm on with Petra and Theo." They were my coworkers. Petra, an aeromancer and light conspiracy theory enthusiast, and Theo, a human former cop and my partner.

"How is Eleanor of Aquitaine?" Petra asked, and the cat actually *rowr*'d a response.

"Good girl," Petra added.

"What's happened?" I asked, trying to steer my evening away from the resident demon.

"We aren't sure," Roger said. "A burst of magic was reported during the day. Looks like around three o'clock in the afternoon."

"Reported by whom?" I asked.

"We've gotten calls from nymphs who called it a 'magicky bass drop' and from a representative of the river trolls who called it a 'big loud.'"

"Checks out," Connor murmured.

"How did you get 'burst of magic' out of that?" Lulu asked, moving closer to the screen.

"ComEd," Roger said. That was Chicago's power supplier. "They recorded a power surge at the same time. There are also complaints about satellite and telecom services going down. None of it lasted for more than a few seconds. Most of the complaints went to the mayor's office, and they were routed back to us."

Connor had grabbed his screen, and I guessed he was sending a message to the Pack to see if they'd experienced anything.

"Was it a demon?" I asked, my heart beating a little faster.

"Not that we've found. The guards didn't see any activity at the wards. And there were no reports of anyone actually *seeing* anything. Just feeling it or its effects."

"Well, there was the UFO sighting," Petra said. "But we're pretty confident a UFO did not land on Soldier Field in order to steal children." She paused. "Because aliens are more interested in tech than bio, really."

"Hmm," I said noncommittally. "What about the fairies? They're magically powerful. They'd almost certainly have felt it."

And maybe their bristly queen, Claudia, would have some insight about what it was.

"Haven't heard from them," Roger said. "But that's not unusual."

"A few Pack members—those who were awake—felt it," Connor said, reading his screen. "No one can say what it was or where it originated. They just felt a sudden burst of energy."

"Something with the ley lines?" I wondered. Three of the world-spanning lines of magical power ran through Chicago. The city's demon wards were powered by cornerstones—big bespelled stones that got their energy from the ley lines and, in turn, helped regulate them.

"What could have affected them?" Theo asked.

"I don't know. Demons? Sorcerers?" I asked, looking at Lulu.

"You're asking if they could affect the ley lines? I mean, I'm not an expert, but I don't know how they could. Ley lines are pure power. I don't think sorcerers could sway them much. And if they'd done something, some kind of spell, I think we'd have felt it."

"So what should we do?" I asked Roger.

"Maybe it's nothing," Roger said. "Just a hitch in the lines because the demon wards were recently triggered. But if it's something more, I don't want it getting worse. I'm thinking patrols around the city. Maybe we won't find anything, but at least we'll have done our due diligence. Wait—you have that dinner tonight, don't you?"

Connor and I were scheduled to have dinner with his parents to celebrate our engagement.

He'd apparently asked for my father's permission despite his seemingly casual proposal, and we'd shared the news with my parents just after he'd proposed. Neither my mom or dad had been surprised, but they had been supportive and thrilled to welcome a shifter into the family.

"We can be late," Connor said.

I looked at him. "You're sure?"

He nodded. "Dinner won't matter much if demons overrun the city."

"I mean, we'll still have to eat," I murmured, but took his point.

"We can be late," he said again, this time with a smile that had me melting a little.

"Connor and I can start here," I said. "We'll talk to the fairies." I'd also need to send a message to my informant. Jonathan Black was half-elf, half-sorcerer, and an attorney with mysterious clients, at least some of whom were criminals. He'd tried to kill me; he'd also saved my life. He was an enigma.

"Petra and I will start here," Theo said, "although my arm would probably not be hella effective against arrows right now."

"Hella *deflective*, anyway," Alexei offered, chewing.

The first demon had triggered the ward that had broken Theo's arm, but a fairy had put an arrow through his leg. He was human, but as brave as they come.

"Sounds good," I said. "Want me to check with the Houses? They won't have been awake, but they may know something."

Chicago, with its three ley lines, collected sups like kids collected comics. It was home to four vampire Houses.

"You take Cadogan and Washington," Theo said. "We'll take Navarre and Grey."

"Got it. And we'll let you know if we find anything on our end. Stay safe out there."

"Same," Theo said. "But immortality probably gives you an advantage there."

He wasn't wrong.

* * *

The breakfast party was disbanded. Alexei took the last bite of his bagel downstairs; Lulu followed him. While Connor showered, I checked in with my parents at Cadogan House and Uncle Malik at Washington House. He wasn't my actual uncle, but my dad's former Second at Cadogan House, and I'd grown up with him and his wife.

Neither House, unfortunately, had anything to offer regarding the magical burst. They'd been unconscious during the day (being vampires), and the human guards who watched over their Houses hadn't felt or reported anything. I also sent a message to Black and didn't get an immediate response, which wasn't especially surprising. He operated on his own schedule.

Then it was my turn in the shower and dressing for a night of who knew what. Connor opted for his preferred jeans, T-shirt, and boots combo; I went for jeans, boots with a stiletto thin enough to double as a weapon, and a couple of thin, layered shirts to combat the coming fall chill. I pulled my long, wavy blond hair into a topknot—the better to fight with—and offered my attention to the second consciousness inside me.

There were two of us in here. In addition to me, my body housed a remnant of the spell that had bound a supernatural creature into my mother's katana two decades ago—and that had bound me to my mother, allowing her to give birth to the world's first vampire child. Lulu's mother, Mallory, had created that spell. The creature, called the Egregore, had been created by a sorcerer named Sorcha Reed. She'd been killed by her creation.

I called the remnant "monster," and its presence was a secret that only Connor knew the full truth about, as I hadn't wanted anyone else—particularly not Aunt Mallory and my parents—to know that I'd been contaminated by Sorcha's magic. Or feel guilty about any of it.

I'd only recently come to understand monster's greatest wish— being reunited with the rest of the Egregore in my mother's sword. Not, as I'd presumed, finishing the Egregore's mission of ravaging Chicago. Now that I'd finally grokked that wish, monster had become . . . naggier. It wanted out, as it frequently reminded me. But in addition to requiring from-scratch and risky magic, putting monster into the sword would require me to make a confession I'd been hiding for years. So that wasn't high on my list.

Checking in with monster usually meant ensuring it wasn't feeling anxious or hyperactive, which usually meant it needed some stretching or exercise of its own. It seemed to enjoy yoga, although not as much as it used to. . . .

Out, it silently said.

Working on it, I told monster silently for approximately the hundredth time in the last week. *It took time to build the spell that put you here, and it's going to take time to get you out again.*

Because I had no idea what I would become if monster was gone, and it also took more bravery than I could spare at the moment, what with the demons.

Let's be honest—they made a convenient excuse for pretty much everything.

TWO

If the pulse of magic had some physical origin in Chicago, we didn't see it as we crossed town. Not that we were entirely sure what we were looking for.

Chicago's mercenary fairies, bereft of their native green lands, had built themselves a castle on the banks of the South Fork of the Chicago River. More defensive fortress than Cinderella's castle, it rose with towers and crenellations. It had seen its share of misery—including a magical attack by one of its own and a visit from a very pissed-off Lulu. The latter had put me on the receiving end of Lulu's fireball, which hadn't been great for my nervous system, but had probably been good for future relations with the fae.

The castle sat at the end of a long stone drive that ran through a wide lawn yellowing with autumn. The gatehouse doors were open, which was not necessarily unusual. But there was no sign of guards, which was. The fae were unmistakably mercenary and rarely left themselves unguarded. Connor parked the SUV he had taken on semipermanent loan from the Pack, given how often we needed a fast ride, and swung the vehicle around so it faced the road.

"Easier exit," he said.

We climbed out carefully, closed the doors as quietly as possible. No one came to check on us, and the air was syrupy with power. If magic were a song, this was sweet and slow, like a blues tune played beneath a whirling fan accompanied by the creak of a porch swing. Not the usual Chicago vibe. An effect of the magical pulse?

"Is that Memphis magic?" I asked as I belted on my katana scabbard. The NAC Pack was historically based in Memphis.

"Some of it might be me," Connor said. He'd come into the full power of an alpha shifter during his first challenge fight a week ago, and he was still adjusting to the sensation.

"Yours is less sweet," I whispered as we approached in the grass to muffle our footsteps. "More pine forest. Less vanilla caramel left in the sun too long."

"Did they make the pulse of magic?" he wondered. "There's so much of it."

"I imagine we'll find out pretty fast."

We reached the gatehouse, walked inside. The magic was even stronger here, even thicker. We walked into the main keep, and caught our first glimpse of fairies. And it wasn't promising. There were a dozen within and around the various stations in the keep— a small garden, a blacksmith's forge, a stone well complete with a rotisserie bucket, and a scattering of chickens. But the fairies were all on the ground.

"Shit," I murmured, and ran toward the closest one. She was a young woman with pale skin and ice blond hair, and she lay at the edge of the garden plot of fall vegetables, including enormous cabbages that rose in leafy rosettes. She was on her back, hair spread beneath her like a halo.

I leaned down. There was no sign of an injury, no blood or bruise. I watched until I saw her chest rise and fall, but the movement was so slight, I thought I'd imagined it. I kept watching until I saw it again. And then, as lightly as I could manage, I touched her hand.

Power rushed me. I snatched my hand away in less than a second, but that small touch was enough to have my fangs descending and my eyes silvering. Colors flashed and became brighter. Everything seemed to sparkle. Was this how fae saw the world?

"Whoa."

"Lis?"

"The whole world is ice cream right now," I said. "If this is how they see things, makes you wonder how they ended up being so mercenary."

For a moment, I let the world be candy colored and sparkling. Then, with a sigh of regret, I stood up and breathed rhythmically, something I'd learned practicing yoga. I did so until the magic dissipated enough to have the colors normalizing again. At least until the prone fairy let out an enormous belch, which sparkled in the air and spilled more magic.

"They're magic drunk," Connor said. "I see glitter everywhere." His eyes changed color, shifting gold to blue as the magic brushed him. "Heady," he added, and reached out an arm to steady himself.

I grabbed him as he swayed. "Do you need to wait in the vehicle?"

He shook his head, stubbornness settling into his face. He wasn't one to back away, and certainly not with alpha magic running through him.

"I'll be fine," he said, and walked a few feet away, putting space between him and the prone fairies.

I took photos of the fairies for the Ombuds; it felt intrusive, given they were unconscious, but if we'd found the source of the magic pulse, Roger needed to know.

The image on my screen blurred as a tremor shook the ground. But that wasn't the only problem. Above us, the tower shuddered.

"Earthquake?" I asked when the world stilled again.

"Magic," Connor said. "A lot of magic." He pulled off his shirt, abdominal muscles clenching with the motion, and for a very fast moment, I thought things were about to get magically sexy.

Then he wrapped the cloth around his face to make an impromptu mask. Smart. Not sexy, except to the extent that he had bared his sculpted abdomen. Which wasn't the point.

"Will that help?" I asked.

Connor waited a beat, blinked a few times. And then his eyes cleared. "Good to go."

"Apparently."

I added "sensitivity to inhaled fairy vapor" to the list of things I knew about my future husband. And then I walked toward the tower, future husband beside me.

The tower was the heart of the castle, and it opened into a great hall with a rush-strewn floor and oversized hearth.

There were more fairies here—maybe a dozen—and all silent, all unconscious. Some in chairs at the long wooden table; some snoring near the fire.

The magic was thicker inside the building and doubly hard to avoid. But when another tremor shook the ground, I knew we'd have to risk it. If the residual magic tumbled the tower to the ground, it would take out all of us. So we either fixed the problem, or we evacuated a lot of drunk fae. I didn't like the odds that we could accomplish either of those on our own.

We took one of the curving staircases to the next level, where Claudia's throne room was located. We stepped over three fairies on the way, one of them snoring softly, the other two with glazed and vacant expressions.

The magic grew stronger and more potent as we rose through the tower, so each spiral of the staircase felt like we were moving deeper into a whirlpool.

We reached the throne room, with its high ceilings and gloriously colorful tapestries, and found the center of the maelstrom. Magic roiled like waves here, and I had to shift some of my energy over to the task of ignoring it. Monster, who wasn't keen on fairies, helped where it could.

A trestle table in the middle of the space was loaded with food. Succulent meats glistened beside tall cakes so delicate that they might have been made of cobwebs and lace. Steam wafted from roasted vegetables, and silver chalices of ale were still topped by foam.

And it all smelled of overripe magic.

"Elisa."

It wasn't until Connor put a hand on my arm that I realized I'd been moving toward the buffet. I dug my nails into my palms until they stung, which helped me ignore the magic, because fairy food and drink were notoriously dangerous. It was a common trap for unwary humans, as any classic fairy tale would tell you. And this felt like the trappiest trap of them all; the table all but sagged with magic.

"Thanks," I said, and dragged my attention from table to plank floor, where fairies lay sprawled or sat against walls, most with mugs in hand, the ale dripping to the floor into sticky puddles.

The building quaked around us, this time hard enough to send platters tumbling to the floor, ceramic splintering as it struck hardwood. The detritus included an entire tray of roasted turkey legs, now scattered forlornly on the floor.

A few feet past the spillage, I saw her. The queen of the fae was at the far end of the room, slumped against a wooden column, her arms banded around it as if it were a flotation device in a magical sea. Her tangled strawberry red hair half-covered her face. Her pale skin looked gray, and her magic spilled an unnatural fog across the floor. I ran to her, dodging bodies and overturned cups, holding my scabbard so it didn't bounce against my leg.

"Claudia," I said sternly. The tower shuddered, tossing portraits and mirrors off the walls and snuffing some of the hundreds of candles that lit the room. I managed to stay upright, but we had to do this fast. I didn't want to be plunged into darkness and trapped in the remains of a fairy tower.

"*Claudia,*" I said again, and this time put glamour behind it. It was a vampire's secret weapon, from a time when blood had to be coerced from humans. I wasn't sure it would work on her—not when her magic was older and stronger than mine—but she jerked her eyes to me.

"Wine," she said, a request, and released her grip on the post to grasp at an overturned chalice.

"No more wine," I said, and kicked the chalice away. She didn't want the wine, but the magic it contained.

Another quake. Stones crunched to the ground outside, the concussions coming faster now. Whatever the fairies had done had begun to tear apart the castle they'd so meticulously constructed—and to bury us with it.

"When you're out of time," Connor said, striding quickly to us, "you go for a classic remedy." Before I could object, he emptied a wooden bucket of water on Claudia's head.

I cursed and jumped back, anticipating a nasty counterattack from a woman who was a flaming narcissist on her better days.

Claudia blinked through a curtain of water and hair, eyes wide and confused. Then she swallowed hard and climbed to her feet, the diaphanous gown clinging to her form.

"The wine," she said. She swayed and put out a hand to steady herself. I think she meant to grab the post again, but the tower swayed like a sapling in the wind, and she caught only air.

Stomach lurching at the shifting floor, I reached out and caught her before she stumbled. I hoped the contact wouldn't trap me in her magic.

My skin buzzed with it, but the glittery edges were gone now. The water had managed to break the spell on her.

"Snap out of it," Connor demanded, "and them, too, or you're going to bring the entire tower down on top of us."

Claudia lifted a dripping hand toward the table, as if to send magic toward it. But before she could, a *crack* split the air as stone succumbed to the magic's pressure, and a section of the wall across from us disintegrated, stone and plaster crumbling to reveal the dark of night outside.

I faced the nightmare possibility we'd all be buried in rubble, but Claudia steadied herself, threw out her hand again. Magic swept across the room; as it traveled, the remnants of food and drink evaporated as the scent of overripe magic dissipated. The rumbling stopped, leaving heavy and cold silence in its wake.

With their magical chains broken, the fairies began to shift. They began to rise and move toward their queen. Claudia stood straight now, brushed a hand through her hair, which dried and fluffed into soft curls. Then that hand trailed the length of her body, drying skin and fabric, clearing her eyes and putting pink back into her cheeks.

She glanced at Connor, shirt still wrapped around his face, the rest of his torso bare. And her gaze lingered, followed the descent of abdominal muscles into the top of his jeans, then over to the black tattoo: *Non ducor; duco.*

Loosely translated: *I am not led. I lead.*

The lust in her eyes quickly surpassed the fading fairy magic.

"Mine," I said quietly, drawing her attention back to me.

It came slowly, her gaze, as if I'd interrupted her perusal of a new fairy confection.

"Lady," said one of her fae, a tall man with brown skin, long braids pulled back at the temples, and a fierce look in his eyes. And that look was directed at us. "Need we address the threat?"

"We aren't the threat. We're the first responders." I looked at Claudia. "What happened?"

"Power. More than I've felt in many seasons."

Literal fairy empowerment was the last thing I needed right now. "The pulse of magic that happened when the sun was up?"

She inclined her head.

It took big power to affect the ley lines. The demon wards drew on them for power, and in return the wards helped regulate the lines' transmission. Roger had said the wards were fine, so how had this happened?

"Where did it come from? What did it?"

"There is only one source," she said. "The ley lines." She crossed her fingers to form a triangle. I presumed that was meant to symbolize their intersection over Chicago.

"Please explain," I said, losing patience.

I wasn't the only one feeling testy. Her eyes had gone flat and cold and nearly dripped with arrogance. Whatever help we'd offered would do only so much to save us.

"Other sups felt it, too," I said, keeping my tone as mild as possible. "You may not be the only ones feeling powerful."

I was telling the truth; we knew they weren't the only sups who'd felt the wave, and I calculated she wouldn't like a potential change to the city's supernatural balance of power. Based on the narrowing of her eyes, I guessed she was calculating whether she might need us in the future and should bother keeping us alive.

"There was a sudden power in the lines," she said, decision

made. "We have been weak of late, and we took advantage of it. We made food and drink of the magic. We feasted."

"Yeah, we saw that part," I said wryly, sarcasm one of my favorite weapons against fear. "How are the lines now?"

"Uninteresting," she said, queenly boredom back in her tone. But there was disappointment beneath it, maybe that the fae couldn't ride a wave of power into a new era of dominion.

"Did a demon cause it?" Connor asked.

"I do not know what caused the surge. I only know its vehicle— the lines—and that we drank much." She looked across the room, gaze vague, and I wondered if she were seeing what had come before we'd arrived, not the ruin of it. The fae would have to deal with what they'd done.

"We'll go," I said.

Claudia made a sound not unlike a growl. I thought she meant to strike out as revenge for our interrupting their festivities, so I turned my body to deflect the coming blow. But no strike came. Instead, she looked regretful.

"It has been many moons," Claudia said. "I do not regret that we experienced this surfeit, although perhaps we went too far." She looked at me, gaze narrowing again. "You have helped us once again. We owe you a boon."

Fairies, like vampires, were very big on debts being owed and paid. And she looked none too thrilled about the transaction.

A woman with pale skin, dark hair, and deeply bowed lips stepped beside her.

"My queen," she said with disdain, "they surely chanced upon us. No boon is owed for following the whims of fate."

"This was not chance," Claudia said. "The bloodletter and her consort would not come here without reason. They came to seek our knowledge, but they stayed to resolve our peril. For that, a boon is owed. And no harm will come to them," she added.

Her people would probably obey her. But they were riding the magic, or grouchy with its absence, and that made our presence risky. It was time to say our farewells.

"We don't need to collect today," I said, and gestured to the broken wall. A mourning dove had flown through and now perched on a rafter, grooming its pearly feathers. "You have other business."

"Yes," Claudia said. "We will repair what we have broken. And we will see what brings the ill wind."

"I want the wind to bring peace and quiet," I murmured when we'd hustled back down the stairs under watchful eyes. Guards had already returned to their positions at the gatehouse, and as we passed, they touched their scabbards, the only threat they dared to make.

We all but leapt into the vehicle, and Connor's eyes kept flitting to the rearview mirror until we cleared the fence around the property and left the fairies behind us.

THREE

"Did you find out why they were unconscious?" Roger asked when I called the team for an update. They'd reviewed the pictures I'd taken.

"They were on a magical bender," I said, and relayed what Claudia had told us.

"The ley lines are normal again?" he asked.

"So Claudia says. And I don't think she'd lie about that. She might have enjoyed the feast, but she understood bringing the tower down around them wouldn't help them regain power. And it's going to take energy to repair the building. Have you learned anything else?"

"No," Theo said. "The vampires of Navarre and Grey were, not surprisingly, also unconscious during the magical burst. And we haven't found anything in the city that looks like it might have caused the jolt."

"The wards are still safe," Roger said, so that was at least some of my worry gone. "I'll give the mayor the answers we've gotten so far. We're bound to learn more."

With the ley lines involved, that seemed inevitable.

"Will dinner with your family be more or less intense than our fairy encounter?" I asked Connor when we were driving to the Keene house.

"Less scary," he said. "Equally intense. They'll be evaluating you, of course."

"Ha ha." Shifters weren't the evaluating type. But I did have a question. "Does this—do *we*—bother your aunt Fallon?"

Fallon Keene was Connor's dad's only sister. She'd given up her claim to the throne to be with a shifter named Jeff Christopher. Although they were both members of the same Pack, he was a tiger while the Keenes were wolves. That had taken her out of the running for Apex.

Not only was I not a shifter. I was a vampire. But much had changed in the last twenty years. Connor still had to prove his entitlement to the throne—physically and mentally—but his relationship with me didn't bar him from trying. There were undoubtedly shifters who didn't trust me, but he was the only son of the Apex. That carried a lot of weight.

"No," he said, and reached over to squeeze my hand. "But I appreciate the question. I think Dad regrets how that whole thing went down, and the Pack has mellowed, too. The world is different. I'm not saying everybody's going to be copacetic; there are assholes in every Pack. But the Keenes understand there are many ways to make a family. And family is what matters."

I couldn't have written a better answer.

The Keene house sat prettily on a corner in a residential neighborhood. It was a Queen Anne–style house, so the exterior had a lot of features: wraparound porch, turret, balcony, and at least five paint colors. It was a big structure, but it glowed with homey comfort, from the buckets of golden mums on the front porch to the wreath on the door.

There were dozens of vehicles parked nearby. "I guess this won't be an intimate affair," I said.

"Mom told me it was only dinner with her and Dad," Connor said. "They aren't the surprise-party type."

"No, but shifters are the drop-in-and-stay-for-dinner type," I pointed out.

"True." He glanced at me, his smile mildly apologetic. "I didn't know."

"I know. You'd have told me." I looked down. I definitely wasn't dressed for a formal human or vampire engagement party, which might have involved champagne and croquettes. But a shifter party was more likely to be beer, barbecue, and blackjack.

Connor wedged the SUV into a spot on the street, switched off the ignition, and glanced at the house. "I don't sense any trouble," he said.

I snorted. "If there were trouble, they'd have already thrown someone through the front window."

"You have a very unique perspective on the Pack you're about to join, Lis." Connor grinned at me, tilted his head. "Now you look paler than usual." He leaned over, slid a hand to the back of my head, and kissed me hard.

"Where I go, you go," he whispered against my lips, leaving them tingling with our combined magic.

We walked inside, the screen door slamming closed behind us, and were immediately greeted by Connor's petite mother, Tonya. He shared her coloring—dark hair and blue eyes—and the dimple at one corner of his mouth.

"I'm sorry," she said, embracing him. "We wanted you all to ourselves, at least for a bit. But then your uncle Eli popped by, and it all spiraled from there."

"It's fine," Connor said, standing a good foot taller than his mother. It seemed a miracle such a small woman had brought such a big man into the world, but she was a shifter, after all. They were strong people.

She let him go and gave me a tender hug. "Welcome to the family."

"It's not official yet," said the man behind her. Gabriel Keene, Connor's dad, stepped into the foyer and put an arm around his wife.

I wasn't sure what to expect from him, given the comment. Unlike most shifters, he generally liked vampires. But a wide, sly grin eased into place on his face. "And she's not nearly drunk enough yet to deal with the likes of us."

"No drinking," Connor said, and slipped his hand into mine, squeezed. "She's on duty and I'm"—he looked at me, unabashed love in his eyes—"wherever she needs me to be."

My heart melted.

Connor's dad beckoned us out of the octagonal foyer and into the den, where Keene family members lounged, watched a game on-screen, or chatted in small groups. I felt as comfortable as a vampire could in a house full of shifters who were still gauging my worthiness for their prince. Which is to say, not very.

The room burst into sound and movement and magic when they realized we'd arrived. Shifters rose, came forward to offer congratulations and slap Connor on the back.

A familiar face found me. It belonged to a tall, lean shifter with dark blond hair long enough to push behind his ears. His smile was kind and wide; he took my hand, pumped it collegially.

"Always good to have a Sullivan and Ombud in the family," the man said. Jeff Christopher was not only Fallon's husband but a longtime friend of my parents. He'd been an assistant Ombud for my grandfather, Chicago's first Ombudsman, and had often worked with my mom when she'd served Cadogan House as Sentinel. Jeff and Connor had gaming in common; they shared a multiplayer quest when they had time.

"Thank you. I'm glad to be here. How are you?" I asked.

His eyes lit with love. "Fallon is pregnant again, and we're thrilled."

Shifters, with their longer-than-human life spans, could conceive well into middle age.

"Congratulations! When is she due?"

"Early next year, so we have a ways to go yet."

The crowd of shifters parted as Fallon ran through them into the hallway. Her face looked a bit green.

Jeff sighed. "Midnight sickness hits hard. I'd better go after her."

"Go," I said with a nod. And found myself quickly surrounded by the arms of another shifter.

"Elisa!" said Daniel Liu, another Pack member and one of Connor's closest friends. "Congratulations." He gave me a hug that might have broken the ribs of a human.

"Thanks, Dan."

He released me and pushed straight dark hair from his dreamy brown eyes. Dan was gorgeous—with light brown skin and high cheekbones—and an unrepentant flirt, but he still managed to find himself single. Based on his recent bar fight with the boyfriend of a lady he'd tried to steal, he didn't make the best decisions in the romantic arena.

"Alexei is with Lulu, so he told me to hug you for both of us."

I doubted that, since Alexei wasn't a hugger.

"I look forward to seeing what you make of the Pack," he said.

"That's Connor's deal. I won't interfere."

"Eh, the Pack is more than business." He gestured to where Tonya stood with Gabriel. She was frowning as she listened to him with obvious intensity. When he finished talking, she leaned in and said something quiet that had him pressing his forehead against hers.

"Love," Dan said, "helps fill the Pack. Keeps it centered. Balanced. And when the shit goes bad—"

"Which, in Chicago, it often does."

He nodded. "Love gives us a place to land."

"Dan, you're going to make me think you're a romantic."

"Lies," he said with a wink. "And you're going to do fine. Just don't forget the love."

That love was everywhere in the Keene house, and Connor and I accepted hugs and congratulations until dinner was ready, which involved old-fashioned meat loaf that tasted like heaven and yeast rolls light enough to float. The family's dining table, which fit twelve, wasn't big enough for this crowd; every spare chair and folding card table in the house had been commandeered, so everyone had a seat. That, I thought, was how you did Pack love.

"A toast," Connor's dad said when plates were heavy with magic and food and glasses were full and ready for clinking.

"Twenty-some-odd years ago," he continued, his glass of whiskey raised, "Tonya gave me the most amazing gift I could have asked for. I still have that Ducati," he added with a wily grin that had the laughter roaring. He leveled his gaze at Connor. "And then she gave me you, and you were a miracle until you hit puberty. And then you were a terror."

"Be honest," Connor's uncle Eli said. "He's my nephew and I love him, but puberty was not the problem. He was *always* a terror."

Connor lifted his bottle of Goose Island root beer, a Chicago specialty, in salute. "You don't know where the boundaries are until you test them."

"Boundaries you did not like," Gabriel said, "which made it very amusing that your first crush was on a girl who followed all the rules." And he looked at me.

I snorted. "I was absolutely not his first crush. He had a new girl every week, and none of them was me."

"He was intimidated," Tonya said with a smile.

"I'm pretty sure Connor Keene has never been intimidated by

anything." I slid my gaze to him, found equal parts arrogance and affection in his return smile.

"I was working up the nerve to ask you out."

"Oh, I'm sure."

"The point," Gabriel said, drawing our attention back, "is that you two have been part of each other's lives nearly since the beginning. I'm glad you've decided to commit to each other, and be there for each other for as long as you may live."

The words might have been serious and hinted at Connor's mortality, but there was no grief in his tone. Just earnest practicality. Shifters were like that.

"It won't be easy," he continued. "Every family in this room has had its share of shit."

"Hear! Hear!" someone called out.

"You'll have your own variety, being who and what you are." He looked at Tonya. "Commitment will give you a confidant, a partner, a shoulder, and a hand."

"And an alibi!" Jeff said, and there was another round of laughter.

"When the need arises," Gabriel agreed, then settled his gaze on us again. Magic swirled in his eyes, like a galaxy's worth of knowledge. "The beginning and the end is you. The beginning and the end is love."

We'd need that love, because the world outside was deadly. We had broken wards, demons, and a vulnerable human population. We'd need every bit of strength we could muster.

There were more hugs, more meat loaf, and a spread of handmade pies that would have impressed even Claudia. Then Connor's parents pulled us into a quiet corner, looked us over.

"We wanted to ask about wedding plans," Connor's dad said, "but you both look beat to shit."

"Demons," I said.

"Apex challenges," Connor said.

"Do you at least have a date in mind?" his mom asked.

I knew she meant well, and given the spark in her eyes, she was probably excited to think about wedding plans for her only son. But . . . demons.

"Not until things are stabilized magically," Connor said. "We don't want to start 'us' until the city is safer." He reached out, embraced her. "But thank you for asking, and thank you for dinner."

"You're welcome," she said.

"No fight tomorrow night, right?" his dad asked.

"Not among shifters," Connor said. "But demons? Who knows."

"That was really nice," I said when we were walking back to the vehicle.

He squeezed our joined hands. "It was," he said, and pulled me against him, held me for a moment in the darkness and the relative quiet. "I guess we have to actually get married now."

"I guess. I'll call my other lovers, Todd and Keith, and let them know."

He flicked my ear, which just made me snort.

"I'm pretty sure one husband will be sufficient," I said. "Probably."

His grin went wicked. "We could pop into the backyard hammock and test my sufficiency."

"You'd wake the neighbors."

"No, Lis," he said, and his smile was slow and sexy and full of magic and promise. "*You'd* wake the neighbors."

There were no Ombud alerts waiting for us and no visible emergencies as we drove back to the town house. We were grateful for that. But we were still wary, because we knew they were coming. We knew the wind, as Claudia said, would blow ill.

We found Lulu and Alexei at home, snoozing at the dining room table. The cat lay on the back of a couch in the den, her legs sprawled and her eyes wary.

Lulu lifted her head, sniffed. "You smell like . . . moldy cotton candy."

"And rotten lettuce," Alexei added. "Why?"

"Fairies," I said, "who, if I have the math right, believe the magical pulse was a temporary boost in the ley lines. And did their best to eat the magic."

"Eat the magic," Lulu repeated as if hearing a foreign phrase for the first time. "Directly or . . . ?"

"Fairy food," I said. "Ale, meats, whatnot."

"Yum," Alexei said.

"Not if you gorge until you're unconscious and you nearly destroy your own castle," I said. "The line was quite a way back from where they actually stopped."

Connor poured a glass of water for himself and handed me a bottle of blood, and we sat down at the table.

I cringed at the label. "Nobody asked for wintergreen."

"We need to order groceries," he said. "You're down to the last bottles."

The bottles I'd been avoiding, he meant. I was fairly certain there was a bottle of "vanilla musk" in the back of the fridge.

"How was the parental dinner?" Lulu asked.

I opted to condense the torture and drank the blood all at once. It made my mouth tingle. And not in a good way. Fortunately, the bottles weren't very large and didn't take long to ingest. Maybe the big providers thought two-liter bottles of blood would be objectionable to humans? Which was illogical, given that keeping vampires well-fed kept us off humans.

"Larger than expected," Connor said. "It turned out to be an extended-family dinner."

"It looks like you survived," Lulu said.

"Everyone was very kind," I said. "Even when we ate the raw deer in the backyard."

Alexei's eyes went wide. "Did I seriously miss that?"

"No," Connor said. "We ate meat loaf at the table like humans."

"But there were pies," I said. "Pies as far as the eyes could see."

"Good reason to get engaged," Alexei said with what I was pretty sure was sincerity.

Lulu got busy inspecting her screen. Which was turned off.

"How's the mural coming along?" I asked.

"Good progress," Lulu said, and held up her hands to look them over. They were mostly clean, but for a few patches of color. "Clint's awesome, as I expected."

Clint Howard was Lulu's boss for this project; he'd hired her specifically to paint a mural.

"Good," I said.

"I totally got us off track," Lulu said. "You said Claudia believes the pulse was in the ley lines?"

"Yup. And no one blew up a ward."

"I know. I checked with my parents."

"How's the reset going?" I asked, and knew that was dangerous territory. The two broken wards hadn't proved to be an easy fix.

"Frustrating. It's Victorian magic, and there's no how-to manual. They're still trying to decipher the spell etched into the machine."

The machine was an antique demon detector that also sprayed them with lightning. The magic only worked once, and there was no physical reset switch, so we had to reverse engineer the magic to get it running again.

Well, the sorcerers did. I mostly ran around with a sword.

"Demonslayer," I murmured, imagining the intro song to my own drama series.

"What?" Connor asked, tilting his head at me. "Did you just say 'demonslayer'?"

I blinked, cleared my throat. "Just wishing there was, you know, a button we could push."

If monster had been capable of a sardonic cough, that would have been its cue.

"Do they have an estimate for when they might be done?" Connor asked, graciously changing the subject.

"'Sometime between half-pissed and never,' my dad says. Whatever that means."

Her dad was "colorful," as my dad liked to say.

"It means not soon," Connor said, linking his hands over his head and stretching from side to side.

"Still sore?" Lulu asked.

"I've been worse," he said. "But thanks for asking."

Lulu nodded, rose. "I'm going to bed. I've got a long night of not demonslaying ahead of me." She smiled at me with obvious amusement.

"Ha ha," I said.

Alexei rose, too, gave us a silent nod, and followed her up.

"Let's join them," Connor said, then shook his head, held up his forearms to form an "X." "Strike that. I just heard it, and it's not what I meant."

"I know what you meant," I said. "Let's fall face-first into bed and go unconscious before we start to worry about what's next."

"Good plan," he decided.

But I still wished I'd had some of that fairy cake.

FOUR

It was the most glorious scent in the world. Not bacon (sorry, Mom); not exotic roses; not expensive, influencer-approved French perfume.

Coffee.

My first stop of the day, via the self-driving Auto I'd ordered for the trip to the Ombuds' South Side office, was Leo's, my favorite Windy City coffee chain. I filled up my honorary "Frequent Roaster" travel mug and, as the boxy vehicle merged back into traffic, scanned the news on my screen. No demon activity during the day—or at least none that was being reported via human media.

Connor was heading to the Pack's Ukrainian Village headquarters. While there wasn't an Apex challenger on the schedule, that didn't mean someone wouldn't pay a surprise visit, hoping to catch him unawares. When he wasn't fighting, he was familiarizing himself with the Pack's business and admin duties. Not things a shifter usually wanted to care about, but crucial for the continuance of the Pack. I was proud of him.

I was shaken from that thought—literally—when the Auto squealed to a sudden hard stop.

I cursed, swept coffee droplets off my black pants. Then glanced up and found an unexpected wall of traffic that hadn't been there seconds before.

"Auto: reason for stop?" I asked it. Autos had access to all the traffic and weather information available, and no human distractions. It shouldn't have needed to stop short.

"Unknown obstacle," it said in its weirdly chipper voice. It sounded like a first-day intern eager to please the senior staff.

I looked up. Ahead of us, cars were packed bumper to bumper. Traffic was barely ever this bad when I was traveling to the office, as I was usually moving against commuter traffic, not stuck in it.

"Auto: Is the obstacle human or supernatural?"

There was a pause. "Vegetal" was its response.

I blinked. "Repeat that."

"The disturbance is vegetal," it said again.

What the hell was a "vegetal" disturbance? A fallen tree in the road? City workers were mowing ditches under the cover of darkness for some reason? Something weird had happened. And in Chicago, weird usually meant supernatural. Lately, it meant demon.

"Auto," I told it, "stop ride." While it processed, I sent a quick message to Theo: AUTO STALLED. WILL BE LATE.

I put my screen away, looked ruefully at my travel mug, and climbed out, closing the door behind me. I ignored the honks and shouts of humans pissed about the traffic, the delay, or the fact that I'd abandoned my ride in the middle of the road.

There was smoke and heat in the astringent scent of split leaves and sap in the air . . . but below it all was something far nastier. Part sulfur, part smoke, both gritty.

Demons.

A woman ran past me screaming, a toddler clutched in her arms. That snapped me out of my daze. I unsheathed my sword and ran forward, passing two more humans who were busy trying to film the incident instead of helping the other humans in harm's way.

"Call the CPD!" I called out, and kept going.

And then I stopped short, just like the Auto had.

An eight-foot-tall supernatural wielded an enormous limb from a nearby oak tree like it was light as a child's toy. His skin was tan with a faintly gold shimmer, and he wore only gym shorts that—let's be honest—didn't match the vibe. He was swinging the branch like an elephant's trunk, slamming it into cars, crumpling hoods and smashing windows. And putting the tang of sulfur into the air.

Demon.

A woman sat cross-legged on the ground beside a vehicle that was sitting precariously on its side. Blood streamed from her forehead, probably related to the spiderweb crack in the windshield.

"Everybody back!" I yelled out, and helped the human to her feet and out of danger. Then I grabbed the collar of another hapless human who was inches away from being thrown onto the asphalt by a flying branch, and shoved him to relative safety.

"Get off the street!" I said, gesturing the humans back.

"I've got civil rights!" another human screamed, screen pointed at the demon.

"But no desire to be civil," I muttered as she tried to start some pushy-shovey, nearly sending me into a young woman trying to drag a stroller from an SUV while keeping hold of two young children.

I pulled the stroller out of the car. "Get the kids away from here," I said, and sent a magical pulse into the woman with the screen. She might have been stubborn, but a little glamour did the trick and had her turning to join the fleeing crowd.

Unfortunately, that magic had been noticed. I wasn't going to have time to update the Ombuds as the demon turned to me, its green eyes glinting in the streetlight.

"Drop the branch," I said, "and leave Chicago in an orderly fashion."

Might as well start by asking nicely.

He released the tree limb, which hit the ground with an audible thud. And for a millisecond, I thought this was going to be manageable.

Naïve vampire.

The demon opened his mouth as if to scream. But there was no sound. Instead, gleaming green vines poured out and stretched and reached for the ground, leaves unfurling as they grew. And then the vines were snaking toward me.

As much as my mind and body wanted to retreat, I didn't have time to be horrified. They moved fast, growing thicker as they sped across the asphalt.

I slashed at one, which oozed a viscous sap the color of blood; then I pivoted to slice at another that was reaching for my boots.

Monster was fully awake now and sent me flashes of instructions from angles that it, apparently, could see better than me. *Slice left, dodge right,* it said as the vines circled me. The help made up for the nagging.

I turned a moment too late to avoid one twisting stem, which roped around my left ankle. Even in boots, I could feel its demonic heat. I stepped on the vine with my right foot, brought my blade across the bit in the middle, and ducked just quickly enough to avoid being impaled by a glossy red thorn that had emerged from the tip of one vine. It was nearly a foot long and looked sharp as my katana. It whistled as it flew overhead. I sliced upward, spilling sap through the air. The lacerated portion of the thorn hit the ground.

I looked back. The demon's mouth was empty, the vines now a bloody mess on the road. But the demon had more tricks.

I turned my body to the side, held up my katana, preparing for the next strike. And flew through the air when something burst through the street, pushing up asphalt in huge, jagged chunks.

I hit the hood and windshield of a nearby SUV, my bones whimpering at the impact. And it took me a moment to get my breath again. I sat up, glanced back at the windshield, and found two grinning teenagers behind the glass. They gave me simultaneous thumbs-up, but before I could even appreciate the support, I was being pulled back down to the street. I hit the asphalt on my knees, the pain singing through my legs. A thick tree root, red as the thorn had been, was now winding its way up my arm from the rip it had made in the road. I twisted and wrenched my arm free, but another root grabbed me by the foot. Then I was on my back, and it was dragging me toward its portal.

I swore loudly, now fully pissed off. I usually tried to rein in the vampiric reactions around terrified humans, but they shouldn't be confused about which one of us was the good guy. So I let my fangs descend and my eyes silver, and I didn't mind when monster added its strength to mine. It might turn my eyes red, and humans—and demon—might see.

Let them. I could just blame it on demon magic.

Unfortunately, the angle was too awkward to use my sword, so I reached up and dug fingers into the root, using vampire strength and everything monster could offer me. That had the root's grip loosening just enough to let me get purchase. I flipped to my feet, regripped my sword, and used both hands to drive it into the root.

The root writhed; the demon screamed.

So the demon could manifest and control a demonic tree root, but the connection ran both ways. Good to know.

I pulled out the sword, spilling more vegetal blood onto the roadway, and drove the blade into the root again. The demon let out another scream, this one nearly drowned out by the scream of approaching sirens; the CPD had finally arrived. I stabbed the root once more before looking up, and found the demon on his knees, dark tears streaming from his eyes.

I swung the fluid off my sword, stalked toward him, and dodged the blow he aimed at my head as he lurched up and forward.

"You get a choice," I said, and raised my sword. "You sigil yourself back into the demon dimension"—I lowered my sword, pointed it at his heart—"or I slice off more of you."

I'd have happily turned him over to the CPD if I thought there was a chance they could safely arrest him. But he'd already hurt people, and even if it managed to knock him out now, there was no guarantee he'd stay that way en route.

Hate boiled in his eyes. "You are no different from us."

"I don't hurt innocents," I said. "And you're running out of time. I don't know what the CPD officers will do when they get here."

I heard footsteps behind me, and held up a hand to hold off the approaching officers. "Stay back," I called out, and didn't take my eyes off the demon. "He's going to do magic."

"Roger that," confirmed a familiar voice. Gwen Robinson was a CPD detective who specialized in supernatural issues; we worked with her often. And she was dating Theo. She stepped beside me, her athletic body tucked into a black pants and blazer. Her skin was medium brown, her curly dark hair was pulled into a tidy bun, and her eyes were all cop.

"Injured humans are that way," I said, gesturing with my free hand.

"We've got them," Gwen said. "And we have the demon oblit-eration spell ready. I've heard it's . . . unpleasant."

I wished that were a real thing, instead of Gwen's very solid improv.

"You heard the woman," I told the demon. "Get out or die."

He bared his teeth, slick and pointed, blood trickling from the corner of his mouth. The power in those drops of blood, even from a few feet away, was remarkable. Some part of me—ancient and visceral—was tempted by them. But the vile scent of demon magic extinguished that interest.

Stone and concrete made grinding noises as roots slunk back beneath the earth, and gravel scritched as he reeled back in the remaining vines. They wrapped around the demon's limbs before being subsumed back into his body. Then he drew a symbol on the inside of his forearm, magic glowing a sickly green-gold as his sigil branded itself into his skin. The smell—singed flesh and sour magic—was stomach turning.

That glow spread, became a magical fire that began to consume his body. He began to burn, to drift into fine, dark ash.

"I will make my way back," he said before disappearing into a column of wispy smoke.

There was a moment of silence, and then the humans who'd stayed to watch—because, again, humans—burst into applause.

I blew out a breath, tossed a handful of salt onto the ground for good measure, and wiped the blade of my sword along my pants leg. It would need a good cleaning, but this would do for now.

Gwen came over, coffee cup in hand, and looked over the mess and destruction. "There's not enough coffee in Chicago for nonsense like this." Then she reached over and pulled a leaf from my hair, let it flutter to the ground.

"Thanks," I said, and watched as CPD units worked through the puzzle of traffic to get vehicles moving again.

"Are you okay?" Gwen asked.

"Sore but alive. Demons suck."

"Rich coming from a vampire."

I looked up at her, managed a smile. "I know, right?"

She held out her coffee. "Want a pick-me-up?"

"No, thanks. I'll get something on the way to the office."

"Friendly suggestion? You might want to clean up a little, too."

I looked down at my torn and sap-covered clothes. "Freaking demons," I murmured, and stalked off to find an Auto.

I checked my screen and found a narrative in texts from Theo: Gwen was on the way; the Ombuds were also on the way; the Ombuds were still several miles away and stuck in the crosstown traffic pileup created by the demon's antics; the CPD officers on duty refused to let them through the barrier around the neighborhood due to "orders"; and after confirming Gwen was on scene, they'd decided to return to the office to keep investigating rather than sitting in an idling car for another hour.

I couldn't fault them for that. Not that there was much they could have done anyway.

When I reached the Ombuds' campus, I detoured to a restroom to clean sap off my hands and clothes, and double-checked for hitchhiking gravel or leaves. Then it was into the main workroom, where Theo, Petra, and I shared desks.

Theo, Roger, and Petra stood in a cluster, eyes on the wall screen. Theo, who had dark brown skin and black hair, wore one of his signature button-down shirts, this time with tiny royal blue–and–white checks, with trim jeans and Oxford shoes. The cast on his arm was a necessary but mostly unstylish addition.

They all looked up when I walked in.

"I'm fine," I said, tossing my jacket on my chair. I lifted my gaze to the screen, where a video of me swinging my sword against the demon was playing.

Theo looked me over, worry furrowing his brow. "Everything in one piece?"

"It is. You okay?"

"Damn traffic," Theo said apologetically. "And damn CPD."

"I imagine you've already had a chat with Gwen," I said with a smile.

"Kid was just trying to do his job," Theo said. "Which was a real kick in the ass."

"It looks like you took down Poison Ivy," Petra said, gesturing to the fight.

"It wasn't actually poison ivy."

"She means the *Batman* character," Theo said.

I put that fact away to surprise Connor with later. Like Theo, he was into the comics thing.

"It was definitely some kind of plant demon," I said, and pointed to the screen. "If he hadn't been trying to kill humans, I'd have appreciated his efforts to green up the city."

"Right?" Petra said. "I was just telling Roger a demon like that could do some real good if it wasn't set on villainy." She did some swiping on a tablet screen, snagged a screenshot of the demon from the video, then shifted the wall-screen image to show a wide color-coded chart.

"What's that?" Theo asked.

"Looks like a database?" I offered.

"Exactly," Petra said. "We're going to track our demons." She gestured at Roger. "His idea to report the ones we came across, both for political and historical purposes, and I added the science and tech. I've already added Rosantine and the guy you found a few days ago." She pulled the screenshot into a box on-screen, and it populated fields with height, weight, skin tone, and other information.

"Is baby diarrhea green really a color?" Roger asked.

"For purposes of this database, yes. If we have to export the data, no. It will become umber." She glanced back at me, gloved fingers poised over glass. Being an aeromancer, she had to be careful who and what she touched.

"What's his strength level?" she asked.

"What's the scale?"

"Human to Mallory Carmichael," Petra said. "And before we argue strongest living sup again, I don't know anyone else who has squeezed a magical dragon into a katana lately. So . . ."

But she hadn't squeezed all of it, had she? I kept the question to myself.

"Physically," I said, "he's stronger than human. I'm not sure if he's stronger than me. Magically, stronger than me or you, but not as strong as Lulu. His magic is very specific, and he's connected to the roots. They're a weakness."

"So you really need axes and pesticides," Roger said.

"Pretty much."

Petra nodded, added the information, giving him a straight score of 38 and a magic score of 51. I worked not to ask how many points I'd earned.

"We'll keep tracking," Roger said. "And maybe we'll learn something from the broader data we didn't know before."

He clapped his hands. "Now that that's done, the daytime report. There's still no unusual ward activity, and there's no indication the magical pulse had a physical ground zero. I'm leaning toward believing the fae—that it was a hitch in the ley lines—while acknowledging they probably haven't told us the whole story."

"The pulse has to be demon related," I said. "It can't be a coincidence that we have two busted demon wards and a hitch, as you said, in the thing that powers them."

"Could a demon have used the ley lines to send a message, maybe?" Theo asked. "To let other demons know the city is available for homesteading?"

"Oh, good," Roger said dryly. "Demon pioneers *and* supernatural colonialism."

"Yeah, that's not great," I said. "But it's probably simpler to use demonic social media, if that's a thing."

Petra snorted. "Human social media is hellscape enough. But I admit I'd check out OKDemon if it existed."

"This demon wasn't hiding who or what he was," I said. "He wasn't trying to stay undetected and avoid getting caught. He engaged in demonic activity on the street in full view of humans, and he was hurting humans, apparently for the fun of it. I saw no remorse. No shame. No boundaries, except the possibility of death."

"Upside," Theo said. "That will make them easier to find and easier to catch."

I appreciated the determination in his voice, but we were going to need more than determination.

"Let's check with the sorcerers," Roger said. "Now would be good," he added when no one moved.

I pulled out my screen and contacted Lulu's mom. She'd been Aunt Mallory forever, but I still felt a little awkward calling her directly. Generational difference, I guess. Plus, I had the Egregore.

"Hey, Elisa!" she said brightly, face on-screen. Like Lulu, she was a small woman. She was pale-skinned and blue-haired, and her smile was warm.

"Hey. I'm at work and wanted to check on the wards."

"Things are moving," Aunt Mallory said, motioning to someone off camera. "We're at the warehouse today. The building has been stabilized and the magic in the machine has been reset, and we should be running tomorrow."

The warehouse housed the demon-detecting machine, one of the two wards Rosantine had triggered.

"Tomorrow?" I said, not a little surprised. I knew she and Lulu's dad, Catcher Bell, and Paige, the Cadogan House librarian, were skilled sorcerers, but I didn't know they'd made that kind of progress.

"Tricky bit was translating the language of symbols etched into the metal. Once we got that and figured out what kind of incantation was used, we were able to build back the spell. As soon as the inspector gives us the go-ahead, we'll kindle it and get her up and running."

"That's amazing," I said, and felt a weight lifting from my shoulders. "What about South Gate?" That was the first ward Rosantine had triggered. I'd been partly responsible for that, and for Rosantine's making her way into Chicago. Granted, at the time we'd thought she was a supernatural informant on the run.

"That's taking longer," Aunt Mallory said. "There's more structural damage, and we can't do the heavy magic work until the stone-and-brick guys finish repairing it. It was in worse shape than the warehouse in terms of, you know, standing up."

"Yeah," I said, and felt that twinge of guilt again.

"Are you okay? You look tired." There was a mom look in her eyes.

"I'm fine."

"Okay. Then I'll get back to it. I'll tell your mom we talked."

"Okay. Thanks." I put the screen away and looked at the others. "You get all that?"

"Live and in person," Petra said. Then she looked ruefully at her spreadsheet. "Bummer if we fix the wards and don't really get to use this."

"But wouldn't it be nice," Roger said, "if we didn't actually have a demon invasion?"

The office screen rang then, and we all looked at Roger.

"You jinxed it," Theo said.

"Let's answer the call first," Roger said, and did so. "Ombudsman."

"Gwen Robinson," said the voice on the other end. Theo stood up a little straighter.

"More killer trees?" Petra asked.

"Not that have been reported to me. But we do have two dead humans in a warehouse."

"Humans?" Roger asked. Purely human matters were outside our jurisdiction. But Gwen wouldn't have called us without a reason.

"Yeah, and homicide thinks it might be an SIH." That was the city's new acronym for a supernatural-involved homicide. "Easier to show than tell," she said. "Put me on-screen."

Roger did the swiping this time, and the image on the overhead screen wobbled as Gwen shifted her screen to point it toward the ground.

"Damn," I murmured at an image of death. Two humans. They were lying facedown and side by side, which was at least a small mercy. Appeared male. They wore no shirts, and their backs bore large circular marks that looked like burns, each at least ten inches across.

And worse, the wounds *smoked*. Thin, oily green-black curls rose from the center of each. I'd seen that smoke—or something close enough to it. I bet it would smell like brimstone and leave an uncomfortable tingle in the air. And it boded nothing good.

"Demon magic," I said. "Send us the directions."

We fueled up with coffee, naturally, and Theo and I drove to the Chicago Industrial Port. It was a complex of storage buildings and lots where the Calumet River met Lake Michigan. Barges docked at the port, and goods being moved across the lake could be unloaded and shipped by truck or rail.

We drove beneath the enormous block letters that identified the port, then drove past building-high stacks of cargo containers.

Above us stretched rails bearing the pinchers that would take the containers on or off ships.

Outside the warehouse, we found Gwen with officers from two CPD cruisers. Two ambulances waited nearby.

We climbed out and walked toward Gwen, passing uniformed officers who were keeping a crowd of port employees several yards back from the taped-off crime scene. Gwen was in conversation with a pale-skinned man in a suit; he had short dark hair and a square jaw. Early fifties, I guessed, with a badge at his waist beside his holstered weapon.

As we approached, his hand went to the butt of his weapon. I disliked him immediately.

"Elisa Sullivan and Theo Martin," Gwen said, gesturing in our direction, "this is Detective Robert Hansen."

He managed a nod. "You sups?"

He knew the answer to that, as Gwen would have told him she'd called us. I didn't like playing cutesy; it wasted time.

Theo, who was very human, simply ignored the question, moved around the man. "Where?" he asked.

"In there," Gwen said, nodding toward the building.

It was big as an airplane hangar, its enormous doors open to reveal the cavernous space inside, where groups of boxes and containers were waiting to be moved somewhere. The building was clean and bright, the concrete floor marked with fluorescent tape to guide forklifts and trucks into position. The warehouse was deep, and a few employees still worked at the other end of it, well away from what had happened here.

The bodies lay about twenty feet inside the door. Either the video hadn't fully captured the bruising or more had appeared since we'd seen it. The wounds on their backs, on the other hand, looked just as bad in real life as they had on-screen.

The magic was undeniable; the air was sharp with it, and the acrid fumes made the eyes water. There was blood on the ground, but the lingering magic and scent of demon eliminated any vampire interest. Even monster stayed quiet, except to remind me how helpful it could be.

"Who are they?" Theo asked.

"Jake Durante and Ernesto País. They worked for Buckley Trade Partners, which owns this building. They've been dead about eight hours."

"Afternoon," Theo said. "During daylight."

"During business hours, I bet." I looked at Gwen. "Is the warehouse open at night?"

"Closes down at nine p.m. Well, normally," she said, noting the open doors and onlookers.

I crouched and reached fingers toward the trail of smoke.

"Don't touch the body," Hansen snapped out.

"Throttle back, Hansen," Gwen said. "It's not her first night on the job. Also, she's not an idiot."

My fingers tingled as they touched the substance, and I pulled them back. I'd found the oily grit I'd been expecting. I rose, showed my hand to Theo and Gwen.

"Demon smut," I said. "I'm not sure how the mark was made, but a demon made it."

Gwen pulled an evidence bag from a nearby forensic kit and held it out to me. "Can you get more?"

I nodded, held the bag to the dark wisp, and then sealed it. The bag felt heavier in hand than it ought to, and I was relieved when I handed it back to her.

"Why would a demon who's necessarily new to Chicago, being the gates were locked, kill two humans?" Theo asked.

"The plant demon was doing it for fun," I said. "But this doesn't look like that."

"Isn't that what they do?" Hansen asked. "Be evil?"

"So do plenty of humans," Gwen said, "as you're aware. Use your brain, or I'll kick you off my crime scene."

"It's not your crime scene," he said stiffly. "It's mine."

"It's theirs," Theo said, pointing to the deceased, the words cold and sharp and not allowing any argument.

"Maybe demons snuck in on a ship," Hansen said. "These guys challenged them, and the demons took them out."

"And nicely placed them here in the heat of the fight, lined up like this?" I shook my head. "This is a display."

"Agreed," Gwen said. "The forensic folks have gotten photos, so help me turn them, Hansen. I want to check their torsos."

He grunted but slipped on gloves. He and Gwen carefully positioned themselves to avoid unnecessary contact, then carefully turned the first man. His face bore no marks of violence. But the wounds to his back weren't the only violations. And killing two humans apparently hadn't been enough for the perpetrator.

Tick.

"Shit," Theo said, the word an exhalation of adrenaline and fear. "Is that a bomb?"

"Shit," Hansen said.

Tick.

The man had been placed atop a small black box attached by colored wires to a block of gray putty.

And the timer read, FIFTY-THREE SECONDS.

FIVE

I wasn't a bomb expert—hell, I wasn't even a bomb *novice*—but that looked like it would do a lot of damage.

"We need to get the bodies out," I said.

"That might trigger the blast," Hansen said, and pointed at two wires that linked the men to the bomb. We'd gotten lucky, apparently, that rolling one over hadn't set it off.

"Shit," Gwen said. "You're right. But let's get pictures." She pulled out her screen to quickly snap shots.

"Everybody out!" I yelled toward the humans still in the building, and pushed Theo toward the doors. "You take the humans outside. Get them away from the building. I'll get the humans inside."

"Lis," he began, but I shook my head.

"I'm immortal," I said. "You aren't."

I didn't wait for a response, but looked around, spotted the fire-alarm switch on the far wall.

Tick.

I ran for it.

The alarm was covered by a glass box. I smashed it with a jacketed elbow, then pulled the switch. The alarm was brilliantly loud, which was great for alerting humans. Bad for allowing me to also hear the ticking of the countdown.

"Let's say thirty seconds," I murmured as Theo, Gwen, and

Hansen shouted instructions to the humans and cops outside, demanding everyone move back from the building.

With them out of the presumptive blast zone, I counted to myself as I ran deeper into the warehouse, looking for humans who hadn't already been moved outside or were ignoring the alarm.

"Everybody out!" I said. "This isn't a drill. Everybody out!"

I snatched heavy-duty ear protectors off one man's head, pulled him out of his seat in a forklift. He swore, but when he recognized the siren, nodded and ran for the door.

Twenty seconds.

A couple of bulky human men took their time emerging from a break room, sodas in hand.

"Fucking drills," one of them murmured, wincing at each screech of the alarm.

"Not a fucking drill," I said. "You've got fifteen seconds until this building blows sky-high and takes everything with it."

I could see they wanted to argue—I was a stranger with a sword—but the alarm kept ringing.

"Run," I said, putting a little glamour into it, and they did.

"Elisa!" Theo had found a bullhorn. "Get out of there!"

I didn't see anyone else, and I was out of time. So I turned back toward the front of the building and ran like my life depended on it. Which . . . you know the drill.

"Eight seconds!" came the call. "Seven. Run faster, vamp!"

I smiled in spite of the circumstances, hurdled one pallet, then another, and finally reached the door.

"Five!" Theo said, standing entirely too close to the building for a mortal.

I grabbed his hand, yanked him forward, and sprinted to get as far as we could from the building in the seconds we had left. We reached a stack of containers, slid to the ground behind them, covered our heads.

"One," Theo said.

There was a moment of intense silence. And then the loudest thing I'd ever heard. The concussion was so powerful, it seemed to rattle my organs, and actually shook the stack of containers. One toppled, and I rolled away before it smashed to the ground in front of us. A storm of debris followed. Glass, metal, and wood rained down. And then a flock of ceramic figurines pelted the ground around us, leaving little weeping angel heads, now divorced from their bodies, to stare up at us accusingly.

When the shower slowed to a light mist of grit, we looked around the corner of the cargo container. The warehouse hadn't been completely leveled, but it was close. Only the back wall remained standing, a break room table still in position, the chairs all upright. Everything else was tossed, charred, or gone in the blast.

"Everybody okay?" Gwen asked.

"Okay here," Theo said, and Hansen's voice echoed the same somewhere farther back.

"Need an ambulance," someone called out.

We emerged from our shelter, crunching angels underfoot, and found a CPD officer pressing down on a wound on an employee's arm.

I looked back. The ambulances already called by Gwen's team to deal with the victims were close and looked only a bit dented, but their access was blocked by the piles of thrown rubble.

"I need some strong arms over here," I said, then picked a spot and started clearing a path.

"Little thing like you is definitely going to need help," Hansen began, and then shut up when I lifted a sheet of corrugated metal, tossed it out of the way.

I looked back at him. "Help or get lost." That must have clicked, because he started lifting, shoving.

It might have been easier with gloves, and I knew my hands would be scraped and sliced by the time we were done, but we didn't have time to wait. We pushed and pulled debris until a couple of EMTs could bring a gurney through. And then the wounded man was placed onto it, wheeled back to the ambulance.

I glanced back, found Hansen watching me. And when I got his nod, knew I had passed his "test." He wasn't the first to require it, wouldn't be the last. So I made no response, went back to the others.

Theo offered me bottles of water and blood.

"I added a mini fridge to the Ombud van," he said. "It's stocked."

"You're a damn good partner," I said. And looked around, wondering if it was better to drink now and replenish my strength, or wait until I wasn't around humans.

"Drink it," Gwen said, drawing my gaze. "They're going to think what they think. And if they aren't comfortable because you eat something different, screw them."

I grinned, drank the entire thing.

Another team was called in to secure the scene, analyze the bomb fragments, and learn what they could forensically. Gwen offered up the pictures she'd taken, and then we regrouped.

"Two human victims," Theo said, "with evidence of multiple wounds. Left in a visible spot, but attached to a bomb to blow the whole thing up if and when someone tried to move them."

"Grim," Gwen said with the flat expression of a cop who had seen plenty of unpleasantness. "Torture is usually for information. And displays like that are usually to send a message."

"There was a delay on the timer," I said. "The killer could have set the bodies to blow as soon as they were moved."

"Instead, the killer gave the humans a chance to evacuate,"

Theo said, turning his gaze back to the building. "But he did not allow time for the building to be saved. Or its contents."

"So it's a business thing?" I wondered. "Some animosity about the warehouse company or what was stored inside it?"

Gwen frowned. "What kind of demon cares about a business dispute?"

"A demon who is capable of prior planning," I said, "and detail work."

"Or a human who's got a demon employee," Theo said, "if that's a thing."

"It's a terrifying thing," Gwen said. "I think I prefer fighting trees."

"Did you know trees can explosively molt their leaves?" Theo asked, and we both looked at him. He just held up his hands. "Sorry. Petra's been studying for *Jeopardy!* again."

"She'd be good at that," Gwen said.

"How did the employees not see this?" I wondered. "If it happened in the middle of the day, how did they miss the deaths, the placement of the bodies, the wiring of a bomb?"

"I don't know yet," Gwen said. "We hadn't started the canvass yet, and then . . ."

"And then *kaboom*," Theo said.

"We'll find out," I said, and gestured to a clump of apparent employees in polo-style shirts with company logos standing nearby. "And start there."

"Take them," Gwen said. "I'll get CPD officers to talk to the other employees, the gate guards, and people in the nearby warehouses." She checked her watch. "Let's meet back here in a couple of hours, and be sure to track who you speak to, so we can check them off the list."

"We will," Theo said. "And keep an eye out."

"Always." Gwen squeezed his hand.

The partner in me wanted to tease him about the tenderness. But I understood the value of those delicate moments in the midst of danger. They made bearing the danger almost worthwhile.

But I was still me and still nosy.

"So you two are . . . ?" I prompted as Theo and I walked to a cluster of employees in their branded shirts.

"Seeing how it goes," he said.

I opted—wisely, I think—not to follow up.

We held out our badges for the humans. They looked wary.

"Theo Martin and Elisa Sullivan," he said. "We aren't cops. We're with the Ombudsman's office."

"Did a vampire blow this shit up?" one of the humans asked.

I took that as my cue. "Did you see a vampire?"

"Nope," said one man. "See one now. You're that Ethan's kid, right? The rich one?"

That interview and the next half dozen involved a lot of questions about vampires and vampire money. They didn't involve a lot of facts about the bombing. According to this group, "Nobody saw nothing." Some hadn't actually seen anything; some probably had, but didn't want trouble.

It took two hours of moving from one cluster of employees to another until we found a few who were willing to talk.

"Mike DeGrazio," said a big man with tan skin and dark hair. "Been working here eighteen years." And his heavy Chicago accent confirmed he'd also spent the years before that in the Windy City.

"Nice to meet you, Mr. DeGrazio." I gestured back to the now-former warehouse. "Did you see anyone who might have been involved in this?"

"Nope," he said, and his answer was so quick, I assumed this interview was going to go like the others.

He must not have liked my narrowed gaze, as he lifted his hands in innocence. "I swear on my mother, god rest her soul. There was a fire near one of the grain elevators, and all but essential staff had to report to help move equipment out of the way."

Well, that was handy timing. Maybe the other employees had been telling the truth.

"When was the fire?" Theo asked, adding notes on his screen.

"Early afternoon. I'm not sure when but it was after lunch."

"Did Mr. Durante or Mr. País help with that fire?" I asked.

"Nah, they work directly for Mr. Buckley, the owner. They're on-site four or five days a week to handle problems." He swallowed down what looked like real distress. "Or they did."

"They have a regular schedule?" Theo asked.

"Not really," the man said. "Mostly come in when it's busy to keep an eye on things."

"Your boss suspicious?" Theo asked.

"Nature of the work," said another of the employees. She had light brown skin and cropped curly gray hair. "I'm Laverne Foley."

"What nature is that, Ms. Foley?" Theo asked.

"Big place, a lot of stuff. Sometimes employees, or just people looking for a freebie, try to steal merchandise. Mr. Buckley runs a tight ship. He pays good, but he doesn't keep thieves on the payroll."

"His men have any trouble lately?" Theo asked.

She glanced at her colleagues, got shakes of the head. "Don't know of anything, but we probably wouldn't. They're very quiet men, if you get what I'm saying."

"Tight-lipped," Mike offered, and she nodded.

"How about unusual things around the warehouse?" I asked. "Or the port, generally?"

"River trolls had a picnic in June," Mike said contemplatively. "Big people, them."

The trolls lived beneath the bridges along the Chicago River.

"They are," I agreed. "How about in the last couple of weeks?"

"Nothing I can think of. Some bigwigs came through yesterday, but they were human, I figure, so . . ." Laverne shrugged it off. But it had been unusual enough for her to notice.

"Bigwigs?" I asked.

"Big white car," she said. "One of those new, sleeked-up models with autodrive. New York plates."

"You see the occupants?"

"Two white guys," Laverne said. "Humans. But I didn't get a close look. Just saw the car when it went by. Attracted attention."

Which had been a mistake if they were connected to the killer. "Why did you think they were human?"

Laverne opened her mouth, closed it again, contemplated. "I guess I just assumed. They didn't do any juju. No fangs or fur."

Demons, of course, could look very human.

Theo failed to hold back a snort. "Laverne," he said, "you've just summarized supernaturals perfectly. What time did you see the car?"

"Maybe noon? Or right after?"

"After," said a third man. "We'd just finished lunch."

"Right!" Laverne said with a nod.

"Your name, sir?" Theo asked.

"They call me Brick."

Little surprise, given how solid he looked. Nearly as big as a refrigerator, with suntanned skin, freckles, and mercilessly parted silver hair.

"So that was before the fire?" I asked.

Brick frowned, scratched his head. "I think so. Security guys will know. They have to keep a log."

Theo nodded. "The CPD is talking to them. Tell me more about the guys from New York."

Unfortunately, we didn't get any more details. The car was flashy, with New York plates; the guys were white and humanoid. The vehicle was unusual enough at the port to be noticed. But then the fire had happened, and all attention had turned to it.

Gwen was fuming when we found her again. "There's no security video. We're going to have to rely on eyewitnesses."

"No video?" Theo asked, glancing around. "There must be dozens of cameras at a place like this."

"Nearly one hundred," she said. "But there was a blip."

"Let me guess," I said, holding up a hand. "It started around lunchtime yesterday."

She lifted her brows. "Give the vamp a prize. How did you know that?"

We told her what we'd gotten from the group of warehouse employees.

"Suspicious," she said. "I'll get word to the uniforms to ask about the vehicle and its occupants."

"Putting all these pieces together, it looks like two people came visiting from New York," Theo said. "They created a distraction to draw attention from the warehouse. During that time, they took out our victims, leaving the bodies behind with an additional weapon."

"And giving us enough time to see it before blowing the building and any evidence to dust," I put in.

"No video of any of it," Theo said. "Nice magic, that."

"Could have been a gadget," Gwen said. "Presuming the plates were legit, if you drive halfway across the country to blow a warehouse, you want to be prepared."

"I don't get it," I said. "Where do potential New York demons fit in? Maybe the blip was magic, but nothing else about this was magical. Not the site, not the victims." I glanced at Gwen. "Buckley?"

"Human as they come," she said. "First name is Felix. We notified the victims' next of kin, and talking to Buckley is next on my list." She looked down at herself. Her dress pants and jacket were stained from the blast. "After a shower and a change," she said, and her smile became amused. "You might want to do the same yourself."

I looked down, realized my clothes weren't in any better shape. "Damn shrapnel."

Theo looked at his watch. "We should touch base with the office. And maybe get food."

"Fine by me," I said, my stomach grumbling despite the location and the inappropriateness. But we'd been there for hours, and I'd cleared a building of people, survived a bomb blast, and cut a path through rubble. And that was in addition to my vegetal fight earlier. Food wasn't an unreasonable need at this point.

"Update Roger," I said. "Then we get Chicago dogs. And if nothing else demonic pops up, we go home."

"Done," Theo said. "You still smell like sap."

"You smell like crushed baby angels."

"Touché," he said. "Touché."

The Chicago dog, with sport peppers and the array of other ingredients, was fantastic. When I was refueled, I decided to make one more stop before heading back to Connor's town house. Not a stop I necessarily wanted to make. But curiosity—and, if I were being honest with myself, irritation—had gotten the best of me.

It bothered me that Jonathan Black hadn't returned my message. He was a broker of information, and a nonresponse from him was weird. Sure, he could have been busy with one of his clients. Maybe he was out of town. Maybe I was just being nosy, in part because I still hadn't decided whether he was friend or enemy.

But the trip served a double purpose: The second demon ward wasn't far from the Prairie Avenue Historic District, the neighborhood where Black made his home. So first I'd drive by the warehouse that housed the demon-detecting machine and check on the sorcerers' progress.

The warehouse was in a series of blocks of bars and shops, and traffic was squeezed into a single lane due to ongoing repairs of the several buildings Rosantine had damaged. I didn't see the sorcerers working—they'd probably already gone home—but the front windows had already been replaced, and a crew was on the roof working beneath spotlights even at this hour. That was all remarkably fast renovation work for Chicago, but officials had apparently decided making the city safe from demons again was worth it, so they'd fast-tracked the permit process.

Traffic eased as I reached the historic district, with its elegant Gilded Age mansions. The houses were big, the lawns wide, and many lots still had separate carriage houses, where horse-drawn buggies might once have been parked out of sight of posh neighbors. Now they held expensive vehicles or served as short-term rental units or houses for newly installed pools—for the ten days a year Chicagoans didn't have to contend with thirty-mile-per-hour winds or freezing cold.

Come to Chicago for the vampires and pizza; stay for the schizophrenic weather.

Black's house was tall and stately, built of pale stone and standing at the edge of a large lot. He lived like most of Chicago's supernaturals—nocturnally. But the windows were dark, the lights off. I didn't see any vehicles parked nearby.

I walked to the porch, climbed up, and paused at the door to listen for sounds of activity and to feel for unusual magic. But other than the low hum of utilities outside, there was nothing. And no magic at all.

Anything? I asked monster.

No.

I saw no security cameras, so I decided to look around outside. I crept down the stairs, waited to ensure that the neighboring houses were still dark. I walked along the side of the house, found literally nothing. Not even a shrub. Grass reached right to the house's exterior walls.

"Not much personality," I murmured.

The yard behind the house was just as empty. No patio, no shrubs. An exterior door led to steps down to a crushed gravel path that led to Black's (presumably former) carriage house.

It was a long structure with two wide, arched doors on the end that faced the street, the doors gorgeously carved. There were high windows along the sides, but unlike the windows in Black's house, they were dusty and smeared with age. I found a few bricks on the ground and piled them up to make a step—while working to ignore the crawling and skittering things that made their home in and around them.

I stepped up, peered into a window. And found nothing. I'd have sworn there was faint magic in the air, but the (definitely former) carriage house was virtually empty. There were a few garden tools and some plastic boxes. Two pieces of furniture— bureaus, given their size and shape—were covered in dustcloths.

I stepped down, looked around. No Black. No magic. No secrets.

At least not ones that I could see.

I messaged Connor when I was on my way back to the town house, advised him I was ready for relaxation. I was welcomed home by the scents of garlic and tomatoes, and found Lulu at the stove. Her short hair was pushed back behind a pearl headband, and she was pouring red wine into a big pot. She didn't cook often, but every once in a while, she found herself in the mood. The dog apparently hadn't done much for my hunger, as my stomach growled noisily.

"Drink?" she asked.

"God, yes," I said.

Without turning around, she pointed at an open wine bottle on the nearby counter. I picked it up, took a drink. My mouth puckered from the dryness. "Nice."

"New-to-me brand," Lulu said. "Dinner will be ready in a few minutes."

"It smells amazing."

"Thanks." For the first time, she glanced back at me and took in the dust and grit and general explodiness of my clothes and hair. And her eyes went huge. "What the hell happened to you?"

"Demons blew up a warehouse."

"While you were in it?"

"Only nearby. Me and Theo."

"You look like you got stuck in a dirt tornado."

Not entirely inaccurate, and the grit was starting to chafe. "Do I have time for a shower?"

"If you're fast." A timer *ding*ed, and she turned back to a boiling pot, which I assumed held pasta.

"Wolves?" I asked.

"Alexei is watching soccer."

"Football," he called out from the den.

"It's soccer in the US, as you know."

Of course he did. But irritating Lulu was one of his hobbies.

"Your shifter is outside. I think he needed some quiet time."

"What happened?" I asked.

"I don't think anything in particular. Just the usual pre-Apex blues." She glanced back, used a finger to gesture at me. "And he doesn't yet know about this. Go take a shower. He'll keep until you're done, and he won't worry so much if you're clean. But don't hold up dinner."

I did as directed. I showered and changed into soft joggers and a crop top in the same pale green fabric. I let my hair air-dry to save time, given even monster was pinging me about hunger now.

"Working on it," I murmured, and went downstairs.

When I didn't find Connor in the den with Alexei, I went outside. Behind the town house was a yard of soft green grass; it was bounded by the brick wall of the building on one side, and covered fences shielded it from view on the others. The space, a rare bit of nature in the rumbling of the city, was one of the reasons he'd bought this place.

Fall was setting in, and the grass was beginning to yellow. Connor sat in an Adirondack chair in the middle of the lawn, hands crossed behind his head as he looked up at the sky. Not many stars were visible inside Chicago city limits, but a few were bright enough to overcome the electric competition.

"Pensive" is how I'd have described him, and that wasn't his usual style.

He held out a hand as I approached, and when I took it, pulled me into the chair on top of him. I relaxed against his chest, breathed in his magic, and buried myself in his warmth. (Admittedly, the crop top was a questionable choice for an outdoor excursion.)

"You okay?" I asked.

"Just taking a moment. You smell nice."

"I used your shampoo."

He snorted. "That explains the forest pine scent." Then he went still. "Why did you shower?"

"Cleanliness is next to godliness?"

"Elisa."

"We'll get to that," I promised. "Let's just have the moment." I closed my eyes.

And nearly jumped out of the seat when Lulu yelled from the doorway, "Come eat, you heathens!"

She'd made a beautiful spread. A platter of spaghetti and red sauce with seared meatballs, topped with a snowfall of freshly grated Parmesan. There was a bottle of wine and an enormous loaf of crusty bread.

"What's the occasion?" I asked as we took seats at the table. Alexei attacked the bread with a serrated knife, then passed around the resulting chunks.

"A good night of work," Lulu said. "The outlines are nearly done, and then we tape and paint."

"And the bakery down the block from the mural gave her the bread," Alexei said with a grin. "So she decided to cook."

"I know how to lure supernaturals," she said. "And we've barely seen each other since Rosantine."

"Where's our resident feline demon?" I asked, looking around.

"Probably peeing in your shoes," Connor said, and loaded my plate with pasta.

"This restaurant has very good service," I said with a smile.

"Don't forget to tip your waiter," he said, voice low and inviting, and kissed me quickly.

"Since I'd like to keep my appetite in order to enjoy this wonderful feast," Lulu said, pouring wine into my glass, "I'm going to change the subject. Elisa, tell us about the warehouse that blew up."

Connor looked torn between fear that I'd been close to injury and fury that someone would have dared to try to injure me. "Explain," he said, voice tight.

"We were called to the Chicago Industrial Port because employees found two dead humans in a warehouse. We moved one of the bodies and discovered the perp had placed a detonator beneath it."

Connor just stared at me. "Elisa."

"I'm fine," I said. "There was a timer." I opted not to tell him how close it had been. "Me, Theo, and Gwen are all fine. I got the other humans out."

His magic was like cold steel, and it sliced through the air.

Lulu cleared her throat. "Should we just—"

"Let Elisa tell us all—and for the first time tonight—what kind of danger she was in?"

I lifted my eyebrows. I surmised he was angry I hadn't sent him a message. But he knew my job was dangerous, and this tone wasn't like him.

"When's your next challenge?" I asked.

"Tomorrow night," he said.

"And your life will be on the line."

He bit back whatever he'd wanted to say next. But his jaw was stiff, and there was anger in his eyes. And, worse, fear.

"Wise man," Lulu murmured, and poured more wine as Connor steepled his hands, elbows on the table, and rested his forehead on his joined fingers. He was composing himself, I knew. And seeing that struggle drained my temper.

"I'm sorry," I said. "I wasn't trying to hide it or make it a surprise. It happened, and we were okay—"

"So it's just one more fucked-up thing in Chicago," Alexei put in, then ate an enormous forkful of pasta. And because he was right, the rest of the tension evaporated.

"Yeah," Connor said, lifting his head and running a hand through his dark waves.

"Who's the challenger?" I asked.

He took a drink of wine. "Leader of a small clan near Green Bay. Thinks we need fresh blood in charge, so the Pack doesn't get stale."

And I could see in his face that he thought the idea had merit.

"Fresh blood is for vamps," Alexei said. "Doesn't matter for shifters."

"I think the system needs change," Connor said. "I think it's time to reconsider whether beating the shit out of someone every few days is a sign of good leadership."

"You're tired," I said.

"Yeah. Of a lot of things."

"That's the sign of good leadership," Alexei said, and we all looked at him. "Doing things right for the Pack. Being strong for the Pack. Putting up with bullshit challenges for the Pack. That matters."

Connor reached out, squeezed Alexei's shoulder.

"You want me at headquarters?" Alexei asked.

Connor shook his head. "Stay with the sorcerers. My thing is simple: I win or I lose."

"If you lose," I said, knowing it was time to lighten the mood, "I will take you to supernatural night at Disney World. You can ride roller coasters until you puke."

"You are such a romantic," he said.

"Speaking of romance," I said, and pulled off a chunk of bread, "let me tell you about Poison Ivy."

Surprising Connor with my second demon attack of the evening maybe hadn't been the best way to soothe him. But they all enjoyed the video, at least.

"Thanks for the spread," Connor told Lulu when dawn was drawing near and it was time to wrap things up. "Not bad for a free meal."

Lulu's smile was thin. "Oh, the meal wasn't free," she said, then pointed to the kitchen . . . and the pile of pans and dishes that awaited us.

"As they say, never look a gift meatball in the mouth," Alexei said.

"Nobody says that," Connor muttered as Alexei took Lulu's hand and they headed for the stairs. "Nobody says that!" he called out again. And was ignored.

He looked back at me. "Rock, paper, scissors."

"Scrub, rinse, dry," I said. "Grab a towel."

SIX

At dusk, we stood in the town house's doorway. I knew how strong Connor was, how determined, how brave. But I still had butterflies about the danger he faced. As he probably did for me.

"I could go with you," I said, as I had before each challenge. But we both knew it wasn't the right move. A vampire at an Apex fight created unnecessary drama, and made the fight less about the future of the Pack and more about our relationship. Yes, they were intertwined, especially if I was "joining" the NAC. But the challenge needed to be about Connor and his opponent.

He must have seen understanding in my eyes as he leaned forward, kissed me lightly. "I'll be fine, I promise. And Dan has my back."

"Good," I said.

"You be careful, too. And work very hard not to get blown up."

"Very hard," I agreed. "On the other hand, every time I almost get blown up at a warehouse, I get a delicious pasta dinner. I'm one for one."

As my Auto pulled up in front of the house, I slid my lips to his ear. "Kick his ass, puppy," I said, and carried my katana to the vehicle.

* * *

I directed the Auto to drive past the fairy castle on the way to the office, just to make sure things seemed relatively normal. There were guards at the gatehouse and the building was intact, so I called that good enough. I wasn't going to tempt fate by getting closer.

We drove smoothly across town; traffic was at its usual pace. But clouds began to thicken overhead, shot through with lightning that had a green tinge I didn't care for. I couldn't think of any nonmagical reason Chicago's sky should look like the background of a dystopian movie.

And it only got worse when I reached the office.

I climbed out of the vehicle and heard something *flap* in the lowering sky. The sound—almost wet?—had me putting a hand on the pommel of my sword.

A really big bird? A human testing the limits of flight?

I walked through the gate of the fence that surrounded the property and toward the parking lot in front of the main building. There was another *flap*—air being pushed, silence being broken. A breeze sour with demon magic stirred the trees at the edge of the property. I stared at the sky, looking for some indication of what I'd heard. But saw nothing.

SOMETHING BIG AND DEMONIC FLYING ABOVE CAMPUS, I messaged the team. COULD USE AN ASSIST AT THE DOOR.

ON OUR WAY, Theo messaged back. WHAT IS "SOMETHING"?

?? was my response.

I caught movement to my left, had my katana unsheathed in seconds. An angle of wing—dark and leathery and tipped with spikes where the wing was jointed—dipped from the clouds. Bat-like wings shouldn't have frightened me. Bats ate fruit or crawly things and were supposed to be friends of vampires.

It slipped down and turned, as maneuverable as a fighter jet. It flew over the trees at the edge of the compound and, with a shriek that would probably haunt my dreams for weeks, banked around again. I still hadn't seen it in any detail. But I saw enough to know that it was big. Much, much bigger than me and spilling magic into the sky.

I gripped my sword in both hands and turned my body to narrow its target.

The demon dived, and I swept my sword in an arc above me, felt it connect. Furious, it spun and pulled its claws back, raking my right shoulder with one razor-sharp tip. The wound burned like fire, like I'd been stabbed with a Fourth of July sparkler, and my arm went numb. My sword fell to the ground. I ducked to grab it as the demon winged back again, picked up the sword with my left hand. While I was far from ambidextrous, I'd trained for this.

Unfortunately, I hadn't trained for a leathery demon with a good thirty-foot wingspan to land in front of me and put its body between me and a building.

And its body was . . . not a wonderland.

The torso between the wings was jet-black and smooth skinned. It stood on two legs, but they were jointed like a dog's back legs and protruded in front of its body. Its head was squarish, with a mouth of gleaming teeth. Its eyes were small and red, its ears just slits.

The demon limped forward, dragging the foot I'd apparently managed to injure. Black blood gleamed like ink beneath the security lights. It was a nightmare.

I rolled my numb shoulder, tried to wake it up, and raised my sword with my left hand.

"This isn't your territory," I told it. "It's a human workplace, and you are very bad for morale."

Limp. Drag. Ooze.

The demon opened its mouth to scream, and the stuff of nightmares would have had nightmares about the consecutive rows and rows of teeth that lined its gullet. And I was supposed to be its meal.

It lunged—faster than it should have been able to on land—and I spun away, tried to put space between us and give myself time to reposition before facing it again. But a hooked claw caught the heel of my boot and pulled with enough force to throw me off-balance. I hit the ground at an angle that at least dislodged the claw. But before I could move, the demon loomed over me, jaws unhinging to show its seemingly infinite dentition.

I rolled over just as a drop of saliva fell, hit my leg, and sizzled. Then burned a hole right through my clothes to bare skin.

"Oh, definitely not," I muttered. I kicked up, but the angle didn't work. Its torso was too far off the ground. Instead, I aimed for its leg while fumbling for my sword, tried to swipe up between myself and the creature. I managed one shot, but that just had more acidic blood pouring over my arm. And that shit hurt.

The demon shrieked again, the sound like metal against metal. Its teeth moved closer. . . .

And then the sky lit up with light that was nearly blinding. Someone had turned on the office's emergency floodlights. The creature, apparently sensitive to light, screamed again and turned around to look for the perpetrator.

Petra stood behind it, a fireball in her hand. "Go home!" she said, and aimed.

The creature flapped its wings, sending a shower of acid and demon-infused air over me as it headed toward the tree line, but it wasn't fast enough to avoid the bolt of lightning that zagged out of Petra's hand. She hit the creature in the back. It screamed and flapped its wings, sending another spray of its caustic blood across the parking lot.

"*Go home!*" Petra demanded again, gathering energy in her hand for round two.

The demon had apparently had enough. It pushed hard, lifted, and disappeared into the night sky.

I lay back on the concrete, breathed. Waited until there were footsteps nearby and a gloved hand in front of my face. It was Petra. I took her hand, hopped to my feet, and rolled my now-tingling shoulder.

"Thanks for the assist," I said.

"Welcome."

"What the fuck was that?" Theo asked as we approached the building's portico.

"Winged demon," I said. "There's something for your chart."

It wasn't the first attack of the day. There had been four reported demon encounters before the sun had gone down. One probably wasn't a demon: A dog had lashed out at a kid chasing it with a stick. The other three demons had caused five human injuries and plenty of property damage, including one who'd worked his way down the Dan Ryan, tossing cars around for fun and enjoyment. Fortunately, there'd been no more human deaths. At least, not beyond the humans at the warehouse. Unfortunately, none of the demons had been captured. So they were still out there wreaking havoc.

"There are still multiple wards in place," I said when we were safely ensconced in the office. "How are the demons managing to avoid them? Are they playing follow-the-leader and mimicking Rosantine's precise route through Chicago?"

"They must be," Roger said. "There haven't been any disturbances at the operating wards. Word has apparently spread."

"Maybe there are more holes than we thought," Petra said, frowning at the map she'd put on-screen. It showed the locations of the defensive wards we'd previously identified through math and logic, and highlighted the two that had already been triggered.

"We've been presuming they provide complete coverage for the city," she continued, "but maybe they don't. Maybe the demons stayed out of Chicago because it was basically a minefield, and that was enough for a while."

"Maybe the ley line surge increased their ability to detect the wards," I said. "Is that a thing?"

Petra shrugged. "No manual. We'd know a lot more if those crazy Victorians had left one."

"The mayor wants us to pull up that welcome mat," Roger said. "But her legal team is concerned about the legalities of cops and Ombuds physically transporting demons out of Chicago—nonmagically, I mean—if they refuse to leave."

"Legalities?" Theo asked.

"There's nothing illegal about their being here," Roger said. "Being a demon, on its own, isn't a crime. At least not yet."

"So we can ask them to leave," Theo said, "but if they decline, we're out of luck?"

"They can still be locked up if they hurt someone or go on a rampage," Petra said. "Right?"

"Of course," Roger said. "They go in the cubes."

Those were the stand-alone concrete cells that filled one of the buildings in our campus. They'd been built specifically to hold supernaturals.

"But they aren't going to agree to be locked up willingly," I said. "And we'd still have to get them here and into the cells without hurting more people. I don't think we have the power for that."

"Sorcerers?" Roger asked.

"Focused on getting the wards fixed," I said. "Well, not Lulu, but this isn't the right job for her."

"Are the sorcerers still on track to get the wards up today?" Theo asked.

"I haven't gotten an update yet, but that's the hope," Roger said.

"Random question," I said. "Has anyone seen or heard from Jonathan Black?"

"What do you mean?"

"I messaged him and went by his house. No response, and the house was dark."

"He has a job," Petra said. "He was probably working."

"Was he?" I asked.

She looked up, blinked. "Well, yeah. He's an attorney. He has clients."

"He says he does," Theo pointed out. "But we've never seen them. So Elisa has a point."

I tapped my sword. "I always do."

"Nice," Theo said, and offered me a fist bump.

I deserved it, accepted it.

"You two were made for each other," Roger said with a grin.

"I'd say he's my work husband, but since he's dating a cop, that doesn't really work."

Theo smiled. "Why do you want to talk to Black?"

"He's supposed to be in the know about supernatural drama, so I want to know what he knows about demons."

"Are you going to tell Connor you went to his house?" Petra asked.

The question made me feel sheepish, which I didn't like. So I gave her a look. "I don't report my movements even to the would-be Apex of the North American Central Pack."

"Connor does not like him," Petra said. "At all."

"*I* don't like him," I said. "Connor viscerally hates him. But he has information."

"He did save your life," Theo pointed out, and sounded as concerned about that as I was. Black, enigma as he was, wasn't the type I wanted to owe.

"Yeah, he did. Where and how he spends his time isn't my business. But there's a lot of crazy shit going on out there. I don't like the idea of his getting tangled up in it."

Theo's screen buzzed. He glanced at it. "Gwen," he said, and answered it. He gave a couple of "yeahs" and then ended the call, looked at me.

"Buckley, the warehouse owner, has been out of the city on business. Multiple stops in Europe, supposedly, and Gwen hasn't been able to reach him."

"Is he avoiding her?" I said.

"Don't know. That's why we're going to his place. If we want to figure out who bombed his warehouse, we need to start with him."

The Gold Coast was one of the poshest and most expensive neighborhoods in Chicago. Just north of downtown, it was edged on the east by Lake Michigan. There were towering high-rise apartment buildings mixed with luxury town houses, big shady trees, and flowers edging the sidewalk. It was also the home of Navarre House, one of the four vampire houses in the city. We passed the stately marble building where its vampires resided, and stopped in front of a tower with a circular drive and valet service. The uniformed valet didn't look thrilled about our parking the van in front of the building.

"You'll need to move that into the garage."

Theo, who'd driven, offered his badge. "I don't actually. This will be a quick trip. But if it gets towed, we'll have to come back tomorrow and the next day and . . ."

"Just go," said the valet, who'd already turned his attention to the next vehicle.

We walked inside, shoes clicking on a floor of matte gray stone dotted here and there with shimmering gold. A security desk was perched in front of a bank of elevators. It was made of pale stone with the same shimmers. The desk's single occupant was lit by an enormous overhead chandelier made of crystal tears that dripped like rain from the ceiling.

Theo held out his badge to her. "Theo Martin and Elisa Sullivan. We're here to see Mr. Buckley."

The human, whose cropped silver hair glimmered in the light, looked both pained and relieved. She leaned forward, glanced around to ensure privacy. "He doesn't live here anymore, I guess."

"He doesn't?" I asked, and her eyes, nearly as pale as her hair, shifted to me.

"No. There's— Well, I'm not sure what to do, and the property manager is in Aruba, and I can't reach my supervisor, and—"

I held up a hand. "Start at the beginning."

"Well, he *did* own it. Like, past tense? But apparently someone else lives there now? Or says they do? But I can't reach my supervisor. . . ." She was repeating herself, and her tone was sliding from uncertain to slightly hysterical.

"Why don't we go up," I suggested, and slipped a little vampire glamour behind it, "and check things out for you? If there's a problem, we'll call the CPD, so your supervisor won't be mad at you. And if there's not, then no harm done."

It took only a second for her to nod. "Mr. Buckley's . . . I mean, the new . . . It's 3011." She pointed toward the bank of the elevators, and the gleaming steel doors parted in invitation.

"Thank you," I said, and we clicked toward them.

"Any bets on what we'll find up there?" Theo asked.

"A bomb or a person who set a bomb."

"Yeah," he said as the elevator glided smoothly upward, its

destination apparently set by the young woman. "You use a little magic on her?"

"A little," I admitted, trying not to feel guilty. I didn't magic humans for convenience. But the bomb was on my mind. Monster echoed its agreement.

When we reached our floor, the elevator chimed its goodbye before beginning its descent again. The foyer matched the decor in the lobby: sleek, gray, crystal. We took the corridor toward 3011, which was four doors down, and Theo knocked.

No answer.

I looked at Theo, who nodded and knocked again. His hand was still poised in front of the door when it swung open.

A demon, magic prickling the air around him, looked back at us. His skin was pale, his eyes the color of a monarch butterfly's wings, his pupils squared like a goat's. He wore an old-fashioned nylon tracksuit, red with white stripes, and his arms seemed a bit too long for his lanky body.

"Hi," Theo said, his voice impeccably calm. "We're looking for Felix Buckley."

The man blinked at us. "Doesn't live here." His voice was deep and heavily accented. Eastern European, at a guess.

"Oh," Theo said, and pulled out his screen as if to double-check something. "That's really weird, because—"

The demon slammed the door closed.

Theo sent a very quick message, presumably to the office, then showed me the screen.

"See?" he said earnestly. "The website says Buckley lives here. I'm not sure how we're going to deliver the goods if we've got the wrong address."

Theo's voice was perfectly plaintive—a man foiled by technology. And perfectly modulated for the demon likely listening through the door and watching through the peephole.

"Yeah, it's very strange," I agreed with a frown, and thumbed off the guard on my katana's scabbard. "Those are some expensive goods. Especially the gold ones."

The door opened again. Tracksuit moved out of the way, then swept a hand into the room.

"Please to enter," he said grandly.

"Oh, thanks," Theo said. "We can just get this cleared . . ."

He trailed off as we walked into the condo. It was a nice space with tall ceilings, good floors, and fancy wainscoting. We paused at the kitchen, which had plenty of marble and high-end appliances, but not much in way of clutter. The counters were empty— not so much as a folded dish towel on the oven handle.

We kept moving, past walls where pictures or artwork had once hung, memorialized now by the rectangular spaces of slightly darker paint.

One of the Guardians who had built Chicago's demon wards said demons spoiled their own nests. If that were true, that wasn't what we saw here. This place had been *unspoiled*—the detritus of humanity stripped away.

We reached the main living space, which opened to expansive views of Chicago's skyline and held the only piece of furniture in the place: a long leather sofa of buttery yellow positioned for a view of that skyline. Arms stretched across the back of that sofa, gaze on the view, sat a demon.

He looked almost human. He had suntanned skin, was wide through the chest, had a medium build. He looked to be in his late fifties. His hair was dark, with slashes of silvery gray. It reached his shoulders, but was slicked back from his well-worn face. His eyes were dark and deep set. But they had the square pupils that marked him as definitely not human.

He was dressed, it seemed, for something fancier than sitting alone on a sofa. He wore a dark suit with a patterned vest and a pocket square, a button-down shirt with the top unfastened, and expensive-looking loafers with little silver buckles.

One of his legs was crossed over the other, and he shifted his gaze to watch us walk toward him. Magic scratched the air, leaving a bitter taste in my mouth. It was unclear whether the seated demon, or the others who stood around the room, had put it there.

"Who do we have here?" he asked, smile wide, as if he was thrilled to have company.

Theo played it very cool. "Theo Martin and Elisa Sullivan. We're from the Ombudsman's office. We're looking for Mr. Buckley, the owner of this condo."

"I'm not Mr. Buckley," the demon said, "but he doesn't own this place anymore. He sold it to me"—he checked a flash old-fashioned wristwatch—"about four hours ago."

"And you are?" Theo asked.

"Dante," the man said with a grin that didn't reach his eyes. "Dantalion is the full name."

"Unusual name," I said.

His gaze slid to mine, and it felt like the movement had scraped the air itself. I didn't like the nerves it set on end. But I held my ground.

"Demons often have unusual names." His gaze was too direct, and there was a dare in it.

I rested my left hand on my katana, watched him watch me, wondered what he would do. If he was concerned by the threat, he made no sign of it.

I could help, monster whispered.

Not the time, I said. I had to keep myself, Theo, and a building full of humans alive.

"Any idea why Mr. Buckley decided to sell? This looks to be a nice place," Theo said, glancing about.

"No idea," Dante said. "I was looking for a property and I found one. Fortunately, he was a motivated seller."

"Odd, as we've had trouble reaching him," I said.

"That is odd," the man said. "Maybe he was concerned you were looking for him and decided liquidation was best."

"So he sold to you," Theo said. "Very unusual. We'd appreciate taking a look at the paperwork."

Dante patted his chest as if feeling for documents. "Unfortunately, I appear to have left that with my attorneys."

"Hmm," Theo said, given we didn't have any basis to demand that information from a lawyer. "Are you aware a commercial building belonging to Mr. Buckley was damaged yesterday?"

"I was not," he said. But nothing in his expression changed. "Isn't that a tragedy." It wasn't a question.

"Two men were killed," Theo said.

"Doubly tragic," Dante said blandly.

"How long have you known Mr. Buckley?" Theo asked.

"For a time. We're business associates."

"It's odd he didn't tell you about the warehouse," I said, "given you're business associates and he sold you this condo a few hours ago."

We both looked at Dante, who hadn't broken a sweat, but didn't look happy about the line of questioning.

"He's not a friend," Dante said. "We've only been involved in discrete business transactions."

"Where are you from?" I asked.

"That's a rude question, isn't it?"

"It's a simple question," I said. "You aren't from Chicago, and I'm sure you know how I know that. So where are you from?"

"New York," he said, practically daring me to make an issue of it.

"You have a vehicle licensed here?" I asked, thinking of the New York plates on the vehicles at the port.

"I don't drive." His smile was thin. "I have drivers."

"And do they have vehicles?"

"You'd have to ask them."

I looked around at the other demons in the room. Half were busy studying the skyline. Half stared back at me with bored expressions. This was like pulling teeth, and it was trying my patience.

"What brings you to Chicago from New York?" Theo asked, probably sensing my growing irritation.

"Business," Dante said.

"What kind of business?"

"Empire building. The kind of business that makes a man wealthy enough to afford this," he said, and flicked a hand toward the windows.

"The name of your company?" Theo asked.

"Don't have one. I'm a sole proprietor. A . . . What do you call it?" He snapped his fingers like a bad-mannered customer.

"Entrepreneur?" offered one of the other demons.

"Right. Entrepreneur," Dante said. "Myself and my associates are looking forward to extended business dealings in Chicago."

"Dante," Theo said, "as I'm sure you're aware, Chicago doesn't have good experiences with demons. So we're going to ask you, politely, to leave town right now."

Dante looked at us for a long time. "No," he finally said, the word falling heavily as a stone.

"Apologies," Theo said. "I asked a question, but should have made a statement." His face went hard. "Get out of Chicago."

"No," Dante said again. He was up before I'd registered his movement, and was suddenly standing in front of me, less than a foot between us. Monster seemed to arch back, like a cat in full hostility mode.

I saw Theo ready to launch forward, but I held up a hand. The demon could do more damage to Theo than to me.

"Vampire," Dante said, darkness spinning in his irises and surrounding me with the smell of acrid smoke. "You should know better."

His words seemed to bounce through my head, echoing within bone and blood. But I worked hard to show no weakness.

"If you're going to tell me vampires should side with demons, let me save you the trouble. Andaras already gave me that speech." I leaned forward, my eyes nearly watering from the bitterness in the air, my heart thumping so loudly, he must've heard it. Sweat, cold and clammy, slicked the back of my neck. "In my city, there are consequences for hurting humans."

He watched me for another long moment, utter disdain in his eyes. I'd seen a similar look in Rosantine's eyes. It was more than just hatred; it was cold loathing wrapped in arrogance with a narcissism chaser. I'd have bet he was imagining ways to hurt me . . . while I was trying to figure out how we could extricate a demon from a condo building without hurting the humans who lived in it. We'd expected to find Mr. Buckley, and we didn't have a contingency plan.

But then Dante stepped back.

I'd called his bluff, and he folded first.

The sociopathy in his expression cleared, replaced by that weird, not quite humanity. "I am surprised you can tell the difference between good demons and bad. I'm a businessperson. I happen to be a demon, like you happen to be a vampire. I'm not leaving, and you can't make me. You don't have the force or the law on your side."

He went back to the sofa, stretched his arms out again, looked not quite human. "She was weak," he said. "I'm not. And I'd be happy to demonstrate my strength. You want to keep me out?" He recrossed one leg over the other. "You should've kept her out first."

"That last shot had good aim," I said when we were standing outside again.

"Yeah," Theo said, and raised his casted arm. "Too good." He looked at me speculatively. "I thought he was going to eat you alive."

"That would have been the finale, if anything." I sucked in a few breaths of lake-washed air and let darkness push away the demon's shadow.

"Let's get some fresh air," Theo said, and gestured toward the sidewalk. "We'll be back in ten," he said to the still-waiting attendant.

"Dante came here for a reason," I said when we were walking down the dark and quiet street. "He can't have been here very long, and we've already found him. He doesn't want to leave, so he opted for politics over violence."

"He has more control than Rosantine," Theo said.

"Yeah," I agreed. "And more magic, and apparently minions, which she didn't have."

"Associates," Theo clarified.

I snorted. "Right. So he and Buckley knew each other before Dante got to Chicago. Because of Rosantine, Dante realizes he's going to be able to get into Chicago. Maybe he asked Buckley for help in getting his 'business' off the ground."

"Good money says his 'business' isn't fully legit."

"Yeah. Seems to me a legit businessman who wanted to build an empire would tell us what he did. Maybe we'd be potential customers."

"Not on an Ombud's salary," Theo muttered.

"Right? Maybe Buckley was supposed to find him a place. For some reason, he decided this was the one he wanted. So he managed to buy it from Buckley, or so he says." I frowned. "So, maybe the warehouse was some kind of warning message: Sell me the condo, or face the consequences? Or a punishment for not selling fast enough? That seems excessive even for Gold Coast real estate."

"The real estate market is a bitch."

"I guess. But why this condo? Why this building?"

"Prestige?" Theo asked. "He seemed pretty pleased with himself. A kingpin's got to have a kingdom."

"We need to find Buckley," I said.

We walked in companionable silence. He stopped to pick up a small white flower, a survivor of early fall, that had fallen to the sidewalk from its small, tidy garden plot.

"You okay?" I asked. "You're not one to inspect the flora."

"I like the flora. But I'm thinking." He placed the flower carefully atop the low wrought iron fence that surrounded the garden. He was taking care of it. His instinct was to save and protect and cherish; Gwen had picked a good partner in Theo.

"About?" I asked.

"Do you think he's right about that good-demon thing? That it's not right—morally, I guess—to demand they all leave?"

"I don't know," I said, and leaned back against the rail. "I think Petra said there were demons who did beneficial things, but that was mostly because humans used their sigils to control them. I don't know how much of that was a demon's nature versus a human's control."

Theo nodded. "That's a point."

"On the other hand, there are not a lot of historical pieces about how great vampires are. Sparkly ones excluded."

Theo smiled. "Supernaturals are a complex bunch."

"Eh, I don't think we're any more complex than humans. Some are good guys; some are not. I'm pretty sure he's not a good guy. And unless we can find the evidence to get him out, it sounds like he plans to stay."

While Theo drove the van back to the office, I watched the sky for winged demons or other obstacles—because that was my life now—and tried to get an update about Connor's fight. I hadn't gotten a message from him, so I bugged Alexei, but he hadn't heard anything either. I stopped myself before messaging Dan, as I wanted him focused on Connor, not babysitting me. I'd just have to keep waiting, which was unfortunate. Patience wasn't one of my virtues.

"So, Dante the demon says he's in town for business," Roger said when we reached the office, sandwiches in tow. He chewed a bite of veggie sub while he contemplated. "And he should be allowed to stay unless he engages in bad behavior."

"Well," Petra said, "until he's caught at it, anyway." She nibbled the edge of a barbecue chip. She'd taken off her gloves to eat, lest she end up with orange-tinted fabric.

"That was his argument," Theo said. "And it lines up with what the mayor was saying."

Roger looked at Petra. "Does he really own that condo?"

"Not according to the county records. But they aren't updated automatically, and there can be a lag depending on when the documents are submitted."

"You're right that we can't take him in the building," Roger said. "There's too much risk."

"Lure him out?" Theo asked, inspecting the components of his sandwich for the second time.

"I told them no mayo," I said.

"I know," he said, and reassembled it. "Just checking the math. Mayo is demon spit."

"I mean, probably not literally," I said, "because it would have burned right through the bread."

"Probably not literally," he agreed.

"We don't have any lures," Roger said, then added dryly, "except property owned by Buckley."

"That we haven't been able to reach Buckley makes me really curious about the condo's sale," Theo said. "If this was some kind of shakedown, why not tell us and get Dante off his back?"

"Maybe he doesn't trust cops," I said. "The devil you know and all that."

"Maybe he's no longer able to talk," Roger said. And the silence that followed confirmed we'd all been thinking the same thing.

I glanced at Petra. "You have any luck learning about Dante?"

"Oh, yeah," Petra said. "That was the easy part. First of all, he's a duke."

"Like a British duke?" Theo asked.

"Like a demon duke. Solomon ranked them." That was King Solomon of religious fame, who had researched, cataloged, and learned to control at least seventy-two demons. A copy of his centuries-old grimoire, the *Key of Solomon*, was easy to find online.

"Solomon said, based on his conversations with demons, that they had this aristocratic hierarchy. Marquises, dukes, et cetera at the top of the pyramid. The higher the ranks, the more powerful the demons, and the larger their legions of lower-ranked demons."

"Legions," Theo repeated, and pushed away the rest of his sandwich, appetite apparently gone.

"What are his strengths?" I asked.

"He can control horses," Petra said. "Use turtle shells to predict the future. Strong as two oxen. And has command of a legion of ten thousand."

Roger nearly choked on his sandwich. "Excuse me?"

"According to Solomon, who wanted to seem like a badass, and the demon, who also wanted to seem like a badass. But I think that's mostly a demon-dimension thing. You don't really get the same fan base when you pop into the human world."

"Minions of some number," I said. "Check."

"This is his sigil," Petra said, and showed us her screen. A sigil was a demon's personal mark, usually made up of lines within a larger circle. It could be used to seal or control the demon, so they didn't share them willingly. We almost hadn't found Rosantine's in time. But Solomon had found Dante's.

"Dante has to know the *Key of Solomon* is out there," Petra said. "So he doesn't care that we know who he is."

"He's not afraid of us," Theo said, sliding a pencil into the end of his cast to scratch his arm. "Doesn't care if we know his sigil, which is basically the key to his destruction."

Problem was, controlling a demon wasn't easy even if you had a sigil. It had taken me, Petra, Lulu, our necromancer friend Ariel, and a cadre of shifters to kick Rosantine out of this world, and we'd only barely managed it. The stronger the demon, the harder to control.

You didn't have to fight demons with magic, of course. You could fight them physically, but with rank-and-file soldiers that wasn't going to be easy.

Me, monster insisted, putting up enough of a metaphysical fight that my vision momentarily doubled.

Stop, I told it, and put magic behind the order—a moment too late to remember that I was just magicking myself.

"You okay?" Theo asked, and offered his pencil.

Petra watched me with narrow-eyed curiosity, but didn't say anything.

"Fine," I said, and rubbed my temples. "Demon-induced migraine." I drank some water and waited for things to stabilize.

"So, what are we going to do about him?" Theo asked.

"I'll check in with the mayor," Roger said. "If she wants to kick them out, we need the legal backing. If she wants to incarcerate them, we're going to need the right gear."

"I want to look at this New York angle," Petra said. "If you have a demon—and a duke at that—living it up in New York with his demonness, someone had to have noticed."

"Not if they were assimilated," Roger pointed out. "Demons don't exactly have a good relationship with humans—especially theologically. Good reason not to advertise where the power is coming from."

Theo nodded. "Maybe makes you feel bigger if you don't tell them about the magic. All those humans just think you're a very capable man."

"Or a very capable mafioso," I said. "And he isn't hiding it here. Does he think he has a free pass because of Rosantine?"

"I'm going to find out," Petra said. "And maybe that will give us some ammunition to get him out."

Maybe it would.

But who was in line behind him?

That question was excellent motivation for me to check with the sorcerers on the wards.

"We have a problem," Aunt Mallory said when she answered my call.

"No problems today. Only opportunities. What's wrong?"

"The machine is repaired. The spell has been kindled here and at South Gate. But they aren't powering up."

"How do you know?" I asked. "I mean, are you throwing demons at them?" It was an honest question, as it hadn't occurred to me to wonder how they'd actually test the magic.

"No," Aunt Mallory said, and I could hear the smile in her voice. "We saved some residue from the Cadogan House lawn."

Casting Rosantine back into the demon dimension had left some of her smut in the yard. "And nothing happened?"

"Bubkes. We're trying to backtrack to find what we might have missed."

"We could come out to you," I said. "Maybe fresh eyes would help."

"We're at the warehouse," Aunt Mallory said, "your mom and I. Your uncle Catcher is with Paige and a few of the Washington House guards at South Gate, but I think we're closer."

"We'll be there in a few," I said, then put my screen away, looked at Petra. "Do you want to zap a machine?"

SEVEN

Imagine the biggest old-fashioned machine—the metal type with gears and cams—that you've ever seen. Build it in black cast iron accented with gold and marked with magical symbols. Have it fill a brick warehouse, and add as its caretaker an earnest gamer whose family history reached back to the machine's very beginnings.

With that, you'd have the start of the warehouse ward. If triggered by a demon, it would shoot a wide column of light into the sky through cantilevered doors in the ceiling. That light would give a faintly green cast to demon skin, and it would shoot lightning at any demons in the vicinity.

Or it had. It apparently was not doing so at present.

My mother—tall and lean, with light skin, straight dark hair, and pale blue eyes—and Aunt Mallory stood with the gamer machinist and gazed up at the ironwork masterpiece.

Hugo looked much healthier than he had the last time I'd seen him, when he'd been coming off a marathon *Jakob's Quest* session—a long-running online RPG—and the bummer of missing his beloved machine's operation. His skin was still pale, but no longer shadowed. His dark hair was still shaggy, but in a way that looked intentionally mod. He wore a Chicago Bears T-shirt with "Monsters" across the front.

He glanced back at me, waved. "Hey, Elisa!"

"Hey, Hugo. You remember Theo and Petra?" We'd left Roger to the running of the office. And something about budgets. He was forever doing something about budgets.

Mom turned, smiled, came over to give me a hug while the others made their greetings.

"So, it's not working?" I asked.

"Dead," Hugo said.

"The cornerstone?" I asked.

"Fine, as far as we can tell." This was from Paige, a sorcerer who happened to live in Cadogan House with her partner, the house librarian. The librarian and I had a complex relationship. As a kid, I'd loved to read books in the House's massive library with a snack in hand. He'd preferred I never darken his door at all.

Paige had milk pale skin and red hair, and there were circles beneath her eyes. Aunt Mallory looked tired, too. Not a surprise, given they'd been working nonstop for nearly a week to get the broken wards online again.

The cornerstone for this ward was in a guarded shed not far from the warehouse. If the machine had been fixed, the cornerstone was still there, and the spell had been reset, it all should have worked.

I looked at the machine, then gestured to Petra. "You want her to light it up?"

Aunt Mallory looked at her. "It's a spark of lightning, right?"

Petra nodded, pulled off a glove, wiggled her fingers. "Yep. How much do you want? There's a ton of energy in the air right now. I'd put my money on a big storm coming."

Aunt Mallory looked at Hugo. "She can take a lot, right?"

Hugo blushed faintly. "Well, yeah. But I think we need to be careful until we figure out what's wrong. We don't want to accidentally trigger anything."

"What will hitting the machine with lightning tell us?" Mom asked.

"We're thinking the machine's connection to the cornerstone might be fried—maybe by that pulse of magic," Aunt Mallory said. "So, while all the parts are in working order, it's not getting power. This will give it some temporary power."

"Is that likely?" Theo asked. "A connection problem?"

"It's possible," Hugo said. "Think about a house with really old wiring. You try to plug in a high-def gaming screen decades after the house was built, and there's a pretty good chance something goes wrong."

"Magically speaking," Paige said, "this mama has really old wiring. That's one of the things we've been trying to fix."

It all sounded simple and logical. Until you remembered we were talking about a Victorian-era magical antidemon system.

"It was a miracle the machine worked at all after all this time," Aunt Mallory said, and grinned at Hugo. "He's the miracle."

Hugo smiled. Yes, his baby was broken, but for the first time in a long time, he could discuss it with others who were as invested in its success as he was.

"Is it worth saving?" Theo wondered, and all heads turned to him. "Not the machine," he clarified, "but the system."

Aunt Mallory and Paige shared a look that said they'd had similar conversations. "It's what we have now," Aunt Mallory said. "No need to reinvent the wheel if we can get it working again."

"I say, let's try Petra's spark," Hugo said. "Sometimes you have to take a chance."

"Good call," Aunt Mallory said, and we followed Hugo to a boxy portion of the machine marked in the scratchy magical symbols that made it run.

"This is the transformer," he said. "Aim here."

"And everyone else step back," Mom said. "Gears shouldn't go flying, but . . ."

Theo and I took extra-large steps backward, nearly to the building's exterior wall.

"This is either going to work or become a shrapnel bomb," Theo said.

"It's Chicago," I said as Petra and the sorcerers talked specifics. "There are so many *other* creative ways it could go badly: spin us all into another dimension, bring interdimensional monsters here—"

"You can stop," Theo said with the faintest of smiles.

When the sorcerers and Hugo moved back, we braced ourselves.

"Ready," Aunt Mallory said, placing a jar of green stuff near the machine. Grass with demon residue, I presumed. "Set," she said, and Petra leaned forward, produced a spark in her hand. "Go!"

The air contracted, and a thin streak of brilliant blue flowed from Petra's hand to the machine. For a moment, there were only the smells of warm grease and oil, and then the gears began to turn. I expected a groan of metal against metal, but Hugo and his family had maintained the machine meticulously. The machine's component parts moved together effortlessly, speed increasing as energy was transferred from one part of the system to another.

Then the ceiling doors began to move, angling upward to make room for the light's beam. That beam was nearly invisible at first, but as the machine's symbols began to glow, light was gathered and condensed into a single beam. Magic peppered the air as machine and beam—a functioning ward—prepared to strike at demons.

But then the column of light flickered, faded. The flywheel slowed, and the gears stopped moving. The machine had already exhausted the energy Petra had fed it.

"First time I've seen it running in a while," Hugo said, voice thick with emotion. "I didn't think it would affect me so much."

"It's your life's work," Petra said with a smile, pulling on her gloves again. "Of course it would."

Paige and Aunt Mallory were still silent. They both stared at the machine, hands on hips and frowns pulling their mouths.

"It runs," Aunt Mallory said.

"It runs," Paige agreed. "But why did it stop?"

"Something missing."

"Mmm-hmm. Connection?"

"Maybe."

They made considering noises.

"They get like this sometimes," Mom said affectionately. "Sorcerer shoptalk."

My screen rang and Alexei's name appeared. My heart began to beat faster, worry potent as the magic in the room.

"What's wrong?" I asked.

"He won and he's okay," Alexei said, and the first wave of panic passed. "Asshole bought magic from a spellseller and tried to use it on Connor. He deflected the worst of it and shifted, but he needs a ride home."

Shifters who were injured while in human form could shift to heal their injuries; unfortunately, the magic didn't work in the reverse, which was why shifters usually fought in human form.

"I'm going to be busy for a while," Alexei added, voice very low and very determined.

"The cheater?" I asked.

"Will be taken care of."

If he was with the Pack . . . "Where's Lulu?"

"Here with me."

"Then I'm on my way." My work apparently wasn't over; I just had a different crisis to deal with.

"Go," Theo said, before I could ask. "Take an Auto, and you can drive Connor home in the Pack's vehicle. We'll get the van back to the office."

"You guys are the best," I said, and put my screen away.

"Give him some scratches for us," Petra said.

"And I'll be online later if he's up for *JQ*," Hugo said.

He and Connor were both fans of *Jakob's Quest*. Hugo was a well-known expert, and they'd played a few campaigns together. I didn't get the appeal, probably because *JQ*—with its quests, supernatural fights, and human rescuing—was too much like my actual job. I was still searching for the hobby that complemented it.

"I'll let him know," I said, and went to find a wolf.

The North American Central Pack had transformed their skill with meat, booze, and barbecue into a successful commercial enterprise. Their headquarters spread through a glass-and-steel building in Ukrainian Village, not far from the Keene house.

The Auto dropped me off in front, where shifters mingled and the magic was a mix of fury, shock, and disgust. Nice that it wasn't directed at me for once.

Dan waited near the door and handed me a key fob for the SUV that waited at the curb. "You're Princess Charming," he said, "and this is your carriage."

"Understood. He's inside?"

Dan nodded. "I'll take you to him."

The crowd parted to let me through, and I felt none of the usual condescension. Maybe meeting an actual Pack enemy, a shark in wolves' clothing, had finally made them realize I was an ally.

I stepped inside; the residue of nonshifter magic was pungent. It smelled like burning plastic. Like something *pretend*.

"What did the magic do?" I asked as Dan walked me back to the back rooms used by the extended Keene family.

"Messed up his vision," Dan said. "Went from blurry to pin-hole to nothing. His dad wanted to call it, but Connor insisted on finishing the fight. Refused to shift, even." Dan smiled mirth-lessly. "And he kicked the guy's ass. Then he shifted afterward, and I think that cleared up the worst of it. But the magic took a lot out of him."

I wondered if the cheater was still breathing, and thought it was better not to ask. "Alexei said the challenger bought the spell?"

Dan nodded. "Claims it was an anonymous online seller. Guy had a little blister pack of the potion hidden in his hand. Barely landed one shitty punch, and that was enough to transfer it to Connor."

"You call the CPD?"

Dan gave me a flat look. "We called you. That was enough."

Either the Keene family had been here for the fight, or they'd come afterward to make sure their prince was okay. There were uncles, aunts, and cousins gathered in the back room like a repeat of the family dinner.

Connor's parents waited at the far end of the room with Alexei—and, of all people, Lulu.

I was furious about the fear in Connor's mother's eyes. As a shifter, she wouldn't have been afraid for him to face a challenger—concerned, sure, but not afraid. Even the most skeptical among them wouldn't have expected this kind of breach of protocol, this kind of cheating, especially from someone trying to prove he was capable of leading the Pack.

There on the floor between his parents was Connor, his coat a thick silver, snoring on his back with paws in the air. The worry I'd been holding in flooded out, and brought tears to my eyes even as I chuckled at his very canine position.

"Has someone taken a picture of this for posterity?" I asked, and knelt beside him.

"Several," Alexei assured me.

Connor twitched, and I wasn't sure if the movement was caused by an aftershock of the magic or a dream. I put a hand on his chest and could feel his body soften. Even monster seemed to relax as I rubbed a gentle circle in Connor's fur.

I looked up at Lulu. "Thoughts?"

"Piece-of-shit asshole shifter," she said, anger not especially contained. Beside her Alexei grunted his agreement. "He said it was only supposed to make the recipient 'a little woozy,'" Lulu continued. "Said he just wanted to make it a 'fair fight.'" She used air quotes. That was the degree of her pissed-offery.

"So either the spell didn't work as intended," I said, "or he's not just a piece-of-shit asshole shifter, but a lying piece-of-shit asshole shifter."

I'd continued petting Connor through that discussion. And apparently hit a good spot, as his back paw scratched rhythmically in the universal language of pets enjoying scritches.

"I haven't seen him do that in years," his dad said, love cracking through some of the icy anger. "Take him home. Let him sleep this off."

"Any suggestions?" I asked, glancing around. "He usually doesn't stay in wolf mode this long around me."

Alexei's smile was thin. "Stay away from the teeth."

I met that smile with one of my own. "His aren't the teeth to worry about."

Alexei wanted to spare Connor the indignity of being carried out of NAC headquarters, so we walked on either side of him as he trotted slowly to the van. The shifters parted for us, and the magic they put into the air said they were relieved he was moving on his own. Other streams of magic bore anger; those shifters were still furious about the blatant cheating and the desecration of a kind of ritual.

Alexei took the driver's seat, Lulu the front passenger seat. I took the second row, and Connor hopped onto the bench seat and immediately put his head on my thigh. And stayed that way the entire drive home.

Once we arrived at the town house, Connor loped inside and into the den, circled twice, and curled into a ball on the thick rug in front of the fireplace.

"Sometimes I have to work to remember he isn't a family pet," Lulu whispered.

"I know, right?"

We heated up leftovers from the night before, and since it wasn't yet time to sign off from work, I checked my messages but found nothing from the Ombuds.

RETRIEVED WOLF, I messaged Theo. HOME AND RESTING.

WE'RE EATING A SLICE WHILE STARING AT VICTORIAN MACHIN-ERY, Theo responded. GLAD HE'S HOME.

I put my screen down, chewed a meatball, glanced at Lulu and Alexei. Lulu ate while penciling in details on a large sketch of her mural. Alexei ate while brooding.

"How did you make it to the NAC building so fast?" I wondered. "Weren't you working on the mural?"

"Apex had a prophecy," Lulu said.

That had me putting down my fork. "He did?"

"Vague," Alexei said. "Or at least what he told me. Just a sense of potential trouble at headquarters."

"You could have called me," I said.

Alexei's expression flattened. "If we called you every time there was *potential* for trouble at the bar, you wouldn't have time to work anywhere else."

"Fair enough," I said, and looked at Lulu. "And you?"

"He dragged me with him," she said, eyebrows furrowed as she redrew a curve to make the arc she wanted.

"Good man," I said, and forked a meatball. "Want?"

Lulu glanced at it, laughed. "Are you rewarding him with meat?"

The meatball was gone before I could answer, and he was chewing happily.

"If it works, it works," I said, and dug in again.

I got the call shortly before dawn, and went outside to take it. The house was beginning to quiet down, but I wasn't sure how this was going to go.

"Well, hello," I said when Jonathan Black's face appeared on-screen. Or mostly. He was outside and standing in shadow, but I could see his pale skin and blond hair.

"I don't have much time," he said. "I've been busy."

I hadn't asked, which made it interesting that he started with an excuse.

"With clients?" I asked politely.

"Manner of speaking," he said, and shifted, a streetlamp putting his face—and the injury that marred it—into sharper focus. There was a long laceration across his left cheek.

"Wrong end of a blade?" I asked.

"I'm fine." His voice was tight. "A client didn't like a result and lashed out. I'm fine."

"What kind of client does that?" I asked, snagging a quick screenshot of his injury.

"A confidential one," he snapped. "Sorry. I'm in a shitty mood."

"Because of your client? Or the city's new demons?"

His eyes widened. "Demons?"

"And demon-involved killings," I said. "You haven't seen the news on-screen?"

"I've been busy," he said again.

"Did you feel the pulse of magic?"

"No. I was asleep. I heard it was due to extra magic in the ley lines."

He'd worked with the fae before, so perhaps Claudia had passed that along. But I pushed a little more. "Did the ones you heard it from know where the extra magic came from? Or who put it there?"

"No one puts magic in the lines. They're natural phenomena." He lifted a shoulder. That move was casual, but the sudden snap of his head wasn't. He peered into the distance, then stepped into the shadows again. Avoiding someone? Hiding from someone?

"Do you need help?" I asked. "I can send a car. Or come get you."

"No. I have to go."

And then the screen went blank.

What had he gotten himself into? Whom was he trying to avoid, and who'd put that nasty cut on his face?

"A lot of retribution being dished out tonight," I murmured, and went back inside.

Eleanor of Aquitaine sat at the threshold, tail swishing nervously.

"What?" I asked, and glanced behind me, wondering if I'd tracked in a demon. But there was only darkness, which was a vampire's bosom friend. I walked in, closed and locked the door.

"Everything is fine," I said.

Apparently satisfied by that or bored by the conversation, she stalked off.

The first floor was empty, so I turned off the lights and checked the security system. Finding a complete absence of demons, I made my way to the master bedroom on the third floor.

Connor, still in wolf form, was stretched out on the bed. Tail to ears, he nearly reached from headboard to footboard.

He blinked his eyes open when I entered, watched me move, but didn't stir.

I put my screen on the bedside table and changed. And when I came back, I found my screen on the floor.

I looked at him. "Seriously?"

He didn't speak or move. But I was absolutely certain I knew why he was looking at me like that—and had apparently batted my screen to the floor.

"He's an informant," I said, and climbed into bed. "I had to take his call."

If a wolf could be sardonic, the low sound he made was a perfect example of it.

"Someone cut him, if that makes you feel better."

Another wolfy grumble—this one had satisfaction in it.

I lay down, and Connor curled beside me. "You okay?" I asked.

He nuzzled his head against my head. Either in reassurance or because he wanted more scritches. I obliged, and we fell asleep together, a girl and her wolf.

EIGHT

I was awoken by heat and touch and the press of lips on my shoulder. I was snuggled into Connor's very human body, which was warm and relaxed behind me. Well, but for the portions that were very much not relaxed, but rigid with desire.

He scraped his teeth against my neck.

"Are you going to bite me?" I asked, voice low in the darkness.

His growl sent delicious frissons down my spine. "Would you like me to?"

"I'm not entirely sure."

He laughed full out now. "Not something a vampire should equivocate on, Lis."

His laughter burned away that little bit of remaining worry about last night's injuries.

"I think you're feeling better now."

His response was somewhere between purr and growl, and it was the precursor to the slow movement of his hands up to my breasts. His fingers were playful, teasing, which assured me he was feeling better.

"I'm glad," I said. "And I'm fully prepared to take advantage of your . . . health."

I rolled over him, enjoyed my first look at his face. His brilliant blue eyes were still drowsy from sleep—or possibly from leftover magic. His beautiful lips were cocked into a half-smile. His hair was a mass of sleep-tousled waves. And he was completely naked.

"I find I'm at your disposal," he said with a grin, and linked his hands behind his head. "Do your best, brat."

"I do love a challenge," I said.

I slid a hand through his curls, stroked his bottom lip with my thumb, then lowered my lips to his mouth, kissed him in bites and nips until he was thoroughly fed up.

He sat up, with me still straddling his waist, and wrapped his arms around me. And his mouth wasn't gentle, but ferocious in its focus. In seeking pleasure and giving it.

His hands found my breasts again, stoked the fire that already burned between us with love and desire and magic. And then his hand was between our bodies, and he found the center of mine. He fueled the fire until I was moving against him.

"That's my girl," he said, and I could hear the smile in his voice. "Take what you need."

And then pleasure was a flame that covered me, consumed me, and left me trembling in his arms.

But I wanted more. I shifted over, away, pulled him down to me. I wanted the cover and heat and weight of his body. His mouth found mine again and, when he joined our bodies, paused with his forehead against mine, shaking with need.

I pushed dark hair from his forehead. "Take what you need," I said.

He kissed me hard, began to move his body, put a hand beneath me to lift me up and increase my pleasure. We moved together, sharing ourselves, bodies undulating in the beautiful darkness of dusk.

"I howl for you," he said. "I fight for you. I *burn* for you."

His voice trembled; then his breath caught. And the agony of pleasure filled his face. That sent me over the edge, both of us tumbling together through the darkness and landing in each other's arms.

"Let's stay here forever," he said.

And then the cat, somewhere beyond the closed bedroom door, made a horrible howling sound.

"She also howls for you," Connor said.

"But out of hatred, not love. And she would definitely not fight for me. Not like you." I glanced up at him, found his eyes closed, a peaceful smile on his face.

"I fight for you," I whispered, and kissed his forehead.

I found Alexei downstairs with Lulu. I'm not sure what was happening between them, except that they were on the couch and hands and lips were moving.

I hadn't even had coffee yet.

I cleared my throat as loudly as I could, which had them splitting apart like guilty teenagers. I covered my eyes as I walked through the kitchen and grabbed my jacket from a chair. "I saw nothing."

"You can stop," Lulu said dryly, but there was a hint of amusement in her voice.

"Really rather wouldn't," I said, and shifted my fingers to look through them. They stood beside each other, but no pink parts were in contact. She looked truly, deliriously happy. He looked ... victorious. Very shifter of him.

I cleared my throat again. "He's sleeping, and I think he needs more rest."

"After the bout you two had," Lulu said with a sly grin, "I don't doubt it."

So, her revenge was swift.

I gave her my steeliest stare, which was probably not convincing given the flush on my cheeks. Then I looked at Alexei. "Are you going with her or staying with Connor tonight?"

"He's staying with Connor," Lulu answered. "Connor needs a hand, and I don't. Clint will be at the site today with some of his people. Safety in numbers and all that."

"All human?"

"Yes, and one supposedly has a black belt in something. The demons don't have any reason to be interested in me, and the violence is only sporadic. So far."

I watched her for a moment. "How long did you work on that speech?"

"Longer than you'd think," she said.

But I liked the confidence. She seemed to be coming back to herself—or digging herself out of the emotional trench she'd been in for a while. And I knew Clint and the mural were part of the reason.

"You keep your screen with you at all times," I said. "That's an order."

"When is that ever an issue?" Alexei muttered, earning a level stare from Lulu that had him grinning delightedly.

"I'll be going, then," I said. "Try to get him to drink one of those disgusting protein shakes." I didn't wait for the snarky response.

It seemed like a coffee (and donuts) kind of dusk, so I took coffee (and donuts) to the Ombuds' office. And I was prepared to use fritters and twists as ammunition against any winged demons that might try to attack me on the way in. But the air was blissfully free of predators. Or predators larger than me, anyway.

I met Theo in the parking lot; he usually beat me into the office since he didn't have to wait until the sun was down to make the trip.

"Donuts?" he asked, falling into step beside me.

"Yup. Take the drinks," I said, and handed him the drink tray.

He accepted it, but wrinkled his nose. "Did you get the almond-syrup monstrosity for Roger again? It smells like lotion."

"I know. But he's addicted to it. And we don't have to do budgets, so I figured we owe him."

"Fair enough," he said.

We walked in to find Roger's and Lulu's gazes on the wall screen. The mayor, who looked trim and efficient in her dark blue suit, had apparently given a press conference about the city's efforts to deal with the demon threat.

With a growl of displeasure, Roger flicked the screen off.

"What's wrong?" Theo asked as we put the food and drinks on a table.

"The mayor recommended humans consider evacuating Chicago."

"Damn," Theo said.

"She's set up a relocation task force. There will be stations across the city to help people in need, and she's asking for mobilization of the National Guard to help keep order on the roads."

"It's not an awful idea," I said.

"No, that part's okay," Roger said. "Unfortunately, she also announced the Ombuds' office will rid the city of demons, which we can't legally do."

"That's been confirmed now?" I asked. "The legality part, I mean."

Roger nodded grimly.

"I appreciate that she's not willing to risk punishing an innocent demon," Theo said, "not that we're seeing a lot of those. But now the public's going to blame us for every new incident and injury."

"And she has a convenient shield," Roger said. He glanced at the drink tray. "You get the Almond Surprise?"

"Even the name is awful," Theo murmured.

"Yep," I said, and pulled off my jacket. It was chilly out there. "It's marked. Help yourself."

"I call any and all donuts with sprinkles," Petra said, but she had gone back to her desk and was fiddling with her screen.

I picked up my own coffee, took a heartening sip. "What else is new beyond our being tossed unceremoniously under the bus?"

"Cook County records now identify Dantalion as the owner of the Buckley town house," Petra said. "Buckley owned it for five years and sold it to Dante, just like Dante said."

"How much did he pay?" I wondered.

"One dollar," she said. "Obviously not fair market value for that condo."

"It's a contract thing," Roger said. "A ceremonial amount when you just want to transfer the property from one person to another."

"So Buckley was freaked out by the warehouse bombing and gave him the condo?" I wondered.

"Or wasn't given a choice," Theo said.

"I talked to Jonathan Black," I said, and sent to the wall screen the picture I'd taken of his face.

Everyone looked up.

"Did Connor do that?" Theo asked.

"No. This was probably while Connor was being hit by cheap magic."

"Oh," Petra said, "I forgot—we found the spellseller's site, turned it over to the CPD's regulatory folks." Her smile was wide and thin and a little sharklike. "They'll do a number on the spellseller."

"Appreciate it. No one should be able to buy that kind of magic."

"The challenger?" Roger asked.

"I didn't ask," I said. "It's better that way."

"And who hurt Black?" Theo asked.

"I don't know. He was very cagey. Seemed worried, and he looked around a lot, like he was trying to avoid the person who'd done the damage."

"Hmm," Roger said contemplatively.

"Yeah," I said, "that was my thought, too: that he's gotten mixed up in something. Maybe one of his clients isn't pleased with his service."

"Odds being what they are," Petra said, "it would be something demony."

"That, too."

My screen signaled. I found Lulu's name blinking at me, and my first thought was she'd gotten an update from her mother about the wards. But wouldn't Aunt Mallory have called me directly?

"What's up?" I asked when I answered.

The first thing I heard was a crash and a sizzle loud enough to make my screen buzz.

"Lulu?"

"Shit! Elisa! I need you. They're fighting at the mural."

There was another crash, and then a very human scream.

"Lulu? What's happening? Who's fighting?"

"Demons. They're fighting each other, and we're stuck, and they're getting closer."

I switched off my rising fear, forced myself to focus on the details. "How many of you?"

"Four. Me, Clint Howard, and two of his assistants. Four."

"I'm on my way. Your people are alive. Do what you have to do to keep them that way."

Roger and Petra would stay at the office, coordinate with Gwen, and deal with any demon incidents that occurred while Theo and I were gone.

I made Theo drive the van; I was too hyped up. In the mean-time, I sent Dad a message, told him to consider locking down Cadogan House, given the mural building was only a few blocks away. Roger called, advised us Gwen and her CPD team were en route. They'd set up a defensive perimeter and were waiting for further directions from us.

It took too long to get to the neighborhood, to the street. We parked on the other end of the block of buildings where the ware-house was located. I climbed out, belted on my katana. The air was so full of demon magic that it felt stiff, like clothes with dried, caked-on mud. And it was pungent enough to make my eyes water.

"Damn," Theo whispered. "Even I can smell that."

"Yeah," I said, "it's not great."

So much demon magic, and no wards had been triggered. Al-though I wasn't sure which of the ones we'd identified were sup-posed to cover this spot. Maybe Hugo's machine? If so, the problem hadn't yet been solved.

I sent Lulu a message: ME AND THEO, ONE BLOCK AWAY AND APPROACHING FROM SOUTH. WHERE R U?

It took seconds for her to respond, and they felt like a lifetime. WE'RE BEHIND MOBILE STORAGE BOX IN ALLEY ON NORTH SIDE OF BLDG. ALLEY IS A DEAD END.

Not for a vampire. EVERYBODY MOBILE?

WE'LL MANAGE, she said.

BE READY, I said. WE'RE MOVING IN.

"I want to get a look first," I whispered, and gestured toward the sidewalk.

We stayed in the shadows at the edge of the sidewalk beyond the reach of streetlamps, and moved toward the street faced by the buildings. Light flashed—leaf green and brilliantly purple— presumably as magic was tossed around. When we reached the edge of the buildings, we peeked around. The street was empty of humans, who'd been smart enough to flee the danger.

A dozen demons had taken up the space the humans had abandoned, and they were fighting with weapons, fists, and magic. One lobbed a red ball of magic that cracked and sparked as it struck a parked car, filling the night with sharp-edged scarlet light. The demons were all humanoid, no winged monsters here. They looked evenly matched, and there didn't appear to be an obvious leader on either side.

"Why are they fighting?" I asked.

"They also want Buckley's condo?"

I hated that that was the only concrete lead we had about demon aspirations.

We could see the floodlights set up to allow Lulu to work at night, and the scaffolding she used to reach higher portions of the building. First priority: get to the alley where Lulu and her coworkers were hiding and get them out safely. Second priority: take the demons down.

But how best to get to Lulu and the others? I looked around, gauging potential routes. Then glanced up and saw one of my favorite architectural features: an old-school fire escape.

I pointed up. "I can go up there and get to the humans from above. But you can't make it up the fire escape with your cast. So you stay here, and I'll bring them to you?"

"I'm not staying here," he said dryly.

"You could go around the back."

Somewhere nearby, glass fractured.

"I'll try to get the humans to you," I decided. "Then you get them to safety, and I'll work with the CPD to get the demons down."

"Don't have time to wait," he said. "I know how to stick to the shadows. I'll go around the front, stay hidden, and meet you there."

"You sure? Gwen will skin me if you get hurt."

He grinned. "And you'll skin me if Lulu gets hurt. No, thank you."

A green fireball flew toward our heads, smashing into the building and knocking bricks from the corner. It hadn't been aimed at us, but the demons were moving closer. We had to move.

"Go," he whispered, and we gave each other understanding nods.

I trusted him to do his part and ran toward the fire escape, jumped, and grabbed the edge of the first landing. I pulled myself up, then took the stairs two at a time until I reached the roof. This one was flat and warm and covered in gravel that scratched beneath my feet.

I ran across to the edge of the next building. I reached the parapet, jumped onto it, and flew across the alley to the warehouse building, ignoring the thirty-foot drop between. I hit the warehouse's roof, sliding in gravel for a few feet until I got purchase. Then I sprinted to the other side of the roof, went to my knees, and looked over the edge.

There, huddled behind a storage container, were Lulu and her crew. One sorcerer and several humans. Magic exploded on the street only a few feet away from them, sending a volley of bricks and dust into the alley.

When the smoke settled, I sent Lulu a message: LOOK UP.

She did, nodded, whispered to the others, who also looked.

I gauged the distance, then stepped over the edge of the building. Vampires and gravity were very old friends, and the three-story descent to the ground below felt like little more than a long step. Albeit a very exhilarating one.

I hit the ground in a crouch, stood up, steadied my katana.

One of the humans squeaked, covered her mouth with a hand, apparently surprised I'd stuck the landing. And then I realized she was looking at me with fear; my fangs had descended, and I hadn't even felt it. Adrenaline and demon magic were a heady combination.

"She won't hurt you," Lulu whispered, her face lit by a burst of magic that had a demon groaning somewhere nearby. Her tone said it wasn't the first time she'd said something like that tonight.

I offered a little wave and smiled (without fangs). "Is everyone okay?"

The younger humans nodded, but didn't look like they meant it. Clint had a gash across his right cheek.

"I'm okay," he said. "It was just glass from the first shot." He tried for a chuckle, but it didn't sound convincing.

Lulu squeezed his arm in support. She looked fine but for the enormous paint splotches across her shirt. "Tipped over a tray on our way down the scaffolding," she said. "They cracked some of the brick. I'm sure it's worse now."

"You'll repaint," Clint said with an effort at a smile.

I appreciated his grit.

"I don't spend much time in the company of supernaturals," he said, "which is clearly something I need to remedy. You're a very exciting bunch."

"In fairness," I said, "this has been a pretty unusual week."

Something hit the container hard, knocking Lulu off her feet and throwing sparks into the air. Before I could offer a hand to pick her up, she was on her feet and moving to the front of the alley. Then a fireball was in her hand. The squeaker squeaked again as Lulu lobbed it toward the fight.

Theo suddenly dodged around her into the shadows of the alley. "Thanks for the cover," he said.

"No problem." She looked at me. "Lots of magic in the air," she explained.

Lulu could only do what was commonly called "blood magic,"

because blood was usually required to kindle it. That requirement was apparently mitigated when the air was full of demonic energy. That might have been concerning, except for the steady look in her eyes.

I nodded, returned that look.

"Thoughts?" Theo asked me.

I glanced around the alley. As Lulu had reported, it dead-ended not far behind us, and there were no doors or windows in the facing buildings. The only ways out were past the demons . . . and up.

"How bad is it out there?" I asked Theo.

"They're pissed about something. It's a full shoot-out."

"What the hell is going on in this city?" I whispered to no one in particular. If he truly wanted to try to build an empire here, maybe Dante would know.

Monster pushed inside me, using what strength it had to demand I let it out. Which wasn't something we could accomplish here even if we didn't have humans to rescue. Which we did.

Not now, I told it. *Fight with me or stay down. There's no way to let you out right now.*

It wasn't convinced, but it had only so many cards to play.

Kind of like our current scenario.

"I could probably manage to get everyone on the roof, but then you're stuck on the roof instead of an alley and hoping the building doesn't fall down in the meantime."

Squealer squealed until Lulu put a hand over her mouth.

"She does that," I said at Theo's blink.

"I'll be the distraction," I told Theo. "You take the humans out to the north. Message Gwen, so she's ready for you." I looked at Lulu. "You go with him."

She nodded. She didn't look thrilled about the idea of sending me into the fight, but like monster, knew her options were limited.

"Cover me with a couple of fireballs on your way out," I said. "But go with your people. They need you."

"CPD will be ready," Theo said, putting his screen away. Gwen had clearly been waiting for a message.

"What are you going to do?" he asked me.

"Play to my strengths," I said, and let my fangs descend.

I went to the edge of the alley, waited as Theo and Lulu corralled the humans and gave instructions. It looked like three of the demons were down, at least from what I could see in the strobe of magic. The others were still fighting, apparently to the death. And for no discernible reason.

"When I give the signal," I said, "fireball."

"What's the signal?" Lulu asked.

"You'll know it when you see it."

"Because you don't know?"

"Not yet. But I will in a minute," I said. And like I was joining a game of double Dutch, I jumped into the fray.

The thing about swords? They were both offensive and defensive weapons. I ran forward with the blade raised and swung at a fireball like a batter at the plate with bases loaded. The magic split and bounced off the gleaming steel, then flew toward the demons. One sliver missed, but the other put a demon on the ground. And in case that wasn't enough to attract their attention, I put fingers in my lips, whistled. The sound echoed off the building fronts and had the demons looking my way.

"Elisa Sullivan," I said with all the bravado I could muster. "Ombudsman and Chicagoan who is concerned that you assholes are breaching the peace and destroying property. If you want to beat the shit out of each other, do it somewhere else. I hear Indianapolis is nice," I said, naming the first city that came to mind. Apologies, Indiana.

I spun my sword. "Who's leaving first?"

They rounded on me together as if suddenly united by their hatred of vampires, Ombuds, or intruders in their fight. I moved as they moved, putting as much space as possible between me and the alley, and rotating my body, so any fireballs sent my way would be aimed away from the rescue route.

Feel free to join in, I told monster as the first demon leapt forward.

I swung hard, a blow that aimed the katana's tip at the demon's belly.

He jumped back just in time to avoid full dissection, but the blade still left a crimson stripe across his shirt. His eyes flashed yellow, and he bared his teeth, then punched magic into the air.

I took an instinctive step backward and nearly moved into the path of another demon's vermillion fireball. I dropped to the ground, felt the needle sting of glass against my palms. The fireball hit the first demon square in the chest and had him flying through the air. He hit the curb with an ominous crunch and went still.

I turned back. The demon who'd thrown the fireball looked satisfied with his shot; they must have been opponents. He was also the most stereotypically demonic demon I'd seen. Cheekbones high and sharp, teeth yellow and pointed, small black whirls of horn at his temples, and skin of burnished gold.

Not of this world. And given his apparent violent tendencies, not welcome in it.

"Human," he said.

"Vampire," I corrected, and lifted my sword. "With steel. Why are you fighting?"

"Dispute," he said, taking a step forward.

"Dispute over what?" I asked, angling the sword for another go.

"Chicago," he said.

I didn't like his answer. I liked it less when he lunged toward me.

I swung my sword. He grabbed the blade with a gilded hand, stopped its arc. I kept the cutting edge carefully sharpened and honed—neither my mom nor Uncle Catcher would have allowed anything else—so the pain must have been intense. Blood dripped from his palm, each drop sizzling as it hit the magicked steel.

Wouldn't complain about an assist, I reminded monster, who filled my limbs with heat and magic and its own piquant frustration.

With its added strength, I wrenched the sword away, slicing open the demon's hand in the process. He grunted and grabbed at the sword again, leaving his flank exposed. I used my momentum to spin the blade back again, and blood welled quickly across his abdomen. But he didn't flinch. Just looked down at me with even stronger rage in his eyes.

"Fucking vampire," he said, and his backhanded slap was fast enough that I couldn't avoid it.

I flew through the air and just managed to catch myself with my hands before face-planting into asphalt. My right cheek screamed with pain; he'd broken something, and the throbbing was powerfully strong.

I ignored more stinging in my palms and tried to climb to my feet, made it back to my knees before my spinning vision nearly pulled me down again. And then the world erupted. Shouts from Gwen ordering the demons to stand down. Lights blazing from a helicopter that was *thwack-thwack*ing its way toward us. And the deep and steady growls of the two wolves who appeared at my side, flanking me and staring down the golden demon.

"Back the fuck off," Gwen said to the demon, moving forward with gun extended.

Lip curled with hatred, the demon shifted its gaze back to me.

"We aren't done," he said. And with a literal puff of fucking smoke, he disappeared.

"Damn it," I said.

While the wolves guarded me, two dozen cops pushed in with weapons pointed at the remaining demons.

One apparently decided the risk of incarceration or death was too great, and he immediately sigiled himself out of Chicago. Two others decided to finish their fight and managed to fireball each other. An excess of gunfire killed one more, but not before he'd thrown a fireball that put a cop on the ground. That left only a few of the original group.

The remaining officers moved in, gleaming neon blue cuffs in their hands.

"Fancy," I said.

"New tech," Gwen said. "Magically enhanced cuffs. They've been in development for safely handling sups for a few years. The mayor escalated deployment."

I surmised that meant some of the testing had been skipped, probably because no one was going to complain about injuries to demons if they turned out to be harmful. Unfortunate for the demons—and any other sups the CPD tried the cuffs on. Not an ideal situation. But then none of this was.

"So we can theoretically transport demons to the cube facility," I said, "assuming we can get the cuffs on and they work."

"That's the idea."

Gwen holstered her weapon and offered me a hand. I took it and worked to stand up, but it took two tries. Connor moved closer, head nuzzling my hip. I let him support me, stood up, looked at Alexei.

"What happened to keeping him at home?" I asked.

Alexei's wolfish stare was bland.

"Are you okay?" Gwen asked. "Your eye's already going purple."

"Damn it," I said, and touched a fingertip to my cheek. Yep. Still fucking hurt. "I'm okay. Demon with a powerful backhand."

Gwen nodded sympathetically. "Sorry it took so long to get here. One of the humans passed out midevacuation, which slowed things down."

"We're all fine now," said Lulu, who walked over to join us. "Sorry you had to take one for us."

"Not your fault they picked this spot," I said—and then thought about that again.

"Unless they thought it would be fun to test a sorcerer?" Lulu asked, voicing my realization. "I've been wondering about that, too."

"I'll ask them."

Theo walked up, cast lifted. "It's fine, and I'm fine. Thanks for asking. Hell of a mess, though."

He looked around the battlefield—two commercial blocks on the edge of Hyde Park—and took in the dented and charred cars, broken windows, spewing fire hydrant, damaged buildings. And Lulu's mural, which looked literally sketchier than before.

"Fixable," she said, absently scratching Alexei's ears. I hadn't noticed that he'd gone to her, but both seemed comforted by their connection. She looked at me. "I need to talk to you, I think."

"You think?" I asked with a smile.

"I might have seen something—," she began.

I felt the wrongness before I saw anything, that sudden tingle in the air. And by then it was already too late. The fireball was already flying, having been launched by the golden demon, who'd reappeared and was grinning through bloody teeth.

The blast hit Lulu's abdomen, and I heard a sharp inhale of breath. And then her eyes rolled, and she went down.

NINE

Lulu!" I screamed, but Alexei got there first, shifting from wolf to human so quickly, there was only a single flash of light and magic and then the transformation was done. He caught Lulu on the way down.

I fell to my knees. The fabric at her torso was scorched, but her skin was intact and unbruised. I tapped her cheeks. "Lulu! Wake up. Come on, Lulu. It's just a little magic. You're fine."

Alexei, Lulu unconscious in his lap, stared down at her in shock.

"*Chicago is ours!*" came a shout from behind us.

I looked back. The gold demon grinned triumphantly, and another fireball was poised in his hand.

"Need an ambulance over here," Theo called out.

I was up—sword in hand—before I'd considered the consequences; my only thought was about the protection of those around me. My only emotion was fury that he'd hurt my friend.

His eyes were daring and without fear; his fireball was in the air within a microsecond. I slashed through it, splitting the magic into a thousand fiery sparks that stung where they hit my skin and peppered the air with sulfur. The bravado in the demon's eyes slipped away. I could feel him attempt to gather magic again, but he'd exhausted his resources, at least temporarily. He instinctively lifted an arm to block my first strike, then screamed and staggered back when blood poured from the gash on his arm. But I didn't stop.

My second slice put him on his knees.

The third finished him. Even a demon couldn't come back from decapitation.

I flicked gore from my sword, sheathed it, and promised it a thorough cleaning later. Then I went back to Lulu. I was breathing heavily from the fight. Her breath was too slow, too shallow.

"Lulu," Alexei said, smoothing his hand over Lulu's hair, her face. "Come on, Bell."

I'd never seen such fear in his eyes. Fear hadn't seemed something that could penetrate his shield. But it had sunk its claws in now.

"I don't see anything wrong with her," I said. "No burns or anything."

"It's a magical injury," Alexei said. "I can feel it."

That was obvious now, and I had missed it in my panic. I closed my eyes to shut out the new chaos rising around us, and put a hand on hers. I felt a vibration. A rattle like a warning from a snake. Something had gotten its teeth into her, and with every second that passed, they seemed to sink deeper.

I opened my eyes again. "Magic," I confirmed. I looked at Alexei, then down at Connor, still in wolf form. "I don't know what to do. I don't know how to help her."

And I'd killed the demon who'd done this.

Panic threatened, and I pushed it down ruthlessly.

Lights flashed as an ambulance drew near; there were no sirens, which made its movements eerier somehow. Then three EMTs were moving toward us, two of them rolling a gurney. One of them, a woman with strong shoulders and light brown skin and her dark hair in shoulder-length twists, looked at Lulu, then Alexei, then Connor. If the humans found anything odd about the man sitting naked on the asphalt, they didn't mention it.

"Shit," she said. "That you, Keene?"

Connor looked at her, gave a yip.

"I'm Callahan," she said. "NAC member." I belatedly recognized the scent of Pack, buried as it was under demon magic. She shifted her steady gaze to me. "And you're Keene's girl."

"Elisa."

The techs began looking Lulu over, getting her vitals.

"She was hit by a demon fireball," I said. "This is some kind of magic."

"Oh?" she asked, and looked back at Lulu. "Give me a sec, Jackson."

She knelt beside Lulu, put a hand over hers. Then yanked it away again like she had been burned. "Damn," she said. "That's . . ."

"Venomous," Alexei said, his face even paler than fear should have made it. And I guessed the magic coursing through her had affected him, too.

So this wasn't just a magical overload but some kind of specifically nasty magic that was dangerous enough to hurt a shifter.

"We need to get her off him," I said, and the EMTs were moving almost instantaneously, slipping Lulu's tiny form onto the gurney.

She looked so small and frail, I thought as tears began to spill.

"Jackson," Callahan said, "get this man some scrubs and a bottle of water."

"You want to shift?" I asked Alexei, my hand on the gurney rail as they positioned Lulu, covered her with a blanket. I was afraid to break that contact.

He looked up at me with devastated eyes. "If I shift, I will tear the rest of them apart. This gives me some control."

I wasn't necessarily opposed to some swift revenge, but spilling more blood wasn't what he needed.

"Okay," I said. "Let me know what you need."

Jackson came back with a water bottle, a blanket, and scrubs for Alexei, then helped lift the gurney into the ambulance. Alexei ignored the blanket and water but pulled on the scrubs and climbed wordlessly into the ambulance with the EMTs.

"You going with?" Theo asked.

I nearly jumped at the sound of his voice; I'd forgotten he was still here.

I wanted to go. I wanted to keep hold of her hand—my sister in every way that mattered—until she woke up and made a juvenile joke about me and Connor.

But that's not what *she* needed. She needed me to figure out how to reverse the magic done to her. And I could do that best out here.

"No. I need to talk to them," I said, shifting my gaze to the bored-looking demons still in those magical cuffs. "But I'll call the Moms." I looked at Connor. "Can you call Dan or someone else you trust to keep watch at the hospital?"

Connor made a soft yip, then trotted through the lingering cops into darkness, presumably to the spot where he and Alexei had left their vehicle and clothes.

"Petra," Theo said.

I looked back at him. "What?"

"Petra can help with Lulu," he explained. "Mallory Carmichael will want to stay with her. But—and I know this is harsh—we need her out there working on the wards. Now more than ever."

It was harsh. But he wasn't wrong. "We aren't going to be able to keep her away from her daughter. But she understands how important the wards are."

He nodded. "I'll ask Petra to visit the hospital. Maybe she can get her cousin to go, too. The doctor."

Petra's cousins were famously and variously successful. One, Dr. Anderson, was an ER physician with training in supernatural biology and a very steady hand with magic.

"Good," I said. "That's good."

I pulled out my screen and stared at it for a moment, preparing for the call I didn't want to make.

It was horrible. There was no other word for it.

Aunt Mallory and Mom, who were still at the warehouse with Hugo, were both crying after I told them what had happened. But Aunt Mallory's eyes cleared when I apologized for failing to keep Lulu safe. And her expression went fierce.

"No," she said, pointing a rainbow-colored fingernail at me. "Don't take away her agency, and don't diminish how much you do. She was working because that work is in her heart. You went to her because she's in yours. Put the blame where it belongs—with the demon who took the shot. May he char in the fires of hell until the heat death of the universe."

"Specific and creative," Mom said, her arm around Aunt Mallory's shoulders. "And she's right. We'll go to the hospital, and maybe we can figure out how to wake her up. You investigate, because you're damn good at it. And figure out what you can."

I nodded, wiped away my tears, and wished Mom were here to give me a hug.

"Let me know if anything changes," I said, and promised I'd update them when I could.

When I put the screen away, Connor was there in jeans and a snug T-shirt, looking significantly less furry than when I'd last seen him.

Wordlessly, he wrapped his arms around me, drew me close, rubbed circles on my back, just as I'd done for him the night before. "She'll be okay," he whispered. "She has an entire support system, including you, to make sure she comes out of this. But if you need to let it out, you can."

I let myself have one long and haggard sob. "Thanks."

"Of course," he said, and didn't let me go. "The world has always been dangerous. But it feels like we're entering a new era. We aren't cowards, but I'd still like to take you home and lock the door."

"Hard same," I said, then pulled back, searched his face. He looked a little more tired than usual, but not horribly so. "You're okay?"

He nodded. "It wasn't the fight I'd expected, but it's the fight I got. And I beat his ass anyway."

"Good," I said. "I'm not going to ask what happened to him. But I am going to find out what happened here. And I'm going to fix it."

"Of course you will," he said as if that were the most obvious thing in the world. And that comforted me down to my bones. "I'm here with you"—he gestured toward Theo, who stood with Gwen near one of the still living demons—"and so are they."

I nodded. "Then let's get this started."

The demons, their wrists glowing from the magical cuffs, sat in the middle of the street, surrounded by CPD officers with weapons. At least the cuffs were working.

Two of the demons sat together; a third was ten feet away and staring daggers at the other two. Parties from opposite sides of the battle, I bet. Which could be handy.

I walked up to the pair. "The demon with gold skin," I said, and rested a hand on the handle of my sword, "what was his name?"

Neither answered.

I had my katana at the heart of the one on my right in seconds. He looked mostly human, but for the crimson fur that sprouted here and there. Demons were a rainbow of villainy.

"Name," I said, "or I force your sigil out of you and bind you to my command for the rest of our natural lives."

"She's immortal," Theo said, voice terribly casual. "So consult your calendar if you need to."

With my free hand, I pulled a handful of salt from my pocket. "I'm the one who commanded Andaras," I said, and let the salt trickle slowly to the ground. "You won't like what I do to you."

"His name was Alarahn. Doesn't matter now. He's dead."

"How do I reverse his magic?" I asked.

"Bring him back to life," the demon said dryly.

I pressed the tip of the blade in a smidge.

The demon winced. "His master could reverse it. Our master."

"And who is that?"

"Dantalion," the demon said.

I stared at him. "What?"

"He's the boss," the demon said, and slid his gaze down to the katana. "You sure you want to mess with that?"

I had to rearrange my mental thoughts. It wasn't entirely surprising that Dante had demonic minions in addition to those we'd seen at the condo; part of his legions, I guessed. But here he wasn't just opposing humans—taking human property or lives. He was, through his soldiers, fighting other demons.

"Why are you fighting one another?"

At his bitter silence, I dug the tip of the blade in more, just enough to draw a drop of sour-smelling blood.

"The upstart," he said, teeth grated as blood stained fabric.

"What upstart?" I asked.

His eyes flashed with magic, and his voice was now a gravelly bass growl. "Someone trying to move in on Dante's territory."

"Since when is Chicago his territory?" Theo asked.

The look the demon gave us was pitying. "Since you opened the doors," he said and smiled widely, revealing teeth that were pointed and yellow.

"So, Dante told you to come over here and beat someone moving in on his—we'll loosely say—'territory,'" Theo said.

"I do as I'm told."

"What's the upstart's name?" Theo asked, prodding the demon again.

"Don't have it. Don't need it." He gestured toward the demon sitting alone. "Ask him who his master is."

I walked to the "upstart's" minion, his dark hair slicked into a 1950s-style wave. He wore jeans with rolled-up cuffs and a white T-shirt. His skin was faintly blue gray. The effect was very zombie James Dean.

"Name?" I asked.

"Don't got one." His voice was raspy and higher than the other demon's, and it carried a thick New Jersey accent.

"Employer?"

He smiled, showing small gray teeth. His magic twitched and jumped, like an insect trying to avoid a slapping hand. "Don't got one."

I sighed and aimed my sword at him; the first demon's blood still sizzled on the blade. That had him looking a little more serious.

"She'd kill me," the demon said.

"She," I said. "Your boss is a woman?"

"Sure."

"What's her name?"

The demon opened his mouth, and we all leaned forward a bit, anticipating an answer.

But then I felt the rise of demon magic all around us, like a foul breeze.

"Incoming demon magic," I warned. "Everybody back!"

I pulled Gwen back with me, and Connor and Theo moved in the same direction.

The demon's brow knit as if in confusion, and he looked down at his feet, which had begun to smoke.

"The fuck?" he asked, and stamped his feet to put out the flame.

But it wasn't human flame. It was magic. And it had smoke flowing off his body, a precursor of the line of white-hot fire that followed it. That line raced upward, leaving copper ash in its wake, until the only things left were his horrified eyes and pompadour. And then they were incinerated, too, and he was metallic dust on the ground.

"What the fuck?" Gwen said softly.

There was a scream, and we all looked at the other two demons, whose boots had begun to smoke. In seconds—two or three— they were both gone. And the attack was repeated on the bodies of the demons who'd died in the fight, so the only things left on the battlefield were piles of shimmering ash and smoke and broken things.

For a good ten seconds, we stood in complete silence.

"All my fucking evidence," Gwen said finally, "literally up in smoke."

"Demon smoke," I said.

"I guess the upstart didn't want his minion naming names," Theo agreed. "And that magic traveled."

"Contagion," Connor said.

"So, let's go see the demon we know," I said. "And we will make him talk."

Gwen would stay at the scene to canvass for human witnesses and oversee the collection of what evidence remained. Connor, Theo, and I took the Pack's SUV to the Gold Coast and the former Buckley condo. I had to put Lulu out of my mind for now and look at the big picture.

"So, Dante isn't the only major demon player in town," I said, thinking aloud. "He and this 'upstart' are . . . what, vying for the same territory? Is this a Sharks and Jets situation?"

"A who and what?" Theo asked.

"Sharks and Jets. Gangs fighting in *West Side Story*—the musical."

"With the dancing?"

"With the dancing."

"Least the demons could do is add a little soft-shoe to the bloodshed," he murmured.

"Someone doesn't seem to like Dante's plan," Connor said, "and is willing to fight him in public in order to stop it."

"Not him," I pointed out. "Only his minions."

"Generals aren't usually on the front line," Connor said.

"Point," I said.

"Maybe there's something related to the buildings where they fought," Theo said. "We know Dante is big on property. I'll have Petra take a look." He pulled out his screen.

"Presuming the minions got the 'upstart' moniker from Dante," Connor said, "Dante doesn't think she's been in business as long as he has."

"Or looking at it the other way, maybe Dante isn't starting his empire from scratch. Maybe he's just relocating one. If he wants to play boss here, maybe he wasn't able to play boss the way he wanted in his hometown."

"New York," Theo said.

"Yep."

"I'll add that to Petra's list."

It seemed to start with Dante. So we'd start there, too.

It was late, and the Gold Coast was quiet enough that we could hear Lake Michigan's waves pounding on the beach to the east. And the buildings were darker than they'd been the last time we'd been here. At the mayor's suggestion, humans had already begun to leave the city—or at least the people who could afford the cost of relocating. They'd locked up their homes, turned off the lights, and headed for higher ground.

Given what we'd just seen, I couldn't blame them.

There was no one in the lobby of Dante's building tonight. The security desk was empty, and we were alone in the elevator on the way up. We found nothing unusual until we reached the Buckley condo. The door was open, and old-fashioned music spilled out. Sinatra, I think, singing about his successes.

Theo and I went inside, Connor behind us. We found more furnishings along the way than we'd seen on our last visit. There were pictures on the walls now and gaudy side tables against the hallway's walls.

There were also more demons, but apparently buzzed on booze and magic, they mostly ignored us. Once again, Dante held court on the sofa near the big window. He wore another suit tonight and was looking down at two demons prostrate on the floor in front of him.

"You'll do what's required," Dante said, either unaware or unconcerned that we'd entered. "Or you'll go back to being nothing."

"You could go back to New York," Theo suggested. "Save us all the trouble."

The room went silent, and all those demon eyes looked back at us with clear malevolence. Then they began to move in, pushing Theo, Connor, and me closer together, like so much prey.

Dante looked very surprised to find us in his apartment. And not happy about it.

"Your showdown was a fucking mess," I said.

I wanted to immediately demand Dante explain the magic that had affected Lulu. Remove it. Give me antidote. But if I started

there, showed that card too early, I'd never get an answer. I had
to pace myself.

Dante's smile was arrogant. "I don't know what you're talking
about."

"Your battle with the upstart in Hyde Park."

That eliminated the smile, which boosted my mood.

"We're sorry to report your team was not victorious," Theo
said. "Only two survivors, so you will not be advancing to the
finals."

"Tough loss," I said, and Theo nodded.

Magic pierced the air. Having felt the demons' magic at the
mural brawl, it was easier to distinguish Dante's. Not in type—his
magic was as corrupted as theirs. But it was stronger. Older.

"Everyone out," Dante said, teeth grinding.

These demons knew when to obey orders, so all but a couple—
probably Dante's lieutenants— hustled out, leaving magic behind
them.

When they were gone, Dante stood. "Two survivors," he said,
and looked bothered by the calculation.

I doubted he cared much about his minions as individuals. But
he did probably care about the loss of troops or the effect on his
burgeoning territory.

"Well, there *were* two survivors," I clarified. "They're gone
now. Handy trick, that thing with the ash."

His stare was blank, and I didn't think he was faking it.
"What ash?"

"Burning up the demons before they could give away too
much," I said. "Very clever of you."

"They burned," he repeated, confusion furrowing his brow.

"Hooves to horns," I said, and cocked my head. "Why did you
kill your own people?"

Fury seemed to choke him. He walked back to the couch, sat,

and then smashed his balled fists into the new coffee table's glass top. It shattered, shards spilling like water droplets and hitting the floor with a shrill crash.

"I didn't kill them," he said, blood dripping from his hands, wisps of smoke rising from them.

"I guess that means the upstart did. Who is she?"

One of the remaining demons offered Dante a handkerchief. He wiped the blood from his fingers, handed back a stained and smoking ball of silk.

"I don't know her name," Dante said. "Only that she has expectations."

"Of you?" I asked.

"Of any demons that came here after Andaras." Rosantine, he meant. "The upstart believes she has claimed Chicago as her own. I disagree."

He leveled his gaze at me. "This wouldn't have happened if you'd been more careful. If you hadn't given all your secrets away."

"My secrets?" I asked, and thought he meant monster. But monster had nothing to do with the demons; whatever questions I had about it, that wasn't one of them. "What secrets would those be?"

Dante rose, stepped around the coffee-table frame and through the broken glass, which crunched like ice beneath his feet. The temperature seemed to increase as he moved, as if he were dragging a bit of hell along with him. I felt Theo and Connor move in behind me, but I held them back with a hand. We were close to something, and I wanted to see it through.

"The wards," he said. "You let Andaras in. You let her breach the wards. If you hadn't, much would be different now, would it not?" He stopped a foot away now; his scent—cologne and burning things—traveled farther.

"You're right," I said. "You wouldn't be here right now."

Dante didn't take that particular bait, but looked at me for a long time, frowning as he stared at me. I expected more insults. But got a question instead.

"The upstart wasn't there?" he asked.

"Not that we saw."

He looked away. "What you're saying—if you're telling the truth—would take power, especially at a distance. I don't think she has that kind of power."

"You've met her?"

"We talked via screen."

"How do you know how much power she had?"

"It was an impression."

"Give me her number."

"It was a disposable." He slid his gaze back to me, and his eyes went hard. "And I don't need others to fight my battles."

"Then you need to take your battles out of Chicago," Theo said, his voice cold. "You've done enough damage here."

Dante's gaze slipped behind me. "The world is changing. Compared to the rest of us, humans are nothing more than meat. Get used to it."

He put magic behind the threat, and it made the air go thick. We were running out of time.

"One of your demons put someone in a magical coma," I said. "How do I fix her?"

He barely blinked. "If she isn't a demon, she's meat, too."

"What do you want in exchange for fixing her?"

His smile was thin. "A kingdom. And you can't give me that. You have bigger problems anyway."

My own frustration was rising. "What would that be?"

He went back to the sofa. Sat. Crossed one leg over the other. "Your defenses," he said, and snapped his fingers. "Poof."

It might've been the magic or the anger or the fear, but something made my back go slick with sweat. "What does that mean? What defenses?"

"The only ones you have, little girl. Didn't you feel it? When the bell was rung? When the magic"—he mimicked running legs with two fingers—"ran away? All of it gone."

"The wards aren't gone," I said.

He clucked his tongue. "For a vampire, you're awfully slow." He moved his gaze to Connor. "Cops and canines, I guess. You'll come running back to me for help before it's all said and done— the devil you know and all that. So I'll give you a hint." He paused for obvious effect. "The quarry," he said, then gestured toward the door. "Get out."

"We aren't leaving," Theo said. "Not without you. Your demons hurt humans, destroyed property."

Dante's gaze was flat. "I've been here for several hours, as I'm sure the security video will confirm. And you said all the demons burned. Where's your evidence?"

When we said nothing, he nodded like we'd proved his point.

"Get the fuck out. Next time, bring a warrant." His laughter was big and rolling. "If you can manage that much."

We were silent as we walked back to the car, and not just because we were followed by "loyal associates" who wanted to ensure we left their master alone.

We were all contemplating what he'd said, trying to wrap our minds around the possibility that *all* the wards were inoperative. And that Chicago was completely vulnerable to any demon who wanted to enter.

When we climbed into the SUV and locked the doors, we gave ourselves another moment of silence. Then I made myself put voice to the fear, as if saying it aloud would diminish its power.

"Is he telling the truth?" I asked. "Are all the wards down?"

"I don't see how," Theo said. "Only two were triggered, and no one has touched the others."

"'When the bell rang,'" I repeated. "Did Dante mean the magic pulse? Is he saying that took down all the wards?"

"That's not possible," Theo said. "Wouldn't the city be inundated with demons?"

"There were more than a dozen demons at tonight's fight alone," Connor added, voice solemn. "And that was just one incident."

Theo said a curse, or a prayer, or some version of both. An appeal to whatever might be watching over us.

"Let's not panic yet," Connor said. "Let's find the facts."

So we drove to the quarry.

It was a former quarry, technically. A place in Chicago where stone had been dragged out of the earth, abandoned, and then turned into a park. The quarry was now a pretty pond, and near it were a meadow and a tall hill with a great view of the city.

We'd thought it might've been a ward location. We'd found no ward there, but we'd managed to lure Rosantine out of hiding—just before she'd animated a set of terrifying animal sculptures that attacked us before meeting their disturbing ends. Mostly in pieces at the bottom of the hill after a very long tumble down the stairs, their vacant eyes staring . . .

I shivered the thought away.

Theo made contact with Roger and Gwen, told them where we were going and why. He also inquired about any unusual activity in the park; none had been reported.

The park was quiet. But it was late, and it was dark, with only streetlights throwing circles across the ground. As we stepped into the grass, Theo turned on his flashlight, moved the beam in an arc over the spots where the remaining animal statues had been; they'd been taken to storage by the city. Which was fine by me.

"Is it just me," Connor asked, "or do demons smell like old cheese?"

I wasn't sure if he was seriously asking or trying to lighten the mood. But the question was less terrifying than the threat we were currently facing, so I ran with it. "Chemical fire and vinegar," I said.

"Sweat and chlorine," Theo said.

So we experienced demons differently.

We walked around the park together, but found no sign of anything unusual related to the wards or otherwise.

"I am forced to ask myself if this is a trap," Connor said.

"We were already in Dante's condo," I pointed out. "There's no point in his sending us somewhere else to be captured."

"That's a good point."

"But what exactly are we looking for?" Theo asked.

"We will know it when we find it."

An hour later, and even with the help of four CPD officers, we'd found nothing.

Well, we'd found trash, a few remaining bits of broken boar (sorry, not sorry), and several abandoned dog toys. But nothing that would clarify Dante's assertion that the wards were done.

Theo picked up a nearly new tennis ball, offered it to Connor. "You want?"

He was absolutely earnest, which was probably why Connor didn't slap the ball out of his hand.

"I'm good, thanks."

Theo chucked it back into the grass.

"Thoughts?" I asked, hands on my hips as I surveyed the land below us, the cops' flashlights still bobbing around beneath trees and under picnic tables.

"I'm wondering if he just wanted us out of his place," Theo said. "Mission accomplished."

"If this had something to do with the breaking of the wards," Connor said, "there must be some connection to the wards here. Why was this originally on the list?"

"Magical criteria," I said. "We were looking for places with very high magic—that would be the wards—next to places with very low magic. That would be the cornerstone." The stones had been spelled to seem magically neutral, so demons couldn't easily detect and destroy them.

"Why did you decide there wasn't one here?"

I wasn't sure what he was getting at. "Demon showed up; ward didn't trigger."

"Are you sure it wasn't just broken? I mean, the system was more than a hundred years old."

I had to pause a beat. "I guess not."

"So, let's assume there's a ward, but a broken one. The ward could be anything—including cursed animal statuary that Rosantine was able to use against you."

"If there's a ward, there's a cornerstone," Theo said. "So that's what we need to find."

"Where are they usually located in relation to the ward?" Connor asked, looking around. "Just outside it, right?"

"Yeah," I said. "The Guardians didn't want them too close together. So not necessarily in the park, but near the park."

We hustled back down the stairs. "Walk the perimeter," Theo said to the mingling group of CPD officers.

"You're looking for a big rock," I added.

The officer in charge nodded. "You're the boss. The vampire. The boss vampire."

"Elisa is fine," I said.

"Big rock," he confirmed, and sent the team in different directions.

"Let's take the sidewalk," I said, because it made a loop around the edge of the park.

Theo took the lead. Beside me, Connor took my hand, squeezed. The affection made me think of Lulu, which had guilt settling in like fog.

"Let it go," Connor said quietly, apparently sensing my concern. "You're working for her. Sitting in a hospital lobby wouldn't help either one of you."

"I know that rationally. But still . . ."

"But still," he agreed, and put an arm around my shoulders. And it tightened at the sudden squeal of tires as a car swerved in the road.

My first instinct was to assume the vehicle was a threat and step in front of Connor and Theo. But the vehicle kept moving, evidently not part of a demonic assassination plot, and disappeared around a corner.

I looked back, realized the vehicle had swerved to avoid a small construction area in the middle of the street. There was some low plastic fencing and a couple of cones—one of them down like a fallen soldier—but none of them were reflective, so the driver would have missed them until he or she was close.

And why weren't they reflective?

Instincts triggered, I stepped off the curb and walked to the spot. Connor and Theo followed behind me.

I pulled back the warped netting, found a hole a good five feet across and six feet deep.

And at the bottom, etched with magical symbols, was a big broken rock.

TEN

It was a cornerstone. A *smashed* cornerstone. Maybe accidentally—some kind of construction work gone awry? But smashed all the same.

"Someone broke the damn cornerstone," Theo said.

"No," I said, "someone broke the entire ward system. That had to be the pulse of magic: the breaking of the stone."

The cornerstones secondarily regulated the ley lines. Stop regulating them, and it was logical you'd get a surge of power.

"That was days ago," Connor said grimly. "They've been down the entire time?"

Theo blew out a breath. "Now we know why the sorcerers couldn't get the machine online."

I wanted to panic—this seemed like a very reasonable time to panic—but knew I didn't have the luxury. So instead I focused, took pictures of the broken stone, the "construction" setup. And sent them to Roger and Petra with a simple message: CORNERSTONE DESTROYED WHEN WE FELT MAGIC PULSE. WARDS DOWN. CITY OPEN TO DEMONS. SPREAD THE WORD FOR ALL SUPS TO BOLO.

The mayor was going to love this.

I put my screen away. "I'm going down there."

Connor and Theo looked at each other, then at me.

"Of course you are," Connor said. "Need a hand?"

I looked into the pit and closed my eyes to double-check for the presence of magic. I felt nothing.

"I'm good," I said, and hopped down.

The stone was probably four feet across. Or had been before it had been snapped roughly in half. The crack was jagged, with lots of chipping. Someone had worked to break it. Not with magic, but with muscle.

Why not with magic? Because it couldn't be broken with magic? Or because the person who'd broken it didn't have any?

I took pictures of the fracture, then studied the hole. The dirt looked roughly hewn, as if it'd been dug out by hand. There were long, sharp marks that I bet were made by a shovel.

So the cornerstone had been buried, and someone had unearthed it by hand, broken it by hand.

Little wonder this ward hadn't worked in the first place; it had been buried under earth and street. That was a risk in having an old magical defense system and not telling anyone about it. Development happened in the meantime. How had the person who'd done this known how to find it?

I squinted, found a little shred of fabric at the blunt end of a tree root halved by the shoveling.

"Yo."

I looked up, found Gwen peering into the hole.

"Evidence bag?" I asked, and after a moment, she tossed one down. I slipped the fabric inside the bag, put it into my pocket.

"Could use a hand getting out," I said.

Connor's face appeared beside Gwen's. "What will you give me?"

"I won't punch you for holding me hostage in a dirt hole."

"Deal," he said agreeably, and held out a hand.

I jumped up, caught it. He pulled, and I levered my feet against the walls, climbed back up into the city. And found a full crime scene team waiting. Floodlights were being set up and there were legitimate barriers around the hole now.

"What did you find?" Gwen asked.

I held up the evidence bag, and the fabric scrap gleamed in the streetlight. This actually *was* reflective.

"Probably something worn by the person that dug that hole and smashed the cornerstone," I said.

"Good work," she said, and held out a hand.

But I closed my fist around the bag. "You need to ask if anyone saw a fake construction crew. I'll help."

Gwen's eyes narrowed. "Don't you want to get to the hospital?"

"Petra messaged," Theo said. "Lulu's in a room now."

"I need to follow this through," I said and, because they were friends as well as colleagues, added, "and I'm not ready to go yet."

Not ready to feel helpless, I meant. Here, at least, I might do some good. And I could keep ahead of the avalanche of fear that was threatening to overtake me. I knew I was on borrowed time.

Theo put a hand on my shoulder, squeezed gently.

"Okay, then," Gwen said, and her gaze shifted to Connor. "You'll know when she needs to quit."

Dawn, I thought. The rising of the sun was when I'd stop.

"Why don't you come with me?" Gwen asked Theo. "We'll look for cams."

"Surveillance video," he said. "I can do that."

We left them to it and looked around. This was a mostly residential neighborhood, but I didn't want to wake up humans in the middle of the night to ask them about roadwork. (Being Chicagoans, of course, they'd have opinions regardless the hour.) But I could see the glow of a convenience store a block away, and pointed it out.

"There," I said.

"You could use some coffee."

"If they have Leo's in a can, I'll take one."

"Of course you will. Something's bothering me," Connor said as we started walking.

I snickered. "Just the one thing?"

"Just one thing about Dante. The rest of the list is plenty long. Why did he tell us about this? He has to know we'll try to fix it—to put the system back."

"I think that goes back to the upstart," I said as we turned a corner. The store was a tiny glowing sliver between larger buildings. "He doesn't want the competition."

"You think he got in, and now he wants to close the door behind him?"

"That's my guess."

We stepped into the shop, a digital bell ringing our arrival. The interior was glaringly bright, and the air smelled like old hot dogs.

The clerk, a young woman with dark hair and big glasses—wide and round—glanced up from her screen, then looked down again. "Dad, there's a lady with a sword out here."

"Find coffee," I told Connor, and walked to the register.

The clerk's father emerged from a door behind the counter, followed by the noise of a droning wall screen. He looked at me, then at my sword, then at me again. "Face and weapon don't match."

I wasn't sure how to take that remark, so I didn't. I pulled out my badge, offered it. "I'm with the Ombudsman's office."

"Hmm," the dad said vaguely, peering at my badge.

Connor joined me, put two cans of coffee on the counter.

"I can't give freebies, even if you're cops."

"Wasn't even going to ask," Connor said with a smile, and offered his credit fob, paid for the goods.

While they worked the transaction and the daughter watched

Connor surreptitiously (couldn't blame her), I began my questions.

"There's a hole in the street a block over. What happened there?"

"No idea," the dad said, handing the fob back to Connor.

"How long has it been there?"

"Week or so."

The girl's face tightened, but she didn't comment.

"You see who dug it or put the cones out?"

"Construction guys, probably," he said.

The screen in the back room beeped, and he looked at his daughter, nodded, disappeared again.

She waited until the door was firmly closed. "He's watching his show. And he doesn't like trouble."

"Neither do we," Connor said, offering his most charming smile. It had worked on many hearts, including mine, over the years.

The human bit her lip, looked back at the closed door, then leaned toward us.

"They dug the hole three or four days ago," she said quietly. "He's called the city every day, complaining it hasn't been fixed and it's not marked well enough."

"You said 'they,'" I said. "Did you see who dug it? Were there multiple people?"

"Oh, I don't know. I just assumed it was a bunch. Big hole, right? And there's always a bunch of people on those crews."

I took the evidence bag from my pocket, held it up. The reflective fabric—already screaming orange—gleamed in the light.

"We found this in the hole," I said. "Probably somebody was wearing it while they worked. Maybe they came in?"

She pushed up her glasses with a knuckle. "I don't know. Maybe?"

"The thing is," Connor said, "we don't think it was official construction work. We think someone was looking for, basically, magical treasure."

"Really?" she asked, and sounded skeptical.

"Really. So, we need to find the people who did it, because there may be"—he leaned forward a little— "supernatural repercussions."

I held up a hand. "We'd better not get into the confidential details," I said, playing the bad cop.

Connor rolled his eyes. "Sometimes you have to do what's right, even if it's not to the letter of the law. Anyway, if you could try again to remember, that could be a big help."

The human sighed, pushed away her screen, and closed her eyes. She chewed on her lip for a moment; then her eyes popped open. "It was a guy."

"Oh, yeah?" Connor asked. "What kind of guy? Tall? Short? Light skin? Dark?"

"Oh." She frowned. "I don't know. I didn't get a good look." She gestured to a shelf of candy beside the door. "I was stocking candy when he came in. I didn't really look at him, just saw the fabric and thought it was crazy bright. Oh!" she added animatedly. "It was a vest thing."

I thought of our female upstart. "You're sure it was a male?"

Her mouth made an O shape. "Well, I assumed it was a guy. But I didn't see his face, I guess. Or her face."

"But he definitely wore a reflective vest?" Connor asked, and she nodded.

"Absolutely."

"What about surveillance cameras?" I asked.

"We don't have any."

"Was your dad working that night?" I asked.

"Wasn't night," she said. "It was daytime. I go to Northwestern, and my class got canceled, so I was here."

That only eliminated vampires. While other sups lived nocturnally, vamps were the only ones physically injured by going into the sun.

"Anything else you can think of?" I asked.

She shook her head.

I nodded. "Okay. Thanks for your time. If you do think of anything, you can call the Ombudsman's office."

"Okay, sure." There was movement behind the door, and she settled back into her pose of boredom. "You should go. Dad hates loiterers."

So we rang our way outside again.

"My sword and my face don't match," I said, sipping my can of coffee as we walked back to the park. Not as good as actual Leo's, but handy in a crunch. "What do you think that means?"

"That you're unique," Connor said, which cleared nothing up.

"How did you think to play up the magic angle?" I asked.

He laughed. "You didn't see? She was reading one of those sexy fairy stories."

I stopped, looked at him. "Sexy fairy stories?"

"Supernatural romance or whatever. Not my bag. But Dan reads them."

Of course he did. Romance was Dan's *raison d'être*.

We met up with Theo and Gwen, offered the evidence bag and reported what we'd learned from the convenience store.

Gwen rubbed her temples. "We are in for, as my aunt Grace would say, a heap of hurt."

"Yep," I agreed. "Any luck with the video?"

"Not so far, but we're going to keep canvassing. The forensic folks have control of the scene now," she said. "So we're thinking about heading to the hospital."

I checked the time. Dawn would be closing in soon, and I

couldn't put off a hospital visit any longer. "Good idea," I said. "Do you want to ride with us?"

"I've got my vehicle," she said. "We'll meet you there."

"Let's go check on your girl," Connor said, and we began that trek together.

Theo and Gwen had beaten us to the hospital, and waited just outside the entrance.

"You okay?" I asked Theo. It had been only a week since he'd been helped inside a medical facility, his broken arm cleaned of magic residue and casted. Demons and wards were picking off my friends one by one.

"I'm fine," he said. He held up his casted arm, made a fist in support.

We were quiet as we walked inside. The lobby smelled as all medical lobbies seemed to—sterile and slightly plastic and tinged with human fear.

"Elevators," Gwen said.

We traversed the wide lobby and took an elevator to the eighth floor. Then there were was another long hallway and a skywalk as we journeyed across the medical complex. It was late, and the buildings were virtually empty.

When we reached the next building, Gwen pushed through a set of double doors and then into a small wing that buzzed with magic. There were supernaturals here, I surmised, and caught sight of a river nymph in a medical gown and bootees shuffling around a corner. The staff seemed to be a mix of human and supernatural, and the central hub of workstations looked shiny and new.

"They still take sups in the ER," Theo explained, "but they're testing the concept of a supernatural ward for nonemergency illnesses."

For which shifters and vampires weren't the target audience. Vampires were immortal and had quick healing abilities, and shifters could shift themselves into relative health.

We followed Gwen to the right and into a small waiting room, and we were immediately engulfed in people. Mom and Dad. Aunt Mallory and Uncle Catcher. Roger and Petra. Clint Howard, who had a bandage on his cheek, but was otherwise up and moving. Alexei wasn't here, and I figured he was in the room with Lulu. Or maybe outside trying to sweat out his anger. But Dan was, and he gave a wave.

They'd all come to see her. And the tears began in earnest now.

"Come here," said Dad, tall and lean and still in his trademark black suit.

He and I had the same green eyes and blond hair, although his was straight to his shoulders. He embraced me, and I got a chance to let go of some of the guilt and fear I'd been holding in.

After a moment, I stepped back, swiped away tears. "Thanks," I said, still a little watery.

"Always," he said, and my mother took his place, squeezing me tightly.

"You are so brave," she said, and kissed my temple.

"Do they know anything?" I asked.

"You guessed correctly," she said. "It's magical, not physical."

But something crossed her face, and I knew there was more. I braced myself for the blow. "What else?"

"She's stable now," Uncle Catcher said.

He was as tall as my dad, but more muscled; his hair was buzzed and his eyes a pale green. He rarely smiled, but he loved his family beyond measure.

"Okay," I said. "But?"

"Everything seems to be slowing," he said. "Her heart rate is slower. Her blood pressure is lower than it was when we got here.

Her oxygen saturation is down." He rubbed a hand over his shorn scalp. "I don't think I've ever said that phrase before tonight."

"They're keeping her as stable as they can," Mom said. "But there seems to be a cumulative reaction to the magic, and they don't know how to reverse that yet."

"We've tried spells," Aunt Mallory said. "To reverse whatever this is or break it. Nothing has worked so far."

"I'm still looking," Petra said, without glancing up from her seat, where she frowned at a large screen. "Easy to find apotropaic demon magic. Harder to find full reversals."

Apotropaic magic was protective; wards fell generally into that category.

I glanced at Roger, not sure if he wanted an update.

"Go see her first," he said. "Then we'll get on the same page and make a plan."

Connor accompanied me to Lulu's room. The door was slightly ajar, and Alexei sat on a stool by Lulu's bed, head down and eyes closed prayerfully. He still wore the scrubs he'd been given by the EMTs.

Connor and I walked in. Alexei didn't stir, but recognition of Connor's presence seemed to move through his muscles. He rubbed a hand across his face. And without a word, he rose and turned into me.

It took a moment of frozen shock for me to realize what he needed. I put my arms around him, held him tight. If he cried, he did it silently. It seemed he wanted only a moment of peace, of oblivion. And then he let go, gave me a nod. Looked at Connor, did the same. And then left us alone in stillness and the quiet.

Lulu lay in the bed, its head raised slightly. Her frame looked tiny under a thin blue blanket. Sensors had been hooked to her arm and slipped across her collarbone and into a gown that was white and sprayed with small pink flowers.

Her eyes were closed. Her face was serene. But the screen beside the bed danced with numbers.

Connor leaned over her, kissed her temple. "Please wake up, because Alexei is experiencing human emotions. And the rest of us must deal with that, and it is a lot. And we love you," he added.

Then he stepped back and kissed my temple. "I'll give you a minute with her. But I'll be right outside."

When he was gone, I sat down on the stool Alexei had vacated; it was still warm from his time at Lulu's bedside. I put a hand on hers and felt the stain of demon magic. It felt potent enough that I pulled my hand back, wondering if I might see some kind of spreading burn. But my skin was unmarred.

"I want to apologize," I began, "but your mom would yell at me, and you tell me not to say ridiculous things. So I won't. But I will tell you that I'm sorry their battle took place near your worksite and damaged it and damaged you. And I'll tell you what I know.

"We think the demons are battling for territory. Dante, the Gold Coast demon, and an unnamed female demon he calls the 'upstart.' We don't know who she is yet. This is all happening because someone found a cornerstone at a ward we didn't know was a ward, dug down to it, and broke it in two. So, that's probably when the ley lines pulsed, and it's probably why your parents haven't been able to get the broken wards going again. Because they're *all* down, and they've apparently been down for days, and none of us knew."

I stopped for breath, pulled up my hair, closed my eyes. Thought about what I'd seen.

"The perp broke the stone by hand, not magic, while wearing fake construction gear, which is such a dick move. And it happened during daylight. So, human? Or, I guess, anyone but a vampire. So, at least that's not our fault."

My stomach growled as a wave of exhaustion hit me. I checked my screen. There was still time before dawn, but not much. And I couldn't remember the last time I'd eaten real food.

"I wish we were at Taco Hole." I squeezed her hand. "And we will be very soon. I promise," I said to seal the deal. And I let the silence fall and sat with my best friend.

I'm not sure when the knock on the door came, but I felt Connor's magic before he stepped inside.

"It's getting close," he said kindly but firmly. "We need to go soon."

"I could sleep here."

"I asked. They don't have sun protection."

That had me sitting up straight. "What? It's a supernatural ward."

"And vampires don't need hospitals," he reminded me.

"Right," I said. "My brain is done."

"And you're hangry."

"I'm not hangry."

His expression was very flat, which made me want to punch him. So, I probably was hangry.

I rose. "I promise," I quietly repeated for Lulu, and followed Connor out.

The crowd in the lobby was still there, but their exhaustion was beginning to show. Dealing with trauma was its own kind of horrible marathon.

"Alexei volunteered to stay with her during the day," Aunt Mallory said. "We're going to get some sleep. We have a lot of ward work ahead of us."

"Is there a chance to repair the cornerstone?" I asked.

"We don't know," she said. "But we're damn well going to try."

"Good luck," I said, and meant it.

"We might move her to Cadogan," Mom said, and she got a nod from Aunt Mallory. "Alexei will need sleep, and it's more secure. Just in case."

As a planner myself, I had no qualms about preparations for "just in case."

"We'll let you know either way," Mom said.

"And I've given everyone the update," Theo said. "So we're all on the same page."

"Good job finding that fabric," Roger said. "I've informed the mayor about the cornerstone."

"How did she take it?"

"She fixed herself a very strong drink."

"Could use one myself," Uncle Catcher murmured.

"There's a good chance the violence we saw tonight is only the precursor," Roger said. "So, in addition to dealing with Dante and the 'upstart' and figuring out what's ailing Lulu, we need to rebuild the defenses and respond to the demons who are already here."

"We're on the defenses," Aunt Mallory said, taking Uncle Catcher's hand. "First thing."

"Your service is greatly appreciated," Roger said. "Especially now."

Aunt Mallory nodded.

"I'd offer to help with the demons," Mom said, "but our deal with the city . . ."

Chicago was fed up with supernatural drama by the time Sorcha Reed brought the Egregore to life. When my parents had bested it, the mayor agreed not to blame them for the damage done in the fight (which wasn't their fault anyway) if they agreed to stand down on battling supernatural problems. The Ombuds got more funding, and my mom, who was pregnant at the time, decided to take a break. She'd been on that break for more than twenty years.

"The Ombuds don't presently have enough staff to deal with this," Roger said. "And the mayor knows it. So, if you're interested, we can ask for a reprieve."

Dad lifted a single eyebrow. It was his signature move. "A reprieve?"

"A temporary lifting of the ban," Roger said. "But only if you're willing. It's not mandatory, and the city has no expectations."

"We'll need to discuss it," Mom said, sliding Dad a glance that pretty clearly said she'd already made up her mind to do it.

I wasn't sure how I felt about that. Glad to have her obviously skilled help. But I didn't want to lose anyone else.

"I need to stay at the House," Dad said. "It's still unsettled."

Because the vampires had been dragged by Rosantine into another dimension, he meant.

Mom nodded. "I know," she said, and they shared a look of understanding. "I can ask some of my . . . former colleagues . . . for help. We'll let you know."

"You'll need a new sword," Dad said.

I was tired, my nerves on edge, and I nearly jolted at the reminder. My mother's sword, locked in the House's armory, held the Egregore. Or most of it.

My parents discussed the available weapons, and monster ached to be part of that conversation. To assert itself. It surged against me, and I worked hard to keep it hidden—while standing amid everyone from whom I was trying to hide that part of myself.

Sweat bloomed, a drop sliding down my face.

"Are you all right?"

I looked at Aunt Mallory, whose face was pinched with concern.

The question ended my parents' discussion and brought everyone's gaze my way.

"I'm tired," I said as Connor stepped beside me, took my hand, squeezed it.

"We should go," he said. "Or the vampires at least. Dawn is getting close."

Dad checked his watch. "I didn't know it was so late."

"Early," Uncle Catcher said wryly, and I had a feeling they'd had this conversation before.

"Go home," Roger said with a nod. "We'll coordinate at the office at dusk."

I nodded. Monster, apparently realizing it wasn't going to win this particular battle, relented. Exhaustion seeped into my bones.

I didn't remember the goodbyes, the drive home, or the walk upstairs. Only landing facedown on the bed. And the world going dark.

For a little while.

And then I was dreaming that I stood before a machine that was spewing demons into the world. I was the only one fighting them. I use sword, fists, and kicks, but they kept coming and I couldn't keep up. Each was more horrific than the last.

So I ran through a park and grassy field and quiet neighborhood and hospital maze. . . . And then I was inside something deep and dark and unfriendly. Monster shifted, slithered, moving like a snake beneath my skin. I tried to climb up and out of the pit, but the walls were sand and they fell away in my hands.

And then the light shifted and I looked up, and Lulu was at the edge of the pit, and she was screaming something down to me, but her voice made no sound. I could hear only a machine whirring in the distance. She screamed again, but I couldn't hear her.

I couldn't hear her.

"Lis."

Connor's voice, gentle even as the sun burned outside, and his hand on my waist, strong and steady.

"You're safe."

And darkness fell again.

ELEVEN

Cadogan House was the fourth vampire house established in the United States, and it had occupied the same stately stone building in Hyde Park since its vampires had settled in Chicago in 1883.

It was a beautiful building, if intimidating in its size, scale, and security. But I was the Master's kid, so the guards let me through to see the sorcerer's kid, who as expected had been moved there for her protection. And with monster already pushing me toward the front portico, I knew I'd face my second threat of the night at only an hour past dusk.

I didn't count the nightmare, but I did count the warning we'd received on waking. Connor's dad had called, which was unusual. I'd still been facedown in pillows—the same position I'd fallen into the night before—when the yelling had begun.

"For fuck's sake," Connor had muttered, stalking across the room. He pulled on jeans, but no shirt or shoes. "We have more important things to deal with right now. If he wants to challenge me, he can get his ass up here. I'm not leaving Chicago." Then he turned to look at me, his eyes brilliantly blue even in the room's dim lighting. "I won't leave her alone to fight this."

Connor went quiet while his dad talked.

"Then I'll deal with it," he said aloud. "If he has questions, he can call me."

He ended the call and paced again, his magic peppering the air. That woke monster and had it offering to fight.

Not now, I told it. Again. And I added monster's need for release—and my lack of time and ability and, frankly, inclination to do anything about that right now—to the list of things I felt guilty about.

"If you want to punch something," I said, "I recommend a demon. They all seem to deserve it."

He strode back to bed, with his "I will take on the fucking world" expression.

"What's happened?"

"You probably got the gist," he said. "Someone wants me to drive to Louisiana to fight him because Chicago is dangerous and unstable. I said no. If he wants to be Apex that much, he should get his ass up here at the least. If he was real Pack, he'd help fight demons."

"Do you—do you have a Southern accent?"

For a moment, he looked stunned. "I don't think so."

"Yes," I said, sitting up. "You were talking in a Southern accent just then."

"I was born in Memphis," he said. "And you're changing the subject."

"Not on purpose." The temporary drawl had me shaken. "What did your dad say?"

"He doesn't like to mix Pack policies and city politics." He put his hands on his hips. "What is the fucking point of trying to become the leader of this community if I don't actually try to lead it? I understand Pack traditions, but there's a time to toe the line and a time to call bullshit. I guess I've gotten to the second one."

I smiled. "I'm proud of you."

He actually flushed a little, this handsome, brilliant, and often wicked fighter of mine, who wanted to do right by his people.

"But . . . ," I added.

"But what?"

"Think of the *food* down there. Boudin. Crawfish étouffée. Oyster po'boys. Pralines. And that's just the beginning. You could go down there, kick his ass, and enjoy one hell of a celebratory dinner." And show off that accent, which apparently came out when he got riled up.

Connor eyed me speculatively. "When were you in Louisiana?"

I waved away the question. "That's not important."

He kept looking at me with that almost Apex stare. And won the staring contest.

"The week before I left for Paris."

His eyes narrowed. "You told me you couldn't go to Louisiana with me. That you didn't have time for Houma or New Orleans because you'd already started college prep work."

"You were taking that brunette. The human. And I didn't want to be a third wheel."

I sounded like such a tight ass. Which wasn't far from the truth. I liked to think I'd mellowed over the last few months. "That human invited herself," he murmured. "But you went anyway?"

"I got a wild hair." Or that had been how Lulu put it. Mostly, I had wanted to look amazing and carefree and to run into him on Bourbon Street as Dixieland jazz *harrumph*ed in the background.

"And?"

And Lulu and I had spent an evening eating the best food the city had to offer. And then bought enormous, frozen boozy concoctions in huge plastic cups, and that had been the end of both of us.

I felt my cheeks going hot. "The weekend didn't turn out like we planned."

He watched me for a moment, and then his cheek dimpled as he smiled that glorious smile. "Elisa Sullivan, did you go to New Orleans to see me?"

"No comment," I said. I did not want to relive the hours spent being nauseated or actually retching in the hotel bathroom.

"Changing the subject again," I said to avoid further humiliation. "So, you declined the trip."

"I did. And I plan to tell him that directly if he asks. And recruit more help."

"For the demons?"

He nodded. "We have muscle. And if vampires can help, so can we."

"You're going to make a damn fine Apex."

"Not soon enough," he murmured.

All that to explain why I stood alone in front of Cadogan House. Because Connor had gone to Pack HQ to deal with the likely fallout of his being rational.

Monster, whom I'd necessarily brought with, hummed with anticipation. Aunt Mallory had already gone to work on the wards, or so Mom had messaged, and her absence reduced some of the risk that monster would be discovered while I was in the House. But not all of it. Vampires could feel magic, and the House was literally full of them. They wouldn't want to hurt me, but they'd want to protect Cadogan House. And what would happen when those things became mutually exclusive?

When Cadogan House and its vampires became my enemies?

This isn't the night, I told monster. *We have to save Lulu first, so you have to stay down.*

I could feel it ignoring me—reaching out toward the basement armory.

No, I said loud and clear and firm.

And then Dad stepped onto the portico and came down the steps toward me.

"Hey," he said. "Are you okay? The guard said you were here, but it's been a few minutes and you didn't come in."

"I'm fine," I said. "Tired." Not a lie. "Worried about Lulu." Not a lie. "Afraid."

Absolute truth.

"She looks very peaceful," he said. "You'll see."

He gave a careful look around, and then put a hand on my back as we walked up the stone steps together. Then we were in the House's big grand foyer, where the colors and decor were crisp and cool, and the air smelled of the enormous white gardenias in a vase on a center pedestal table. The vampires at the security desk nodded as I followed Dad to his office in the House's administrative wing.

"Where is she?" I asked, as we clearly weren't heading in the direction of the dorm rooms.

"The guest suite on the second floor," he said. "We have a guard stationed outside."

"Good," I said as we stepped into his office, which was sleek and efficient but in a welcoming way.

Mom stood inside, one hand on her hip, and she talked on her screen. "Okay," she said. "I'll talk to Scott and Morgan and Malik and coordinate."

They were Chicago's other three Master vampires and the leaders of their houses: Grey, Navarre, and Washington, respectively.

"Thanks, Roger," Mom added, then ended the call.

She looked at me and smiled, but that expression faded to concern, which had me directing every defense I could muster against a breach by monster.

"Hey," she said. "Are you all right?"

She searched my face. I didn't know what she saw, or if she saw monster, but her expression didn't change.

"Nightmares," I said. "Still a little groggy."

Truth.

Despite my defenses, monster kicked, and I kicked back. The armory was beneath us, and we could both feel the buzz of the sword and the creature it held. And that buzz seemed stronger than the last time I'd been here. Was I more sensitive to it because I knew more about its relationship to monster, or had it actually gotten stronger? Maybe because of the pulse of magic? Or the unregulated ley lines?

And then I realized what I was hearing: They were calling to each other. The monster in me and the monster in the sword were communicating.

"You do look a little tired," Mom said. Her voice was smooth and relaxed, which was a harsh contrast to my racing thoughts and galloping heart. "And your magic seems . . . frazzled."

Wait, I told it. *You have to wait.*

But it was tired of being patient.

"I am frazzled," I admitted.

"Do you want some blood or food? Or you could take a nap."

I felt disconnected, like I was experiencing three conversations at once: me and Mom, me and monster, monster and the thing it wanted.

"I have to get to the office after this," I said over the roaring in my ears. "But thanks."

She nodded. "That was Roger on-screen." Her gaze slid carefully, neutrally, to my dad's face. "The mayor has agreed to temporarily suspend the contract."

Dad sighed, and I expected they'd had several conversations about this since I'd seen them last. And he wasn't happy about the results, but resigned to it.

"You'll be careful," he said.

"Obviously. In the course of helping our daughter save the city."

Good strategy, I thought, actively trying to disconnect my mind from monster's. And hoping that would give me some space.

"I'll coordinate with Roger," she told me.

"That's great. Thanks for the help."

"Of course. And I'm excited to get out there again. Training in the gym just isn't the same."

"I'll go see Lulu, so I can get to the office and help with that," I said. "Is Alexei still here?"

"He left a few minutes ago. He wanted to shower and change clothes."

Good. He would have needed a break.

"Okay, then. I'll come by before I leave."

And I tried not to run out of the office.

I left them to what sounded like further negotiations for Mom's reengagement as Sentinel.

I walked carefully to the staircase, focusing all my attention on the stairs leading up to the second floor—not those running down to the basement. And then I lurched forward and only just managed to grab the newel post instead of hurtling fifteen feet to the floor below.

Monster had *moved* me.

"Ms. Sullivan?" a vampire at the security desk asked, and I heard her chair scrape back.

No, I told it, and plastered on my best smile, looked back. "I'm fine," I said, locking my knees to stay upright. "Tripped over my own feet. New shoes," I added, and made what I'd said sound like truth.

"Oh, okay," the vampire said, then tended to a ringing screen.

Lulu has to be safe first, I told monster again. *You can't just jump out of me. There will be a process to get you out. Be patient.*

That had it backing down, at least for now. But it didn't diminish the low hum of its conversation with the monster in the sword.

I made it to the second floor without further incident, and then went down the quiet hallway to the guest suite. Outside the door, I found a guard standing at attention with his sword belted. He nodded at me, then turned his gaze back to the hallway and watched for threats.

"Doctor took a break," he said. "She'll be back in five."

I couldn't spare much more time than that. So I opened the door.

The magic was thick. I assumed that was a side effect of the magic done to Lulu, as it bore the sour tang of demon. This wasn't a symptom I'd seen before, but then it was my first experience with a demon-induced coma.

I wasn't sure if I needed to worry about it, but I'd tell the doctor. She was human and wouldn't have noticed it. Because I wasn't sure what it would do to monster, I left the door open, looked back at the guard.

"The room needs to air out," I told him, then walked across the small room—bed, nightstand, bookshelf, dresser, and assorted medical devices monitoring Lulu—to the window. I cracked it open, let a cool breeze blow in, waited until some of the magic dissipated.

When the magic had thinned, I sat on the edge of the bed. Lulu wore blue pajamas with white piping around the hems. Her eyes were closed and her feet were tucked into fuzzy socks.

"There's nothing new to report," I told her. "But it's only a little past sunset. You're in Cadogan House, in case you wondered why it smells like pizza and Armani."

She would've at least chuckled at that, if she'd been awake.

"Alexei was here all night. I haven't asked, because I know you're still figuring it out, but I thought you should know that he's been watching over you. I'm pretty sure you're the one for him, Lulu.

"You were in my dream last night," I continued. "I was stuck in a well or something and you were screaming down at me. But I couldn't hear you."

I watched her in silence for a moment, half-expecting her to sit up and explain what she'd been screaming about. But she didn't move or react.

And still I wondered: Could she have really been trying to tell me something?

"That's crazy talk," I murmured. There were undoubtedly supernaturals who could travel in dreams; she wasn't one of them.

I sat with her in silence for a few more minutes, then rose. "I have to get to work. Nail the bad guy, rescue the princess, all that jazz. Stay with me," I told her. "I'm going as fast as I can, and you have to stay with me in the meantime."

I closed the window and stepped into the hallway, where I found a woman standing with the guard. She had light brown skin and dark hair pulled into a tidy topknot. Her eyes were dark brown and wide and full of knowledge. She wore a white doctor's jacket over scrubs and sneakers. This was Dr. Anderson, Petra's cousin.

"Elisa," she said.

"Dr. Anderson. You're making House calls now?"

"Clever," she said. "And in this case, yes. She's a friend of Petra's and I'm a very curious woman. The circumstances are unusual."

"She seems stable."

"She is, for now." She frowned. "I think it's partly being in this House. She's still shedding magic."

I nodded. "I opened the window. It was thick in here."

"Good thought. Her vitals have remained stable. I think Cadogan House's own magic is having some sort of reverse osmosis effect; it's actually pulling out some of the demon magic. It's fascinating stuff. Second to patient welfare, of course, but fascinating." Then she narrowed her eyes. "You look peaky. You need blood."

"I'll keep that in mind," I said, resisting the urge to tell her I was aware how to vampire, because I knew she was trying to be helpful.

I left them in the hallway, walked to the staircase again. I took the stairs two at a time to the first floor, ordering the Auto as I did. I wanted out of the House before anything else went haywire.

I made it to the foyer. And that's when it struck.

Monster hadn't been considering. It had been *waiting*. And this time it had me grabbing the newel post and taking that first step down into the basement.

I suddenly had no control over my body. I used what little strength I could muster to try to look casual—and prevent the vampires at the front desk from alerting the House's guards that I looked unbalanced.

I was sweating and terrified by the time we reached the basement. I tried again to reason with monster, explain what would happen if we were caught. But its demeanor—in addition to "suddenly fucking intent on the armory"—remained jarringly positive.

For you, it said, making me stride down the hallway even as I fought it.

We passed the guards' office, the doors thankfully closed. Inside, someone was giving instructions about responding to a hypothetical demon attack.

As we reached the armory's locked door, I realized how this had happened. It was the haze of demon magic in Lulu's room. Somehow, maybe because I was worried and exhausted, monster had managed to take in that magical miasma and use it to increase its own strength.

And then my hand was on the door handle, turning. I felt monster's stark disappointment, its bright frustration, that the door was locked.

And then monster was moving my hand to the palm plate. I pushed back against it, beads of sweat rolling down my face as I tried to resist its remarkable strength. My arm shook with the force of our struggle, and I could smell the brimstone our battle was putting into the air.

I was sweating out the residue of demon magic, the excess power that was seeping out of Lulu and into Cadogan House.

Help you, monster said, apparently baffled that I was fighting against what it believed was an act of kindness.

The vampires will stop us, I said. *They won't let you take the sword. They'll think we're a threat.*

It didn't believe that or was too high on magic to care. With a final push, it shoved my hand against the plate. The light turned green, and the lock disengaged.

The door opened.

The sword lay on a bed of red brocade silk on a table in the middle of the room. It was a gently curved blade of folded steel, its handle wrapped in bumpy ray skin, its brilliantly red, lacquered scabbard lying beside it. The katana had been forged by a master bladesmith, magicked by Uncle Catcher, and tempered with my mom's blood. And then magicked again by Aunt Mallory to hold the Egregore.

We were moving toward it, my feet shuffling as I tried for purchase to slow our journey.

The demon magic was finite; we hadn't been in Lulu's room very long. Monster couldn't use it to fight me forever, so maybe I could stall.

An entire wall of the armory held katanas on horizontal racks. I looked at them, focused my gaze in attention there. *The one on my table is my father's,* I lied. *He doesn't fight anymore. They put my mom's sword with the others to make it harder to find in case of an intruder.*

I could feel monster's confusion, and it took seconds to consider.

I heard the door down the hall open. The guards were probably wondering who was in the armory.

They will hurt us, I pleaded, narrowing my gaze on a sword with chartreuse leather wrapped around the handle. *That's the one you want,* I said, and stared at it.

There were steps moving down the hallway.

I will ask Lulu as soon as she's awake. Not like this.

But it refused to believe the chartreuse sword was the correct one, and it was totally unswayed by the possibility we were in danger. It was turning me around, back to my mother's sword and the magic that surrounded it.

I felt monster's joy, its relief at the possibility of reunion. Of being made whole. Its emotion was as sharp as the edge of my mother's katana.

More footsteps outside moving closer.

In its impatience to get to the sword, monster hadn't closed the door.

My hand reached out, inches from the gleaming steel. And I knew what I had to do.

Voices, multiple, were only a few feet outside.

I'm sorry, I told it—and myself—and poured glamour into monster. And, thus, into me.

TWELVE

Secondary demon magic did not beat vampire glamour. In the wave of magic that covered me, monster let go of its control. I snatched back my hand and fell to my knees.

"Lis?"

I nearly retched from the barrage of magic that echoed inside my body like a scream, bruising me from the inside.

Dad knelt beside me. "Lis? What's wrong?"

I had to wait to speak, and then let myself sob while monster, either out of magic or awareness that its chance had passed, slipped down again, lonely and miserable. *But alive,* I reminded it, and turned my attention back to the room.

And once again, I lied.

"I thought, maybe with a different weapon, I could beat the demons. And then I came down here and realized how ridiculous that was. I'm sorry," I added, and wiped away tears. "I'm having a bit of a breakdown."

And my heart is beginning to collapse from the weight of so many lies. Although, like the others I'd told, there was at least a kernel of truth in this one.

Dad nodded to the guards in the doorway, and they left us alone, closing the door. Still in his suit, he sat on the floor beside me and looked around this room of latent violence.

For a moment, I thought I was in the clear.

"Your mother worries about you," he said.

I had only a second to decide whether to let the tears flow again or to soothe his fears.

"I'm managing," I said, pulling myself together. "It's just a lot right now. I'm glad she's going to help with the demons."

"I didn't mean the demons," he said quietly, and I felt monster's attention again. But it had spent the magic it had collected in Lulu's room, and could only watch and wait.

"Then what did you mean?"

"We don't know, Lis."

But they'd talked about it together. About what they believed was wrong with me. And that was a new kind of pain.

"Not Connor," Dad said, "whom we know and trust. Not work, because you thrive at it. It's your mission."

I hadn't thought about it that way, but I didn't think he was wrong.

"You and Lulu aren't fighting, at least as far as we know." He looked at me. "So, we are out of ideas."

I felt more relief than I should have that my parents were baffled and didn't understand my problems. Because I didn't want them to understand.

I cleared my throat as the silence stretched on. Dad, a strategic and patient man, had four hundred years of experience in waiting out humans. He'd keep waiting until I answered the question one way or another.

"I'm not ready to talk about it yet."

Dad was also really good at controlling his expression; he'd given me his patented chilly stare more than a time or two, especially when I was a teenager. But a flash of surprise widened his eyes before he schooled his features again.

"Are you sick?"

"No," I said quickly, as I didn't like the anxious magic that accompanied the question. "I'm . . ." I cleared my throat. "I'm just working through some things. But I'm safe and healthy." I put a hand on his. "You don't need to worry."

I could see his frustration. Both my parents were fixers. They weren't passive; they attacked problems. If something was dangerous, they eliminated it. If someone was hurting, they healed them. But this wasn't their problem, or I didn't want it to be.

"Is this one of those things I have to let you handle, even though I don't like it?"

I smiled at him. I loved Mom, but Dad understood me in a different way.

"Unfortunately yes," I said, and took the handkerchief he offered me, wiped my eyes, pushed back my hair, and tried for something close to "composed."

He smiled, but his expression was tight, and his magic still seemed wary. "Then that's what I'll do. Even though it goes very much against my nature. And your mother's."

"I know."

He nodded, looked around the room. "You're welcome to take any weapons you think would be useful."

The variety of weapons was wide. But I didn't think anything here would stop a demon.

"It wouldn't help," I said, and rose. I offered him a hand, helped him to his feet, extended the handkerchief.

"Keep it," he said. "Just in case you need it."

Then he frowned, leaned toward me, sniffed.

"Lulu is shedding demon magic," I explained. "I opened the window for a bit, and Dr. Anderson is aware of it. But I don't know how bad the exposure might be for anyone who gets too close for too long."

He frowned. "That's concerning. I'll speak to the doctor about it."

I nodded. "Let me know if anything changes."

"We will. Where are you going next?"

Next, monster and I were going to have words. And then, "To the office. We have to coordinate—or I need to catch up on everyone else's coordination." Because I'd already had shifter, sorcerer, and monster crises tonight, and they'd put me behind schedule.

"Then I wish you good fighting. And take care of yourself." He embraced me. "We love you, Lis. Whatever it is, we love you."

I took an Auto to Promontory Point, a small peninsula that stretched out into Lake Michigan. It was empty at this time of night, and I walked alone to the expanse of inky water, watched waves lap in and roll out until my breathing slowed. And when I was calm again, I tore into monster.

"Do you have any idea how dangerous that was?" I asked it in a fierce whisper. I needed to speak aloud to put my thoughts together, but I didn't want to find a video of myself online screaming at Lake Michigan.

"Do you think it will all be fun and games and happy reunions? That I'll tell them who you are and they'll invite you back into the House? I know you want to reunite with the rest of you. But who knows what the rest of you wants? The Egregore—the thing that you're part of—nearly destroyed Chicago." It had hurt people, ruined buildings before it was bound into my mother's sword. Or at least mostly bound.

"In twenty years, it hasn't escaped. My parents protect this city. That's what they do. And even if they let Lulu take you out of me, the odds are low that you're getting close to that sword."

Monster and I had been through much together. But right now I was feeling a lot less conflicted about its possible removal.

It was still furious, but I could feel its doubt creeping in. Good. Welcome to my decade.

"The point is, we have to be careful. We have to plan. Because we'll only get one shot."

After virtually inhaling food and blood, I took an Auto to the office. Monster was quiet, and this time I knew better than to assume it had tuned out. I'd have to avoid demon magic as much as possible, and I had no idea what to do about Lulu—except avoid Cadogan House.

Traffic was light, more humans having departed during the day in response to the mayor's statement. And good timing, as there had been demon attacks on Michigan Avenue and a suburban mall, where a coordinated band of demons robbed a dozen humans and some stores before a police shoot-out left two civilians, two demons, and two cops dead.

We were in a full-out siege.

There weren't many cars on the road, but entirely too many of them were being driven by humans with too much ego or too little sense. People hung out windows with weapons in hand and streamed enormous "Take Back Chicago!" flags from the backs of trucks. I didn't begrudge them their loyalty to the city, but if I'd been human, I'd have been lying low until the scourge was swept clean. I wouldn't have been advertising my defenselessness.

Monster said nothing during the ride, which was fine by me.

I found Petra, Roger, and Theo in the workroom, their gazes on the wall screen. Petra's demon matrix was up there, and it had enough demons listed now that the document required serious scrolling to get to the end. I didn't bother taking off my jacket. I doubted I'd be here long.

I was surprised—and a little relieved—to see Jeff Christopher with them.

"New recruit?" I asked, moving to stand beside him. "Or re-recruit?"

"Temporary volunteer," Jeff said.

"He did this data entry," Petra said.

"We get a pretty good accuracy rating using AI and machine learning to pull demon information from videos and news reports. That gives us a first draft, at least."

"Hell of a time-saver," Theo said with a nod. "And it's appreciated."

"Anything I can do, I'll do," Jeff said, then looked at me. "How's Lulu?"

"Unconscious but stable." I looked at Petra. "Your doctor cousin is in with her."

"I know. She told me. Said Cadogan House is helping Lulu shed demon magic." She tilted her head. "That why you look weird?"

"Part of it," I said. "But I'll do until margarita time." If we had time for margaritas, what with the demon siege.

"Then let's get to business," Roger said.

At that, Petra shifted the screen to show demon statistics from the night before.

"They're increasing," Roger said. "More demons, more incidents. The vampires are assisting with ongoing incidents. Gwen, with the help of some surprisingly cooperative Feds, is working to process and hold the demons captured thus far."

"Holding them?" I asked.

"They've built a containment facility and transport vehicles that have some sort of flux capacitor. Still in the testing stage."

"I'm pretty sure that's not what it's called," I said.

"Whatever it's called, it has a membrane with a shifting magnetic field that absorbs magic. And we're running out of cubes here, so . . ."

"You said they're still testing it?" Theo asked.

"It apparently got too absorbent with a couple of deceased supernaturals they tested it on. Sucked the magic right out of their bodies."

"Damn," I said grimly, imagining supernatural husks on the floors of the cells. "That's horrible. And I'm sure these will be used only for good, and not to attempt to turn other supernaturals into humans." My voice was as dry as I could make it.

"Of course they will," Petra said, her voice equally dry.

"The wards?" I asked.

"Nothing yet," Theo said. "They're trying alternate ways to reconnect the ley lines."

"What about Dante?"

"The CPD is surveilling him," Theo said. "He hasn't done anything interesting. Still no word from Buckley."

"Anything from the New York or mob angle?" I asked.

"I took that one," Jeff said. "Found some online chatter about changes in the New York Mob's leadership structure, but nothing I could link to Dante specifically or demons generally. If he was a higher-up, no one is talking about him online."

I looked at Theo. "Any more incidents of the demon burning and copper ash? And sorry about the twenty questions. I'm playing catch-up."

"It happened once during the day," Theo said. "A couple of demons got into it. The survivor was turned to ash, and the incident was captured on a surveillance camera. We're trying to get the video feed. The owner is demanding paperwork in triplicate before releasing it."

"Do we know whose side the loser was on?" I wondered.

"Not yet," Theo said.

"Before you ask," Petra said, her voice tight, "there's nothing on her yet either."

I realized how tired she looked. Her face was wan, her dark hair was in a messy (for her) bun, and her eyes were a little puffy.

"Have you slept?" I asked her.

"Not much. Too wired. But I'm going to crash at dawn. Just want to make it until then."

"Take a break when you need to," Roger said kindly.

"Yep" was all she managed. "Oh, there is something. But it's nothing. Literally. There was no official construction at the quarry ward. That means city, ComEd, or anything else. So whoever got down to the cornerstone did it on purpose."

As I had suspected.

"Anything else?" Roger asked when silence settled again.

We looked around, shook our heads.

"Then we discuss priorities," he said, nodding at Petra, who put another image on-screen. This one was a list.

1. Fix Lulu
2. Fix wards
3. Rid city of remaining demons

"I'd be happiest if they all happened simultaneously," Roger said, "but I don't have infinite wishes, so . . . we figure out what Lulu needs, and we wake her up. We get the wards fixed, so we stop the infiltration of violent demons. And we deal with demon issues as they arise."

If only a list could be conquered so easily.

My screen buzzed and I checked it, in case it was an update from Connor or one about Lulu's condition. But it was a message from Jonathan Black. It was an address, nothing more.

I frowned.

"What is it?" Theo asked.

"I'm not sure. Jonathan Black just sent me an address. That's it."

Theo's brows lifted before settling into low suspicion. Which I figured was the appropriate response. And I sent the appropriate return message to Black: WHAT AND WHY?

"Where?" Petra asked.

I read out the address, and she put a map on-screen, then zoomed in to a location just west of the Loop on the edge of new developments and town houses.

The address corresponded to an empty lot, or at least that was what it had been when the satellite snapped the shot. And I didn't see anything Black would be interested in—or that he'd think we'd be interested in.

"A ward location?" Roger wondered.

Petra shook her head. "That's not even on the list of potential sites."

"Weird place to suggest if he wants a meet," Theo said. "He's been to our office before. Surely he's not trying to lure us out there."

"I don't think that's his style," I said. "He'd have picked something—I don't know—grander." And he hadn't yet responded to my message. This was all very sketchy.

"He's not our enemy," Petra said, "based on current facts." But she didn't sound entirely convinced.

Roger deliberated in silence. "Check it out," he said to me and Theo. "But be careful. If you smell something off, don't even get out of the vehicle. Just keep driving. I'll call Gwen."

We looked at each other, nodded.

"Petra and Jeff can work on the research," Roger said, "after they've had food."

"I really don't need . . . ," Petra began, but trailed off when the receptionist brought in a stack of pizza boxes. And the scent was outrageous.

"To-go slice," Theo said, and we each grabbed one, folded it, and dashed.

I debated whether to tell Black we were en route, but opted not to. Even if he wanted to meet us, which seemed unlikely, this would give us a chance to scope out the location first.

We rolled quietly past the address, found a weedy vacant lot. Theo parked up the street, and we could smell what Black had apparently wanted us to find before we'd trekked back to the lot.

Death.

A lot of death.

"Shit," Theo said as we looked over the field.

I guessed there'd been a gas station here once, but the concrete pad and poles were all that remained now. In addition to broken glass, trash, and knee-high weeds gone golden with the end of summer. And a dozen demons lying among the refuse.

All, at least from our vantage point, looked dead. And that death looked as if it had been violent: blood, viscera, and dark wounds made by magic. And that was only what we could see from the street. There was still demon magic in the air. Not enough, I hoped, to help monster take over.

I crouched near one demon, found his fingers bruised and obviously broken. There was a gash on his forehead, and at the edges of that gash was a dark line of singed skin. Some kind of burn?

I regretted the need, but leaned forward, sniffed near that wound. The demon magic was stronger there.

I rose. "Yours have burn marks?" I asked Theo, who stood fifteen feet away.

He looked down. "This guy has a fireball-sized hole in his torso. And the edges look burned." He spoke smoothly, and I was grateful for his experience as a cop and his acclimation to horrors like this. I was also glad Lulu hadn't taken that kind of shot.

He pointed to another body. "This one's got burn marks on her shoulder. Made a fucking mess of it. They're recently dead. They can't have been here long."

"No decay," I agreed.

The woman at my feet was the first female demon I'd seen since Rosantine; I'd been beginning to wonder if they mostly presented male. She wore jeans, a tank top, and sneakers. Nothing fancy, unlike the male closest to her, who wore a suit. A variety of demons, and a variety of styles.

Theo walked back to me, screen in hand. "I'm telling Gwen. And I count thirteen."

"Someone's lucky number?"

"I guess. Another territorial dispute?"

"Maybe," I said. "They're all dressed differently. Look different. But all were killed about the same time. All were put here about the same time, and there's no sign of a demon battle in this lot. There are no scorch or magic marks on the ground, and there's not enough magic in the air to indicate the battle happened here."

"So, why move them here?" Theo wondered.

I looked around, saw no building on this part of the block likely to have security cameras. "Privacy. There are probably no cameras trained on this lot."

Theo was quiet for a beat. "How deep is Black in this? I mean, he led us here."

"This is demon magic," I said. "He's not a demon."

While I was sure about that, it occurred to me for the first time that I hadn't really seen Black use magic. I'd sensed it around him, but I hadn't seen him toss a fireball or kindle a spell. Certainly nothing with this kind of power.

"Maybe a demon is his client," Theo said. "The one who cut him."

"Yeah, that thought occurred to me. But if so, why would he send us here? Doesn't that implicate his boss?"

"Hmm," Theo said. "Maybe there's a third major player. Someone we don't even know about yet."

"No," I said sternly. "Don't even joke about that. You'll jinx us."

"We need to talk to Black," Theo said. "I doubt he just stumbled across this empty lot full of bodies. Either someone told him about it, or he saw the dump happen. Either way, he knows who was involved."

I checked my screen again, found no response to my earlier message, and sent another one. As Theo moved to another body, I crouched down, looked over the demon at my feet. He had very dark skin and a torso wound, the edges crisped from the flash of magic.

But near his hand was something very pale. I leaned in closer, holding my breath, and saw what looked like a square of paper. Careful not to touch or disturb the body—only the evidence that the body was holding, which probably wasn't better from a forensic perspective—I slipped out the paper. It was card stock, thick and crumpled.

And then I heard Theo's low curse.

"What?" I asked, standing and looking around for the threat. But it wasn't a threat to us.

Like outside the mural building, the bodies had begun to burn, and the air began to sour with the scent of demon magic.

Demon fire sprang up in each body, and the field began to dance with flames that weren't really fire. And magic transformed bodies to glittering metallic ash.

We both dodged flames and ran for the sidewalk, trying not to get wrapped in the magic.

"Shit," Theo said, looking at his screen. "We haven't even been here for ten minutes."

"Did you get pictures?"

"A few, but they're shit. Fuck," he said, and kicked a discarded box. It sailed halfheartedly for a few feet before landing again to no applause. "We should've known. We just fucking talked about it, and we should've taken pictures as soon as we got here."

"We didn't know they'd be incinerated," I said, but without much enthusiasm. Because he was right. We had known incineration was a risk, and we should have dealt with it immediately.

I looked back at him. "Tell her it was my fault. Then she can't take it out on you." I meant Gwen, but it occurred to me that the same sentiment would have worked for Petra.

He gave me a sardonic grunt. And then frowned. "Why now?"

"Why now what?"

"We were thinking this copper-ash dissolving trick might be a way to punish losers or keep minions from giving up their secrets. But we were only standing here. We weren't trying to make anyone talk."

"Bodies tell their own stories," I said. "With forensics, with evidence."

And I remembered the paper still clenched in my hand. I opened my fingers, glanced down.

There, written in tiny, scratchy script, was a note.

> Buckley:
> You took what was mine when you left
> New York. I'm taking it back.
> —D

Theo came over, read over my shoulder, whistled. "Where did you find that?"

"Clutched in the hand of a demon who is now dust."

"Damn," he said. "I mean, we have to verify, but if Dante is the

'D,' that appears to confirm he and Buckley knew each other before Dante came to Chicago. And had some strife."

"Yeah," I said. "He said he and Buckley were business associates. So, what did Buckley take from him?"

"Not the condo," Theo said. "Dante's not in the purchase history."

"Maybe the condo is the payback," I said. "That would explain the one-dollar purchase price. Pay only what's necessary for the paperwork."

A car door slammed, and we looked up. Gwen strode forward in a lavender suit with a rip in the left shoulder and bloodstains on the right arm; she had hell in her eyes.

"You tell her," I said, changing my mind.

"*You agreed,*" Theo whispered fiercely.

"I only offered. You didn't accept my offer, so I take it back."

"Coward," he murmured, and walked toward Gwen.

"Would you like to tell me why I had to haul ass from five miles out to see"—she cast her gaze over Theo's shoulder—"an empty lot?"

"Well," he began with a sigh, "it wasn't empty before."

She was surprisingly magnanimous about the fact that we'd lost evidence without documenting it first. The note and Theo's pictures helped. And I think she felt a little bad for us.

"You have to tell Petra," she said. "That will be worse."

"Still not it," I said quickly before Theo could. A textbook case of situational cowardice.

"I'm intrigued by the note," Gwen said, looking at it through an evidence bag while her team collected samples from the field. "I don't know if it's fake or planted, but I am intrigued."

I could maybe help there. I pulled up the realty sales contract

Petra had provided; it bore Dante's signature. I looked it over, then showed the screen to Gwen and Theo.

"The note's handwriting is comparable to his signature on the contract," I said. "And the note sure does sound like a threat."

"It might be just enough for a search warrant if we can find a friendly judge who hasn't left the city. When I thought about the apocalypse," she added after a moment, "I hadn't really considered the bureaucratic challenges."

"We're all doing the best we can," I said thoughtfully.

But Gwen just gave me a look.

"Too soon?" I asked.

"Too soon."

We gave her a report about what we'd seen before the evidence had been burned away, and she coordinated with the forensic team and the district attorney. I'd taken to pacing back and forth on the pitted sidewalk while she talked. Finding a judge was, as she predicted, proving to be a problem. The roster was lean right now, and the judges she'd managed to find apparently weren't eager to risk pissing off a demon. Apocalypse problems were weird.

While I waited, I called and messaged Black again, and got nothing. He'd gone silent again. By order of his client or because he wasn't able to respond?

"Let's just go talk to Dante," I said, stopping in front of Theo. "He's linked to this one way or the other, and if the upstart is doing this to his people, he may be feeling revengy."

"You can't force your way in," Gwen said.

"I know. But we have information he may want."

"He seemed surprised by the copper-ash magic," Theo said with a nod. "If these are his people, he may not know they're down, or how. That gives us leverage."

I hoped it would be enough.

THIRTEEN

Monster had been well-behaved at the lot, but we were entering a demon's lair—or at least a demon's million-dollar condo—and the risk of it acting out seemed high.

We need him to help us if we're going to wake her up, I told it. *So, you have to behave.*

I got its vague agreement, which I figured was good enough for now.

The security desk was empty again. The elevator doors opened as we neared them, and a cluster of demons emerged, Dante at their center.

Theo held up his badge, focused his gaze on Dante. "We need to talk."

Demons shifted restlessly, like fighters waiting for the bell to ring. Or for Dante's order to dispense with us.

Dante's jaw tightened, but he maintained his composure after a quick glance around—maybe remembering he was in a semipublic space. Violence wouldn't help his efforts to present himself as a legit businessman.

He worked his jaw, as if trying to dislodge an unpleasant taste. "You bring a warrant?"

"In process," Theo said. "But you'll want to talk to us."

He extended his screen, which showed a picture of one of the demons he'd managed to photograph.

Dante paused, then gestured to his minions to give him room. He stepped forward, studied the image.

"There are a dozen more just like this," Theo said. "All dead and left in a field. We know you put them there."

Dante looked genuinely surprised—and then angry. "I didn't put anyone there. I've been here."

Theo glanced blandly at the other demons. "Powerful guy like you has people to do the work for him."

Dante ran a hand over his slicked-back hair. "I wouldn't kill my people."

That confirmed one suspicion.

"I want to see them," he said.

"They're gone," Theo confirmed. "Left in place only long enough for us to get a look, and then destroyed."

There was only fury in Dante's gaze now. Magic was a whisper around us, pungent and prickly.

"What did your minions fight over today?" I asked. "What part of Chicago is the upstart trying to take? Where are her head-quarters? Tell us who she is," I said, "and we'll bring her in."

Frustration, or at least that's what I thought it was, curled Dante's lip. "I've already told you, I don't have a name."

"Then give us a state," Theo said. "If she's not from Chicago, where is she from?"

"California," he said.

"Where in California?" I asked.

"I don't know."

"We found your note to Buckley in the hand of one of the dead demons. It said you'd be taking back what Buckley took from you. So, what did he take? And where is he now?"

Dante looked confused now, uncertain. As if unnerved by his uncertainty, his minions glanced around, shifted on their feet.

"Who had the note?" Dante asked.

I described the demon who'd held it. "He's gone now. Turned to ash like the others."

Dante stepped closer to us, which was entirely too close. I shoved Theo behind me.

"You're lying," Dante said.

"About what? We obviously didn't make up the note; you haven't denied it." I cocked my head. "So, what did Buckley take from you? Money? Things? People? Did he steal from you in New York and run to Chicago?" I thought of the property records Petra had found. "He bought that condo, what, five years ago? So, maybe that's when he set up shop here. Was it with your money? And being a demon, you couldn't follow him. But now you're here, so you decided to take back whatever it was. And had to punish him a little, right, by blowing up the warehouse?"

Dante's eyes glowed yellow with anger, the color bright enough to leave spots in my vision.

Then he murmured something in a language I didn't understand, the sounds short and harsh and full of power. I took a step backward and closer to Theo as magic began to pool at our feet, a gray-green miasma.

Stay down, I reminded monster. *And do not collect demon magic. It hurts me, which hurts you.*

"Stop using magic," I said aloud to Dante, my voice as hard as I could manage. "We are sworn Ombuds, and if you hurt us, you won't survive the night."

"I don't have to hurt you," he said. "I just have to let you hurt yourselves."

And the enchantment or spell or incantation, or whatever the demon equivalent was, grew stronger. I pulled salt from my pocket, tossed it at our feet, and watched it spark and evaporate in the mist.

"You think that's going to stop me?" Dante asked. "We are older than humanity. Older than the fetid pools you crawled out of. And you haven't gotten any smarter."

Any pretense of him being a businessman was gone now. Dante's eyes gleamed with magic and age and the deep narcissism of the powerful. His magic grew deep along with the mist, the floor no longer visible beneath it.

Then he threw back his head, roared his displeasure. The sound was a wave that covered us with power and shook the stone beneath our feet. The crystals in the chandelier above the lobby clanged cacophonously as they vibrated. An enormous canvas fell from a wall, and ceramic pots holding palm trees shattered, sending dirt spilling to the floor. The trees toppled and bounced, and spiderweb cracks appeared in the nearest window.

Then Dante lowered his head, and the sound stopped, but left a ringing in my ears. Apparently done with us, he turned toward the main doors, minions clearing a path through the mess he'd made.

"Tell me how to save my friend," I said, my last-ditch effort to get something, anything, I could use for Lulu.

He stopped, looked back. "She's not worth saving."

Maybe it was fury or fear or adrenaline or the effect of his magic. But I had my sword in hand in less than a second and was striding toward him. And I'd have used the blade to threaten a cure out of him . . . if he hadn't tossed me back through the air without so much as a flick of his hand.

I dropped the katana, which clattered to the floor, and I hit the wall of the elevator bank several feet behind me with force enough to have it cracking from the impact. There was a blissful nanosecond before the pain signals circulated, and then I hit the floor, bounced, and felt the collision from teeth to toes.

I heard Theo call my name, but held up a hand to stop him from coming closer. I wanted to keep my position between him and the demons.

I tried to stand, but my legs wouldn't support me. My vision blurred, and I slipped to the floor. I'd have to wait for the pain to subside and the healing to begin; in the meantime, I'd be vulnerable. I lifted my gaze to check the demons' advance, but they remained where they were, halfway to the door. Maybe they assumed Dante had finished me off, and concluded Theo posed no threat.

Or maybe they were leaving the finishing to Dante.

"Want us to find her, boss?" someone asked.

Dante's gaze snapped, narrowed at the one who had asked the question.

"How?" he asked flatly. "We don't have any way to reach her."

"Maybe back to the beginning," one of the demons said. "The first place we met her people. Maybe her HQ is near there."

Name the damn place, I thought. Tell me where to find the upstart. Because as much as we needed Dante put away—after he fixed Lulu—we needed Dante's demonic competitor even more. Her body count was higher.

Dante considered his minion's suggestion. "Let's go," he said.

I prepared myself for the pain of standing up to follow the demon's trail. Maybe Gwen's people would surveil Dante and all the minions, if they had enough resources. Theo must've had the same idea, as he caught my gaze, nodded his readiness.

But then Dante turned back to me, that reptilian shadow across his skin. He glanced at Theo, and his smile was gleefully malicious.

"Didn't bring a warrant," he said. "And he won't be following me out. Vampires are predators, as much as they prefer to deny it. *Remember,*" he added in a low, gravelly drawl. And then he was out the door.

Murmuring another curse, he directed it at me, still stuck on the floor.

My blood began to tingle from the magic in the air, and that portended nothing good. I tried to climb to my feet but didn't have the strength to stand yet. The magic had wicked away my strength, leaving only pain.

"Get out of here!" I told Theo. "You have to follow them."

"I'm not leaving you like this!" he called out, and although he was only twenty or thirty feet away, his voice sounded far away and hollow, like it had traversed a great distance to reach me.

With a hand on the cracked wall for support, I made it to my knees. The effort had sweat pouring down my face.

"I don't know what he's done," I said, "but he's aimed it at me, and I think it's going to be ugly. I don't want you getting hurt."

The tingling turned to heat . . . and then to hunger. Not for food, and not just for blood . . .

But for prey.

Vampires are predators, Dante had said. *Remember.* I was never unaware of who or what I was. My identity was me; I was my identity, and that was vampire. But like most, I didn't take blood from humans without their consent unless it was necessary to save their lives. And I'd done that only once.

Dante had decided to change the score.

My fangs descended and my eyes silvered. Pain ebbed as it was replaced by an all-consuming thirst.

"Theo," I managed weakly, "you have to get out."

The miasma was thick enough that I couldn't see him or anything else now.

Outside, monster said. *Get outside.*

Part of me knew that was the right thing to do. But that part was only a whisper, and it was drowned out by need, which made my stomach ache with pain. I'd always been careful to eat and drink when necessary, so I wouldn't become irrationally hungry. This hunger was beyond thought and morality. And Dante had sent me there with one bit of magic.

"Theo," I said again, this time my tone all sweet and enticing, "I need you."

I remained perfectly, predatorily still, and I could hear his hesitation, his uncertainty.

And the strong, quick beat of his heart.

"I'm here," I called out, another wave of hunger threatening to send me back to the floor. But I ignored it, then climbed to my feet and found myself steady.

And so thirsty.

"Elisa?"

His voice was unsure, and the "me" that had been shoved down by demon magic hated that I had made him sound that way. And yet . . .

"Theo," I called again, "over here!"

I sniffed the air, searching for humans, and felt him draw nearer.

Wake up. That was monster again. And unlike the last time we'd been inundated with demon magic, monster was urging me to fight back against it.

I pushed with the energy I had, but I still hadn't recovered from being tossed like a rag doll across the lobby. And the possibility began to creep into my mind that I might never be strong enough to fight this demon.

I ignored that, tried to break through the haze of magic. But with each step, I felt that hunger sync deeply into the real me, until it was me. Until there was no more me.

Just an aching desperation.

"Theo?" I said, voice plaintive and helpless, and knew from the echoing footsteps that he was close. I threw out a hand and touched his arm. He jerked beneath my grasp—prey aware the trap had been sprung—and tried to pull free.

But even injured, I was stronger than a human.

No, monster said, trying to keep me hungry.

"Elisa."

Theo's face came into view through the mist. His wide pupils. His beating pulse at the base of his throat. It raced, his heart, and I knew the taste would be electric and tinged with adrenaline.

"No," Theo said, voice hard. Coplike. "This isn't you. Stop this."

Stop, monster echoed. *Not you.*

But I didn't hear them—not really. His heart was a timpani drum, and he was my salvation. The relief was so close now, and I put my free hand on his shoulder as he tried to pull away. I drew him toward me, fangs bared.

But something inside me pushed, shifted, stretched.

Monster, using its consciousness to fight me from the inside, metaphysically punched me.

I shoved Theo away and fell to my knees, screaming; it felt like my body was being pummeled from the inside.

My stomach revolted, and I retched until my body was empty.

When that was done, I reassessed. I hurt, and I was dizzy. But I was me again. Because monster had attacked me from within to keep me from doing something wrong. Maybe because it knew I would regret it. Maybe because it feared we wouldn't survive punishment for the violation.

And I was grateful for the help.

We're even, I told it.

And passed out.

*   *   *

I couldn't look him in the eye.

The CPD and an ambulance arrived, both called by a human security guard who had apparently been monitoring the lobby from behind a locked door. Couldn't blame him for that, but I bet he was rethinking his career choice.

I sat on the back of the open ambulance, feet dangling, while the EMTs checked my pulse and asked me inane questions to ensure I'd recovered my senses. Theo stood nearby, arms crossed and face inscrutable as he watched us. And I really wished I could have scrut-ed it, because I couldn't manage eye contact with someone I'd nearly drunk from, even if only because I'd been under the influence of demon magic.

"You're fine," one of the EMTs announced, snapping off his gloves.

"Blood?" asked the second, offering me a bottle. Did they keep it on board ambulances now in the event of vampire emergencies?

"Ombud-involved incident," the other EMT said, packing away gear. "We have it ready just in case."

"Thank you," I said. "I appreciate the gesture, but I'm not . . ." I didn't want to say "hungry." "In need," I finished. The thought of blood held zero appeal.

"Your call," the second EMT said, and put the bottle back in a cooler in an interior side panel.

Theo walked closer. "Could you give us a moment?"

The EMTs nodded. "Sure," said the first. "Need to write this up."

They left us alone in simmering awkwardness.

"I'm so sorry," I said, looking at my hands. "It was demon magic—the predator thing—and I couldn't control myself."

There was silence for a moment, and I braced myself to be dumped as his partner.

"I'm not mad at you. I'm worried."

That had me looking up. "What?"

"I know that wasn't you. You don't even like to drink from bottles in front of people because it might freak them out."

That was true.

"Besides, you did control it. You reined it in, and that looked like it hurt. But you hit that wall really hard. That sound—I'm not likely to forget that anytime soon. And yes, I know you heal. But still . . . he tossed you across the room. And didn't break a sweat doing it."

His fear was the same as mine: that even an immortal like me wasn't enough to stop the demons.

"I'm okay. The demon magic was tough. But yeah, I'll heal."

"And in the meantime, you look like you've been through a war zone." He took my hand, frowned at the bruises that had bloomed in ugly colors. "Just . . . be sure to tell Connor I didn't do this."

For the first time in a while, I grinned. "He'll know. You're a hell of a partner."

"Tell him that, too. Just in case."

We were both emotionally exhausted. I was physically exhausted, too, from the beating and having been used as a marionette by two temperamental supernaturals. I debated going home early, but settled for a refresh at a late-night breakfast joint not far from the condo. It was fancier than the typical Ombud lunch spot, but it was close and we both needed a break.

Coffee and bacon later, I was feeling more myself.

We checked in with our respective partners; Connor reported he was still at headquarters, and would like a very large beer after work. I could relate.

Dad advised me that Mom had taken down two demons harassing humans on the L—Chicago's elevated train. And someone had, of course, recorded the incident, so Theo and I watched the video as we walked back to the vehicle.

I'd seen her practice before, sparring with Dad or the Cadogan guards. But since she had been officially out of commission, that was for fun or exercise. This was street fighting—or above-street fighting anyway—and it was different. She was fast. The moves were less precise than in the House training room, but more fluid. Dad had said she danced when she fought, and I could see that in the way she moved the sword, swung her body. The demons—minions, by the look of it—hadn't stood a chance against her.

"You fight like her," Theo said, then sipped from a to-go cup of coffee. "Not exactly like her," he added, responding to my dubious expression. "But you can tell she trained you. You're more deliberate, though."

"Deliberate?" I asked. "What do you mean?"

"You're a planner," he said, tapping his head. "You fight like you're playing chess, responding to the opponents' moves and whatever. She doesn't seem so predictive. But the core is the same."

I nodded, considered his analysis. I'd never thought about my fighting that way, at least consciously. But it made sense.

"What about you?" I asked as we climbed inside our vehicle. "What's your fighting style?"

"Mortal," he said with a grin, and started the vehicle. "Stay away from the shooty and pointy parts."

FOURTEEN

We'd been planning to go back to the office and strategize, check on Petra's research. But because this night intended to be one shit sandwich after another, my mother's call interrupted us.

"Lulu?" I asked immediately.

"Fine," my mother said. "I'm not calling about that."

"Then what—," I began.

Before I finished the sentence, something made a low, mournful sound behind her.

"Was that a whale?" Theo asked.

I wondered the same thing, but didn't think it was possible, due to Illinois being landlocked.

"Are you at the aquarium?" I asked.

"No," Mom said. And then there were more sounds—an impact, a crash, and a splash.

"Wacker and Wabash," she said. "Catcher accidentally tripped a ward. Get here as fast as you can."

Theo and I were improperly excited on the way over. Not just to find out who had made the noise, but because one of the wards had been at least temporarily operational. That warmed the cockles of my still aching heart. We knew a ward near the Chicago

River existed. It was one of the spots we'd (correctly) identified. But we weren't sure how it operated, as it hadn't yet been triggered by a demon.

The drive downtown was . . . strange. It seemed every uniformed person in Illinois—local deputies to National Guard—was in the city tonight, protecting businesses to prevent looting, guarding wards to prevent the destruction of additional cornerstones, working with vampires to stop ongoing demon attacks, and helping to relocate humans out of danger zones.

And then there was the magic. Maybe it was the demons. Maybe it was the ley lines now unbounded by the cornerstones. Whatever the reason, the city seemed to be wilding. Tree limbs stretched over city streets so they looked like ancient forest paths. Dead flowers had rebloomed, and cottontail rabbits—a Midwestern fixture—hopped down sidewalks, apparently unafraid of human eyes.

When we reached the intersection my mother had named, we parked on the street, which was nearly empty of vehicles anyway. The Wabash Avenue bascule bridge crossed the Chicago River here; the bridge was flanked on the north and the south by sleek glass buildings. But the bridge wasn't a bridge any longer. It was now just two chunks of concrete that extended out from each side of the riverbank, the breached ends jagged. The middle of the structure was simply gone.

We walked to where Mom stood with Aunt Mallory and Uncle Catcher, and found no glowing pillars of light or attacking ghosts. The three of them looked healthy and safe.

"What happened to the bridge?" I asked.

Mom and Aunt Mallory looked at Uncle Catcher with equally bland expressions.

"The wards were powered by the cornerstones," he said. "It's a big magical daisy chain, so you break a connection to one, and the entire system goes down. We were testing spells to reconnect the wards to the ley lines one ward at a time, starting with this one. And we apparently triggered it."

"And that broke the bridge?" I asked, confused.

"Not exactly," he said.

"Why don't you just fix the bridge with magic?" Theo asked.

"We can use magic to move the chunks of concrete out of the water," Aunt Mallory said, "but that wouldn't make the bridge structurally sound. That would require engineers."

And we didn't need emergency vehicles in the river because their drivers thought the bridge had been fixed.

"And the ward didn't break the bridge," Mom said. "The triggering woke something up."

"Something?" I asked.

She looked toward the river. "A demon ward's Guardian."

I walked over to the rail that separated the street from the river below, and looked down at the dark water. I saw nothing for a moment, but then something glinted, reflecting the overhead streetlights. But it was gone in a second, and I wasn't sure if I'd actually seen something or just a trick of light on the water. And then I saw it again. It was long and dark and sleek, with skin the iridescent color of spilled gasoline: blues and violets and greens waving together. And then it submerged again.

"Whoa," I said. "It's big."

"Is it a snake?" Theo asked beside me at the rail. His voice was low. "I really hate snakes."

"We aren't sure," Mom said. "We just know it didn't like the spell. It was literally triggered."

"The ward was created more than a hundred years ago," Theo said. "How long does whatever this is live?"

"Apparently a while," Mom said.

"Did you call the CPD?" Theo asked, glancing back. There were no CPD or emergency vehicles nearby.

"Roger did," Mom said. "We talked to him, and he talked to Gwen. She suggested not bringing in any human cops, given it's not really our enemy and they aren't really equipped to handle underwater creatures." She looked at Theo, smiled a little. "Other than skilled Ombuds, of course."

"Of course."

"And there aren't any demons nearby, so we aren't certain how much more activity there will be anyway."

The water rippled, and instinct had me grabbing Theo's arm to nudge him prophylactically back from the railing . . . which I did a millisecond before the creature launched into the air: thirty feet of wet and claws and a mouth of dripping teeth longer than my arm—

I yanked Theo back hard enough to have us both toppling to the ground—and just out of the reach of those jaws.

The creature roared, blowing back our hair, but even stretched to its max, it was still a foot short of reaching us. It looked like a cross between a snake and a shark—or maybe like an ancient oceanic dinosaur. Its body was wider than its long tail, and its fins were elongated. Its head was viper shaped, its eyes ovals with wide pupils. It smelled of dark and wet and apparently made its home in the depths of the river.

It wasn't unusual for humans to claim they'd seen a monster in the lake or the river. But that usually turned out to be trash, abandoned kayaks, or snakehead fish, which were nightmare fuel in their own right. I wondered if any human had gotten it right and actually seen this guy.

I glanced at Aunt Mallory and my mom, both of whom seemed really unfazed considering we'd all just learned the Chicago River had its own Loch Ness monster. This was going to make Petra's week.

"Aren't you freaked out?" I asked.

Mom lifted a shoulder. "I mean, it's not great. But I think the dragon was worse."

Aunt Mallory nodded. "The Egregore was much worse."

While monster seemed unbothered by the sentiment, hearing things like that made me wish I could crawl inside myself and disappear.

The leviathan broke the water surface with a clap of sound and a spray of water, then slapped its tail and hit the rail where we'd stood moments before. With the horrible screech of wrenched metal, it ripped away a section of balusters, and dragged a chunk of sidewalk and retaining wall into the water. It made a deep, bass roar before diving into the water again.

"How do we calm it down?" I asked, looking back at the Moms. "We can't let it keep doing this. And we can't kill it for helping."

"Yeah," Theo said. "It was probably just hanging out in its fish fortress."

"Cretaceous castle," Mom said.

"Monster mansion," Theo countered.

The creature leapt from the water—fans stretched like moist wings—and bared its teeth at us. Then it slapped the rail hard enough to warp the metal. It roared before hitting the water again, then slid under with hardly a splash. And the rail gleamed with dark, iridescent blood.

"It's hurting itself," I said.

"It will probably keep fighting until it kills the demon, or the demon is gone, or the demon destroys it." Uncle Catcher's voice was grim.

"There has to be some kind of prearranged signal, so it will know when to stop attacking," I said. "Something the Guardians did."

"This is why you should always leave instructions for your replacement," Theo said. "It's common courtesy."

"Have you tried—I don't know—talking to it?" I asked.

They all looked at me like the suggestion was insane.

"Considering our biology and jobs, not really our place to get judgy about supernaturals."

"This is now a rescue mission," I said. "Saving the creature from himself."

Theo pulled out his screen. "Petra," he said a second later. "Chicago river monster. How do you send it back to its home or put it back to sleep or whatever?"

Her squeal of excitement was loud enough for all of us to hear.

"Lizard lair," Aunt Mallory quietly offered.

I guessed she was the kind of worn down and tired in which everything had better be funny or she wouldn't be able to stop the tears. And I wished I had more to offer her.

"Dino den," Theo murmured.

"Oooh," Petra said. "Is that the fourth ward? A river monster?"

"A leviathan," I suggested. "Big, wet, pointy bits."

"Did you sing to it?" Petra asked, and we all looked at one another.

"No?" Mom said. "Should we?"

"Well, I'm not there"—and she sounded very disappointed about that—"so I'm going off my personal research, but usually your undersea supernaturals are responsive to sound."

"I told you that you should've talked to it," I said.

"Did setting off the ward make some kind of noise?" Petra asked.

"Bells," Uncle Catcher told Petra. "Sounded like church bells."

"That could do it. That's probably the trigger the Guardians established for it. The sensor, which is probably near the bells, is triggered by demon magic, and when it sounds, the leviathan—let's call him Levi—comes up to attack. Wait—are there demons near you?"

"Uncle Catcher accidentally tripped the ward with a test spell," I explained, leaving Uncle Catcher to mutter his objections.

"It's destroyed the Wabash Avenue bridge," I said, "and taken chunks out of the Riverwalk, and it's hurting itself in the process. So, we need to make it stop."

"Well," Petra said. "Thinking it through, we need it to go back to its resting state. To think the demon has been vanquished and it can go back into this good night."

"Right," Mom said. "I mean, that sounds right."

This was the first time we'd encountered a ward that incorporated a living creature. It was new territory.

"*Manual,*" Theo intoned, drawing out each syllable for emphasis.

"And the human who found it first would've sold it to the highest demon bidder," Uncle Catcher said. He wasn't much of a philanthropist.

"Point," Theo conceded.

"Back to the sound thing," Petra said. "Start with asking it to leave."

"In English?" I asked.

"Unless you speak leviathan, yes." Petra's voice was remarkably matter-of-fact.

"Maybe George knows," Mom said.

"George?" Petra asked.

"A river troll," Mom said, and pointed to the next bridge downriver. "I've met him before."

"It's possible he knows how to communicate with Levi," Aunt Mallory said.

"Thanks, Petra," Theo said. "We'll do what we can here and keep you posted."

I could tell from his voice that he was running out of patience with magical hijinks. That was the problem of being on supernatural hijinks patrol. There wasn't an off switch and wouldn't be one until the wards were fixed.

Mom looked at us. "Who wants to talk to the nice monster?"

"I'll try," I said. "You go talk to George, since you know him."

I also wanted to talk to George, as I'd never met a river troll, but I was the best candidate for this. Theo was mortal, and Lulu needed her parents.

Mom looked at me, then at the missing chunk of railing, then at me again. The parental battle was clear on her face, but she nodded, then looked at Uncle Catcher. "Keep working on the wards." Then to Aunt Mallory: "Brainstorm a backup spell. I'll be back," she said, and strode down the street.

"Thoughts?" I asked as Levi surfaced again and jumped into the air—beautifully, I had to admit, at least until his tail whipped the head off a statue mounted to one of the towers at the end of the next bridge.

"Stay out of range?" Theo offered, worry in his eyes.

"That's a goal," I said. I blew out a breath and walked to the part of the railing that was still wet with Levi's blood.

First thing, find it under the water. I closed my eyes, hoping I'd hear it coming if I missed the timing, and opened myself to the magic. I concentrated on the world beyond, stretching until I could sense the creature's magic in the water.

And it was miraculous. A rainbow of shimmering power in the river's dark depths, the colors moving and blending like puddles of wet paint as they flew through the water. That was the goal, I thought. To live a life in your own prism of joy, even when sur-rounded by darkness.

I could've stood there for hours just watching the colors move. And I wondered—a moment too late—if that was how Levi lured prey into the range of those remarkable jaws.

When I finally opened my eyes, I was staring into Levi's. And then its teeth were on my arm, and Aunt Mallory screamed, and Levi and I were diving.

The water's chill hurt first. Any residual pain from my encounter with Dante was gone, replaced by the piercing objection of muscles to freezing water. The pain triggered my desire to suck in air, and I had to bite my mouth shut to keep from breath-ing in the river. I wouldn't have much time before my last breath was exhausted. And even a vampire wouldn't come back from that.

I could see nothing as Levi pulled me through the darkness, and I had to stem the rising panic. It was night, and even the glow from downtown Chicago's copious streetlights didn't reach the murky depths of the river. Levi's teeth were still clamped on my arm—not chewing, but gripping—and I wondered if it simply meant to drown me. Maybe the Guardians had taught it that was the appropriate end for demon invaders.

I pulled my arm, trying to tear it free of Levi's maw. When that didn't work, I tried to wrench around and strike the creature with my free hand, but couldn't get enough leverage to turn against the force of the water. So I half-turned and kicked and landed a shot on Levi's snout. He threw his head in the opposite direction, causing his claws to rip through my flesh; my blood spilled from the wounds into the water.

Levi circled to a stop, regarded me with one big unblinking eye—its pupil dilating, contracting, dilating. And then, as my lungs began to scream for air . . . it literally spit me out. I was torn between relief and insult, and I desperately hoped I'd survive, not least because I didn't want "coughed up by the river monster" as my epitaph.

And then it was pushing me up toward the surface with its muzzle. My vision was going dotty from lack of oxygen, and I wasn't sure if the spots in my vision were glimmers of streetlights overhead or hints of the beginning of asphyxia.

A large hairy hand hauled me up and out of the water, and two deep-set eyes blinked at me. It was a humanoid person with a squat nose and a thick neck. He was over six feet tall, with square shoulders and a barrel chest. He'd pulled me onto a platform made of woven driftwood and sticks and water bottles—stuff probably foraged from the river itself. I looked up, found the bottom of the bridge above us.

I sucked in air, pushed sopping hair from my eyes. "George?" I asked when I'd gotten some of my breath back.

"He was my dad. I'm Bjorn."

I nodded. "I'm sorry for your loss. And thanks for helping me up."

He nodded.

"Did my mother talk to you?"

Bjorn shook his head. Maybe she'd looked for George, hadn't found him in his old home.

"I think it spit me out because I'm a vampire. Because I didn't taste the way it expected. I mean, I didn't taste like demon."

"Maybe."

"The creature," I said. "Does it have a name, if you know?"

"Ambrosia."

It took me a moment to wrap my mind around that. "Okay," I said. "We think it was triggered by the demon ward, and we aren't sure how to calm it down again."

His stare was steady and unblinking. "Did you talk to it?"

I was going to start screaming. "I tried," I said. "But it pulled me into the water."

He watched me for a second. "Yeah."

Not loquacious, this one.

"So maybe I could try to talk to it now. Do you know how to do that from here?" Because I really didn't want to go back into the water. Even monster was cold.

Before I could prepare myself, he put two fingers into his mouth and let fly a whistle that had my ears ringing. It sent a visible wave of sound across the water.

And then we waited.

"Do you have any fruit?" he asked.

"Oh, well, no. Not at the moment." River trolls liked fruit, I belatedly remembered, and it was often used to pay them for services or cooperation. "I can find you some when we're done here?" There were still grocery stores operating for the humans who hadn't left.

He shrugged, which I took to mean he wouldn't object if a fruit basket found its way to his doorstep.

There were rumblings below the water, and then Ambrosia broke the surface. Or its eyes anyway—the rest of its body was still hidden.

Bjorn nudged me with an elbow.

"Hi," I said, very aware of the sound of my voice. "I'm Elisa. I'm an Ombudsman and we're trying to get the demons out of Chicago. I'm sorry we accidentally triggered the ward. We're trying to fix the system, but that didn't go well."

It—she? they?—stared at me unblinkingly.

Was I supposed to keep going? Pause for questions? River monster etiquette had not been covered in my cultural para-anthropology class.

"We don't want you to injure yourself any further."

Still nothing.

I looked at Bjorn, whose thoughtful gaze stayed on Ambrosia.

You hear anything? I asked monster. If part of an Egregore could metaphysically shrug, it did that.

I cleared my throat. "So, you can go back to your evening now. And thanks for your service. And for not eating me."

And then its deep and rumbling voice was in my head.

I don't eat vampires.

I was thrilled by the response, even though there'd been way too many creatures in my head this week.

"Thank you," I said aloud, as it had clearly heard me before.

There are demons in Chicago.

"There are. Not here, though."

They are without regard.

I thought that summed the species up pretty well.

"The Guardians' wards are currently broken. Someone smashed one of the cornerstones, and we're trying to fix them. Would you like an update if we're able to do that?"

Agreeable, it said, its voice echoing in my head even as it slipped beneath the water, leaving barely a ripple on the surface.

I glanced at Bjorn. "I don't suppose you have any advice about the wards?"

"They are not built for the city that stands today."

"Truer words," I murmured. "Have you seen any demons?"

"No. They haven't been fighting here."

"Are you the river troll who reported feeling the magical pulse?"

"No, but it was a brother of mine. The ley lines have no regulation. The city is rewilding."

I nodded. "I saw that. Chicago is a kind of supernatural."

"Of course it is. The magic makes it so."

*   *   *

I climbed up to street level, using the handholds Bjorn pointed out, all cleverly hidden so they were visible only from eye level. And not from above or below, so curious humans on the street or in boats on the water couldn't use them or disturb him.

Mom was waiting. She pulled off my dripping jacket and threw her own around my shoulders.

"So, I met George's son Bjorn," I said, and told them what I'd learned.

"Why did the Guardians think demons were going to be in the water?" Theo asked. "Are there mer-demons?"

That was when I finally realized the "where" of the wards. We thought they were geographical, with each ward protecting a certain chunk of the city. But that wasn't the full story.

"Not in the water," I said, glancing at him. "*On* it. The ward was built to protect against demons coming into Chicago by water."

"By water," Theo murmured, and his face changed the second he got it. "The wards are transportation oriented."

"Transportation?" Aunt Mallory asked. "What about the quarry?"

"Trying to stop demons from tunneling in, maybe," I said. "The quarry was still operating when the wards were established."

"South Gate is for demons coming in by road," Mom said. "Or, at that time, carriage or horse."

"And the warehouse—maybe intended for flying demons?" Uncle Catcher guessed.

"The beam goes up into the air," I said with a nod, "and it shoots lightning."

"Transportation," Uncle Catcher murmured. "I want to think about that." He wandered a few steps away to ponder.

"That means you did good," Aunt Mallory said.

I didn't know if that was true right now, but I'd make it true in the end one way or the other.

"Go home," Mom said. "You both look beat."

Theo and I looked at each other, then back at the skyline. There was still so much to do, and tomorrow would only add new challenges. Resting felt like stealing time.

"You can't save the world on your own," Mom said. "Let us help shoulder the burden."

"You saved humans on the L tonight."

Mom's smile was wide. "We did."

"The mayor is going to be pissed," Theo said, kicking a chunk of rock off the sidewalk, probably so no one would trip on it. I appreciated the small kindness.

"Probably," Mom agreed. "Officials always get mad when we solve problems we didn't create." That was said with a *definite tone.* "But as soon as someone offers me a better, easier, faster, clearer option, I'll be happy to take it."

"Truth," Theo said with a nod.

Mom's screen signaled, and she pulled it out. "Hello, Mr. Ombudsman," she said. "You're on speaker with, well, pretty much everybody. We were just about to report in." She gave him an update about the river monster.

"We got close to fixing the wards," Aunt Mallory said.

Uncle Catcher sniffed. "Not close. We triggered it. One hundred percent successful. But only temporarily."

"I know you're eager to get back to your daughter," Roger said. "If you need to go, please do. At some point, the mayor is going to have to make some hard decisions about who she wants to allow into the city and how she's going to enforce those limits."

"Yeah," Aunt Mallory said, "she is." She reached out to Uncle Catcher and my mother, and took their hands. "But in the meantime, we have to keep Chicago standing. It has to start by closing the door to demons. We'll do our best," she said.

"I know you will," Roger said. "And Chicago appreciates it."

I was nearly dry by the time I made it back to the town house. The lights were on, but the first floor was empty. A note on the counter read, simply, "Outside." I put my still-damp jacket on the chair to dry, grabbed a throw blanket for the chill, and headed into the backyard. I needed a shower, but it could wait a bit.

A small fire shone in a brick firepit on the side patio, and a cooler was on the ground in front of it. Connor sat in the low Adirondack chair, beer in his clasped hands. He stared at the flames like they might tell him the answers he needed.

He glanced up at the sound of my footsteps, took in my damp hair and the blanket. Wordlessly, he leaned over, pulled another beer from the cooler, popped the cap, and offered the beer to me.

I took the seat next to his, accepted the beer, our fingertips holding that contact for an extra beat.

I didn't want to give voice to troublesome things. But the sun wouldn't give us another chance to release the day's frustrations. And I knew we'd need a fresh start tomorrow, not a rehashing of tonight.

"We'll say it quick," I said. "Your night, twenty-five words or less. Then I'll go. Then we put it away."

He looked at me, nodded, the move spilling a dark wave of hair over his brow. "I had to debate my worth with assholes who contribute nothing to the Pack."

I gave him a moment, but he said nothing else. "Fourteen words," I calculated. "Short and to the point. My turn." I took a breath, tried to mentally condense the evening. "Monster freaked at Cadogan House. I lied to Dad. Dante nearly made me bite Theo. I swam with a river monster. Lulu is still spelled. And fuck demonkind," I added, although that put me three words over the limit.

Connor watched me for a moment, his anger fading into concern. "Quite a fucking night," he said after a solid minute.

"Which I hope never to repeat." I leaned over, clinked my bottle against his. "A toast to the good guys."

"May we stay that way," he agreed.

We stared at the flames until the fire died to an orange glow. While the earth spun toward the rising sun, we sat together in silence and let the world move around us. There would be time for talking, for considering, for planning tomorrow. But this part of tonight was for acceptance and quiet. And us.

FIFTEEN

Water surrounded me. Covered me. But this time I could breathe, and sunlight shimmered across the surface, spilling light and shadow across the bottom of the pool I was in. It didn't seem to matter that I'd never been in a pool in sunlight, nor seen that shimmering. It all looked very real.

I pushed off the bottom and swam toward the breaking surface. But I emerged into darkness and violence and blood. Demons with human bodies and reptilian faces fought with vampires and shifters, while a dozen leviathans, swift and graceful as birds, soared through the sky above us.

Then something was being pushed into my hand. I looked over, found Lulu in her pajamas at my side. I was curling my fingers around the handle of my katana. She opened her mouth to scream something at me, but as before she made no sound.

She stomped her feet in frustration, then took a few steps backward, giving herself room. She held up her hand, two fingers extended.

"Two?" I asked.

Lulu rolled her eyes, made the sign again.

"I've got the two," I said. "Two what?"

She turned and ran inside the nearest building, and I followed her, thinking she wanted to show me something. And then we were in a classroom, with "Test Today" in enormous letters on the board at the front of the room, sun streaming through windows.

Oh, god. We had a test? Had I even studied for this class? I couldn't remember anything about the room, probably because I hadn't attended this kind of human school.

Lulu was at the desk beside mine, and she was holding up two fingers again.

"I don't understand, Lulu. It looks like you're trying to play charades."

She nearly jumped out of her chair, gave me two huge thumbs-up.

"You're serious."

She held up two fingers again.

I rolled my eyes but played along. "Two words."

She nodded, held up one finger.

"First word."

Another thumbs-up. Now she stood up, the room expanding and morphing around her into some sort of gymnasium. She stretched her arms wide.

"Something big," I said.

She nodded, then moved her arm up and down, her wrist fluid.

"Painting," I said.

She nodded, made that keep-going gesture.

"Big painting. Mural!"

She pointed at me with one hand, and used the other hand to put a finger on her nose. I'd guessed correctly.

But then there was a crash as an SUV drove through the gymnasium's wall. Connor got out, wearing the same pajamas as Lulu. He offered me a long skewer with a marshmallow on the end.

"Hungry?" he asked.

My stomach growled, and hunger had the dream dissolving. I awoke, blinked, looked around. The bedroom was dark, but I knew the sun was still high. I could feel it in my bones.

I crawled into Connor. "I don't like charades," I murmured, and slept again.

Our first stop after sunset was for meat.

Not, unfortunately, for us. We'd settled for bagels and protein drinks on the way to NAC headquarters. The Pack was donating food to human first responders, and Connor had offered to make the delivery to the relocation center closest to the Ombuds' office.

It was a small gesture on our end—dropping off food—but at least it was something. Things kept getting worse, despite the human exodus. During the day, demons had attacked a bus of humans headed out of the city, their only apparent motivation the sheer enjoyment of terrorizing the human passengers. They'd rolled the bus, forcing humans to pick their way into the street, and then called down dozens of crows and ravens to peck and harass them. Emergency crews made it to the scene before there'd been any fatalities, but fifteen humans were injured, some severely, and only two of the demons were caught. They didn't burn, but they refused to talk about Dante, the upstart, or the cornerstones.

"Freedom," one of them had said. "We are here for freedom."

Their kind of freedom scared the hell out of me.

We had no wards to keep them out. Lulu was still unconscious in Cadogan House. My mother would put her life on the line again tonight. I hadn't been strong enough to fight Dante competitively, much less defeat him. And I was still healing from yesterday's battles. My hip ached from the condo, and although the punctures had healed, my arm was one huge bruise where Ambrosia's teeth had sunk in.

"Stop this," said a voice behind me accompanied by a motorized hum.

While Connor had continued on to the Pack's commercial

kitchens, I'd stopped in front of the brilliantly colored mural Lulu had painted inside the building.

But I didn't think that was what Berna meant. She was Connor's aunt, although I wasn't sure if that was an honorary title or a genetic one. She'd been a fixture at Pack headquarters even when my mom had been Cadogan's Sentinel, although she now roamed the halls on a mobility scooter.

She drew closer, pale face pinched, hair bleached a bright contrast to her dark brows, and wagged her finger at me.

"No wallowing," she said in her Ukrainian accent. "Is waste of time."

"I'm not wallowing," I said, and sounded pouty even to my ears. "I just don't know how to fix this."

She snorted, and the sound was so filled with sarcasm that it made me feel a little better.

"You are young and strong and immortal, and you have nephew, who is very strong." She flexed a biceps in illustration. "Wait until time is right to fix." She lifted her shoulder. "Or you won't."

"I need to fix Lulu now," I said.

Berna's brows shot up. "Why?"

"Because she is my responsibility."

Berna snorted again. "She is her own responsibility, and her parents'. Let them worry about her. You fix city."

I wasn't sure that assignment was better. "Does it ever stop?"

"Life is assortment candy box," she said philosophically, and waved goodbye as she rolled down the hall.

Connor came out of the kitchen pushing a tall cart filled with foil-covered trays.

"Feeding the entire city?" I asked.

"A good part of it. We know what greases the right palms."

"Nice," I said at the barbecue pun.

"Did I hear Aunt Berna?"

"'Life is assortment candy box,' she says."

He blinked. "Box of chocolates."

"Yep. You never know which demons you're going to get."

We loaded the trays into the back of the SUV. And when we closed the back door, found a stranger standing near us.

I nearly moved in front of Connor to protect him before realizing the stranger was a shifter, not a demon. But not, given his unfamiliar magic, part of the NAC.

He was about Connor's height, but on the slender side. His skin was suntanned, and his chin-length dark hair was pushed behind his ears. His eyes were brown and deep set, with dark brows and long lashes. His expression was unreadable.

I felt the cold twist of Connor's magic, then the angry heat. But his body language didn't change.

"Swift," Connor said.

"Keene," the man said, then shifted his gaze to me.

"Kieran Swift," Connor said. "Elisa Sullivan."

This was the nephew of the Western Pack Apex, Robin Swift. At least he wasn't another challenger. Or so I presumed.

"Strange time to visit Chicago," Connor said, voice bland.

I wasn't sure if Kieran and Connor were close. But it didn't sound like they were bosom friends.

"Strange times all around." Swift glanced at the back of the SUV. "You running deliveries now?" There was mild sarcasm in his voice.

"Is that any of your business?" Connor's tone was light, but his magic was biting.

So maybe enemies?

"No," Kieran said. "But I find myself curious about what's

happening in Chicago lately. And wondering how it might affect my people."

He didn't specify which "happenings" had interested him, but it was easy enough to guess. Odds were good he'd come to find out why Connor had rejected the challenge earlier this week and if the Pack was in danger of imploding or becoming dictatorial. But Connor's gaze stayed steady.

"You're here to help with the demons, then?" Connor asked, the challenge obvious in his eyes. "Because that's the most important happening in Chicago right now."

Kieran met Connor's gaze and made his own silent evaluation—including a pinprick of magic that I guessed was intended to measure Connor's strength.

"Absolutely," Kieran said after a moment. "Where do we start?"

We started with the drop-off, and Kieran helped us carry trays into the empty storefront the city was using as an emergency response center. I let Kieran sit in the SUV's front-passenger seat for the ride, and I sat behind Connor—all the better to watch Swift's face as we drove. He noticed the damage done already as we passed but made no mention of it. He sat in silence the entire way. Was he considering what he saw, I wondered, or testing Connor to see who would bite first? Connor didn't speak a word either, so the silence was thick and uncomfortable.

Shifters, I thought ruefully. They thought vampires were dramatic, but they had their own passive-aggressive plays.

When the SUV was unloaded and we climbed in again, I took the front seat, dialed up the office.

"Evening," Theo said.

"Hey. I've got Connor and Kieran Swift of the Western Pack. We just finished a food drop-off."

Theo would know the guest was unusual. But he was a cop, so he also knew how to surmise silently. "Got it. I'm sorry to report Felix Buckley was found dead during the day."

Not entirely surprising, but still a bummer. "In Chicago?"

"Yeah. Magic wounds. No evidence he was killed by Dante, but the forensic people are looking. He was in a tiny apartment on the North Side. Looks like he'd holed up in there."

"Trying to avoid more of Dante's payback?"

"All signs point to yes. Fortunately, that was enough for a judge to give us a search warrant."

"Not an arrest warrant?"

"Not without direct evidence tying Dante to the death. The 'D' on the note wasn't enough. We're heading to the condo now. Where are you?"

"East Side ERC."

"We can pick you up there. Perhaps when they're done, your shifter friends would like to tussle with a mess of demons currently running wild through Grant Park?"

Connor glanced at Kieran, brows lifted. Kieran nodded at the silent invite.

"We'll handle it," Connor said.

"Petra will email you the details," Theo said. "Elisa, we'll be there in ten."

"Ombuds cooperating with a CPD officer," Kieran said, and sounded surprised to hear it.

"They don't call or cooperate out West?" I asked.

"They don't. Marin County police generally prefer to pretend supernaturals don't exist."

"Not a luxury we have in Chicago," I said. "And we need all the help we can get. So, thanks for heading all the way out here to offer your support." My voice was exceedingly pleasant.

I climbed out of the SUV, went to the other side of the vehicle, and kissed Connor through the open driver's-side window. "Be careful. Who knows what kind of germs they carry."

He smiled. "We will, and same to you."

"Always," I said, and kissed him again for good measure.

Then I shifted my gaze to Kieran, who watched us with an expression that wasn't as light as friendly curiosity, but wasn't as antagonistic as full suspicion. Skepticism, maybe.

"I don't care why you're here," I said, giving voice to the thing we were all thinking about. "And unlike Connor, I don't have to be diplomatic. If you put him in danger, you'll answer to me." I smiled, with fangs. "And I bite."

Fortunately, Gwen was driving a CPD cruiser, as I'd have had a very uncomfortable time trying to fold myself into the backseat of her tiny convertible. Instead, I played perp behind bulletproof glass, and talked to her and Theo through the tiny perforations. I was glad Kieran didn't witness that, as it would've taken some of the shine away from my fantastic parting line.

"Kieran Swift, eh?" Theo asked. "Goodwill mission?"

"The pretense seems to be he's here to help with demon management."

"You don't think so?" Gwen asked, meeting my gaze in the rearview mirror.

"I think he's here to evaluate Connor's power and determine whether Connor's avoiding challenges because he's not strong enough to win."

"Dangerous presumption," Theo said.

"Fortunately for him, Connor is not an asshole. But I'm not expecting much out of the demon patrol. Wouldn't surprise me if he stood by and watched. Many shifters have an irritating habit of letting other people handle their problems."

"Anything new with Lulu?" Gwen asked.

"No change. Alexei and Aunt Mallory are taking shifts."

"Hopefully this will help," she said. "We don't have enough to convince a judge to give us an arrest warrant—or not those still in town, anyway—but who knows what goodies we can find in his condo?"

"Crappy art and lizard-skin shoes."

"Not taking that bet," Theo said.

"How pissed is the mayor?" I wondered.

"Honestly, she seemed more angry she missed the chance to actually see Ambrosia for herself. She's talking about a theme park."

"No," I said flatly. Business development could go only so far.

We passed a panel van hand-painted with conspiracy theories about demons: They were fake, and the siege was a ruse to get humans out of Chicago. Or they were real and created by government labs. We were invited to visit the driver's "demon truths" social media pages.

"People will believe any damn thing," Theo murmured. "And back to the point, the mayor seems to realize this is really the Guardians' fault, if anyone's. So, the sorcerers are in the clear."

"She also heard about your bath," Gwen said, and nudged Theo. "Show her."

"Show me what?"

"Nothing," Theo said. "It's nothing."

It took only ten seconds of Gwen's stony silence to have him reaching for his screen. He found what he was looking for, held it up to the glass between us.

It was a picture of me fresh out of the Chicago River, hair and clothes wet and plastered. "River-dragged Goth" was not a good look for me.

"Who took that?" I demanded. "And where would they like to be bitten first?"

"Hey, the mayor's pity is very handy in these times," Theo said, putting his screen away again.

"Were you just not going to show me that?"

"I was kind of hoping Connor would do it first. And I'm glad you're behind that glass," he said, giving it a friendly tap.

"Changing the subject," I said, "I assume we don't have an update on the wards?"

"Not yet," Theo said. "But a message from Catcher sounded optimistic. He said, and I quote, 'Maybe something tonight.'"

"For him, that is optimistic." I'd known him my entire life, and I'd probably seen him smile three times. And that might've been generous.

Gwen pulled up to the condo building where CPD cruisers were already parked. Paige stood outside, talking to the officers in one of them.

"Magical backup," Theo said. "Just in case."

We walked toward the building, my body giving a post-traumatic shudder at the idea of going in again. Or maybe that was monster. My mind wasn't thrilled either, but maybe Paige could help if the demon magic got heavy.

"He in there?" Gwen asked when we reached the cops; they hadn't bothered to hide themselves.

"Don't think so," said a cop I knew from such supernatural hijinks as "Fairies attempt to take Chicago."

"Hey, Hammett," I said.

He was the leader of a SWAT unit. I gave him a nod, and he smiled back. He was a little shorter than me, but all muscle, and wore dark fatigues like the rest of his team.

"How's it going, Sullivan? You look drier today."

I growled. "Did everybody see the picture?"

His grin was wide and unabashed. "It spread like wildfire. Anyway, we watched him leave about ten minutes ago. The field team says he's headed downtown. They haven't reported a final destination yet."

I tried and failed to be disappointed Dante wasn't here. At this point, I had to face the likelihood that I couldn't beat him physically, not with his level of magic, so that wasn't going to be the route to unenchanting Lulu. It was going to take evidence and leverage. And getting that would be easier if he wasn't here.

"Then let's get in and get out," Gwen said. "And keep an eye out."

"Of course," Hammett said, then gave me a wink. "Stay away from pools and fountains."

"Let me know when you've booked that stand-up gig," I said with a flat smile.

"You okay?" Theo asked as we pushed into the lobby.

"Fine," I said. "For now." And I gave monster another warning: *We need Lulu, and this is our best chance. So, stay down.*

"Some magic in the lobby," Paige said behind us. "But residual."

"Let us know when it's fresh," Gwen said.

The security desk was empty, so we moved smoothly to the elevators and then up to the demon's floor.

"Well," Gwen said when the doors opened, "looks like they've rearranged things."

The hallway, once classily (and lightly) decorated, now looked like a flea market. Random objects—lamps, pictures, stacked chairs, ugly vases—filled the entire space, but for a narrow, serpentine walking path.

"The condo board must be pissed," Theo said.

"I don't think there's a human left in the building other than us," Gwen said. "They all got out. But I'm sure they'll be back, and angry letters will be drafted."

It occurred to me then that she didn't sound like she believed there would be a solution. It sounded more like she'd settled in for a long ride—like demon response was her new normal. I'd been treating it more like a flare-up, because I'd been assuming the sorcerers would fix the wards and the demons already in town would be given an ultimatum—cooperate or get out. That was one reason, monster and Lulu being two more, but I was impatient to find a fix.

Was I being naïve? Was this life now?

"Hey."

I looked up, found Theo looking back at me.

"Coming," I said, and followed him.

There was more decor in the condo, too. Not in any style that I could see, other than "a lot." There was also more residual demon magic, but no booby traps or words. I guess Dante hadn't expected us to secure a search warrant. Maybe he'd found a few judges to pay off, just in case. Whatever the reason, we could be gloriously nosy.

"All right," Gwen said. "Cameras on for your protection and mine."

Some of the cops chuckled as they switched on tiny lapel cameras that would record the search.

"We are here to execute a duly authorized search warrant," she said, holding up her screen, where the text was printed. "We will search thoroughly and damage nothing. Any claims for damage, verified by video evidence, can be made to your local precinct. We are authorized to obtain any material—electronic, physical, or supernatural—that potentially pertains to the deaths of humans or demons within the city of Chicago over the last week, or to the magic used on Lulu Bell." She looked over the cops, me, and Theo. "Let's make it a clean search, and let's get what we came for."

Teams took rooms. I started in the kitchen, helping a uniform search through drawers, behind drawers, underneath drawers.

The cupboards were still bare. I wasn't entirely sure what demons ate—but whatever it was, they hadn't eaten it in this kitchen.

After finding nothing, I walked through the living room and considered its hoarding. Because that was what it looked like—the obsessive gathering of stuff Dante didn't need now and probably wouldn't use in the future. There were built-in bookshelves along one wall, but they were empty of books or personal effects. Just empty frames, empty vases, chunks of decorative stone.

"He's like a bowerbird, huh?"

The question came from a thickly Chicago-accented voice, and I turned to find a petite, curvy woman in uniform. She had pale skin, a mound of dark curls on her head, and a brilliant smile.

"Sorry?" I said.

"Bowerbird," she repeated, and looked at me. "Little birds that live—maybe in Australia? The guys build a nest for the ladies to show off. But it's not just twigs. They collect stuff—plastic, glass, rocks, what have you, and make little collections. All to find mates."

"Huh," I said. "I don't know about mates, but it does look like he was trying to show off." If that was right, was he doing it for someone else—to impress the upstart—or to reassure himself that he was winning the territorial war?

I wandered down a hallway. On the left was a bathroom full of grooming products; there was an empty bedroom on the right. Dante hadn't bothered to fill this part yet, or maybe he just hadn't gotten around to it. The master bedroom was at the end of the hall. CPD officers were working through the cabinets of the connected bathroom; the cabinets were stocked with what looked from a quick glance like more hoarded grooming supplies.

That a demon was obsessive about his looks wasn't a surprise. Since Dante was obsessive and tended to favor flashy suits, I walked through the bathroom to the master closet. It was enormous—bigger than the first bedroom I'd passed. Not yet overflowing with clothes, but he'd made a good start. Two dozen suit jackets hung in one section, all in shades of black, gray, and silver. The wall of shoes was bigger than the kitchen in the loft I'd shared with Lulu.

"You can do suits," said one of the forensic techs, pointing to the rack. "Check pockets, linings."

I nodded but kept staring at the shoes, and then realized I wasn't just *looking* at them. I was *feeling* them.

I pulled on a new pair of gloves, walked closer. Then closed my eyes, opened myself to the magic. That wasn't difficult to do, standing in the middle of a demon's wardrobe. Looking for *unusual* magic amid the cloud of power that clung to the fabric was the tricky part.

I moved a hand across the shelves, forcing myself to focus on one pair at a time. And stopped when I felt a twang of something.

I opened my eyes, looked at a pair of forest green dress shoes with a reptile texture. Very carefully, I lifted one, looked it over, checked beneath the leather tongue for contraband. And was a little disturbed that I was putting a hand in a demon's size thirteens. But an Ombudsman had to do what an Ombudsman had to do.

There was nothing in the shoe, so I turned it over. And light shimmered as it caught the gleaming copper ash embedded in the tread.

"I need an evidence bag," I said. "I think I've got something."

"What is it?"

I nearly jumped at Gwen's voice. I hadn't realized she'd sidled up right beside me.

"Good lord," I said. "Don't startle a woman holding a demon shoe."

"Bet you've never said that before," she said with a smile as she held out an open evidence bag. "What have you got?"

"Demon ash," I said when the shoe and its mate and their residual evidence were safely sealed inside the bag. Then I flipped the package over, so she could see. "The copper kind."

She looked it over with pursed lips. "Good. We didn't see him at the empty lot or the Hyde Park shoot-out. But this puts him at a demon death site. Is that his magic?"

I wanted it to be. I wanted, needed, leverage to make him fix Lulu. But facts were facts.

"I don't think so," I said. "It feels different from the rest."

"Can't win them all," she said, offering the bag to a tech who placed it carefully in the tub used to carry out what we found.

"It's not enough," I said.

"To nail him? Maybe not. But it's enough to drag him in for questioning. Judges don't like liars. Especially those with dead demon on their shoes. And we may find more."

Raised voices echoed from the front room, and we left the techs to the hunt.

Four demons, including a couple I recognized from my prior condo visit, had entered. They were staring down two uniforms, including the petite one from earlier. The cops put on brave faces, but their fear permeated the air. And I was sure I wasn't the only one who could tell.

"Problem?" Gwen asked, moving in, one hand on the butt of her holstered weapon.

"What are you doing in Mr. Dante's place?" a demon asked.

"Executing a warrant," I said, stepping beside Gwen. "Just as he asked us to do."

"You got no right—"

"We have every right," Gwen said, offering her screen with her free hand. "A duly authorized warrant. We get to search and take what we want."

Her smile went thin, and I imagined it had scared the attitude out of more than a few supernaturals and humans.

Unfortunately, demons were a different breed. One of them stepped forward or made a move to do so. But these were minions, not royalty, and I got there faster, had my sword at its throat.

"I wouldn't," I said, and bobbed my head toward the other cops in the room, who were all at attention and ready to draw down. That included former cops: Theo looked furious that the demon had even considered stepping toward Gwen.

"Even if they let you live," I said, "interfering with a warrant will put you in supernatural lockdown. You've heard of the Feds' new magic-siphoning containment cells, haven't you?"

That put a hint of uncertainty in their expressions.

"If we have to lock you up, do you think the other supernaturals will be nice to you?"

The one in front of me—my gleaming sword at his throat—stepped back.

"Wise," I said, but kept the blade lifted. "Who wants to tell us who the upstart is?"

More looking around. Before they could play dumb, I held up a hand. "If you don't tell us, I'm going to tell Dante that you spilled all the details about his business dealings in New York. Especially the illegal parts. I doubt he's going to like that very much."

"That's blackmail!" one of the demons said.

"Technically," Gwen said, "it's extortion. But that's close enough."

"First one who tells us is off the naughty list," I said.

"We don't know her name," one of them said. And like an experiment in jail room snitching, they all jumped in, trying to be the one who delivered the best news first.

"Not very loyal, are they?" Gwen asked.

"Loyalty only goes so far when you're immoral," I said. "Quiet!" I put glamour behind the command, and it took only a bit for the din to die away.

"You," I said, pointing at the first one who'd spoken. "Go."

"We don't know her name. But she told the boss that she was taking over Chicago, that it was her territory, and the boss better step in line."

None of that was new. "Last night, some of you were going to look for her at the place where you met her minions before. Where is that?"

"Big park downtown."

My heart pounded. "Grant Park?"

"Sure."

"I'm on it," Theo said before I could ask him to warn Connor or send someone to do it, since he and Kieran and the others were also at the park—and probably not in human form.

"Was she there?" I asked, ignoring the worry that wanted me to run for the car.

The demons shook their heads. "Didn't show," one of them said.

"Where are her headquarters?" Gwen asked.

"Near that park?" the first demon asked, obviously unsure.

"Does she have social media?"

There were shrugs all around.

"What's she look like?" Gwen asked.

"She's hot," one of the demons called out.

That had me stopping. "She's hot? You've seen her?"

"Well, no. But she had a good voice."

"So you've heard her voice, but you've never seen her in person?" I wondered.

They shrugged. "She has people to do that."

Minions, he meant.

"Why'd your boss kill Buckley?" Gwen asked quickly, given they were all being very cooperative.

"He didn't," the demon said. "He had Azod do it."

SIXTEEN

That was almost too easy," Gwen said with a sigh, when the Feds had been called and a sputtering Azod was hauled out in neon blue cuffs.

"Good ploy, though," I said, "throwing that question out there so casually."

"You were having so much fun as good cop. I wanted to play, too."

Unfortunately, after grilling the demons for another half hour, we got nothing else useful. Dante told his minions only so much, and given they weren't the brightest bulbs in the demonic marquee, I could sympathize. But we had Grant Park, and we had a murder suspect.

Theo came back from the hallway, where he'd been working to reach Connor.

"There are vamps at Grant Park, too," he said. "Washington and Gray. They've been fighting demon minions with the wolves. They haven't seen anyone who seems to be in charge, but they'll keep an eye out."

"It's a long shot," I said. "We have nothing other than a California demon who doesn't show her face and wants to make it big in Chicago."

"And maybe a human who broke the cornerstone on their behalf?" Gwen said.

Theo and I both looked at her. "What do you mean?" I asked.

"The other wards were working when the cornerstone was broken, and Rosantine was the only demon in Chicago before that happened. So, it couldn't have been a demon that broke the cornerstone. It couldn't have been a vampire, because it happened in daylight. And probably not a supernatural, because the work was done manually. A sup wouldn't have wasted time doing all that work in public."

"You have a point," I said, and scratched my healing arm. Then felt sudden sympathy for Theo, given the many times I'd teased him for doing the same thing.

I looked at Gwen. "Any sign of Jonathan Black?"

"He hasn't been home since he sent you the message," Gwen said. "We've been watching his house."

Gwen's screen signaled. She checked it, lifted her brows. "But we have found someone else. Turns out, our aristocratic demon is on a lake cruise."

Cruises on Lake Michigan and the Chicago River were popular tourist activities, and large ships hosted weddings and corporate booze cruises. The lake ships usually traveled parallel to the shore, giving passengers a view of the skyline.

"Convenient that he's doing it after the river ward was disengaged," I said. Not that it was working but for the single burst of functionality that had woken Ambrosia.

"If we can get an arrest warrant, it would be a handy spot to bring him in." Gwen's gaze was vacant as she considered. "Out on the water, there are fewer people to hurt."

"I don't want to go swimming again," I said. "And I don't think we're powerful enough to take him."

"Maybe Paige or Mallory can give you some kind of magical Teflon, so the demon stuff slides off," Theo suggested.

"I don't know if that's a thing," I said. But the idea of confronting Dante protected by a magical shield was intriguing.

"I need to talk to people and coordinate," Gwen said. "So, you have time to ask. But we have to move quickly. Those lake cruises have start and end points."

"Maybe the surveillance crew could find out our window."

She nodded. "I'll get on that. Find out about the magic."

"Demon Teflon," Petra said. "That's exactly what you need." She was back in the office and on video eating cheese balls with one hand, fingers of the other one flying over her screen.

"Yeah, and I need it pretty much immediately. Is that a thing?"

"I don't see why not. But I don't know the specifics."

"I'll ask Aunt Mallory," I said. "Can you get me information about the boat, the crew, that kind of thing?"

"Of course. You really going to tussle with him?"

"I'm hoping there will be zero tussling. But he will be cornered, and that will be dangerous."

"All the better he's offshore, then."

I left her to work and contacted my mom.

"I need demon repellent," I said, "and soon."

It was a truth universally acknowledged that a mother was going to have Some Thoughts about her kid putting herself in harm's way (again).

"How soon?" she asked.

"Half an hour? Dante's cornered," I said, "but we don't have much time to take advantage of it."

"I'll talk to Mallory and call you back in five," Mom said, and the screen went blank. She wouldn't mess around with my safety, which I appreciated.

"Thanks," I said to no one, then looked at Theo. "If we get him, we're going to need the Feds to take him. I don't think our cubes are strong enough."

"On it," he said, and pulled out his screen.

Petra sent boat schematics, and I studied them while everyone else made calls. The ship was huge—nearly two hundred feet long, with two stories above the water and one below. Dante would probably be on the top deck, lapping up the luxury and eating or drinking or otherwise doing what demons like to do. Other than making Chicago generally unlivable for humans.

"Feds will have transport here in under an hour," Theo said, sliding his screen into his pocket as he returned.

Handy but disconcerting. I didn't want magic-siphoning tech that close to me.

Gwen came back. "It's a four-hour cruise. They left about half an hour ago."

"Pretty good window," Theo said.

"Yeah, although our ride out to the ship will take some of that time. Fortunately, the coast guard has a boat. And one of the security personnel on the cruise ship is former CPD, so they're coordinating."

"That's lucky," Theo said, then told her about the Feds.

My screen rang. "Discuss our entry and exit points," I told him. "I'm going to discuss magic."

"We can do a saltwater spritz," Aunt Mallory began. She'd turned on video, and the circles under her eyes looked darker and deeper than they had the day before.

"Which means?"

"We hose you and your team down with salt water laced with a few other ingredients. I'm thinking rosemary and lemon."

"And then you'll roast us with nice potatoes?"

She smiled, which was what I'd been going for. "Maybe after

battling the demon. But it's not one hundred percent. It will give you a thin layer of protection and lessen the effect of big magic."

I'd have to get the team's okay for a pre-op shower, but that was probably workable. "Anything stronger?"

The screen shifted to show my mom. "She's working on some amulets to help deflect the magic," Mom said. "But she'll be able to manage only a couple of those in the time we've got and with the stuff she has on hand."

"A couple is better than none. Thanks."

"You're welcome. We'll talk to Gwen about the delivery."

I saw in her face that she wanted to go with me in order to protect me.

"Wards are more important," I said. "We can't make a dent in the scourge until they close the doors. And the fewer supernaturals on that boat, the better. To demons, we're weapons."

Dante's ship had embarked from Navy Pier, a tourist attraction that stretched into the Chicago River and held the famous Chicago Ferris wheel, in addition to restaurants and event venues. There wouldn't be many humans out, so we waited there for the coast guard ship and to get our magical vaccinations.

Aunt Mallory didn't spray us down with a hose, but the pesticide canister and sprayer didn't seem much better.

"It was clean," she said. "I promise."

I nodded, closed my eyes as a cool mist that smelled like a day spa was sprayed on my face, clothes, hands, feet. The same was done to the seven others who would board the coast guard's boat—me, Theo, Gwen, and four cops. More cops would follow in CPD boats, and the Feds would be waiting at the dock with their transport.

When we'd been spritzed, Aunt Mallory walked down the line,

frowning as she surveyed us. "You'll do. Don't wash your hands until you're done. The demon bane will wash off."

"Demon bane sounds much cooler than demon marinade," Gwen murmured. "But it doesn't make me feel better."

"You'll be fine," Theo promised. "Demons don't seem to notice us much."

"And now your medals of honor, so to speak," Aunt Mallory said, pulling a folded piece of emerald fabric from her pocket. It looked like silk, and I wondered if she kept magical supplies in her vehicle. Like a charm caboodle.

She opened the fabric, pulled a chain from a small glass vial. "I'm told this one's for you," she said, slipping it over Gwen's head.

"And for you," she said, pulling out a second one and holding it up for me.

A silver disk gleamed in the streetlight, and I recognized it immediately. It was my mother's Saint George medal. He was the patron saint of warriors; the medal had been given to her when she joined the Red Guard, a no-longer-secret organization that had been established as a check on Master vampires in the House system.

A small twig also hung from the chain. As far as I was aware, that wasn't a gift from anyone.

"Something from your mom and Chicago to help boost the magic," Aunt Mallory said, and I looked at my mom, nodded. She nodded back.

"Do we need to do anything?" Gwen asked. "I mean, to turn them on?"

"Nope. Just keep them on your person. They're warded successfully," Aunt Mallory said dourly, so I didn't need to ask how the city ward repairs were going. "They will give you little umbrellas of protection. And like with the spritz, they may not completely block the big stuff. It depends on how powerful the demon taking the shot is. But they should significantly minimize the effects."

"Thanks for the rush," I said. "I know you have a lot on your mind."

"Exactly why I prefer to think about other things," Aunt Mallory said.

"Random question," I said, as someone handed me a very bright orange life vest. "Have you been having weird dreams lately?"

Her brows lifted. "No more than usual. Why?"

"Never mind," I said.

"All right," Gwen called out, "let's get started." She waited a moment for quiet. "There are currently seven demons aboard," she continued when she had everyone's attention. "That includes Dante. You've all got the floor plan, and the host staff reports they're sitting in a conversation area on the upper deck. There are couches and chairs facing the windows."

"How often does the host go in?" Theo asked.

"Every fifteen minutes or so, unless someone calls her up. There's a bar on that deck, but Dante didn't pay to staff it."

"Wanted the privacy?" I wondered.

"That would be my guess. I think you go in from the front and let him see you," she said to me. "While he's reacting to that, we'll come in from the back."

"He'll probably try to use magic," I said. "So, be prepared for it, but remember we've been treated. If he really wants to play businessman, he'll come with us without incident."

"And if he doesn't?" a cop asked.

"Then use Tasers if you need to, and magic cuffs when they're down," Gwen said. "The minions, his people, shouldn't be as much of a problem. But he's strong, so keep him in your line of sight as much as possible. We cuff them. We bring them down-stairs. We get them into the boat and back to the dock. The Feds will take custody formally when we reach it." She looked around. "Any questions?"

No one had any, or at least no one wanted to raise any here.

"All right, then," Gwen said, "time to climb aboard."

Despite my unfortunate run-in with Chicago's water system the night before, it was exhilarating to be out on the lake. (Or it was after I thought to pull back my hair after five minutes of it blinding me.) I didn't often get the chance to see the skyline. Modern glass skyscrapers gleamed beside older, more stoic buildings. Lights twinkled and steam rose. It looked magical from this angle, and I could imagine the city was a sparkling fairyland.

We drew close to the cruise ship, a giant glass behemoth. The long row of windows on the top deck glowed with light, and music was audible across the water.

"You ever been on one of those?" Theo asked.

"Nope. You?"

"Once, for a wedding. It's like being in a club, except the club moves."

We were already running without lights, and the captain cut the engine as we neared the ship. Our momentum carried us to a spot where a man on deck signaled with a green flashlight. There were rungs along the side of the ship to the upper deck. And they rose and fell several feet as the swells moved beneath us.

"I'll be here in the boat if you need me," Theo whispered, lifting his casted arm.

"Sorry," Gwen said. "I didn't even think about how you'd get aboard."

"No worries," he said, giving her a soft smile. Then he shifted that smile to me. "Go get him, and let's wake her up."

I gave him the most confident nod I could manage, then turned my attention back to the ship. I gauged the time of the swells, and when the boat started to rise, I grabbed a rung on the ship and jumped over.

My boot slipped, sending my right knee hard against the rung, but I was buzzing with adrenaline and barely felt it. I hung on through another swell, got purchase on the rungs, and climbed. And thanked whatever gods might be listening that I wasn't swimming again.

"I am not a demon," I murmured to any leviathans that might have been listening.

Hand over hand, one rung at a time, I made my way to the boat's open deck. A human hand reached out and helped me climb aboard. I moved out of the way, breathed out, got my bearings. And while the music of Dante's party made the deck underfoot vibrate, I gave monster a reminder.

We need Lulu awake. He is the key to that.

I got nothing but a sullen metaphysical nod. I wasn't sure if it had entered the adolescent phase or if it was truly resigned to the fact that we needed Lulu in order to move forward.

I wasn't sure if *I* was resigned to that fact—to telling Lulu what lurked beneath my skin.

When we were all on deck, the man who'd helped us over leaned in.

"I'm Chuck," he said quietly. He wore a polo shirt and a windbreaker with the ship's name embroidered on the pocket. "I'm the second mate. The federal authorities have confirmed their transport is ready and waiting. So, you just have to get the demons to them."

One of our cops, a nervous-looking sort, nodded vigorously, and I hoped this wasn't his first op.

"We've got it," Gwen said with a comforting air of authority. "Stairs?" She pointed to the right.

Chuck nodded. "Front of the ship is called the bow, and that's the forestair," he said, correctly assuming we were not up on maritime lingo. Then he pointed behind himself. "That's the stern and the aft stair. They're upstairs. Please don't fuck up my ship."

"We'll do everything in our power to keep demons from doing that," Gwen said, then nodded at us. "You know your assignments. Let's go."

And then we were moving. I headed right. I would go in with two cops at my back. Gwen and the others would go the other way and close off the demons' means of escape.

Quietly, and as swiftly as I dared on a bobbing ship, we made our way toward the bow, then into the stairway that wound up to the next deck. And when we reached it, nearly ran into a waitress who stood there, tray in hand.

She opened her mouth to squeal in surprise, but I covered it with a hand. "We're here to help," I said quietly. "I think the captain told you about us."

When she nodded, I moved my hand.

"Nearly gave me a heart attack," she whispered, then gestured to the glass doors a few feet away. "They're in there."

Dim overhead lights were on, in addition to the colored strobes that I guessed were supposed to add atmosphere. Even here on the deck, with the wind blowing around the lake scents outside the closed doors of the party room, I smelled cigars and brimstone.

I held out a hand. "Give me your tray."

"Gladly," the waitress said, and handed it over. Her fingers were shaking, and she wiped them on the short apron tied around her waist. "Not even supposed to be my shift, but freaking no one else is in town, so I had to take it. And I get freaking cops and demons. No offense," she added.

"None taken," I said sincerely. She hadn't included me in that list. "They bothering you?"

"No. Just weird. Like they think they're some kind of Mafia, but look around," she said, waving her hands. "It's just them on a booze cruise, which isn't very impressive. Anyway, not my business. I just want to be somewhere else."

"There a staff break room or something?" I asked, and she nodded. "Good, go down there. Someone will let you know when this is all done."

And I hoped, for the sake of this woman with her shaking hands and tidy apron, that we'd do it safely.

"Clear," the cop behind me said when the human had made it down the stairs.

"Stay back," I said, then flipped off the thumb guard on my katana, adjusted my tray, and put on a brilliant smile. And then I pushed open the doors.

The scents were stronger with the doors open, and the shed magic felt like a curtain I had to push through. The demons were situated in the conversation area, Dante in the middle of a sofa, his preferred position. They all ignored me until I reached them; apparently they assumed I was a server with another round of drinks, which was perfect.

"Hello," I said, and pretended to stumble, showering drinks and glasses onto the nearest demon. He bolted to his feet at the shock of ice and insult. Glass shattered, and booze spilled across the floor.

"Oh, my gosh," I said, covering my mouth with my hands. "I'm so sorry! I'm such a klutz. Let me help you," I said.

And as all the other demons looked my way, I picked up a cocktail napkin and stooped to swab at his feet. He still swore loudly at my incompetence, which gave Gwen and the others time to come in and block the doors.

When the music fell silent and the lights were turned up, I stood, met her eyes. "The floor is yours," I told her.

"Dantalion aka Dante," Gwen said, staring at him, "you are severely under arrest for conspiracy to murder Felix Buckley, Jake Durante, and Ernesto País. You have the right to remain silent, but please feel free to say something incriminating, so we can dispense with the niceties."

She worked through the recitation of Dante's rights; the other demons waited in stillness for some order from their master. For a moment, the only other sound was the *plink* of spilled tequila dripping from a coffee table.

"You've got the wrong person," Dante said. Then he stroked his jaw, eyes skittering across the room, no doubt looking for exits.

Or giving silent instructions to his crew. Because all hell broke loose.

The demon nearest me jumped up, ready to brawl.

I snatched up the drink tray, swung it like a baseball bat. The demon fell back onto the sofa, out cold.

The next one hopped up, and I tossed aside the tray, unsheathed my sword, and aimed. I sliced diagonally, managed to catch his arm before he pivoted. I jumped onto the coffee table, used a two-handed downward arc.

He blocked it with magic—some kind of buzzing barrier that made the blade bounce an inch above his skin. Then he opened his mouth and *literally exhaled magic*—a blue-black mist of particles that flew toward me like horizontal sleet, a Chicago wintertime favorite. I swept a few particles away with my sword, but the others hit me. And while I braced for their assault, they bounced on the floor like pearls from a broken necklace.

We both looked down at my chest. His magic had done nothing.

"Way to go, Aunt Mallory," I whispered, and grinned at him. "You're going to have to do this the old-fashioned way."

"Behind you!" someone called out, and I spun just in time to avoid being hit across the back with a stacking chair.

"Oh, you aren't even trying," I said, and clucked my tongue at the demon who wielded the chair.

I used my sword to bat it away, and when the demon dropped it, I kicked him in the stomach. He stumbled back but stayed upright, then put his head down and simply barreled toward me. I brought my sword low, spun up and around as he reached me, and caught him in the chest. The laceration was deep and filled the air with sourness. Screaming, he went down with a thud.

I stepped over him, flicked demon gunk from the blade, and looked up to check the rest of the fight. His hands in the air, Dante stood with Gwen, surrounded by cops. He wore a slightly baffled expression, as if unsure what move to make.

The other cops were fighting the handful of demons who hadn't yet given up. In other words, the situation seemed to be contained.

Which is exactly when you get overconfident.

I felt magic gathering behind me, and began to turn an instant too late. The demon I'd sliced wasn't dead and had apparently figured out the limits of our protective magicking. His magic was a wavering flame that struck me in the chest—the same spot in which I'd hit him. He opted for volume this time and used so much power that it pushed right past the barrier to seep through to my skin. Then it overtook that barrier, too, and weighed on my lungs like a midnight incubus. I had to concentrate in order to breathe.

His bit of magic was, unfortunately, enough to turn the tide. The knowledge of how to breach our defenses somehow spread silently through the room, as if carried by a wave of magic. Two cops started coughing, their breathing also impeded, and I guessed where this was headed.

I sucked in the biggest breath I could and used that air to shout, "Our shield is down! Use weapons!"

That had the cops pulling and firing Tasers at the demons closest to them. One demon hit the floor, didn't move. Another jolted, but went in for round two. I looked back at the demon who'd magicked me; his brilliantly yellow teeth were bared in a nasty grin.

Any help you can give would be appreciated, I told monster, grateful I didn't have to say the words aloud.

Monster's response was shockingly physical, and my breath came easier, not at full capacity but better. I wasn't sure how it had managed that trick—maybe using the demon's magic against it?—but I decided to keep the improvement to myself. I was on my knees already, and I dropped my head like I was gasping for air. The demon leaned over me, spilling his sour-milk scent.

"Not so tough, are you? Can't even do magic." His voice was gravelly and hard and edged with glee.

"Not much," I said honestly, and then launched my fist into his solar plexus.

He hit his knees in front of me, struggling for air. So, naturally, I punched him in the face. Cartilage crunched and he screamed as oily blood leaked from his broken nose.

"Whoops!" I said. "Guess I was feeling better than I thought."

His eyes closed against the pain, and I grabbed one of his wrists, twisted, and put him down on the floor. "Cuffs!" I called out, and someone tossed me a pair. I ignored the burn I got from holding them—being supernatural and all—and snapped them onto his hands.

With a hand on the edge of a sofa for support, I rose. Dante was the only demon left standing now, and he was still surrounded by cops. I walked to the group, met Gwen's gaze, got her nod.

"How do I wake up Lulu Bell?" I asked him.

"Who?"

"The sorcerer. The one your minion fireballed at the street fight in Hyde Park. Information, or you leave here a lot less conscious than you came in."

His laugh was chummy. "You have the wrong idea here. We were just on a nice boat ride, and you bust in with talk about an arrest."

"Demon ash all over your possessions," Gwen said blandly, as if repeating this fact for the third or fourth time. "And a confession from your associate, Mr. Azod, that you instructed him to kill Felix Buckley. You also instructed him and a demon named Menzos to kill the two humans at Mr. Buckley's warehouse and plant a bomb. Payback is a bitch."

"I didn't," Dante said. "It's a conspiracy against me." He looked at me with bald accusation in his eyes. "She's out to get me."

Gwen rolled her eyes. "Try again."

He looked around for support, but all his colleagues were down. He might've tried magic, but seemed to realize that human weapons might do significant damage to him first. So he loosened his tongue.

"The ley lines have gone crazy. And they're making us do horrible things."

Gwen glanced at me. "Do you think they brought this garbage from New York?"

"Maybe that's the reason he left," I said. "Knew the NYPD was sick of his flimsy excuses."

"Look, I'm not saying we haven't made some mistakes," Dante said, "the ley lines being what they are—"

Gwen ignored him. "I think he's the one that put down all those demons at the empty lot."

"The upstart did that," he insisted.

"The person with no name who you've never seen?" Gwen shook her head. "I'm not buying that excuse. I wonder if the Feds' new buildings can actually suck the magic right out of demons like him. Or maybe they'll just bind him, so he can do their bidding for a few millennia."

"No Gold Coast condo," I said. "No more life of luxury."

"They were my demons!" Dante said. "Why would I kill them?"

"Who were they fighting?"

"The upstart!"

Gwen and I rolled our eyes. She gestured to the windows. "The Feds are waiting. Let's just take him in."

"Okay, maybe one of my people killed Buckley, but he wasn't a nice guy. Do you know what he ran through that port?"

"Ceramic angels," I said, and suppressed a shiver at the memory. "You had the warehouse blown, remember? We saw what was in the crates."

"That wasn't me. I wasn't there."

"Your people were," Gwen said, and moved her finger in a circling let's-wrap-this-up gesture.

"Tell me how to wake up my friend," I said, "and maybe I can pull some strings."

I saw the fire in his eyes and knew he wasn't going to surrender. Going gently into that good night wasn't demon style. Especially not this demon. And he intended to go out with a bang.

"Incoming!" I called out as sulfur and magic mixed in the air. I shoved Gwen down, pivoted to face Dante, and had my sword out when he sent the first volley of magic.

I angled the blade toward the fireball, which struck the steel, bounced, split, and did no damage to anyone I cared about.

"You're done," I said. "You want to help yourself, you'll tell us everything you know about the upstart."

He pulled residual magic into himself with such intensity that he lifted a breeze in the room. I wasn't sure what he intended to do, but I didn't think our magical pretreat was going to be strong enough to resist it.

"Get out!" I told Gwen and the others, and braced myself to take on whatever he was preparing, because I wasn't going to let him spread it over the mortals.

Dante lifted his hand, his power strong enough to warp the air above his fingers. I locked my knees and held up my sword . . . and then a single shot rang out.

It took too long to register what I'd seen, what I'd heard. What had happened. And by then Dante was slumped on the floor, blood pooling from the hole in his chest.

I looked back. The nervous cop, face now pale, still held his gun in two shaking hands.

"Gwen, deal with him!" I said, and turned back to Dante. I ripped his shirt open, but the arterial blood was pumping from the wound in spurts.

"No," I said. "No. You will not die."

His grin, now bloody, was ferocious. "Not worth it," he said, and went still.

I hit my knees, blood ringing in my ears as I stared at the trail of blood slicking its way across the floor.

How would we get Lulu back now? How would we save her when the only demon who had the answers was dead on the goddamned floor a few feet away? How would I tell my mother?

Was Lulu supposed to be a sacrifice? The cost of Chicago with one less demon?

Because that was unacceptable.

I'd bring Dante back to life if that was what it took. Maybe

Mallory could do it. Or Catcher. Or I'd figure out how to go back in time, toss the damn gun overboard. Or further back and I'd keep Lulu from working on the mural the night of the demon attack.

I didn't know how long I kneeled there as people moved around me, rounding up the minions, who'd become aimless and slow now that their master had been slain. They'd be sent to the Feds' facility, never to be seen again.

I surged to my feet, grabbed one of the demons by the lapels. "One of Dante's minions put someone in a coma. How do I bring her out of it? How do I fix her?"

His gaze was vacant, glassy, and he didn't so much as shift at the sound of my voice. I shook him violently until a hand was on my arm.

"Elisa."

Gwen, beside me, removed my fisted hands from the demon's clothing. "This isn't the way."

I slid my gaze to the nervous cop, who was standing in a corner, his face now gone faintly green and regret plain in his eyes. And I remembered when I'd killed the demon who'd spelled Lulu, and I couldn't bring myself to blame that cop for his response to a potential onslaught of demon magic.

Gwen must have seen my grief. She sighed. "Just hang on, Elisa. We'll get this figured out. I swear it."

I hoped she was right.

As we rode back to the shore, I was numb, sitting alone on a bench seat in the coast guard boat. With my head in my hands, I tried to figure out what to do next. Time passed, and then we reached the shore, and I had no memory of the ride itself. I stepped onto land, nearly stumbled to the ground, stupid with grief.

I heard my screen buzz, squeezed my eyes shut. I knew it

would be Aunt Mallory asking if Dante had given us instructions for waking Lulu up. Instead of a solution, I had to give a mother her nightmare. I considered just tossing the screen into the lake instead. But I did the right thing and pulled it out.

Found not a call but a single short message.

SHE'S AWAKE.

SEVENTEEN

I left the booking to Theo, Gwen, and the Feds, and took an Auto to Hyde Park. I was out of the vehicle before it stopped. I left the door open behind me, and I ran toward the House. This time, even monster was wise enough to try to tamp down its frenetic excitement.

I waved a hand at the security desk, took the stairs two at a time. I nearly slipped to my knees when I took a corner at a speed too fast for hardwood. My mother reached out an arm before I drifted into her like a Japanese street racer.

"You run like your mom when she smells barbecue," Uncle Catcher said with what I was pretty sure was a smile.

"You can look in," Aunt Mallory said, "but she's sleeping."

That had me tensing again. "Sleeping?"

"She woke up, said hi, said she really needed a nap, and fell asleep," Mom said.

"But how do you know she's not—"

Before I could finish the question, a snore louder than a river monster's roar—which was a comparison I could use now—issued from the room, even with the door closed.

"Never needed a baby cam," Uncle Catcher said. "We just listened for that."

Mom looked alarmed. "That was really loud. You're sure she can breathe?"

"It's not respiratory," Aunt Mallory said, putting a comforting hand on my mom's arm. "The doctors thought it was related to her dreams. Maybe some kind of communication."

I'd heard her snore, but she didn't do it often and never loud enough that I'd worried about her breathing. But it was very Lulu to turn her dreams into a vehicle for artistic expression.

"Speaking of pizza," Mom said, "why don't we get some food? It's been a long night, and her body probably needs a reset. Let's give her a little time before waking her up again."

It had been hours since I'd eaten, and food sounded amazing.

But we hadn't been talking about pizza.

The Cadogan House cafeteria wasn't your average plastic-tray-and-casserole type of place. There were fast-food options, but the House's head chef, Margot, made sure there were fancier and healthier options, too, including an ample supply of bottled blood.

The cafeteria served two meals per night in the summer months when evenings were short, and three in the winter when nights were long and we could be active longer. Tonight's choices ran the gamut from salmon and roasted brussels sprouts to club sandwiches.

Feeling at least a little victorious, I opted for the latter, and had no reason to be shy about drinking blood here. That was definitely a benefit of growing up in a vampire house; I might've felt like an outsider because of monster, but never for my fangs.

Aunt Mallory had opted to wait upstairs with Lulu; I guessed she wanted a bit of quiet. Mom, Uncle Catcher, and Dad, who'd joined us after wrapping up a meeting, sat with me at a table.

I managed one bite of my sandwich before my screen rang. I

found a message from Connor: DEMONS CORRALLED. HEARD
LULU AWAKE AND DANTE DEAD. DINNER WITH SWIFT AT HQ, THEN
HOME. STAY SAFE.

He was safe. Everyone I loved was safe, at least in this beautiful, singular moment. Which did great things for my appetite.

"How's it going with the wards?" I asked.

"They're crap," Uncle Catcher said.

Well, maybe not singularly safe. But pretty safe, at least.

"Paige got the crack in the broken cornerstone mostly healed,
so we spent most of the night trying to reestablish the cornerstone–
ley line link. Nothing worked. It might be easier if we had a manual, but even then . . ." He shrugged, ate a forkful of kale. For
some reason.

"They were built on the fly," I said. "No sorcerers in Chicago,
so the Guardians used whatever magic or spells they could cobble
together. Kind of a miracle they lasted this long."

"Very much so," Uncle Catcher said. "And I know what it's like
to magic under pressure. So I don't fault them for the effort. But
the magic is the Victorian equivalent of duct tape and crossed
fingers."

"The machine is well-built," I said, feeling defensive on Hugo's
behalf.

"Not magic," Uncle Catcher pointed out. "Amazing crafts-
manship but built by human hands. Or at least with human tech."

"So, what do you do, then?"

Mom and Uncle Catcher shared a glance that said they'd discussed the answer to that question.

"We have to talk to Roger and the mayor," Mom said.

"But if they're good with it, we scrap the entire system," Uncle
Catcher said.

I stopped midbite, put the triangle of sandwich on my plate. A
piece of bacon bounced out, as if relieved by last-second reprieve.

"Scrap it?" I asked. "Like, no more demon wards?"

"Demon wards," Uncle Catcher continued. "But not like this. A single integrated system rather than a piecemeal mess."

"How?" my dad asked, cutting a slice of pizza with a knife and fork. Because Dad.

"Bubble," Uncle Catcher said. "Or at least that's how we're conceptualizing it." He glanced at me. "You heard about the Feds' technology—with a shifting matrix that absorbs magic?"

I nodded. "And that it's dangerous and not fully tested."

"Yeah, we aren't going to use it per se," he said. "But I was intrigued by the idea. Part of the problem with the old system is that it's not limited to bad acts—namely, doing demon magic. It's triggered by demons who could, at least theoretically, not be assholes."

"Spike and Angel," Mom offered, and Uncle Catcher nodded.

"Do I know them?" I asked, and the look the three of them— family all—gave me could have frozen water.

"I have failed you as a parent," Mom said, shaking her head.

Buffy the Vampire Slayer," Dad said with a smile. "I don't think you liked that show."

"Oh, you're talking about the not-quite-bad guys in the screen show," I said. "Right."

"The point is," Uncle Catcher continued, "we judge the sin and not the sinner. A bubble protects the city against demon magic, with several fail-safes."

"And a manual," I said. "Please, don't forget the manual."

He smiled. "Naturally. The bubble will be magical, so, yeah, it could potentially be vulnerable to attack. But with a good manual, future sorcerers can easily recreate it, strengthen it. The system would be stable. Without ghosts, animal statuary, or river monsters required."

"How long?" I asked. "If the mayor says yes."

"That's the best part," he said, leaning forward. "Between me,

Mallory, Paige, and the strength of the ley lines, I'm pretty sure we could have it in place tomorrow."

The door to Lulu's room was open when we went back upstairs; Aunt Mallory was sitting on the edge of Lulu's bed. Lulu was sitting up, looking better rested than she had since I'd returned to Chicago.

Relief flooded me and filled my eyes with tears.

I waited in the doorway while Uncle Catcher rushed in, gave them time to be together.

"You did good," Dad said.

"I didn't do that," I clarified. "It must have been Dante's death—that must've released his minions' pending magic. And I didn't kill him."

"You gave them hope," Mom said. "You kept Mallory calm, because she believed you when you said you'd fix it. You took the steps that got us here."

I nodded, appreciating the gesture. "Team effort" was all I could manage to say.

Mom snickered, looked at Dad. "She is your daughter."

"Talented and humble?" Dad asked with a grin as he leaned against the wall, arms crossed.

"Goal oriented," Mom said, smoothing a hand over my hair. "And not entirely happy when she doesn't meet those goals, even if the outcome is still good."

I had no defense against that, because she was exactly right. There was a reason Connor had called me "brat" growing up.

"She's all yours," Aunt Mallory said, eyes red from joyful tears, as she and Uncle Catcher stepped into the doorway. Then she surprised me by embracing me, squeezing tight. "Thank you," she said quietly, then wiped her cheeks when she pulled back. "Go talk to her."

"Go ahead," Mom said, and I walked in, sat down on the bed.

Lulu watched me with careful consideration—she was well rested—and seemed to be waiting for me to say something.

I felt monster edge out a toe, preparing to pounce, when I shut it ruthlessly down. *Not tonight,* I told it. *It's nearly dawn and she just woke up.* I was reaching the limit on reasonable excuses, and I worried what monster might do if it wasn't released. But even if I accepted the possibility that it would have to be released at some point, this wasn't the time.

"You're crap at charades," Lulu said, breaking the silence.

"That was real? I wasn't sure."

"Of course it was. I couldn't speak—something to do with the magic—but I could move, which I tried to do with you. You have a lot of stress dreams."

The words came out quickly, like she'd been holding them in the entire time she'd been asleep.

"I do," I agreed. "Are you feeling okay?"

"Fine," she said. "I mean, I feel well rested, but also like I just had four double espressos and want to sleep for a week. I'm sure that's just an adjustment."

"We didn't know how to wake you up, and I was freaked out. I was angry and scared"—I paused—"and the demon that spelled you was about to unleash another fireball."

"You killed him?" she asked quietly, and squeezed my hand when I nodded.

"We managed to corner Dante, but he wouldn't tell us anything. And then he was killed in the op."

"Aristocrats and their minions have a weird relationship," she said. "Some kind of magical symbiosis. Dante probably could've broken the spell if he'd wanted to."

I nodded. "I think I might have been close at the end, but then a literal shot was fired. Did your parents tell you about the river monster?"

"Yeah. Did it really try to eat you?" She picked at her blanket, fingers nervously working the fabric with that excess of energy.

"Not exactly. But the spitting out was one hundred percent accurate."

"Hate that I missed that."

"Alexei was here a lot," I said. "He and your parents took turns on Lulu duty."

A flush rose high on her cheeks. "Yeah, Mom mentioned that."

"I guess you two are officially an item now."

"Let's not go crazy," she said, but looked like she found that idea very agreeable.

"What were the charades about, anyway?"

"Huh? Oh. Sorry. My brain is everywhere at once." She closed her eyes, squeezed them. Opened them again after a moment. And when she did, there was alarm in her expression. She grabbed my hand. "Shit, the demon. Dante."

"What about him?"

"He was at the Hyde Park battle when I was working on the mural. Or right before." She tapped the side of her head with a fingertip as if trying to settle some pieces in a place.

"Dante? No, he wasn't there."

"Before you got there," she said. "I didn't know it was him, but one of the cops showed us a picture after they got us out of the alley, and I recognized him."

That confirmed, if posthumously, that Dante had been aware of the attack before it happened and had probably set some of it in motion. Maybe he'd gone back when it was over, and that's when he'd gotten the copper ash on his shoes. But I couldn't think how we could use that information now.

"Okay," I said. "I'll add that to his file. Maybe it will lead us somewhere."

"No," she said. "No. That wasn't it. That wasn't the important part."

She let go of my arm, closed her eyes again, went back to kneading the blanket. For a good minute she sat like that, working to straighten out her memories.

And then her eyes popped open. And I didn't like what I saw in them.

"Ariel's boyfriend. No, ex-boyfriend."

"Jonathan Black?"

"Him!" she said. "Him. He was there, too. At the mural building."

I thought she must've been confused. "He was there?"

"Yeah, and he was talking to Dante. He was arguing with Dante?"

I wasn't sure if the buzzing in my blood was anger or confusion, but I guessed that the buzzing was likely to continue for a while. "What were they talking about?"

"Demons," she said, frowning as she looked away. "Something about demons and . . . Oh! They were arguing about the cornerstone."

Just before she'd been hit, Lulu had told me she needed to talk to me about something, and there'd been worry in her eyes. I'd thought she'd been hit accidentally, maybe because the demon had been aiming at me.

But maybe I'd been wrong. Maybe the demon who'd shot her had heard what she said. And maybe they'd taken aim at her.

I was running out of Cadogan House a moment later, my Auto already on the way. I reached the sidewalk as it reached the curb, and I jumped inside. It was already programmed for Black's Prairie Avenue house. I wasn't sure what I'd find there, but I knew I'd find something.

Black had known the cornerstone had been destroyed before we did. How? Because he'd been involved? Because a demon to whom he had some connection—maybe the person who'd hurt him—had done it? If so, why hadn't he just told us? Did he think that was too dangerous, or did he want to ride that wave of power?

I half-thought I'd find him dead inside the mansion, with the front door left open by the upstart so I could confirm what she'd done and that she had the power to do it. And I'd still have no leads.

I closed my eyes, put my head back, and tried to think.

The upstart was powerful, a demon with her own minions and the ability to destroy them if she wanted.

"Why hasn't she shown her face?" I asked quietly.

"Showing face," Auto said, and I opened my eyes to find an animated assistant had appeared on the windshield.

"Hi. I'm Karen. How can I help?"

"You can't. Go away."

"Goodbye," it said, and blinked off again.

And unlike Karen, I thought, our upstart wasn't graceful in defeat. Not when she was incinerating dead demons.

The Auto rolled to a stop. I climbed out, closed the door, and, as I surveyed the house, imagined Karen giving me the middle finger as the vehicle drove away.

I walked up the sidewalk. The house was dark (again), and the front door wasn't cracked open. There was no sign anyone had forced their way inside. I put an ear to it. Heard nothing.

I checked the door, found it locked. I very seriously considered breaking it open, but I didn't want to jeopardize the CPD's work by screwing up any evidence that might be in there. So I walked down the steps and, for the second time this week, stalked around to the back of Black's house.

A light was on in the carriage house, the windows aglow with it.

I stuck to the shadows, crept toward it. And felt monster's sudden alarm a millisecond too late.

Something hit me in the back—big and solid. I hit the ground and rolled, and found myself staring up at a demon. He was short and square of build, and all of him looked to be muscle. He had a humanoid face, but with squat, squarish features. The short black horns left no question about his demonic origins.

But I couldn't feel his magic; there was no sourness in the air. Why not?

He lifted his weapon—a literal two-by-four—to strike me again. I rolled onto my back and, when he came down to strike, kicked out and up. I didn't quite hit my ultrasensitive target, but he was surprised enough by the move that he dropped the lumber, shifted to the side.

I could feel monster's sudden and sharp rising energy now, and I wasn't sure why it was agitated. Not, I thought, because of the demon, who had some moves, but seemed to be another minion. But I didn't have time to think about it.

I took advantage of the demon's loss of balance and jumped back to my feet, then spun into a kick that had the demon flying back. He fell to the ground, grunted, stood up.

"Not so fast," I said, unsheathing my sword and advancing. I had him on the ground in two swipes, and this time, he didn't get up.

Monster was still itchy, and I looked around and found Jonathan Black in the square of light cast by the carriage house.

"Good to see you alive," I said, carefully wiping the blade of my sword. But I didn't resheathe it. Not yet. "You're a hard man to find."

Black stared back at me with an unreadable expression.

Careful, monster said. And I trusted its judgment, even if I didn't understand the situation.

"Since you're walking around your own property, I guess I don't need to ask if one of your clients is holding you hostage." I gestured back to the demon on the ground. "What the hell is going on?"

"You have something that doesn't belong to you."

I blinked at him. The sword was the only thing I had. "What?"

He strode toward me, and I raised my sword, kept it aimed at his heart, and decided to skip the preliminaries.

He didn't look like a man who'd been held hostage or forced to do things against his will. He looked angry, and rage boiled in his magic, which felt different from how it had in the past. Newer somehow. More vibrant but less clean.

So I skipped the preliminaries.

"How did you know about the broken cornerstone?" I asked him.

He watched me for a moment, ignoring the sword pointed at his heart. "Because I fucking broke it."

I stared at him. "What? Why would you do that?"

"Because it was time."

He tilted his head at me, and although I couldn't feel his magic, I knew he was using it. Partly to search me for the thing he thought I had, and partly to hide his magic. He'd done it before. Had he been the reason I couldn't feel the demon's magic? If so, what kind of game was he playing?

"Time for what?" I asked.

"For a change in Chicago."

Goose bumps rose on my arms as he dropped that curtain, and magic filled the air. And I couldn't distinguish between the earthy potency of his elfish magic and the peppery bite of the sorcery I'd never seen him use. And over it all, the sourness of demon magic.

Instinctively, I looked around, thinking the power was spilling from a hoard nearby. But we were alone.

"What have you done?" I quietly asked. "Did you make a deal with them?" A nearly literal deal with the devil.

"I didn't need a deal with them. I used them, because that's why they exist: to be used by someone more powerful."

"Are you working for the upstart?"

He blinked. "What?"

"Dante's competitor. The demon who hurt you, it was trying to take over Chicago. Was that your client?"

"That's what he calls her?" Black muttered. "I didn't know that." Then he settled his gaze on me again. "None of you get it."

"Because you've been refusing to talk," I pointed out. "So, enlighten me."

"I broke the cornerstone. I opened the door for the demons, because it was time I got mine. Dante was worthless. A thug who thought he was entitled to the triangle." He put a hand on his chest. "My triangle."

"Triangle," I murmured, and thought of the symbol Claudia had made with her fingers. "You're talking about Chicago? Because the ley lines cross here?"

"What else?"

I stared at him. "You're saying *you* were Dante's competitor? You're the upstart?"

He pulled out his screen, swiped fingers across it. And a woman's voice filled the air. *This is my city, my turf. I claimed it first. If you want to fight, we will. But I have powerful friends.*

While I stared at him, he turned his screen off, put it away. "Deepfake," he said. "Very easy to set up."

"You killed the demons at the empty lot. And you sent us the address because . . ." He waited while I thought it through. "Because you found the note from Dante and wanted us to know he'd killed Buckley. And think he'd killed the demons."

"They were uncooperative" was all he said about the many dead.

"Why so secretive? Why not show Dante who you were?"

"The time wasn't right," he said cryptically.

That one took me a second. "Because he was more powerful than you," I said. "Because you aren't a demon, and you knew he wouldn't agree to you being in charge."

He rushed me, faster than I've ever seen a supernatural move; he pushed my blade aside, pushed me down. I hit the ground, rolled, came up, sword pointed.

This one's on me, I told monster. *Feel free to jump in if you want to play.*

But as Black and I circled each other, monster stayed down. After so much indiscretion, why was it afraid now? Even if Black thought I had unusual power, he couldn't know who or what monster was.

"It's mine," he said, reaching for me.

I jumped aside, barely avoiding his hand, and sliced back with my blade. He turned, grabbed the wrist of my sword arm, twisted.

The pain was hard and sharp. I hung on until tears rose, but the sword fell from my shaking fingers, hit the ground.

He released me, and I kicked, trying to push it out of his reach. But he put a foot over the blade before I could reach it, and that had me scrambling back. He was dangerous enough on his own, much less with a honed blade in his hands.

"It's my right. My due."

That sounded like an elf thing. "Due from whom?"

There was a story here, but he was giving me only the dangling threads of it, and that wasn't enough to make sense of what he was saying.

That question seemed to enrage him. He flipped my sword into the air, caught it, wrapped his fingers around the handle. Then pointed the blade at my heart.

"Give it back," he said.

"I don't have anything of yours!" I yelled out the words, putting magic behind them. But that was the wrong thing to do.

Black opened his mouth, screamed out fury that rose like a column of boiling magic into the sky. And then he lowered his gaze back to me. "I was never one of you. Even with Ariel. Never quite enough."

I scrambled to my feet and moved backward. I didn't like backing away from him—or anyone else. It felt cowardly. But I knew I was outmatched and I'd need more strength to beat him.

"It's my turn," he said. "I've waited long enough."

His eyes bright with power, he held my sword horizontally in front of him. And he snapped the blade in two.

Because I'd tempered that steel with my own blood, I felt the shock of magic like needles in my bones. I clutched my chest, the pain not really there, but just as keen. Then he tossed the shards to the ground, the blade going flat and dull as the power seeped away.

Where had this strength—enough to allow him to snap magicked steel in half with his bare hands—come from?

He reached out a hand, and the earth shook, dirt rippling as he used it to pull me toward him. I turned to run, but the ground rebelled again, growing up into a mound that tripped me and sent me sprawling. I rose to my knees, crawled over cold earth, but it moved like a treadmill beneath me, and I felt him getting closer.

Down! Monster warned, and I went flat as that damned board whistled overhead. I should've splintered it when I'd had the chance.

I kicked, caught Black's shin, and was relieved by his grunt of pain. The board came down again, and I rolled to the side, then onto my back and aimed the heel of my boot at it. I put as much strength as I could muster into the strike. The board cracked, the sound splitting the darkness.

Black just tossed the pieces aside, and before I could evade him, he grabbed the front of my shirt and hauled me high enough that my toes didn't touch the ground.

He stared at me, nostrils flaring and teeth bared, and I had to work to keep the fear down. But I wasn't giving up to him— whatever he had done—without a fight. I put my arms between his, pushed, broke his hold, and dropped back to my feet. I aimed a right hook, but he caught my fist, tossed it away with force enough to have me stumbling backward. He grabbed my other wrist, twisted my arm back and up. Pain was a red-hot flare.

"Give it to me."

"I don't have *anything*," I said through the automatic tears triggered by the searing pain. With my arm caught, I tried to use the rest of my body. I stomped at his foot, but he avoided me; a kick to his shin made contact.

With a roar of fury, he released my arm, pushed me back against the building. I hit it, my wrist and shoulder singing in relief, but I knew that pain would be back.

I turned as quickly as I could, and a spinning kick caught his chin, had his head snapping back. He was stronger now, but he wasn't a trained fighter. He caught himself before falling, then reset and came in with fury. I spun away just as he hit the carriage house, one of its walls cracking from the impact. I tried a crescent kick this time, but he grabbed my ankle, twisted. I hit the ground hard again, grabbed a handful of dirt, and, when he tried to roll me over, tossed it into his face.

He screamed, threw out a blind backhand that had my head

snapping to the side, and I knew the pain would suck in the milli-second before it registered. But that was only the beginning. I was still down and vulnerable, and he kicked me hard in the side.

I nearly lost my breath from the shock. Another kick had me rolling into a ball—his moves were so fast, I could barely defend myself. And I wondered if this was how I was going to die.

I heard screaming, thought it was me, realized it was sirens. Cops. Someone had called the CPD.

Their approach made Black pause, and I took the opportunity I'd been given, scissored my legs between his. I twisted and had him tumbling to the ground.

It took two pitiful tries to get to my feet, but I managed to do so just before being blinded by brilliant white lights.

And I felt him before I could see him.

"Connor," I said before falling again. A door opened and then he was near me, catching me before I hit the ground.

"Black," I said. "Tell the CPD to find Black."

Because I knew he was already gone.

"You could have called me," Connor said when we were in the town house and I was in a hot bath to soothe the aches.

"Someone did call you," I pointed out, sinking down to my chin in fragrant bubbling water. "Thanks for the rescue."

Connor sat on the floor beside the beautiful copper tub, legs stretched in front of him, arms crossed. "Black is the upstart?"

"Supposedly, he's the one who's been acting as the upstart. But I don't get it. The upstart has minions. How could he control de-mons or convince them to follow him? We're missing something."

"We'll find him," Connor said.

But that wasn't the thing that worried me. "He broke my sword in half," I said. "I'm not strong enough to fight him even when we do."

"We'll get you another weapon," he said. "And you won't fight him alone. You'll get the sorcerers together—"

"Even then, I don't know," I said. "I still feel like he's holding back."

"You think that he's controlled by someone, that you're only getting a sample of their magic?"

I shook my head. "I thought maybe a client had his leash, but not anymore. I think this is all him. And where did his power come from? How did he get it so suddenly?"

"And what's the thing of yours that he wants?"

I let silence follow that question for a moment. "It has to be monster, doesn't it?" I quietly asked.

"But why?" Connor asked. "Maybe he's confused it with some sort of elf magic? He's half-elf, and your mom was kidnapped by elves, wasn't she?"

"Along with your uncle Jeff, yeah. But that was before I was born. I don't know why he'd think monster was elvish."

"Feeling that you have unique magic might be enough," Connor said.

"He's power hungry," I said quietly. "He'd have heard about Sorcha, about her strength and the fact that she nearly took control of the city. Maybe he thinks I have some of her magic. That's technically correct, given she made the Egregore. But how would he know that? Sorcha was killed nearly a year before I was born."

"He doesn't have to know its source," Connor said. "And given the timing, he might have concluded it was related to the Egregore. Maybe he's made a posthumous mentor out of her. You should check with your parents, just in case they know something. And warn them."

"I know. And I will."

"We'll get him."

Silence fell, and I dropped my head back, closed my eyes. "If he wants monster, we can't tell Lulu or anyone else. And we can't put it back into the sword. Not until he's put away. Or put down."

I felt monster's immediate anger, immediate grief.

It's for you, I silently told monster. *I swear it.* "If he thinks Lulu knows, he'll hurt her."

"And if monster's in an object, it would be easier for him to take."

I nodded. "Puts me in one hell of a position. And monster, too. I was worried about having to tell Lulu. Afraid of what she'd think of me when I confessed what monster was. Now I can't let it out, and that doesn't feel any better."

Connor blew out a long, slow breath. "I don't like him."

That lifted a corner of my mouth. "I'm aware. Tell me about Kieran Swift."

"He's okay," Connor said. "Seems genuinely interested in helping with demons, even if that's not his only reason for being here. Secondary reason at best."

"Everyone is obsessed with you, puppy."

He snorted.

"Did he conclude you're a stand-up guy?"

"He concluded he doesn't like chewing on demons, Goose Island root beer is legit, and I'm not an asshole."

"I concur with the last two. No experience with the first one. But I'd guess . . . sour milk?"

"Up the vile meter ten or fifteen notches, and you're there." He grinned. "But chasing them was a hell of a lot of fun."

"Are they Black's minions?"

He sat up a little, looked at me. "I don't know. They didn't say. They looked like they were— I don't know the right term."

"Free agents?"

He smiled. "That works. They looked to be in control of them-

selves. I'm not sure if that's better or worse than their being led—
or misled—by Black. And you're right," he added after a moment.

"Usually yes. But in particular?"

"I don't see him leading self-centered demons. What would
they possibly think is in it for them?"

That was the million-dollar question.

"Move over," he said, standing up.

"What?"

By way of answer, he stripped off his shirt, bearing stacked
muscles under taut skin. And then his hands were at the button
on his jeans.

"No way," I said with the laugh. "This tub is way too small for
two people."

"Let's test that," he said, and stepped into the water.

EIGHTEEN

Dusk had us getting the gang back together or, more specifically, ensuring that the city's resident sorcerers—Lulu and Paige—had a protected space to work with the out-of-towners—Lulu's parents—on their "bubble ward."

Lulu looked, TBH, amazing. Pink cheeked and bushy tailed, and not just because of the gumiho plush pinned to the messenger bag she'd paired with jeans and a striped long-sleeved T-shirt. She had reportedly eaten two bagels and a mess of hot-sauce-covered eggs for breakfast, much to Alexei's joy and amusement, him being an aficionado of all things spicy.

He, Connor, and Kieran Swift had also joined us. Swift looked well rested after last night's demon hunt and barbecue dinner. "And visiting every bar still open near the Keene house," Connor had told me; Swift had been invited to stay with the family, being shifter royalty and all.

With the mayor's approval, the sorcerers had picked Grant Park as the spot to kindle the new ward. It was well within city limits, easy to access, and defensible from the lake on the east side. A demon would have to get past the actual bubble in order to get to the place where its magic had been first kindled. But unlike the Guardians' version, this ward wasn't tied to geographic features. So, even if the grass on which we stood was bulldozed, it wouldn't affect the bubble. Or so Lulu's parents had explained to me, Roger, Petra, Gwen, my mom, and two representatives from the mayor's office.

The wolves stood inside a circle of two dozen CPD uniforms and barricade tape. Four powerful sorcerers made quite a demon-friendly target, and we weren't taking chances. A human crowd was gathering outside the perimeter, but there was no hostile magic in the air. Not now, anyway.

My mom had brought me a sword from Cadogan House. It was perfectly fine, with a gorgeous Damascus pattern in the steel. But it wasn't mine, and it felt heavy and dead in my hand.

I couldn't dwell on that, because monster got twitchy if the concept of a sword even skidded through my mind. It was eager to get out, even as I worried its exit would leave the city even more vulnerable than it already was.

And something else was bothering me: Black had proved himself to be even more dangerous than I'd believed. I had no idea what he'd do next or how much magic he was capable of. If I couldn't defeat Black even with monster, how could I possibly defeat him without it?

"Are all the tags in place?" Uncle Catcher asked as the other Ombuds and I sipped from coffee cups and tried to stay out of the way. We were liaising and watching out for Jonathan Black. But if he felt this accumulation of magic, he hadn't shown his face yet.

"The pins were placed," Gwen confirmed with a nod, "per your very detailed instructions."

While the bubble wasn't tied to geographic generators, Uncle Catcher had given the CPD a map of spots to be "tagged" with spelled metallic spray paint. As he had now explained twice to the mayor's people, the tags were necessary only to give the bubble its initial parameters, like magical muscle memory. The paint would wear off, but the protection wouldn't be affected. If changes needed to be made later—if the city's boundaries changed dramatically—new marks could be placed.

Paige, who'd been a magical archivist for the sorcerers' union, would compile a manual with all the necessary information and documents. And that manual, in both paper and screen forms, would be stored in Cadogan House, with a backup held by the city.

"And remind us what will happen to the demons already inside city limits?" asked one of the mayor's people. "They won't be vaporized, right?" He looked up, apparently anticipating the risk of demon bits falling from the clouds.

"*Per my email,*" Uncle Catcher said, mimicking the bureaucrat's aggressive passive-aggressive tone, "the bubble won't affect demons already in town. It will keep demons from entering."

"That's our job, Miles," Gwen told the man. "But it will be easier to do that job without new demon arrivals."

Miles didn't look satisfied by the answer.

"One hundred percent chance he did not read that email," Theo murmured.

"He never does," Roger said quietly. "He prefers to complain that we're hiding information we've already provided. And when we point out that we already told him, he says we didn't send the message correctly or it was unclear or he wanted to be sure we understood what we planned to do."

I caught a whiff of something spicy in the air, and went on full alert. "Demons?"

"No, that's my drink," Petra said. "It's a PSL."

"Early for pumpkin spice, isn't it?" Roger asked.

"Yeah, but that's not what this is. Wrong kind of PSL. This is a Paranormal Spice Latte."

I didn't ask. Because that seemed best.

While the sorcerers got into position to cast the spell, Roger's screen buzzed. He pulled it out, glanced at the screen.

"Problem?" Theo asked at his frown.

"Another story about drama on Lake Michigan and in one of Chicago's 'finest neighborhoods,'" he said, scanning it. Then he muttered a curse. "And someone gave the reporter Black's name. Says he's a person of interest in the investigation."

"Not it," Theo, Petra, and I said simultaneously.

Roger looked up, considered. "I bet the mayor did it. She wants Chicago on the road to normalcy, and she can't do that if there's an ongoing territorial war. Dante is dead. Black is the hot new story. The faster he's caught, the better her approval rating."

I wanted to get Black under wraps even faster than she did, I bet. And it was entirely possible someone from her office had leaked his name.

"Still no sign of him," Roger said, then glanced at me. "But we'll find him."

"I know." And I hoped I'd have some idea what to do about him by then.

"Okay," Uncle Catcher called out. "We're ready to get started."

The sorcerers gathered together in an expanse of grass, each at a cardinal direction point, and facing inward. We'd made the same kind of circle when we'd sealed Rosantine. They each poured salt into the empty spaces between them, then began a series of hand gestures. The air glowed pale yellow with a complex magic that smelled a little bit citrusy, but layered with cedar and ocean water and something sweet.

Something pale and iridescent shimmered in the air between them.

A soap bubble. Or it looked like a soap bubble. It expanded, nearly touching the sorcerers as it filled the center of their circle. Then it grew to cover them completely. It would take about an hour for the bubble to move across the city, and we'd stay in place until it was done.

As the magic spread, I wished the Guardians could have been here to see the continuation of their efforts, and I wondered if they'd have been thrilled that their own system had lasted so long or irritated this crew was scrapping it.

And then the bubble's iridescent sheen wavered.

"Uh-oh," Petra said.

With a *pop* of pressure that made my ears ache, the bubble of magic literally burst. Somewhere across the park a wolf yelped in surprise at the noise. I wondered who it was and pitied what would probably be merciless teasing for that perceived show of weakness.

It began to rain glitter. We covered the lids of our coffee cups as we were dusted with the residue of the magic. The sorcerers regrouped—with Uncle Catcher stomping forward—to dissect the problem and plan for another start.

"I mean, it's not the worst thing that's come out of a failed demon ward," Theo said, raising his casted arm. "Exhibit A right here."

"And I didn't have to push an animal down a flight of stairs," I agreed.

While the sorcerers talked, Miles frantically swiped at his screen, apparently eager to report the failure to the mayor.

"Can we help?" Roger asked when Uncle Catcher approached us.

"No. Not an unexpected problem. Just an irritating one."

"What exactly was the cause of the failure?" Miles asked primly. "It will need to be included in the record."

Uncle Catcher squeezed the muscle in his jaw so hard, I thought he might crack a tooth. And then he stepped toward Miles. He was a big man—muscular and tall. Miles was short and lean, with only the political repercussions as a defense. But Uncle Catcher apparently remembered them, and he managed to unlock his jaw.

"We are developing a novel form of citywide demon ward without a spell or a schematic. The need for adjustments was expected. And we will use this run to calibrate and perfect the next one."

It was a perfectly politic answer, and I wondered if Aunt Mallory had been giving him lessons. Or maybe he had just learned the necessity as a professor. He probably had department chairs and deans to placate.

"Right," Miles said with an arrogant nod. "I thought as much."

Apparently unaware of the danger he was in, he dismissed the sorcerer who'd nearly pummeled him by returning his attention to his screen.

Uncle Catcher blinked in surprise, then turned on his heel and joined the sorcerers again.

"And so," Theo began in the voice of a nature documentarian, "the predator is swayed by the defensive dance undertaken by its prey, and it moves off into the night, hoping for a better hunt tomorrow."

Twenty minutes later, the sorcerers still hadn't started on round two, so we took a collective break.

"Can I talk to you for a sec?" Petra asked me.

"Of course. What's up?"

"It's about Black," she said. "I feel like I should apologize for not believing you."

I lifted my brows. "Believing me?"

"I mean, you had a vibe about him at the beginning, and I was all 'But he's so cute.' And in the meantime he's, like, plotting our general demise."

So many places to start on that one. "There was nothing to believe," I said. "Having a vibe doesn't mean there's anything actually wrong with him. It's just a matter of taste. And I've been wrong anyway; he saved my life after that, and he seemed to really care about Ariel."

"Right?" she asked with emphasis, her expression shifting from apology to confusion. "Do you think something happened to him?"

"What do you mean?"

"I don't know. Maybe something like how meeting an alien can totally screw up your worldview."

I didn't think aliens were at issue, but she did have a point. Black had gone from saving my life to trying to kill me and accusing me of theft.

"Maybe he was hiding it all along," I said. "I don't think he ever really liked me. But maybe there's more there. You said you looked into his background?"

"Yeah," she said. "But I didn't find much."

"Dig more," I suggested. "Find out whatever you can, especially about his clients and the people he's worked with. Maybe that will help us figure out what has pissed him off and how we can stop him."

And maybe there was one more trick up my very stylish sleeve.

"I need to take a ride," I said.

"Where to?" Petra asked.

"To collect on a debt."

Connor shifted back to human form and donned his clothes, and I explained my idea to Roger, and we left Swift in Alexei's care.

"Why are we doing this?" he asked, sounding very leery, which was understandable.

"Because we need answers. And we don't have a lot of sources. And depending on what Black has gotten himself into, we may not have a lot of time. Claudia owes me a favor."

"Which she'll try to sneak her way out of," Connor said, drumming his fingers on the steering wheel. He wasn't nervous, but on alert, which was also understandable. "You think he has something big planned."

"I think there's been a lot of magical foreplay. If he really wants to be supernatural king, or kingpin, of Chicago, wouldn't there be an enthronement ceremony at least?"

Giving voice to the possibility that Black had something big planned settled something inside me, because I realized that was the reason I was feeling so on edge. While Gwen thought demon fighting was her new forever gig, I was afraid we were heading toward a more cataclysmic conclusion.

Connor reached over, put a hand on mine. "One step at a time," he said. "That's all we have to do."

The trip to the fairy castle was rougher than it had been earlier in the week—literally. The road was missing chunks of asphalt, nearby apartment buildings had lost windows, and storefronts were boarded up. Chicago was looking more and more like a postapocalyptic landscape.

We saw no sign of Black or his magic—whatever that might be—as we crossed town. Not that we knew what to look for.

The fairy castle, either immune to demon destruction or protected against it, stood tall and stark against the sky. Torches had been lit, all the walls had been repaired, and when we climbed out of the vehicle, the air smelled of woodsmoke.

I took the lead on foot to the gate, where guards stood at attention. They made no move to stop us as we walked in, but a half dozen fae met us inside the gatehouse.

"We'd like to see her," I said.

The fairy in front—tall and gaunt and long haired—looked me over.

"She owes you a boon," he said after a moment. "You may attend her."

It was possibly the easiest entry we'd ever had into the fairy castle—at least among the times the fairies had been awake and sober.

Three of the guards took the lead as we moved into the keep; the other three stayed behind us. Boon or not, Claudia was taking no chances in these times.

We found her in the great hall, seated at the head of a long table. A dozen fairies, including a human handmaiden, attended her. A dozen more danced to the sounds of a flute and a stringed instrument—a lute, maybe?—their dance steps nearly silent on the rush-strewn floor.

We were led to the head of the table. A few fairy eyes were on us, but not those of the fairies in the empty spot in the room performing a kind of line dance. If they were bothered by what was happening in the world outside, they didn't show it. To the contrary, they looked happy and relaxed.

I felt monster's mild irritation and agreed with the sentiment. It was difficult not to feel envious of their party.

In addition to the handmaiden, who stood just behind the queen, a beautiful woman and an equally handsome man were seated on either side of Claudia; they took turns offering her grapes while she sipped from a goblet. Tonight Claudia's gown was a pale, frosted lavender strategically embroidered with violets and ivy. Her hair was braided and wound into a crown and studded with amethysts. With her hair up, she looked younger than she usually did, but no less formidable.

"Bloodletter," she said, pausing for a sip of wine, "you are impatient. You might have held your boon for a millennium."

"Chicago may not last that long."

"But the world will survive it," she said, drawing her gaze away from her apparent lovers to take a look at us. There was appreci-

ation in her eyes when she glanced at Connor and mild disappointment when she looked at me.

"I can make you as beautiful as we are," she said, "and improve
that dour clothing."

"She is beautiful," Connor said, and her smile went dim.

"The wolf has teeth," she said, and held out a hand, waved at
the carafes and bottles that filled the table. "You may drink from
my vessels."

I mean, come on. That wasn't even subtle.

"No, thanks," Connor said before I could decline on his behalf.
"Then you'd owe her another boon."

Claudia's eyes narrowed, but a caress from her female lover
had her relaxing again. So she was back to her normal, prickly
self.

"Ask," she said, turning her gaze to the dancers.

"How do we defeat the demons?" I opted for a broad question,
afraid a narrower one would result in a "Monkey's Paw"–type
answer. But I still missed the mark.

She rolled her eyes. "Demons will never be defeated. Not as
long as they are lured from their dimension by the furies and fol-
lies of humans."

"Then . . . how do I defeat Jonathan Black?"

She shook her head. "You ask questions predicated on knowledge you do not have. It is not a method that eludes you; it is the
information."

The information? We needed all sorts of it.

"Who does Jonathan Black work for?" Connor asked, and was
rewarded with a less pitying look.

"The wolf prowls closer. But I believe you know he works for
no one."

I had the urge to slap the goblet out of her hand for clearly having information we needed and demanding we play her game to get it. But she did it because she was fairy; there was no point in punishing her for that.

Since my temper—or monster's—was rising, I looked down, tried to think.

Black had been angry with me. Why? Because I'd interfered with his plans? Not just generally but because he believed I had something he was owed. Something he should've had.

So what was that thing?

No, I thought, that wasn't the important question. It mattered less what it was than why he believed he should have it.

I looked up at Claudia, found her gaze on me, curiosity dancing there.

"Who is Jonathan Black?" I asked.

She watched me a moment longer and then, almost imperceptibly, inclined her head.

"Read your history," she said. "And remember—sorcerers love fire."

We were escorted out of the hall after she made that pronouncement. And if those escorts had any idea what she meant, they didn't tell us.

"What do you think she meant by that?" I asked.

"That we need Petra."

I nodded. "I asked her to look into Black's history. Wasn't much there previously, but she's very good at digging."

My screen buzzed, and I found a message from Aunt Mallory: IT'S HEADING YOUR WAY.

"It?" Connor asked, glancing around for whatever threat that might have been.

We felt it, the shift in air pressure, the faint and quick scent of magic. I looked up, saw a brief iridescent shimmer. And then the world stilled again.

The demon wards were in place.

For a moment, standing in front of the vehicle in front of the fairy castle, I closed my eyes and let myself breathe.

We wouldn't know for sure if the defenses were fully operational until they actually repelled a demon trying to get through. But if they did, this was the first step toward normalcy.

My screen buzzed, and I answered the call. Heard only screaming at first and was afraid someone had been squished by the bubble, one new problem instantaneously replacing the other. But then I heard Lulu's voice.

"We did it! It worked!" The shouts must have been from her parents.

"We felt it! Congratulations."

"Thank you. We are stoked and hyped up and let's celebrate." And she kept talking before I could remind her of the problems we hadn't yet solved.

"Pizza," she continued. "I want a pie as big as a table. Meet us at Ralphio's in thirty."

Ralphio's was a Chicago dive famous for the size of its pizzas and the fact that it never closed. Although I wasn't sure how the demon apocalypse would affect their business hours.

"You're sure it's open?"

"Yep. I checked."

It wasn't near our loft, so I hadn't been there often. But we were celebrating Lulu, so at Connor's nod, I relented.

"We'll meet you there. But then it's back to work."

"Scout's honor," she said.

"You weren't a scout," I pointed out, but she'd already ended the call.

*   *   *

We were pulling into the gravel parking lot at Ralphio's when my screen signaled. I pulled it out and found the message I knew would come sooner or later.

BE PREPARED TO GIVE BACK WHAT YOU TOOK. IT'S ONLY A MATTER OF TIME.

It was sent from a screen account with its contact information blocked, so it was barely worth sending to the team. But I did so anyway, and I showed Connor the message.

"I have something to give him," he said darkly.

"Let's skip that, and go eat."

Connor leaned over and nipped at my ear, which sent amazing heat down my spine.

"Food now," I said. "But later, do that again."

Lulu, Alexei, and Kieran were stuffed into a corner booth in the restaurant's hazy light. The seating area was small, dark, old, and hot. The kitchen was small enough that the enormous oven was visible from every seat; the bustling staff wore jeans and vintage tees. But the smell was absolute heaven. Grease and meat and garlic and yeast, as they made their dough on-site every day.

"We ordered the kitchen sink," Lulu said as I slid into the booth beside her. Connor slid in beside me.

There weren't many others in the restaurant, and most were humans. They'd taken notice of our presence and watched us warily.

"Should we announce we aren't demons?" I wondered.

"Wouldn't help," Kieran said. "Conspiracy theorists are already yelling about the demon ward, how it's a government mind-control device."

"First the fluoride, then the demon ward," Lulu said, voice exceedingly dry. "What will the government do next?"

"Do you know how peaceful and quiet the city would be with

mind control?" I asked. "Zero crime. Fully educated populace. Everybody does their fair share."

"Or billionaires turn the rest of us into serfs," Kieran said grimly.

"You are the life of the party, Swift," I said.

His smile was thin. "You want optimism, stick to the NAC. You want hard realism, come out West."

Connor snorted, then smiled beatifically at the person who brought a plastic pitcher of water and a stack of red plastic cups.

"Water all around," the waitress said. "Anything else?"

We all declined. The kitchen sink—a pizza with literally everything they had on it—would take all the internal capacity we could spare.

"You guys don't party?" I asked Kieran after sticking the offered bendy straw into my drink. Because even a vampire needed to relax now and again.

"We have our moments," Kieran said. And didn't sound like he knew firsthand what a party actually involved.

"They're hippies," Alexei said, reading a drink menu to pass the time before the pizza arrived.

"We aren't hippies," Kieran said. There was no insult in his voice. Just a kind of polite logic. "We're conservationists."

"Burning Wolf creates tons of trash." This from Alexei again.

"Burning Wolf?" I asked.

"Burning Man without man," Connor said. He stretched out his legs beneath the table, one thigh against mine, my skin warming from the contact.

"Or celebrities," Kieran said. "Or endorsements."

"Or desert," Alexei said, looking up. "It's in Yosemite."

"Fancy," Lulu said.

"Very relaxed," Kieran countered. "And clean."

"We're just giving you crap," Lulu said. She had taken a kids' menu and was coloring over an outline of Chicago with enormous flowers.

I was getting the sense that either the Swift family were sticklers for the rules—something near my own heart—or his shifters were just different from those in the NAC.

Connor leaned over. "If you're thinking about defecting, brat, unthink it."

"Nothing to defect from," I said. "I'm not Pack."

Alexei snorted. Kieran cleared his throat. And I went on alert. I looked at Connor. "What?" I asked. "I'm not."

"You have alpha all over you," Lulu said, then glanced up. "Ooh, that would be a great band name—alpha all over you."

I had no idea how to respond to that, so I just kept looking at Connor. He was smiling at me, slow and easy and sexy.

"Explain," I said.

"I have alpha-level power," he said, and gave Swift a not-very-subtle look, a reminder of his aptitude for Apex of the NAC. And then he looked back at me. "You are mine and vice versa. My magic is stronger now. Strong enough to mark."

"To mark me?" I didn't like the canine sound of that.

"You're in the bubble of his protection," Lulu said. "You can't feel it? It's kind of obvious."

I shook my head. I hadn't felt it. But my magic had come from a mix of sources over the past few days. Was I so out of sync with my own body that I hadn't recognized Pack magic mixed with mine?

"And the Pack?" I prompted.

"Everyone else knows you're his, too," Swift said. "They've seen and heard it, and now they've felt it, too."

I shifted uneasily. Something about this scraped against my sense of independence, which had been feeling especially vulnerable this week. Before I could comment further, two of the waitstaff carried over the biggest pizza I'd ever seen in real life. It nearly filled the table, and it had Swift and Lulu scrambling to move napkin dispensers and cheese shakers out of the way.

I'd have sworn on my lifetime coffee card that the table groaned under the weight of the pizza.

"Careful," one of the waiters said. "It's hot. Enjoy!"

And they left us staring goggle-eyed at the sheer enormity of the thing. For a moment, there was only silence.

"I assume this is Alexei's order," I said, and glanced around. "Did you order some for us, too?"

Since he'd already taken a slice and was chewing near boiling cheese and toppings, a grin was his only response.

We had no room for plates, so we ate rectangular slices right off the pan.

"I hear you enjoy demon eating," I told Swift, eager to change the subject.

"I plead the Fifth," he said.

"No demons were actually ingested," Connor said. "They'd taste like dirty soap and sour pickles."

"Old milk and gasoline," Alexei said.

Swift shook his head. "Sauerkraut and charcoal."

"You guys have quite the palate," Lulu said, stirring her drink with a straw. "Paranormal gourmands."

"I think that would be my parents," I said.

"Truth," Connor said.

"So, not so much demon eating," I corrected myself, and eyed Swift speculatively. "Did you learn what you came here to learn?"

"It's been educational," he said after a moment. "But I'm not the decision-maker."

"And what decision would that be?" Connor asked.

Swift lifted his gaze to Connor, and they stared at each other for a moment. "Who to support as Apex."

Alexei sighed. "Not the Western's business."

Swift lifted his shoulder. "Like I said, I'm not in charge."

But he was the nephew of the current Apex, who had no children, if I remembered my Pack information correctly. That put him in the running for the position. That said, I didn't sense around him the type of power Connor now shone with. Maybe he hadn't yet come into his own.

"If you want to be," Connor said, leveling his gaze at Swift, "you'll need to learn when not to say shit like that."

Swift frowned. "You've been accommodating and honest. I'm just trying to do the same. I'm not in charge of the Western, and do I think this trip is insulting to the NAC? Maybe. But we share a long border, and it's not unreasonable he wants reassurance."

"You have it," I said. "You've seen him, and you know who he is."

Swift nodded, but his eyes told a different story. And he didn't look thrilled about that tale.

We ate and chatted, but I could feel Connor's gaze on me; he was checking my emotional temperature. When the pizza was demolished—shifters could do some damage to a meat-covered pie—and we separated to go to our respective vehicles, Connor pulled me aside.

"Do you want to hit me, yell at me, or feel extremely honored to be my fiancée?"

There was enough sheepishness in his voice that I didn't slug him. But it was close.

"I've experienced a lot of unrequested boundary violations this week," I said. "Not from you, but from monster and fairies and demon magic and a river monster. I guess I'm feeling a little vulnerable."

He leaned in. "Thank you for telling me that. And I'm sorry I didn't mention the magic before." He rubbed the back of his neck, smiled. "I assumed you could feel it, but apparently you can't."

I shook my head.

"It's there. Close your eyes."

I rolled my shoulders and did so, there in the parking lot beneath the single overhead light, and I heard the hum of moths attracted to its brilliance.

I let my senses expand from my body outward, and when my mind was open and aware, I turned back toward Connor. His magic felt bright, warm, peppery with earthy power. And beside it, in cool contrast, was my own, pale and iridescent. Monster was like a knot in the grain of it, a thick spot in the pattern.

"Look in a little more," he said, and I felt further, past vampire and Egregore to the shimmering edge of gold that nested inside it. Not my magic, but his. The Pack's magic mixed into my aura. It was there, even if I couldn't sense it right now without the extra effort.

I opened my eyes, found him watching me with just a tiny mode of worry.

"I feel like I've had spinach in my teeth all week and no one told me."

His expression flattened. "Pack magic is spinach?"

"In this analogy, yes." I breathed out, tried to focus my swirling thoughts. "I already feel like I'm on the verge of losing myself, because I don't know what I might be without monster. It's just a lot."

His brow furrowed. In worry, not in anger. But still . . . I could feel the gap between us now, like shining light through a cracked door.

"I just need time," I said.

"Okay," he said. "Let's go home." He unlocked the vehicle.

"I need to go to the office."

He met my gaze over the hood. "That's the first place Black will look. Have the Ombuds come to the town house if you want. I'm pretty sure he doesn't know where I live. And I'll feel better if I'm with you."

I wanted to argue, to reassert my sense of self, but he was right about all of it.

"Okay," I said, and climbed into the vehicle. And stared at that new edge of magic all the way home.

Lulu had already set out research materials—electronic and analog—by the time we returned. And Alexei was at the espresso machine preparing an array of drinks. They knew how to support an Ombud.

Gwen and Theo were in the field. Roger and Petra were at the office, but they'd secured the building and were comfortable there. While it was possible Black would look for me there, I didn't think he'd harm them if he found me absent. Not because he was kind, but he wouldn't see much benefit in it.

Petra had shared her demon identification chart with Lulu, and she was digging into their adventures in Chicago, in hopes it would lead us to Black's larger plan.

I was poring over the minimal background information Petra had been able to find on Black; even with her remarkable honey-badger-level extraction skills, there wasn't much. But I was distracted, and my brain kept returning to the extra magic I was carrying. I hadn't asked for either monster's or the Pack's, and I was feeling very conflicted about both.

Focus, I told myself, and turned back to my screen.

Black didn't have any social media, an office site, or a physical office location. There was no biographical information about him online other than a form he had completed to register a business—Black Consulting LLC. Frankly, it sounded like the kind of fake business mobsters would use to hide funds, but Black had no criminal record. Not even a speeding ticket, which was suspicious at best. I also found no reviews of his business from satisfied or furious customers, nothing about his family or life before Chicago. Jonathan Black was a ghost. And I concluded he'd wiped his online history.

I needed to think big picture. He had destroyed a cornerstone and allowed demons into Chicago because he thought the city needed a change. But he was a sorcerer, or at least he had sorcerer genetics in addition to elf genetics.

He was one hundred percent supernatural. So why hadn't we seen it before now?

"Is his magic broken?" I asked aloud to no one in particular.

Lulu, gummy worm hanging from her mouth, looked at me. "Who?"

"Black."

"Oh. I don't know." She bit the worm in half, chewed. "I haven't been around him much."

"He's used his power to hide his parentage—the fact that he's both elf and sorcerer. But until last night, I hadn't seen him actively use magic, much less magic of that magnitude. Could the fact that he had only one sorcerer parent have limited his skills? Or made them—I don't know—latent?"

"I don't know," Lulu said. "Possibly, depending how the elf and sorcerer magic mixed. But I don't know anyone else with that parentage to ask."

But we knew someone who knew Black.

"Do me a favor," I said. "Call Ariel. Ask her if she saw him use magic."

Connor, who was reviewing the other half of the demon incident reports, looked up. "What would that tell you?"

"I'm trying to find his motivation, because that might help us predict what's next. Two supernatural parents and limited usable magic were the motivation for, maybe, some rage."

"And a desire to get magic out of you," Connor said.

"Wait—what?" Lulu stopped, screen in hand, and looked at me. "What does that mean—that he's trying to get magic out of you?"

Connor's wince was nearly instantaneous, but I caught it.

And I lied. "I think it's related to his magic not working. He thinks he can take magic out of other people."

"Has he tried it on anyone else?"

"He didn't try it on me," I said. "He just keeps saying it."

She narrowed her eyes at me, but that was it. "Weird," she said.

"Yeah, I'm also confused."

Lulu watched me for another second before pulling out her screen, swiping. "Ariel," she said a moment later, putting the screen down with the speaker engaged. "I'm with Elisa and the wolves. We need to talk to you about Jonathan Black."

There was a pause. "What about him?" Ariel asked.

"Did he use magic?"

"What?"

"We're wondering if his magic is fully functional," Lulu explained. "Did you see him use it?"

"I mean, we didn't date for very long. But it was very . . . I guess you'd say human. We had dinner or went to a show or the Art Institute. He liked fancy."

I nodded. That checked out.

"I could feel that he was supernatural, although he didn't do magic. He didn't say it was broken or anything. Really, we didn't talk about magic much. He didn't want me to hang out with the coven. I didn't like that, but looking back . . ."

Ariel trailed off. Her discomfort was understandable, as her witchy friends thought killing supernaturals was the only way to stave off the upcoming apocalypse. Their leader was apparently correct about the end, if not the means.

"Although there was one weird thing," Ariel said.

"What weird thing?" Connor asked, stretching his arms over his head and giving us all a beautiful view of his prime biceps. It wasn't a purposeful tease; he didn't really need to try to be seductive. It was in every movement of his body.

Ariel paused. "He wanted to know if I could transmit magic from the deceased."

"Transmit magic?" I asked.

"Instead of communicating messages. He wanted to know if I could bring a dead person's magic into this world and give it to someone else."

"Did he say whose magic he wanted you to take?" I asked.

"We didn't get that far. I told him I couldn't do it. I don't think *anyone* could do it."

That had to be Sorcha. She was gone, and Black had wanted Ariel to transfer Sorcha's magic to him. Did he think that was the solution to his magical problems?

"Did he say why?" I asked.

"Just that it was a waste that magic couldn't be redistributed."

"Anything else?" Lulu asked.

"No," Ariel said. "I need to go. I have a client shortly."

"Thanks, Ariel," I said.

"Sure. Hey," she added, "be careful of him. He always seemed to be on the edge. Like he was waiting for something."

An opportunity, I thought. That was what he was waiting for.

We said our goodbyes, and I went back to my search. When I was out of ideas, I went back to the "clue" Claudia had given us.

"Sorcerers love fire" didn't mean anything specific to anyone I asked, other than the potential link to Chicago's Great Fire, which had been started by a sorcerer. But a sample size of one didn't make for a pattern.

I started by searching the exact wording. Few humans were

privy to the real source of the Great Fire, so at least I didn't have to wade through that. But I did have to wade through dozens of search results related to Rambath, the fire mage of Lyrfront, who was an expert in fire sorcery. In *Jakob's Quest*.

"Rambath," I said, testing the waters.

"Fire mage of Lyrfront," Connor said without looking up. Then he paused, met my gaze. "No way does Black play *JQ*."

"Because there aren't any sociopathic gamers?"

"I think he's mostly Elisa-pathic," Lulu said, then offered her bag. "Gummy worm?"

"I'm good."

"Gaming attracts all kinds," Connor said. "But *JQ* requires a lot of sacrifice and teamwork. I don't think he's the type."

"He's definitely a single-player type," Alexei agreed.

Dead end there, so I added "Chicago" to the search. And on the fourth page of the results, I found an article from nearly twenty years ago.

HOME OF ACCUSED SORCERER BURNS, read the headline. ARSON SUSPECTED.

That had me swiping and then screaming at a pay wall and uploading my credit information to pay for a thousand words that might be totally irrelevant.

And then I started reading, and it wasn't irrelevant at all.

And I kept looking and found more articles, and a story began to piece itself together.

"What is it?" I heard Lulu ask. "You're practically vomiting magic."

I held up a finger, holding her off until I got to the end of the article I was scanning. Then I looked up. "You are not going to fucking believe this."

NINETEEN

When Roger and Petra were dialed in (Theo was still in the field with Gwen), I told them the story.

Once upon a time, an evil sorceress named Sorcha Reed murdered her (equally evil) husband. She gathered up all of the hard and painful emotions that Chicagoans sent into the world every day, and she made those emotions sentient. She gave them physical form.

She called that creature the Egregore.

The Reeds had lived in a sprawling old mansion in the Prairie Avenue Historic District, the same neighborhood where Black now lived. Photos from before and after the fire showed flowers, balloons, and other mementos left by those who apparently worshipped (some literally) Sorcha or who hoped she might perform posthumous miracles. Proving, once again, that humans were deeply fucked up.

The Reed house burned to the ground about twelve years after Sorcha's death. It had been empty at the time of the fire; the Reeds had had no children, but some legal issue had kept part of the Reeds' large fortune, including the house, tied up in a Dickensian legal knot, so the house couldn't be sold or passed on to a fourth cousin.

The house stood, at least for a few years, like a monument to their evil. The fire was determined to be arson because accelerants had been found at the scene. But there was no suspect, and the authorities had no idea who might've waited more than a decade to take out some grievance against the couple.

"The house was razed a few months later, when the investigation was complete. No suspect was ever found. The lot was empty for a long time. Until a few years ago, when this house was built on that empty lot."

I showed them the picture I'd found.

Of Jonathan Black's house.

"I don't know what this means," Roger said.

"In the abstract," I said, "maybe not much. But when you put the pieces together, and going by our office motto that there are no coincidences, a sorcerer with a mysterious past chose to build his house on the same spot where a powerful and notorious sorceress had previously lived."

"Wait," Connor said. "I thought his house was old."

"It's not," Petra said, her frown visible on-screen. "Built only a few years ago according to the county website."

"To build in that neighborhood," Roger said, "you'd have to go through a lot of hoops. The house would have to look era appropriate or the builder wouldn't be able to get the permits."

"So, we think Black had some kind of obsession with Sorcha?" Lulu asked.

"Maybe not with her," I said. "Maybe her *magic*. If we're right that something's weird about his magic, maybe he thought there was something in her magic, and in that spot, that would help him."

"You've been to the house," Connor pointed out. "Did you see anything?"

"I've been *in* the house," I clarified. And remembering that I had watched Black munch breadsticks in his tidy kitchen made me feel doubly unnerved. "It's pretty and well decorated, although it wasn't all unpacked the last time I was in it. He told me he'd just bought it. Looks like that was a lie."

And then I thought about that walk around his yard. "The carriage house, though," I murmured, and I looked at Connor. "Did you feel anything around the carriage house?"

He shook his head. "There was too much demon in the air to notice anything, but I wasn't there long. Did you?"

"Yeah, it was light, though. And it wasn't any particular flavor of magic. Just magic."

"Wait," Petra said. "What carriage house?" There was silence for a moment while she perused her screen. "On the west side?"

I had to orient myself to my mental map of the city. "Yeah. Edge of the property, I bet."

"Got it. Boom," she said. "According to the county records, that structure is original. I mean, it was part of the Reed house, and it wasn't burned in the fire."

"That's our spot," I said, and stood up.

"Where are you going?" Connor asked.

"To Black's place and that carriage house. To see what's in there."

"He could be waiting for you."

It would definitely be a problem if he was there with more demon friends. But he wouldn't know we'd found this link, at least not yet.

"Roger," I said, "is he at the house?"

"The CPD has a car sitting at it," Roger said. "He hasn't been seen tonight."

"He doesn't yet know that we know about the house's history. And we need to take a look before he figures out we do."

"I'll get my jacket," Connor said, and stood up.

I glanced at Alexei and Lulu, who were already closing books and capping pens. "You sure you're up for this?" I asked Lulu, thinking her mom was going to kill me if she got hurt again.

"I'm good," she said, and Alexei nodded his assent.

"Get Swift," Connor told him. "He enjoyed the last round."

"There might be nothing to see," I pointed out.

"In which case, he's off for the rest of the night." He leaned in, kissed me hard. "We all do what we have to do, right?"

Roger cleared his throat.

"The camera is rolling," Petra reminded us, and Connor gave her a wide grin.

"Do you want us there?" Roger asked.

"Better idea," I said. "It seems to me Black's clean history isn't coincidental. Maybe he wiped it or had someone do it for him. Maybe that someone works for the court system."

"Oooh, sealed records," Petra said, rubbing her hands together gleefully. "That's a fun puzzle."

"I'll make the necessary calls and alert Gwen," Roger said.

"Have the surveillance team ready to roll if he does show up. They may need to follow him somewhere else."

"We'll get it done," Roger said. "Be careful, and keep us posted."

I wouldn't say the ride back to Black's neighborhood was uncomfortably silent, but it certainly wasn't chatty. I could feel Connor's anticipation and worry. I felt that way, too, and not just because I'd added another layer to my magical jawbreaker.

The main house and the carriage house were both empty when we drove past quietly. We parked a block away, waited outside the vehicle to test the air for magic. The neighborhood was dark and quiet but for the calls of crickets and katydids.

"Anything?" I asked the group.

"No sulfur," Lulu said.

And when no one suggested anything different, we started for the house on foot.

We met with Swift at the end of the block.

"You see or feel anything?" Connor asked, and Swift shook his head.

"All clear." He gestured to the vehicle across the street. "There's your surveillance."

Connor nodded, glanced at me. "Your dance, Lis."

A reminder, I thought, of his acknowledgment of my autonomy. I appreciated the gesture, so I brushed my fingers against his. And liked the happiness that sparked in his eyes.

"Lulu, you and Alexei hang under that tree," I said, pointing to a maple just beyond Black's property line. "Keep an eye out for Black or demons."

They nodded, walked to their spot.

"You take the front of the house," I told Swift. "There're no trees out there, so stick to the shadows."

"Got it," he said, and ambled off.

"Guess that leaves us," Connor said, and took my hand.

We approached the property from the side. The carriage house doors were open. We crept closer, then with the privacy fence at our backs, we paused to wait and watch for movement. But I saw nothing and felt no magic.

Someone had been here to open the door. And the surveillance team hadn't mentioned anyone doing so.

I got a very bad feeling about that, and after pulling out my screen, I turned toward Connor to block as much light as possible, and sent Roger a message: PING YOUR SURVEILLANCE TEAM AGAIN. DOORS OPEN ON CARRIAGE HOUSE; SOMEONE WAS HERE.

I'LL MAKE CONTACT, he confirmed.

I showed the messages to Connor, got his nod. His expression was grim, as were my feelings. Had the surveillance crew missed someone, or was the surveillance crew out of commission?

I put the screen away, looked back at the carriage house, and tried to tell if anything looked different from the last time I'd been there. But beyond the open doors I didn't see anything. The exterior was pretty nondescript, so I was sure I'd have noticed any changes.

Satisfied we were alone, I nodded to Connor and we moved closer, sticking to the grass instead of the gravel driveway. I pointed to a spot at the threshold, then at Connor, meaning he should wait here. I didn't want to be surprised, especially with my back to the door.

He nodded, crossed his arms, and leaned back against the threshold.

Good puppy, I mouthed, and got a very dissatisfied scowl.

I turned my attention to the interior. The furniture I'd seen through the window was still here, and it didn't look disturbed. The structure had a dirt floor, and there were marks where someone had come through, but no obvious path, at least not to my eye. But like last night, I could feel that faint twinge of magic. So, where was it coming from?

I walked to the other end of the structure, then back. I had a vague sense the magic was stronger in the middle of the room, but it was faint enough that I didn't trust my perception of it. So I requested backup via text message. Less than a minute later, Lulu walked in.

Her eyes went wide. "What do we have here?"

I looked around, had no idea what she'd seen. I looked at Connor, who lifted his shoulder and gave me what I thought of as his "It's Lulu" face.

"What?" I asked.

"A lot of cool old stuff," she said, lifting a corner of the blanket that covered one of the bureaus. "Empire style. Nice."

"Magic and demons now, please," I said, lowering the cover into place again. "Dumpster diving later."

"Dumpster diving in a vintage carriage house is the best kind."

"It smells a lot less like garbage," I admitted. Because I'd done my share of picking through trash during her teenage recycled-art phase.

"Magic," she said. "Yes."

Frowning, she looked at the walls and the ceiling before stepping into the center of the space. She pulled a penlight out of her pocket, flipped it on. The light shone pale blue until she aimed it at the ground, which glittered like diamonds.

"What is that?" I asked. When she didn't answer, I looked back at her. There was something very sad in her expression.

"Demon ash," she said. "The remains of demons."

When she slid the beam across the floor and back, the glittering continued nearly to the edges of the room.

We were standing on a demon-killing floor.

All three of us were quiet. Demons weren't friends to any of us, but neither was death. We had that in common with them.

I had to wait for the shock and horror and sadness to wear away before I could think again.

"This isn't the coppery ash we've seen before," I said, crouching down and trying to disturb it (them?) as little as possible. "And it doesn't smell like demon magic in here."

"Not now," Lulu said, crouching beside me.

She found a small piece of wood, gathered up some of the ash. It glittered like the demon remains we had seen elsewhere, but the color was wrong. It was onyx, not copper, and it was virtually magicless.

"He's done something to it," Lulu said. "Or to them."

"Not just killed them," Connor said, "but stripped them of their power."

My eyes widened. "Is that possible?"

By way of answer, Lulu just gestured to the floor. She took a square piece of paper from her pocket and slid into it some of the ash she had gathered; then she folded the paper up into a little packet. "For Petra to test," she said. Then she stood up.

"So, you get copper ash when you kill a demon with magic," I said. "And you get this magically empty ash when the magic is taken out of them."

"That would be my guess," Lulu said.

"And why do it?"

"Because he wants to use it for himself," Connor said. "He wants more or better power than he has."

Lulu nodded. "It's a way to make himself stronger."

More evidence there was something wrong with his magic.

"How do you strip the magic out of a demon?" I wondered, working hard not to think about the possibility Black had tried to do that to me and monster.

"No idea," Lulu said, "except that it requires death."

"So, he breaks the cornerstone," I said, "lets the demons in. Maybe plans to use some as minions, but that doesn't work like he thought it would, because Dante's in town. So he engages Dante in a battle for control of the city."

"Why would they follow Black?" Connor asked. "He isn't a demon. What's their incentive?"

"Maybe it's a carrot-and-stick thing," Lulu said. "And this is the stick."

"Or maybe he played the kingpin like Dante and promised them something," I said. "Part of the city or money or magic. Whatever he offered, the fight with Dante wasn't going well, and it was attracting a lot of attention. So he decided to use the demons differently. But maybe he had to practice first," I murmured. And I wondered if the demons we'd found at the empty lot had been his first unsuccessful venture. He'd killed them, but hadn't managed to strip their magic away.

"He's been unbuilding an army," Connor said quietly, "taking it apart so he could have its strength."

"But for what?" I wondered. "I mean, big picture. What is he going to try to do?"

My screen buzzed, sending a jolt of shock and adrenaline through me. It was Petra calling.

"Talk quickly and quietly," I told her as Lulu and Connor drew close.

"I found another property."

"Owned by Black?"

"Owned by Sorcha and Adrien Reed. It's the only property in Chicago still officially under their names."

"Where is it?"

"Practically on top of a ley line," she said.

"Send me the address," I said. "We'll check it out."

"Anything at his house?" Roger asked, and I told him what we'd found.

"What is he trying to do?"

"Be the most powerful," Connor suggested. "Be in charge. Isn't that what all this is? He's digging up some way to get stronger, same as he was doing with Ariel. She was a potential tool. He's insecure, and he's been wanting applause for a long time." He looked at me. "Especially from you."

I shook my head. "No, he doesn't."

"He has a thing for you," Connor said again. "You don't see it. And I'm not saying his feelings aren't complicated, but still . . ."

"Wait," Roger said. "I just heard from Gwen. The CPD can't reach the surveillance unit."

We all looked in the direction of the car at the curb, and the silence was ominous.

"So much has happened here," I said quietly. "If they saw anything, they'd have reported it."

"Yeah," Connor said. "So Black made sure they didn't see it or couldn't report it."

"We'll take a look," I told Roger. "And you might want to have emergency units on standby."

We ended the call, walked in silence toward the vehicle, where Swift joined us. The windows and windshield were tinted, so I knocked on the window with a knuckle. Waited. Knocked again. And knew what I'd find when I opened the door.

"Stay alert," I said quietly, and used the hem of my shirt to grab the door handle so I would not leave extra fingerprints. I opened the car door carefully, and knew immediately nothing in the vehicle posed a threat to us.

There were two cops in the front seats of the vehicle. And they were dead.

Both stared straight ahead. There were no obvious wounds, no sign of a struggle. Their seat belts were still fastened. There was magic in the vehicle, but not a type I immediately recognized.

I touched the neck of the man in the driver's seat. No pulse, but his skin hadn't completely lost its warmth. Carefully, I leaned over and checked the other.

"Both dead," I said quietly. "Magic of some kind, and not very long ago. They aren't cold yet." I stepped back and looked at Lulu. "Would you be able to tell me what magic was used?"

"I can try," she said, her expression grim. I didn't like to ask her. She hadn't used her magic for a long time in part because she wanted to avoid drama. I didn't like the idea of laying two bodies at her feet now, but we needed information.

I moved out of the way and she took my place, then leaned down and looked in. I watched her face, saw a flash of horror and pity, followed by determination. She lifted her fingers toward the driver, but didn't touch him. Just let her fingers drift an inch above his body.

"A shot of magic," she confirmed. "I think magic might have stopped his heart."

"Who did it?" I asked.

"Not a demon," she said. "This is sorcery, but with a margin of something else." She stood up and looked back at me. "Do you remember those markers that made a gold or silver outline? Like the ink color would be pink, but when you wrote with them, the lines had metallic edges?"

I knew what she meant. I'd gone through an analog phase as a teenager—pens and stickers and paper planners. But I couldn't remember the last time I'd used a marker. Probably to put my name on bottles of blood I kept in the loft refrigerator, even though there'd been no chance that Lulu would accidentally grab one.

"Yeah," I said. "Why?"

"That's the margin of demon here."

"Black," I said. "Using the magic he stripped from demons to power his broken sorcery."

"That's my thinking," Lulu said. "But this is all new territory." For us and for Chicago. And I intended to put a stop to it.

DECEASED, I messaged to Roger. SEND THE CPD IN. WE'LL WAIT WITH THEM.

Because they didn't need to be alone anymore.

"If Jonathan Black wasn't already public enemy number one," Connor said when the deceased had been taken away and we'd climbed back into the SUV for the hop to the second Reed property, "he is now. The CPD doesn't look warmly on cop killers."

"What do you think they saw?" Swift wondered.

"Something Black didn't want them to see," I said, "or tell about."

"Demon genocide?" Connor wondered, tone short, magic furious. Like me, he abhorred pointless violence.

"He wouldn't have wanted them to see him at all," Lulu pointed out. "There's a pending arrest warrant. But he probably also wouldn't have wanted them to see what he was doing magically. Because knowing would have made it easier to stop him."

It didn't take us long to reach the other Reed property, which was only a couple of miles away. And there wasn't much to see: just a metal storage building on a scrap of land.

We stepped out of the vehicle, sniffed for demon magic. It was definitely present, but the wind had picked up, so it was hard to tell how much of the sourness was from current magic versus past bad acts.

The building, about sixty feet long and twenty feet high at the eaves, sat on a concrete pad. A security light was mounted on a tall pole a dozen feet away, and it cast a wide circle of light on the main door, which was situated in the middle of one end of the building. The structure looked well maintained; it didn't show its twenty-plus years of age. No obvious rust, and the grass had been recently cut. Maybe, as with Hugo's machine, there was some kind of maintenance contract.

There weren't any windows and, with the front door closed, no way to tell if Black was in there. But if he was, he wasn't actively doing magic.

"Keypad," Connor whispered beside me. "Next to the door. The light is red, so it's engaged."

His eyesight was better than mine, which rankled for some reason. At least I got to take advantage of it, which was nearly as good.

"I don't see any other way in," I whispered, "unless the Packs have a secret skill of tunneling through concrete."

Connor and Swift both shook their heads.

Brakes squealed nearby, and I was glad we'd stuck to the shadows of a tall hedge near the property line. We slunk back farther against it.

An older-model sedan with New York plates—probably "borrowed" from Dante—pulled into the gravel driveway.

The driver's-side door opened, and a demon emerged. Ditto the front passenger door. Then a second vehicle pulled in behind the first, and four more demons climbed out.

One of the demons from the front car opened the back passenger door, and Jonathan Black stepped out. He wore a black suit, white button-down shirt, no tie. His hair had either been oiled back or was still damp from the shower he'd probably needed after what he'd done in the carriage house.

There's your damned upstart, I thought, complete with minions who've probably been scared into doing his bidding by what he'd done to their friends.

Black went suddenly still, looked around, and glanced toward our tight knot.

"Check the perimeter," he said, and pulled out his screen while his demons began to walk around the yard. One of them headed right for us.

Then I scented blood.

I snapped my gaze to the others, found Lulu wincing at a red welling on her finger.

One of us—the vampire one—should've been warned about the certain surprise presence of a certain ingestible substance.

Lulu's magic was of the old eldritch variety, the type that needed blood for kindling. Usually, by the time we needed her magic, blood had already been shed. But not now, and not yet. Her lips moved as she whispered some bit of arcane magic, and used her blood-tipped finger to draw symbols in the air. The air felt momentarily thick, and then magic settled around us.

The demon who approached us was physically unique even by

supernatural standards. Nearly eight feet tall with skin the color of cranberries. No hair, and the irises around his slitted pupils were bright yellow. He looked stereotypically demonic, although that image was ruined by the very cheap cologne that surrounded him like a funky cloud. He patrolled to the end of the property next door, then began walking right toward us.

He stopped inches from Kieran and sniffed the air, nostrils flaring widely as he searched for some anomaly. That anomaly was, of course, the five of us.

To his credit, Kieran didn't move, even though instinct probably would've had him putting space between them. I wondered if his heart was beating as wildly as mine.

Maybe we didn't need to hunch there in the dark, hiding ourselves. The five of us to six demons gave us fine odds. But Black was a wild card. If he could stop a human's heart without much effort, what might he do to us?

The demon ultimately passed, and we all breathed a sigh of relief. We waited until the majority followed Black into the building and closed the door. One stayed outside to guard the entrance.

A storm was drawing nearer, with sharp, daggerlike clouds moving swiftly toward us. And I didn't think it was meteorological.

It was magical.

"Get ready," I whispered.

"Yeah," Swift said quietly as magic permeated the air. "He's doing something very big in there."

"Ley lines," Lulu said; her eyes had gone glassy. "He's trying to do something with the ley lines."

"Kill more demons?" Connor asked.

She shook her head. "I don't know. I can't tell. But the magic has that demon edge again."

"We have to at least look," I said. "Maybe we don't have enough power to take him in, but we have to see what he's up to and stop him if we can."

I knew Connor wanted to argue that would be too dangerous, but Black posed a danger to the entire city. Especially with the magic he was gathering. And mine wasn't the only family in town.

"Next life," he said, "no marrying an Ombud."

"Anyone have X-ray vision?" I asked.

Swift snorted. "We are not Kal-El," he whispered.

I could practically hear Connor's heart beating faster. "You a Superman fan?" he asked.

"Yeah," Swift whispered carefully. "You, too?"

Connor nodded, held back a grin—badly—while sliding a glance at me. "I'd love to discuss this more, but she's impatient."

"Just imagine *Action Comics* Number One is in that building," I said. "That'll keep you motivated."

"Now you're just flirting with me," Connor said. "Since we don't have X-ray vision, Alexei and I can take the guard." He looked over at Lulu. "Can you give Elisa a shield, so she can look in?"

"Better if Lulu looked in," I thought aloud. "She'll know what she's looking at."

"No," Alexei said, the first words he'd spoken in a while. "She's just now conscious again."

"Try to take a picture?" Lulu suggested.

I nodded. "I'll call an audible on that one."

"I thought we said no more flirting?" Connor's grin was just for me.

I kissed him hard. "Go," I said. "Distract."

Alexei was already naked and changing to shifter form, the light and magic of that transformation echoing the red in the clouds above us. Once in wolf form, he ran toward the demon, but whipped past him. Connor, still in human form, was there by the time the demon turned to look, and he did some sort of pressure-point move that had the demon slumping to the ground.

"That was faster than I thought it was going to be," I said.

Lulu grinned. "That's what she said."

"Stay here," I told Lulu and Swift, and crept over to the door, checked the keypad. The light was red. I leaned in closer, stared at the buttons. And saw fingerprints on only one of them. I took a guess, keyed in 0-0-0-0.

"Villains are so predictable," I murmured as the lock disengaged. With Connor keeping watch at my back, I edged open the door and looked inside.

The building was one long space, all of it empty except for Black and his demons—and the light show that filled the air above them.

A circle, at least ten feet across, had been rendered in red light, and it rotated vertically in the middle of the room. Magical symbols were arranged around it in thin red lines. This wasn't a sigil—or not a demon's personal symbol, anyway. It looked more like someone had taken a compass and a zodiac calendar and mashed them together.

A cone of greenish light funneled down through a gap in the roof and into the circular symbol; it was flowing directly from a ley line. I could feel the massive volume of power even at the door.

Black stood in front of the symbol. His jacket was gone, his shirt open, his skin glowing red as power poured over him. Three of his demons were positioned around him. But they weren't privy to the flowing magic—they were contributing to it. The demons' arms were extended, their eyes closed, their bodies vibrating as magic flowed from them and the ley line into the symbol. And from the symbol, that magic poured into Black.

The symbol was some sort of magic transmission device, and he was filling himself up.

I thought I'd fibbed by telling Lulu that Black wanted to absorb magic from others. But I'd been horribly, surprisingly right.

And we had to stop him.

I pulled out my screen, took a photo of the room, the symbol. And then glanced down. On-screen, Black was surrounded by wisps of black smoke, and as the symbol turned and power funneled down, that smoke grew thicker. It slipped inside him, putting black streaks across his skin that weren't visible in real life.

When Black screamed, I dropped my screen, but caught it an inch before it hit concrete—and gave away my position.

The demons who weren't part of the circle looked around nervously. Black's scream had them jittery. They might have followed him in there as loyal minions, but that loyalty, probably purchased with threats, had a limit. And they probably passed that limit as they watched Black use their brethren.

Black was sweating now, his body slicked with perspiration. And he was shaking, either from the effort of maintaining the symbol or the effect of the power.

We needed to stop him. Maybe have Lulu throw a fireball into the symbol to break it up. But I wasn't sure what that might do to the ley line. And a ley line disaster was the last thing we needed right now.

The funnel seemed to thicken—growing wider and more opaque—and Black screamed again as the building shuddered. The symbol flickered from the excess of power. Irregularities in the ley line, probably.

Lightning cracked around us, giving the ambient magic a harsh red glow. The symbol flickered, and then another burst of lightning cracked, the loudest sound I'd ever heard. The symbol flashed, the brightest thing I'd ever seen, and its lines began to break.

The spell was falling apart.

The center wasn't holding.

The ley line, clearly too powerful to be harnessed this way, fractured the symbol into shards of light and magic that blew across the room, and the green column disappeared. I saw two demons drop before I instinctively let go of the door and turned away. Then the building's front wall bowed in from the force of the sudden vacuum.

As the wall began to splinter, Connor grabbed my arm. "Run!"

We ran toward the hedge, hit the shadow line as the front wall of the building exploded, sending sheets of knife-edged steel spinning through the air and smashing into the demons' vehicles. The building's door flew above our heads, landing somewhere in the yard next door.

A few demons staggered out, looked around. Some of them saw their chance and took off at a run. And then Black appeared in the smoking hole where the front of the building had been. He stalked out, clothes torn, skin bloodied, hair mussed. He was visibly trailing black smoke now.

I repeated what I had done for myself earlier and felt for his aura. That metallic margin Lulu had seen was thicker now, an onyx edge encircling his virulently red magic.

Black approached a demon trying to open the door of the front vehicle, which was now wedged shut by a large piece of steel. Black picked the demon up, tossed him down to the concrete. The demon tried a fireball, but he was bleeding and injured, and it didn't do much.

Black batted the fireball aside and held out his hand. Black smoke began to gather.

"It wasn't my fault!" the demon said, his voice an insectile whine.

I knew Black would kill him, and it wouldn't be self-defense but murder, demon or not.

I cursed, looked at Lulu.

"Cover me," I said, waited for her nod, and was up and out of the shadows, sword drawn, before anyone else realized what I was doing.

A fireball flew overhead, landed inches from the demon on the ground. He squealed, tried to scoot away.

Black turned his attention to me. For a second, his eyes widened in surprise. Then they hardened, and he stepped closer. "You did this."

Fake some bravado, I ordered myself as the demon scampered away. A crap result for our team, but easier on the conscience.

"No," I said lightly. "The ley line did this. The light show was rad, but your circle wasn't strong enough to hold it."

"Liar," he said, but didn't put much force behind it.

"What are you trying to do?" I asked.

"Claim my right."

"Sorcha's right, you mean?"

There was a flash of surprise in his eyes. And that was followed by deep and burning hatred.

"Yeah, we figured out the property-ownership thing. Why are you so obsessed with her? Are you looking for a mentor? Because you know she's dead, right? Killed by her own magic."

She'd literally been eaten by the Egregore dragon she created.

He didn't like the question, given he pitched a smoking ball of magic toward me. I dodged, used my sword as a shield to deflect the edge of the magic that I wasn't fast enough to avoid. The contact sent a blaze of heat down the blade, but I made myself keep my fingers around the handle. Skin would grow back, after all.

"Was the symbol her idea?" I asked. "Or her creation? Is that what you found in this building? I hope she had insurance."

"You don't know anything. None of you do." When his gaze flicked behind me, I knew the others had moved out of the shadows and revealed themselves, which wasn't part of my plan. Granted, I hadn't told them my plan.

"So, enlighten me. Why the obsession with Sorcha? Why the Reed properties? Why try to take her magic posthumously?"

"Because it should've been mine."

I lifted my brows. "Because you're her powerful successor come to finish what she started?" My voice was dry, baiting.

And he bit. "Because she's my mother."

TWENTY

I stared at him—could only stare—and wondered what fucked-up twist of fate had brought us together with the Egregore between us.

"What?" I asked.

"My mother," he said again, the words a curse. "Treacherous bitch that she was, Sorcha Reed was my mother."

My brain was still spinning. "She didn't have children."

I had meant that as a statement of what we'd all been led to believe, not an insult. Weirdly, the villain with the insecurity complex sure took it as one.

He threw another bolt of smoke, and this one dodged when I dodged, weaved when I weaved. And when I feinted right, it had sentience enough to ignore the fake. It hit me in the back, hot as fire and sharp as an arrow, and sent barbs of glass-edged agony through my legs. They nearly buckled, and it was only by using my sword as a cane that I managed to stay upright. I was sweating, but my mouth was desert dry.

"Her unacknowledged son," Black said, the smoke again sneaking beneath his skin, clearly visible now.

So when he'd said the magic I had was his "due," he'd meant biologically.

"Unacknowledged," he continued, "because she couldn't be bothered with a halfling."

Because she was racist or because his being a half sorcerer wasn't enough to keep his magic running?

"I'm sorry," I said, and meant it. "Your father?"

"I don't know him."

"Did that affect your magic?" I asked. When I saw his eyes, I braced for the hit I knew was coming.

But it wasn't wisps of black smoke this time. It was Black. With some sort of demon quickness, he rushed over and grabbed my arms. I felt a burst of shifter magic.

"Stay back!" I said.

Black's gaze shifted to look behind me, and I wished the others had stayed in the shadows. I was the only immortal one in the group.

"You brought a motley crew. Unpracticed sorcerers. Dogs. And someone new."

Welcome to Chicago, Swift, I thought ruefully.

"Your attention span is very short," I said, willing Black to turn his focus back to me again.

Black's face was inches from mine now. Magic swirled in his eyes like ink, the same glittery obsidian that now tattooed his skin.

"Are you giving yourself up to demon magic?" I asked so only he could hear.

"This is the only way."

"To do what?"

"To live," he said. "I am broken. She broke me—she and the man who contributed only genetic material. So, when I learned who I was, I had to go my own way."

"How old were you?"

"Thirteen."

A quick calculation told me that was approximately when the Reeds' house had been burned down. I'd wondered how far he'd gone.

"This isn't the way," I said.

"It's been so easy for you, hasn't it?"

His eyes searched mine, his magic a flurry of emotions. But he hadn't hurt me. Yet. So I kept him talking.

"Easy?" I asked.

"The child of privilege, of power. Of magic."

He used one hand to grip my chin. I tried to move, but he'd managed to pin me in place with magic. I fought back against the sudden claustrophobia of his imprisonment. I wanted to get information, but not this way.

"Unhand me," I said, "or you will lose that hand to my blade."

There was another burst of magic behind me. Another fight had begun.

Black's fingers gripped harder, and his gaze searched deeper, staring through me to the thing that he wanted, but wasn't sure I possessed.

Monster crouched low, evidently certain that I was a better ally than Black.

"I see what you are," he said, "and what you have. And it doesn't belong to you."

"It doesn't belong to you either," I said, feeling suddenly very protective of monster. "It belongs to no one."

I felt its joy at that admission, and then its horror as Black's fingers on my chin, digging into flesh, began to reach down magically, spearing through my aura to what lay beneath.

To monster.

There was a flash of success in Black's eyes as I sweated beneath his fingers and tried to push past his magic to escape him. But he'd just drunk from a ley line, and he was riding that power. Having found monster, he was like a child with a kite, trying to spool monster toward him. Trying to rip monster out of my body.

I screamed, as I felt like he was ripping organs from my chest. "Not. Yours."

That was all I managed in the midst of having a layer of my innermost self physically peeled away. I grabbed monster with as much inner strength as I could manage, held it tight. It didn't resist. It wanted freedom, and understood that was not what Black was offering. Black didn't care about its sentience. Black wanted its essence—the magic his mother had created.

The pain was unimaginable, the fear just as keen. Black's ley line experiment might have been ended—or at least slowed—by the destruction of the building and the magic Sorcha had apparently planted there. But if he took monster, he'd have part of a creature that Sorcha had managed to make sentient.

"No," I said, pouring all the strength I had left into holding on to monster.

"She is my mother. Her magic belongs to me," he said, nails drawing blood along my jaw.

And that was his mistake.

Magic was now a full riot behind us. Black looked up, loosening his grip and the chain of his power. I knocked his hand away from my face, then kicked him in the side. But his other hand still gripped my sword wrist, and that tightened. He spun me in front of him as Connor rushed us.

Connor looked like an avenging angel. Beautiful and fallen and furious. His eyes widened instantaneously when he realized Black intended to use me as a shield. And in that moment, I heard his voice in my head, clear as the ringing of a bell.

Down.

I didn't stop to think, but dropped to my knees. Connor hit Black, who dropped my arm. They rolled, and Connor bloodied

Black's nose with a wicked punch. They rolled again, and Black threw back an arm, gathered black smoke into his hand. A blue fireball flew from behind me, struck the ground near Black's hand, causing his smoke to transform into steam.

I wanted to jump in, but was afraid I'd hurt Connor in that tangle of limbs. And my vision was blurry, presumably from Black's attempt to split me open.

The sound of sirens cut through the air. Connor landed another punch before jumping to his feet. Black's left eye was swollen and already turning purple. His mouth was a mess.

I aimed my replacement sword at him, but got too close. Black grabbed my ankle and searched for another route to monster. I was frozen by that magic, but Connor ripped me away as CPD units and one federal vehicle pulled over the curb and onto the grass in front of us.

"Hands up!" someone yelled out.

"You're done," Connor said to Black, teeth bared and blood trickling from a cut on his forehead.

Black glanced at the cops now moving toward us.

The fireball was moving before I saw him gather it. It flew toward me, and I braced for the impact. But Connor spun me again, and it struck him in the back.

I heard the sharp intake of breath, saw the sudden shock of fear and confusion in his eyes. Then he slid to the ground.

"Connor!" I screamed, ignoring the chaos igniting around us as officers spilled out of their vehicles.

I dropped to my knees, rolled him over. His eyes were closed and his face had gone gray, and my heart all but stopped beating. I ignored running footsteps and yelling, and checked for a pulse, found nothing.

I wasn't sure if human CPR was right for shifters. So I did the only thing I could think of. I slapped him.

"Connor Keene, wake up!" Tears were rolling now, but I didn't feel them. "Wake up!" I screamed again.

Then I tried CPR, breathing air into his lungs and beginning chest compressions. Part of me wondered why no one else came to help me, but I kept counting and didn't stop to ask.

"*Breathe,*" I told him. "Breathe, or I swear to god, I will hunt you down in whatever dimension you're in and kick your ass myself. You are not going out because of Jonathan Black."

Or because I failed to protect you.

Or because you threw yourself in front of me.

We protect each other. But how was I going to do that? How could I do that as strong as Black was now?

Another round of breathing and chest compressions, even though fear threatened to constrict my airways into uselessness.

And then Connor sucked in a breath.

I helped him turn to the side as he breathed in oxygen and coughed out wisps of smoke.

There were more tears now, and I wasn't sure if they were all from relief or fear or absolute fucking fury that Jonathan Black had hurt Connor.

After a moment, Connor glanced up at me. He still looked pale, but he was awake and breathing.

"You look relieved, brat," he said, glancing up at me. He shifted, winced. "Did you break my ribs?"

I sobbed, pressed a kiss to his lips, then lowered my forehead to his as more tears slipped from my eyes. "I thought that was it. I thought you were gone."

"I'm here," he said, but his voice was hoarse.

I knuckled away tears, pointed a finger at him. "You are *not* allowed to die."

Even seconds after cheating death, he chuckled. "I'm not immortal, Lis."

"No," I said. "You misunderstand. *I will not allow you to die*. I'll figure something out."

There were curses behind us, so I stopped contemplating how to immortalize a shifter and looked back.

Gwen, Alexei, cops, Lulu, Swift, Hammett. All were alive, if a little bruised. And all looked Very Fucking Displeased.

"Stay here," I said.

"Damn. Thought I might get in a quick jog."

"You would," I said, and kissed him again, letting my lips linger against his, searing the contact into my mind.

I rose, walked toward the others. "What happened?"

"Black," Gwen said. "He's gone. Again."

How was I going to get him back? How was I going to stop him? The questions echoed in my head, but no answers followed. Well, other than monster's gentle prodding that it wanted to go home.

I turned back and found Lulu staring at me, eyes wide and bewildered.

And I knew what she'd seen.

And I dreaded what was to come.

Connor and I had apparently missed a show of light and magic while he'd been unconscious and I'd been trying to bring him back. Lulu and Black had exchanged fireballs while officers ran for cover, but he'd managed to poof himself away.

"I'm sorry," Gwen said, but I shook my head.

"This isn't on you," I said. "He used demons and a ley line like a water fountain. He's more powerful than all of us."

We returned to the town house, and I got Connor, who was suffering through his second magical attack of the week, into bed and ran a hand through his hair until his body relaxed. When I was sure he was asleep, I sent an update to my parents about Black's connection to Sorcha, and warned them to be careful.

Then I opened the bedroom door. And found Lulu staring at me. "We need to talk. Right now."

I guess it's time, I told monster, my heart beating like a drum. And swallowed hard.

"Okay," I said, and followed her to the room she was using.

She closed the door behind me, locked it. I wouldn't say I was afraid of Lulu, but I certainly wasn't comforted by that. The magic peppering the air said she was hurt and angry. And I knew why, because I knew what she'd seen on the Reeds' property: Jonathan Black trying to rip monster out of me.

"I know you've had a shit night," she said. "But you need to tell me what the hell's going on."

I swallowed hard, nodded, afraid—rationally or not—that I was about to end our friendship.

"There's something . . . ," I began, and realized I hadn't imagined the actual telling of it nearly enough. Only the emotional consequences. So I cleared my throat and tried again. "It started with the Egregore."

That had her brows rising. But she didn't speak. Just stood there stiffly.

"I'm not alone in my body. There's something—someone, I guess—in here, too. I think it happened when the Egregore was bound. A fragment stayed behind that wants to be reunited with the rest of the Egregore. That's what Black was trying to take from me."

Before I could move, she wrapped her arms around me, squeezed the breath from my lungs.

"I know," she said.

Not since Han Solo had uttered those words had a woman been so shocked to hear them.

I pulled back, stared at her. "I . . . What? What do you mean, you know?"

"I know about the something inside you. It's obvious, Lis."

That, for some reason, offended me. Maybe because I'd tried so hard to hide it. "How is it obvious?"

Lulu's stare was flat. "Well, you get red eyes when you fight like you're some kind of modern-day berserker. And I'm a sorcerer, and I've met vampires before. I know what vampire feels like. You feel more like . . . a vampire plus one."

"This isn't how I thought this would go," I murmured.

She crossed her arms. "Why didn't you tell me?"

"I didn't want to hurt you."

Her eyes narrowed with anger. "How would something that's part of you hurt me?"

That made tears well. "You have a no-drama rule, remember? And this is magical nonsense dropped right into your lap. It seemed cruel to tell you, because you didn't want any magic or supernatural stuff, and I was double the fun. I was trying to respect that boundary."

"Oh, well, thank you. But I think we're past the halcyon days of no drama. Not with demons in town."

"Yeah."

After a moment, she cleared her throat. "I think we both messed up."

"Yeah," I said. "Best friends are supposed to tell each other everything. We did not pass that test."

"On the other hand, we were trying to do the right things for each other. And we did tell each other eventually; it just took us a couple of decades."

It was my turn to hug her. "I love you, Lulu."

"I love you, too, Elisa." Then she punched me in the arm. "But I'm pissed you told me only because you *had* to."

"You only told me about your magic because you had to."

She opened her mouth, closed it again. "You aren't wrong."

"I know," I said with a Solo-esque smile.

Lulu went to the bed, sat down, and patted a spot beside her. "Sit," she said, and I obeyed. "Do your parents know?"

I shook my head. "I haven't told them. I was afraid they'd take it personally, see it as some kind of failure on their part. That they'd failed to protect me. I think my mom suspects there's something, but she doesn't know what. Connor knows. And his aunt, because she guessed when we were in Minnesota. That's it, until now."

I thought of all the times we'd lied to each other—or protected ourselves to protect each other—simultaneously. So much time wasted, even with the best of intentions. Now we'd be walking a new path together. Hopefully one that, if no less treacherous, would bring us closer together. Because even if we'd been honest with each other, being who we were—vampire and sorcerer—was still risky in a world where humans were in the majority.

Maybe one day we could just *be* different. Maybe we wouldn't have to hide or change or pretend to be something that didn't feel like *us*. Maybe we wouldn't have to feel guilty or weird or shamed about those differences. We just could . . . be.

"So, Black," she began. "He tried to rip it out of you."

"Yeah. Hurt like a son of a bitch." I rubbed my chest where it still felt sore, like my scalp after wearing a ponytail for too long. Stretched in the wrong direction. "Monster didn't want to go."

"Monster?"

"That's what I call it," I said, and felt a little sheepish. "It wants to go back into the sword." At that, I felt monster's enthusiastic approval.

"Well, that's better than Black having it. He's got enough magic as it is. We had to hold him back, you know," Lulu said after a moment.

"Black?" I asked, looking over at her.

"Connor. We had to hold him back from lunging for you and Black when he was working his magic. And it was a close call. I might have used magic on him." She made a little grimace. "But I knew you didn't want him getting hurt."

"And I'm immortal."

She nodded. "I know. And I know you were prepared to take that hit for all of us. So, thank you."

"You're welcome. Thanks for keeping him safe."

"He loves you fiercely," she said. "Not something I ever thought I'd say about Connor Keene where you were concerned."

"But life is a candy assortment."

She didn't skip a beat. "It is. It really is."

"I don't have the strength to stop Black, Lulu. Not with the power he's drawn now."

"I don't think anyone else can beat him either."

That put an uncomfortable flutter in my chest. "Is that supposed to make me feel better?"

Lulu grimaced. "It was, yes. So you didn't blame yourself specifically. But it mostly sounded hopeless. Sorry about that."

Monster tugged at my consciousness again, and Lulu jolted. "I felt that!"

"What?" I asked.

"Monster. I felt its magic."

"It's prodding me to go home. Into the sword."

"Hmm," she said, and looked me over. Then she narrowed her gaze and looked a little more. "Hmm."

"Hmm what?"

"Hmm, maybe it has the right idea. As it is—and I'm not going to mince words here—Black's strong enough to steal it from you. I'm not saying you wouldn't put up a fight, but he'd win. And if he gets monster, I think we're all in trouble. It's not just a spell or a scrap of magic. It's part of a sentient creature. That's exponentially more magic."

"So, bad."

"Bad," she agreed. "But if we let it go home, you put a lot of power into a single weapon."

Monster's excitement had the effervescence of just uncorked champagne.

"It's the Egregore, though. Isn't that dangerous?"

"How long have you known about monster?"

"Longer than I'm willing to tell you," I admitted with a grin. "You scare me."

"Has it killed you in that time?"

I just lifted my hands. "I appear to be alive."

"Not killed. Roger. But it's grown up with you," she said. "What was that like?"

"It helps me fight sometimes. Gives me hints about threats. And recently, at Cadogan House, it took over my consciousness in order to get to the sword."

Lulu's eyes went huge. "What?"

"Yep. In the armory, with the guards and my dad banging on the door. It was the night I got my replacement sword."

She whistled. "It really wants back in that sword. Has it tried to hurt you?"

"Well, no. I mean, we've gotten into some scrapes, but it wasn't to hurt me." Monster felt mollified by that conclusion and irritated that I had taken so long to get there. "It wasn't to hurt me," I whispered again, and tears nearly fell again.

"I didn't think so," Lulu said. "Monster is inside you, has been inside you, and hasn't tried to hurt you. If it were your enemy, it would have taken you out long ago."

"Are you sure it wasn't only trying to protect itself? Keeping me alive to keep it alive?" I felt its responding huff.

"Who says it needed you to stay alive?" Lulu asked.

I simply stared at her. "What?"

She leaned toward me, voice low. "Don't think of yourself as a fortunate vessel, but a locked box. If you live, it can't get out without magical assistance. But if you die, if you shuffle off that mortal coil, it probably can."

"Well, shit" was the only thing I could think to say. Monster was supremely self-satisfied. I felt like an idiot.

"The point is, it's not your enemy. Maybe we should do what it's suggesting." She turned to look at me. "Maybe what you need to defeat Jonathan Black is a kick-ass, magically infused weapon."

I had no doubt she could feel the exuberant burst of magic that followed that suggestion.

"Do you think you can do that? Get monster back into the sword?"

She folded her legs beneath her. "Well, I won't say I haven't given some thought to getting the plus-one out of you. But I didn't know where I was going to stick it, because I wasn't sure what it was. Now I know."

"Monster would like you to know it does not approve of being 'stuck' somewhere."

Lulu patted my leg. "No worries. We'll get everyone into their appropriate vessels," she said a little louder than necessary as if she was trying to permeate my belly to speak directly to monster.

"Can you do it by dusk?"

She looked ready to voice an immediate objection. Then she looked thoughtful. "Maybe. But you're going to have to tell them—your parents and mine."

TWENTY-ONE

G irl," Petra said via screen.

"This had better be extremely important news," I grumbled, looking down at the steaming breakfast Connor put in front of me. Part of me—the part that contemplated the possibility I'd be completely changing my consciousness later tonight—was nauseated by the thought of eating. The other part of me was vampire.

I put the screen on speaker. "We're eating," I said. "So the noises you hear will be chewing."

"People? Are you eating people?"

"Eggs, bacon, pancakes," Connor put in.

"Jealous."

Alexei had already tucked into a stack of pancakes tall enough to hide behind. Lulu's plate was seventy percent bacon. Connor went for volume. I went for a smorgasbord—a little of everything.

"I ate two bowls of steel-cut oats with chia," Petra said, "so we're all rocking breakfast tonight. Anyway, Jonathan Black."

That had me pausing midbite. "Sighting?"

"No, he was mercifully quiet last night. But, after approximately a googol of calls, I found a sealed court record."

"Murder?" Lulu and Connor asked simultaneously.

"Adoption."

"Makes sense," I said, "given he wasn't raised by his biological parents."

"Yep. He was adopted as an infant by humans and raised without incident, apparently. Good schools, soccer lessons, the whole deal. The adoption was sealed. And then, at thirteen, he wanted to find out about his biological parents. His adoptive parents weren't thrilled about it, at least according to the counseling records in the file, but they agreed because it was important to him. Sorcha was, of course, gone by then. But he got her name."

"Did he get the elf's name?"

"Not that I can find. I don't know if Sorcha identified him."

"I wish the damned elves would come and pick him up," I murmured.

"Wouldn't want him," Alexei said, flooding his pancakes with syrup. "He's 'other' to them now."

Unfortunately, Alexei was probably right. Elves were notoriously xenophobic, and they designated everyone who wasn't an elf as "other." I presumed that also applied to elves who had non-elf parentage.

"What happened after he found out?" I asked.

"Well, the Reeds' house burned down the day after he found out who his mother was."

"I knew it," I said.

"I mean, I don't have any hard evidence," Petra said. "Like we talked about, the investigators didn't make a conclusion about motive. But it happened the day after he found out who she was."

"Rage," Connor said. "He was enraged."

"About what?" Lulu asked. "I'm pretty sure most adopted kids don't go around torching houses."

"No, but he's a narcissist with broken magic," I said.

"The only thing in the file after the arson is a history of counseling sessions," Petra said.

"Would that be unusual?" I asked. "Sounds like something you'd expect when a kid is working through emotional stuff."

"*Daily* counseling sessions," she clarified. "No notes of those discussions, but I did some searching, and the psych was a specialist in kids with violent tendencies."

"Hmm," I said, and pushed eggs around on my plate. "Do the records say anything about magic? His or hers?"

Petra blinked. "No. They actually don't. I thought that was weird."

"His magic wasn't fully functional," I said. "He learned he was special, the son of an infamous sorceress, but still couldn't do magic. And since she was gone, he couldn't ask her about it. He got angry—Sorcha and elf levels of angry—and burned down the house. And I bet he's been trying to figure out how to fix himself with remnants of her magic or spells since then."

"Cold," Connor said. "They're both cold."

"And cursed by their self-centeredness." I looked back at the screen. "What about the red-light symbol that we saw in the building? Anything interesting there?"

"It's actually an old alchemical symbol," Petra said. "But there's no indication he picked it up from Sorcha. Could have, but no indication of it."

"I think Rosantine coming to Chicago was a trigger for him. It, maybe, opened his eyes to the possibilities."

Connor shook his head. "Go back further. Maybe to Ariel and her coven telling him about the end of the world."

"Good point. And then Rosantine comes. He sees how powerful she is. He learns about the cornerstones, decides to open the door to demons in Chicago. Maybe he starts the process because he's impressed by her power and wants some powerful minions," I added, pushing back my plate.

"They can do magic for him," Connor said.

"And they do. But he doesn't like that. He's not powerful enough to control them. So, he killed a few, turned them into copper ash. Did it at first to keep the demons quiet or to eliminate the enemy. And then he saw the potential."

"The empty lot," Petra said. "That was his first attempt at taking power en masse."

"That's what I'm thinking," I said. "A first try that didn't work. So he decided to use it to his advantage—frame Dante and then get rid of the evidence."

"How does this help us get him?" Alexei asked quietly.

"I have no idea. I need to let my thoughts percolate like a good cup of coffee. Anything else from your end?" I asked Petra.

"No, but I'll let you know."

"Then we'll do the same," I said, and ended the call.

"I'm going to get back to work," Lulu said, glancing at me. "I'm nearly ready with the magic."

I nodded, wished I had more time. Was surprised and touched by monster's gentle assurances, Lulu's kind smile, and Connor's hand on my knee.

"It's going to be fine," Lulu said. "I probably won't even turn you into a toad."

"Are you all right?" Connor asked when we were alone.

"I don't know what I am. Sad. Terrified. Excited."

"Good," Connor said, brushing a lock of hair away from my face. "You're planning to change a fundamental part of your life. At least one of the voices inside you will be gone."

"Ha ha. What if I'm not me anymore?"

"You mean, like a brain-eating parasite has taken you over and subbed its personality for yours?"

"Is this a *JQ* thing?"

"Yes, but that's not the point. You are you, Lis. And yeah,

you've had to adapt because you have monster. It has, too. But the core of you is still one hundred percent brat."

"That doesn't make me feel better. What if I'm not as strong? Or as fast?"

"You'll adapt again if you have to. But this is nonsense talk, because you aren't going to get weaker by having a—sorry, monster—parasite exorcised. Don't stay in a bad situation just because you aren't sure what comes next."

Monster had no comment to that.

"You're going to come out the other side. I promise you that. And then I'll be there waiting for you when you do."

"Thanks. But if new Elisa wants to go in a different romantic direction, I may not be able to stop her."

"Try it," he said. "Monster and I will team up to get you back."

Lulu appeared at the bottom of the stairs.

"I'm ready," she said.

And that was that.

We drove to Cadogan House in silence. Connor, Alexei, Lulu, and me in the Pack's SUV. We'd told my parents we were coming and needed to talk, and asked that they invite Lulu's parents.

Monster wasn't a literal physical presence inside my body. But it felt like we were embracing the entire trip. Holding each other as we journeyed toward our crossroads.

Like me, it was nervous, excited, scared. It had spent most of its existence inside of me; I was the universe in which it lived. Now that would change. And if we didn't work the magic correctly, or if my parents objected, it could be the end for at least one of us.

It will work, I told it, because that's what it needed to hear, so that was what I needed to say.

* * *

When I sat down in my father's office and they all looked at me, I decided the best way to discuss monster was to show them.

"Monster," I said to it, but aloud this time. "Show yourself, please."

There was no hesitation now, not as eager as it was to reunite with its other half.

I knew my eyes had gone red, and I sat up a little straighter as it stretched inside me.

Aunt Mallory was the first to react; she leaned close, eyes slightly unfocused, probably because she was seeing a change in my magic. Not just mine and the Pack's, but monster's, too.

I looked at my parents, saw only bafflement. But they hadn't bolted yet, so that was something.

"This is monster," I said. "Or that's what I call it. It's a little piece of the Egregore that got stuck to me during the binding spell. And it's been living inside me ever since."

For a moment, there was only silence as the parents stared at me.

"Well, fuck."

We all looked at Aunt Mallory, who was now frowning as she stared at me.

"You're right," she said, but her brow was furrowed in confusion. "But I'm not sure how you're right."

"I'm sorry," Mom said. "I still don't understand."

"Back to my eyes," I whispered, and monster let them shift back to normal. "It's like a second consciousness—*is* a second consciousness. It is aware, sentient, emotional. Doesn't like demons. Likes fighting. And wants to go home."

"Home?" Dad asked. It was the first thing he'd said.

"Into the sword with its other half. I think it's lonely."

"I still don't understand," Mom said. "How long has this been going on?"

And when she asked that, I knew she hadn't meant that she didn't understand the magical possibility. She lived in Chicago, had been Sentinel of Cadogan House. She had seen some shit.

But she didn't understand how this could've gone on without her knowing. Or without me telling her.

"Since I was a teenager," I said. "That was the first time I became aware of it. But it's been there forever."

"She just told me last night," Lulu said, trying to ease that particular ache.

"Does it hurt you?" Dad asked, a wrinkle of concern between his eyes.

"Not usually on purpose. It's been a pretty good companion. But circumstances being what they are, it needs out. I need it to get out." I looked at Mom. "This was the thing I wasn't ready to tell you about."

"That's why you always wanted to hear the story of the dragon," Mom said.

I nodded.

Wordlessly, Mom rose and left the room. And my worst fear had come true. I had horrified her. Learning the truth about who I was had horrified her.

"I thought there was something," Aunt Mallory said. "But only, like, residue from the spell because it was so closely connected to who you are."

"That's not wrong," I said. "It's just not all of it. It took me a long time to figure it out. I didn't really get it until Rosantine took Cadogan House. Monster grieved. And when the House came back, it let me understand why."

I didn't mention the years in between, during which I'd thought it wanted to grab the sword and start killing. That had been my error and not monster's fault. Also my parents would freak.

"It's weird," Aunt Mallory agreed. And looked like something was bothering her.

Not, I thought with much relief, because I was wrong or bad, but because the magic was odd. I didn't disagree with that either.

Mom came back in, and I steeled myself for anger or disappointment. But she was carrying an old-fashioned bell-shaped glass bowl, its dark brown contents topped with a pleated mound of whipped cream.

"What's this?" I asked when she handed it to me.

She crouched down, looked up at me. "Chocolate milkshake with a swirl of mocha and whipped cream."

Memories flooded my eyes with tears. The last time she'd brought me a chocolate milkshake, I'd been sad that I wasn't going to have a senior prom. I'd been tutored as a kid, so it wasn't like I expected the full balloons-and-band routine. But I'd also discovered Connor was dating a human and she'd invited him to her prom.

The time before that, I'd broken my arm while trying a complicated spinning kick. My arm had healed quickly, but I'd been so frustrated with my lack of progress that I wanted to quit training to fight altogether.

There was a time before that and a time before that. Chocolate shakes had marked chapters in our lives, and had been my mother's little trick to heal my heart with chocolate.

"We love you," she said, still crouching in front of me. "Not *regardless* of who you are, but *because* of who you are. Because you're you. And you are ours."

Tears welled in her eyes now, and although I didn't take my

eyes from her—my beautiful mom with her pale blue eyes, now gone silver—I could hear Aunt Mallory sniffling to my left.

"Why didn't you tell us?" she asked.

I took a sip of the milkshake, which gave me a moment to compose myself. It was stunningly good. The only thing possibly better than coffee was coffee with chocolate.

"I was afraid you'd feel guilty or that I'd remind you of the Egregore and all the . . . pain of that time."

Heat flared in my mom's eyes, and she stood up. "You were trying to protect us. But you didn't need to do that. We can take care of ourselves, and you don't have to worry yourself over us." The heat in her eyes, I realized, was a ferocious kind of love.

I swallowed and looked at Aunt Mallory. "I also wasn't sure if this was a mistake in the magic, and I didn't want to put that on you."

"Oh, sweetheart," she said, her voice so kind that tears started to flow again.

"Both of you," Dad said, rising to stand next to Mom and looking between me and Lulu, "have tried so hard for so long to protect us from yourselves. Put those burdens down. You don't have to hide yourselves from us."

"You could have told us," Mom said kindly. "And that's the last thing I'll say about that, because it's in the past. You didn't tell us, which means you braved this on your own for all these years." She paused to compose herself. "You're a brave and strong woman. And don't let anyone tell you different."

"It wasn't a mistake."

We all looked at Aunt Mallory, whose expression had cleared. And now she looked surprised.

"What?" I asked, and my chest felt funny.

"I mean, god knows and evidence shows I can make a mistake. But I don't think this was a mistake. The spell was to bind the Egregore into the sword, right?" She looked around at us for confirmation. "And because Merit was holding the sword, a little of that magic got passed to her."

"And boom, nine months plus later, Elisa," Lulu said.

"Yep. But nothing about that process would put part of the Egregore into Elisa. You can't accidentally make a cat out of a toaster."

An extremely Mallory Carmichael example. Or at least I assumed it was only an example, and not something she'd learned by trial and error.

"So how did it get there?" Lulu asked. "Could Sorcha have done it?"

"She was dead at that point," Mom said quietly.

There was silence for a moment. And then I understood.

"The Egregore did it," I said, and felt monster's agreement.

"What?" Dad asked. "How?"

Tell me if I'm veering away, I told monster. "Maybe it wanted revenge?" I proposed, and then winced when monster metaphysically kicked me. "Ow," I said aloud, and rubbed my abdomen. Then found Mom looking at me curiously, one corner of her mouth raised.

"It kicked you, didn't it?"

"Yeah," I said, startled that she guessed so quickly.

"I know that because I carried you for nine-plus months." She was grinning full out now, and that expression had me feeling a lot of relief. "You kicked me the entire time."

"Maybe she was under the influence of monster," Lulu said with a smile.

"Anyhoo, it didn't like that answer. It wanted freedom," I finally said, and felt warmth spread in my abdomen. Monster approved. "Maybe it knew what was coming and tried to split itself into two pieces. Or did it accidentally because it was trying to squeeze all of itself somewhere else, but didn't quite manage it."

Everyone looked down at my abdomen, as if monster might pop out *Alien*-style and give an answer.

"No response," I said. "I don't think monster has all the details about that part of it. But I don't think it disagrees."

"So, that begs the real question," Dad said. "What do you do next?"

"None of us are strong enough to beat Jonathan Black alone, and probably not even together. But if I had a sword that was magically enhanced—not just by a sorcerer, but by a sorcerer even more powerful than him—I bet I could do it. And more important, *it* thinks it can beat Black."

The room went very quiet. And the parents went very still.

"You want to reverse Humpty Dumpty the Egregore?" Uncle Catcher asked. "Absolutely not."

"We aren't going to let it loose," Lulu said. Monster didn't feel good about that, but understood that total freedom wasn't on the table. "We're going to reunite two parts of a creature that was created and then forcibly torn apart in the span of a week."

"It tried to break Chicago," Mom said.

"In fairness," I said, "it didn't try to break anything. A sorcerer did. The Egregore is just a creature. Not good. Not evil. But broken because of everything that happened then. And it doesn't want out. It wants to go home."

"Into the sword," Dad said, and I nodded.

"It's been protecting Elisa," Lulu said, and told them the conclusion we'd reached the night before. "Including against Jonathan Black, who tried to take it from her last night."

I gave her a Very Mean look.

"Excuse me?" my mother said, and looked angry enough to bite.

"He thinks he's entitled to it because of Sorcha," I said.

"Sorry," Aunt Mallory said, "but why would Black think that?"

"He's Sorcha Reed's unacknowledged son," Lulu said.

Aunt Mallory nearly spewed her coffee. "What?" she demanded, wiping away at chin dribble.

"Did I not tell you?" Mom asked, and when Aunt Mallory turned furious eyes on her, she added, "Guess not. I'm sorry. I honestly thought I had." She ran a hand through her hair. "This week has been a lot."

"Details," Aunt Mallory said.

"We don't have all of them," I said, "but it sounds like Sorcha had an affair with an elf, and Black was the result. He grew up with a human family and didn't know about his magic for a long time. Petra found the records. He had them unsealed with his adoptive parents' support. But Sorcha was already gone. He was thirteen." Then I told them about the arson.

"I remember the fire at the Reed house," Dad said. "But I didn't think much of it since the Reeds had been gone for years by then."

"I thought it was just deserts," Mom said. "And we think . . . what? He wants monster because it 'belonged' to his biological mother?"

"I think in part," I said. "And maybe because he thinks it will fix his magic, which seems to be broken. Or was before he started eating demon and ley line magic."

Mom and Dad sat down again. Mom crossed her arms, frowned as she considered what I'd said. Dad's posture was pretty much the same. After spending more than twenty years together, some of their habits had merged.

"What are you thinking?" Aunt Mallory asked. Not a challenge but a serious query about magic.

"Elisa thinks it can rejoin itself in the sword. So we just have to get it out of her and then into the steel."

Uncle Catcher scratched his chin. "You're thinking a lure?"

"Trust me," I said. "It doesn't need a lure."

"That's why you were in the armory," Dad said quietly.

The sadness in his eyes made my throat ache. But I knew I wasn't the one to make him sad. Not really.

"Yeah. It's been pesky in Cadogan House for a while. But it's been louder since we brought the House back."

"It doesn't need a lure," Lulu repeated. "But it needs a road. A magical path it can follow."

"Preferably one-way," Uncle Catcher said, "so it has only one potential destination."

Lulu nodded. "That's my thought. I'm calling it an antisundering spell."

"Because it puts back together what was split," Dad said, nodding. "Very nice."

"You might feel different when it's out," Mom said, looking at me with concern. "I mean, physically. After its being there for so long."

I might be weaker with monster gone. And I knew I'd miss its constant company. But none of that mattered now.

I nodded. "I know. But it's time."

A round of hugs and tears and milkshake tasting followed. And then it was time for whatever came next.

"We need to use the armory," I said.

"Do you need help?" Aunt Mallory asked.

Lulu looked at me. "I think we need to do this ourselves. But more important, you need to stay out of the room. Just in case."

"Just in case of what?" I asked, and heard panic in my voice.

"You turn into a half-dragon. Dragon face on your body, or vice versa."

Her lips were twitching, and I nearly pinched her. But Connor took my hand, squeezed.

"Nothing bad is going to happen as far as monster is concerned," Lulu said. "But we're running up against Sorcha's magic. And she is bad-news bears. I don't think there's any way she could affect things now, but . . ."

"But Black is eating demons," I said again. "I don't think he understands enough about the mechanics of monster or the Egregore to try to hit the House. But he's not in his right mind, and it's better if you're outside on guard."

"We will be," Mom said with what I thought of as her Sentinel look. Ferocity and courage in her eyes and a little bit of a smirk at the mouth as if she were ready to leap into a dangerous fight and throw out some snark along the way.

"I'm not sure how I'll feel afterward," I said. "Probably weak. So, if you have blood ready, that might be good."

"Or coffee," Connor said with a smile.

"Do what you need to do," Dad said. "But, please, don't destroy the House. It's having a very hard month."

TWENTY-TWO

And then it was just Connor, Alexei, Lulu, and me in the armory. We'd closed and locked the door, just in case.

It was a new generation of Chicago's protectors in the room this time. Not taking something out, but putting something back.

Alexei whistled as he surveyed the hundreds of weapons ready for use—from ribboned pikes to katanas to guns. The latter were rarely used unless the enemy was similarly armed.

"Can we take souvenirs?" he asked, gazing lovingly at a set of viciously sharp throwing stars.

I looked at Mom's sword, which lay atop a table on its bed of silk, and felt monster's excitement become palpable.

"Is the House vibrating?" I asked.

"No," Lulu said quietly. "That's the magic surrounding the sword. I can feel it, too, a little."

But not just magic. There was hope, too. A promise very nearly fulfilled.

"How are you feeling?" she asked.

"Nervous." I glanced at her. "Not about you. About the separation. About what I'm about to become and what we're about to unleash."

Monster tried to reassure me, but it was mostly relieved at the possibility of what was about to happen and trying not to scare me off. It felt . . . overjoyed. And it seemed appropriate that I should offer it some last words.

Thanks for not killing me or getting me killed, I told it.

If internal magical consciousnesses could snort, monster did. And I felt the faint warmth of what might have been affection. And impatience.

"Come here," Lulu said, and I walked over, positioned myself beside the table. The vibration was stronger the closer I moved.

"You promise we aren't going to loose the Egregore on Chicago? *Ouch*," I added when monster paranormally pinched me.

"Are you talking to me or it?" Lulu asked.

"Yes."

"Then for my part, yes, I'm sure. Adding a missing piece to the puzzle doesn't make the scene in the puzzle come to life. It just completes the puzzle. And you're stalling."

I totally was.

I looked at Connor, who nodded. "You'll be fine, Lis. And we're here, whatever happens."

"*Aww*," Lulu said sweetly. "Now back up," she told Connor. "Alexei," she prompted, and he came forward with the materials that Lulu had gathered.

"My mom went the alchemy route, so we're doing the same." This time, it was Lulu who looked at a friend for support, and that friend was Alexei. She got his steady, barely there nod in return, and nodded confidently.

"Now who's stalling?" I murmured.

As if to prove me wrong, she made a blue flame appear over a small silver bowl. She tossed in what looked like flakes of salt; the flame flashed yellow, then settled again. She added a drop of something that made the room smell green and metallic.

"Hold out your hand," she said, and when I did, she jabbed a slender needle into my fingertip. "Not blood magic. Just an ID check."

She squeezed my finger over the bowl, so one drop, then two fell into it.

The blue flame shifted to purple, and magic settled over the room. Not the excited, hivelike buzz of vampires from the House, but something calmer, more serene. The lap of cool water at a sandy shoreline. The ring of crystal.

It was Lulu's magic—the flavor of her power. And there was nothing evil in it. Strong, yes, and old, but clear and tranquil and unmalicious.

She murmured something, a chant with a rhythmic cadence, and then swept up a slender bamboo paintbrush. She dipped it into the substance in the bowl and began to paint symbols in the air, flourishes that glowed white as she drew the brush along, the previous mark fading even as she began the next.

Something rattled, and I looked up sharply. The sword vibrated on the table—visibly now—and I felt the answer pulse inside me. Not like the violence Black had used or when monster had nearly been dragged along with Cadogan House into another dimension. This was an invitation, a path back to its home.

The sensation of its exit was a cold prickle, and I could feel the metaphysical void left inside me. And that void was . . . expansive. I had no idea how much room monster had taken up. And I wondered how keenly I'd feel that absence.

I hope you find peace, I told it.

And then the world rippled—the entire House shuddered—as if something had settled into place. Something powerful long denied.

Magic. Strength.

My body trembled and I nearly stumbled. I reached out to the table to steady myself.

That ripple of magic, of power, wasn't the sword. It was *me*.

"Lis—," Connor said, and I felt him move forward, but held up a hand.

"I'm fine," I managed. "Give me a minute."

And we all waited for my body to adjust to its new magical reality. When my legs were less wobbly, I looked up at Lulu, the question in my eyes.

"You were holding it in for a really long time," she said gently, and I nodded.

For more than a decade, as long as I'd felt monster's existence, I'd worked to keep it hidden. I'd pushed it down, and that had required energy. A lot of it. A lot of power that I hadn't even known—not consciously—that I'd been using. That I'd been capable of using.

"What are you talking about?" Connor asked.

"Elisa has more power than we knew. Than *she* knew," Lulu said quietly. "She'd just been unconsciously using it to keep monster in check."

Nodding, I rose to my feet, my heart racing. But that wasn't magic; that was just emotional adjustment.

Connor stepped forward now, offered a hand. I took it, squeezed. I could feel his magic now surrounding me, that bit of bright power he'd added to my aura. It was beautiful. And it was love.

Connor's eyes widened. "Damn, Lis."

But there was no horror or concern in his eyes. There was only awe and love and a hint of excitement.

"You can tell?"

"Yeah. You feel less . . . constrained." He tilted his head. "Maybe that's why you were so bratty?"

"Ha," I said, and had to work not to giggle. I was feeling giddy and, yeah, a little more free than I had before. I didn't doubt some of that would fade as I adjusted, but for now, I felt amazing.

"Maybe you'll need less caffeine," Lulu said.

"How dare you."

"Same old Lis," she said with a smile.

"Hey," Alexei said. "The sword."

We all looked over at it.

It was no longer vibrating. It was now *hovering* a good six inches over the table, its silvery magic rippling the air above it.

"Careful," Connor and Lulu said simultaneously as I put a hand over the metal—and felt its brilliance even from inches away.

"Hello," I said, smiling at the sheer joy that seemed to emanate from the blade. The Egregore was whole, happy, and aware. And knew I wasn't its enemy.

I felt its answering smile, and then it literally jumped into my hand. Magic flowed through us like a loop. Like a continuum. Like a circuit finally closed. She made the offer; I could wield her if I wished. We would fight together against Chicago's enemies.

Yes, I said, and the world rippled again, and this time the sound was as clear as striking crystal.

I felt the word—the name—as much as heard it.

Bloodletter.

It was the name Claudia had given vampires, had called me and my parents. And it was the name the sword now chose for itself.

For you, monster had said the night it had pushed me into the armory against my will. Had it known then what would happen?

I felt its warm, satisfied smugness all the way to the handle.

"I'm not sure if a semisentient sword is an improvement," I murmured, and felt its answering flash of humor.

I also wasn't sure how I felt about communicating with a semisentient sword. I could have asked Lulu's dad, but that would have required me to tell more of the tale, and I wasn't up for that. It seemed needless to expose the family, extended and otherwise, to a pain that had, at least for now, been soothed. I had no doubt we'd find new trouble together.

For now, there was one more step. I didn't know all the details of tempering a sword, of solidifying that bond between fighter and steel. I lifted my free hand, sliced the blade across my palm. The pain was bright but overshadowed by the blade's ripple and shimmer and the warmth that blossomed through my chest.

"Bloodletter," I said quietly.

The sword shuddered in my hand.

Now I had a weapon.

I opened the armory door with the sword in hand, and found my parents in the hallway outside, along with half a dozen guards. So much for keeping their distance.

They watched carefully as we walked out, eyes widening as they realized the source of the buzzing magic was me.

"Sorry about the shaking," I said. "That was . . . me, I guess."

Mom walked toward me, her eyes on mine. Then she reached out, put a hand on my cheek. Her pale blue eyes went wide.

"I don't think Amit is the strongest vampire in the world any longer," she said.

She was smiling, but I saw the shadows in her eyes. Where there was a strongest vampire, there was someone who wasn't . . . and wanted to be.

Dad moved forward next. He glanced behind me at the open armory, assuring himself that everything was copacetic. "An adjustment?"

"It had a little more effect than I thought," Lulu said with a smile. "Everything's fine now."

I nodded, looked down at the sword in my hand, and felt the sword's answering grin. "I think I need to use the sword. For a while."

Mom looked down at the sword, one she'd tempered with her own blood and wielded for years before the Egregore had been bound into it.

I extended the sword to her. "Do you want it?"

She looked at it for a moment, and I wondered at the memories that passed behind her eyes. Times that she'd fought with the sword, that they'd been joint combatants in awful fights, including against the Egregore.

She held out a hand, and the motion actually had the sword moving away from her, like magnets repelling each other.

"Whoa," Aunt Mallory said. "I don't think that's your sword anymore."

Mom's eyes cleared, and she grinned at me. "No, it's not. It's chosen you. And it's feeling very strongly about that sentiment." She embraced me, kissed my temple. "Be careful with each other."

TWENTY-THREE

Theo, Petra, and Roger watched me carefully as I walked in, Lulu and Connor behind me. They all glanced down at my vermilion scabbard, which wasn't an accessory I'd carried before.

"You look different," Theo said, rising from his office chair.

"You are glowing," Petra added, rushing toward me. "And not in some metaphorical way. Like your energy is intense."

"So, it's kind of a long story," I began, but then told them the entire thing anyway. And included jazz hands at the end. Because even though they were also my family, even I wasn't used to who I was.

"You did that," Petra said with such awe in her voice, I wasn't sure how to take it. "The pulse."

"One of us did," I said, and put my hand on the pommel. "I'm not sure which."

"You had your radioactive spider," Theo said.

"Pretty much," Connor agreed, which saved me the trouble of trying to figure out which comic book or gaming character Theo meant. Probably an arachnid one?

Roger scratched his head. "Should we salute you or something?"

"I tripped on the sidewalk on the way in here," I said, and that was enough to put them all at ease. Omnipotence weirded humans out.

Roger gestured toward the sword. "You're sure it's safe?"

A fair question; the Ombudsman wouldn't want to risk an eldritch monster emerging from one of his employee's work gear.

"Safer now than it was before," Lulu said. "The monster is more securely bound because the sword's magic is back in place. And it's chosen Elisa."

"Chosen?" Theo asked.

I held out the sword, glanced at Petra. "Try to take it."

Fearlessly, she reached out a hand. Even sheathed, the sword shifted away from her with a deep *thrum*.

"Amazeballs," she said, and moved her hand around, watching wide-eyed as the sword avoided it. "It won't let anyone else use it."

"That seems to be the case," I said.

Roger nodded. "Good. You saw the reports?"

"Yeah. I don't suppose Gwen managed to bring Black in just before I got here?"

"Unfortunately not," Theo said. He sat down, swiveled small arcs in his chair.

"We still have to find him, and we still have to shut him down." Roger's voice was firm. "If we don't, the CPD will be authorized to shoot demons on sight and ask questions later to prevent him from getting stronger."

"And they'll shoot anyone they think is a demon," Petra said. "We don't need that."

"Nope," Roger said.

"So, what do we do?" Petra asked. "And that's not hypothetical. I'm honestly asking. Do you think you can beat Black with that sword?"

"One on one and a physical fight? Fuck yes," I said, and that had them grinning. "But I can't do magic. He can still beat me that way, and as we know, no ward is perfect."

"Hypnosis," Petra said. "We convince him not to be such a mood killer."

"Pretty sure he won't agree to that and not easy to trick him into sitting down for a talk sesh," Theo said.

"He wants monster, right?" Roger asked, gaze dropping to the sword. "But I guess that won't work now that it's been relocated fully into the sword."

I frowned. "I mean, he doesn't know we did the spell. But, yeah, he may be able to tell that the magic is in the sword and no longer in me."

"What if we hid it?" Lulu said, eyes narrowed with purpose. "Or faked it?"

"What do you mean?" Theo asked.

"It would be pretty easy to spell Elisa so it seems like she still has monster. A facsimile spell, maybe. I can talk to my parents."

"Okay," Roger said. "Maybe it would work as a lure, but how do we use that to put him down?"

"The sword and I will handle that," I said.

Another shiver from the sword, but this one was more like a purr. I patted the pommel soothingly, and wondered if I now had an actual Tamagotchi.

"And the sorcerers can help," Lulu said. "While we're making the facsimile spell, maybe we could add something to help ensure you can beat him. Oooh! Maybe we combine it with a siphon spell to pull out some of the magic he's been absorbing?"

"Magical regurgitation?" Connor asked.

"Yeah. That will tip the odds a little more toward Elisa and her sword. I mean, presuming it's possible." Lulu looked at Petra. "What do you think?"

Petra's lips were pursed as she considered. "Theoretically, yes. If he can use a spell to suck the magic in, we should be able to push it out again. Like, I don't know, blowing bubbles in milk. Shall we work on that?"

"Yes, please," Lulu said.

"I have no objection to reducing his power," I said. "Having a sword strong enough to beat him is one thing, but I still have to avoid what he's dishing out. And we have to make sure he can be safely incarcerated."

"I like this plan."

We looked up, found Gwen in the doorway. She wore jeans and a CPD T-shirt today, and I wasn't sure if she was dressed for relaxation or for mixing it up with villains. Probably the latter, given the weapon holstered at her waist.

"Hey," Theo said, his eyes warming. He rose to meet her. "I didn't know you were coming by."

"I was in the neighborhood," she said, and squeezed the hand he offered her. But she shook her head, held up her free hand. "Okay, that's a lie. I heard someone got magically swole." She looked me over, her scan pausing at the scabbard on my belt.

"It's locked away," Theo said on my behalf. "I'll give you all the details later. It is a long story."

"Took like fifteen straight minutes," Roger said with a grin.

"You're all awful," I said. "But I love you anyway."

"Okay," she said with a nod, her final determination.

I felt like I'd won a prize: I'd gained her confidence.

"Petra and Lulu are going to figure out a way to pry some of the extra magic out of Black," I said. "And then it's go time."

"And if the magic doers can make that happen, how do we get him to where we need him to be?" Gwen asked.

"Monster is the lure," Connor said. "When we tell Black we're ready to deal, he's gonna come running."

My screen buzzed, and I pulled it out. Then my blood went cold.

It was a message from an unknown number, with a single image of Kieran Swift. He stood against a building, arms spread and bound by gleaming chains. Probably silver, which was kryptonite to shifters.

Then a second message appeared—a single phrase.

COME GET HIM.

I showed Connor and the team. This time, I was the one who had to hold Connor back. And it wasn't easy. He was a shifter in his prime, with the power of an alpha, and Black had threatened Pack. Maybe not his Pack, but Pack all the same.

I moved in front of him, a physical barrier between him and the door. And he did not like that.

"This is my problem," he said, "and I will fix it."

"No," I said, "this is *our* problem, and we will fix it when our plan is ready. Remember that Black doesn't care about Swift or you."

I immediately felt guilty when I remembered the curiosity in Black's gaze when he'd seen Swift the night before. Was that when he'd concocted his plan?

"He cares about monster and incidentally me. He cares about himself most of all. He thinks this will get us where he wants us to be, so he can proceed to take Sorcha's magic out of me." The sword shimmied.

Petra was already on her screen with the sorcerers. Roger and Theo searched for data in the picture or the file that might tell us where Swift was being held.

"You need to call your dad and tell him we'll get Swift back. And then the Pack is going to have to give us room."

His eyes flashed like those of a predator in moonlight, a plain warning that I would ignore at my own peril. "The Pack will do what it has to do."

"Run full on into a trap? Put more shifters in danger?"

Connor's lips curled. Magic rolled off his body, thickening the air in the room.

Not one to miss a chance, Petra took off her gloves and wiggled her fingers in the air, presumably to collect Connor's magic. A good idea, given the possibility we'd need a bolt from her later.

Connor looked down at me, and this time he let me see the conflict in his eyes. The fury, fear, and grief multiplied by all-American adrenaline.

"You know you can trust us to get him to safety."

I put a hand on Connor's chest, felt his heart beating a fast tattoo as his body prepared to fight. With my hand there, a reminder he didn't have to fight alone, it began to slow.

"You want some scritches?"

He growled.

"Not yet ready for sarcasm. Acknowledged. Let's use our brains," I said. "How could Black have gotten Swift?"

"Went willingly," Connor said. "Or was alone."

"Agreed. I don't think Black's brave enough to take on the entire Pack by himself. He might be powerful enough, but he's not brave enough."

And we hadn't heard from anyone that other shifters had been injured or found dead.

"Maybe Swift went out for a run," I said. "Shifters like exercising, even solo. Maybe Black was watching him, doing some surveilling, saw Swift jogging. Black decided he'd make a good bargaining chip. Used magic to pick him up and take him to wherever that is." I gestured to my screen. "And kept him alive, because he wanted me—us—to have an incentive to hurry. To go in so hard and quick that we ignored the risks and consequences. Which we aren't going to do."

Connor's chest tensed against my hand.

"Call your dad," I said again. "Get Alexei and Lulu over here. We'll put together a plan to get Swift back in one piece. Buy us as much time as you can."

"We've got a location," Theo announced. He gestured to the wall screen, where the image of Kieran Swift was now displayed.

I took Connor's hand, squeezed hard as fury had him stiffening again.

"How do you know?" I asked.

I scanned the image left to right, then up and down, trying to understand what Theo had seen. But I found nothing familiar. The wall behind Swift was empty—blue corrugated steel, it looked like. Not unlike the paneling on the Reeds' building.

"GPS information in the file?" Connor asked.

"No, Black was smart enough to delete the metadata before he sent it. This was trickier."

Theo zoomed in on a link of silver chain that bound Swift to the pole, and he kept zooming in until we could see a faint reflection in the metal. It was the vague outline of a large yellow block letter.

"Chicago Industrial Port," I said, and my own adrenaline started pumping.

"Give the vampire a prize," Theo said. "Fortunately for us, the image has a ridiculously high resolution."

"How could he do this there?" Connor asked.

"The entire facility has been closed since the explosion," Theo said. "The forensic work is done, but there aren't enough humans left to run the place, and demons are still on the loose."

I turned to put the image at my back; then I envisioned the sign visible in front of me but at a slight angle.

"Swift is on the opposite side of the facility from the Buckley warehouse," I concluded.

"If there's ever geographic Chicago *Jeopardy!*," Roger said, "I want you on my team."

"Done," I said. "In the unlikely event."

The door burst open. Lulu came in first, followed by her parents.

"One wonders about the security of this building," Roger said with a smile. "What's the good word?"

"We've got something," Lulu said, moving to me. "It's not a guarantee—that little a-hole is sneaky. But we think it will work."

"Odds?" Connor asked.

"Sixty-eight percent," Uncle Catcher said. "He'll definitely think it's monster. He'll try to take it out, and that's where the risk comes in. The spell has to be completely uploaded for him to be completely depleted of demon and ley line magic. If he thinks something is amiss, he may stop midway."

And if he stopped midway, he might not be beatable. But we were on the clock, so we had what we had.

"We'll make it work," I said. "How long will it take you to set up?"

"We're ready when you are," Lulu said.

I glanced at Roger, got his nod. I looked up at Connor, and he squeezed my hand. Even Bloodletter bounced. It had no love for Jonathan Black.

"Now would be good," I said. "Let's finish this."

Roger and Theo coordinated with Gwen. Petra would provide backup. Connor and a few wolves he trusted, including Alexei and Dan, would also help, and they discussed protocol among themselves.

I pulled Lulu aside. "How bad is it going to be?"

"How bad is what going to be?"

I gave her a flat look. "We have to pretend Black is pulling out of me a sentience that's been there for two decades. The new thing won't have been there that long, but he's still going to try to drag it out. How bad is that going to hurt?"

"Not great. Maybe ripping a Band-Aid off a yeti?"

I nodded. That wouldn't be fun, but I'd live through it. "Anything else your parents don't want me to worry about?" It was the danger of well-meaning parents.

"You're going to be vulnerable while he's in there, so you want it to go as quickly as possibly. Don't distract him with too much fighting back. I mean, make it look realistic, but you want him to download as fast as he can." She glanced at the sword. "Maybe throw some energy his way. He doesn't know what the Egregore really feels like. But he knows what the *sword's* magic feels like."

It jiggled.

"How did you get your virus to feel like monster?" I asked.

"My mom ponied up some blood," Lulu said. "It was her magic, so her essence is part of monster's essence."

This was a very tangled web.

For the second time that week, I submitted to bespelling, which sounded more arch and Gothic than it actually was. I sipped a green sports drink while Lulu, with her mom's guidance and her dad's supervision, drew symbols on my arms with fragrant oil.

"This is the atmospheric magic," Lulu said. "It gives the right tang."

I nearly choked on green drink. "I don't think I want tang about my person, thanks."

"Six or eight showers and you'll be fine," Uncle Catcher said.

I was sixty-eight percent sure he was joking.

I felt heavier in the vehicle en route to the port, like the magic had added physical mass. Add that to monster's new position, and I was feeling a little unbalanced. And a little worried I hadn't had time to practice using Bloodletter. While it was nearly identical in weight and length to my sword—the one Black had snapped—the handle's diameter was different. Maybe only by millimeters but different. That could make a big difference in a martial art that relied in part on muscle memory.

"Don't get broken in half," I whispered to it, "or get me broken in half."

If a sword could snort, it did that.

"You know where you're supposed to go?" I asked Connor.

He sat beside me, arms folded and eyes closed, one curl over his forehead. He looked surprisingly relaxed. "I know," he said, and regarded me with the one eye he bothered to open. "I know that you're prepared and that you've gone through the scenarios a dozen times in your head. Now we get to bury him."

I knew his casual vibe was partly to keep me calm, which was one of his particular skills. I was the list maker, the box checker. At least until the fight started and the adrenaline began to flow.

I nodded, unsure. I still felt like I'd missed something.

Connor leaned over, lips brushing against my ear. "And when this is over," he said, voice low and full of magic, "we discuss wedding and honeymoon plans."

The tone, the words, the promising brush of skin against skin were enough to have my heart beating faster for an entirely different reason now.

"Quit flirting," I said. "Or I'll start talking about *Avengers* again."

"More flirting is not a deterrent," he said with a grin, and nipped my ear.

The port looked, even in the best light, like a zombie-movie setting. It was empty and silent, all movement stopped. Forklifts had been abandoned midload, their boxes perched in midair.

We stopped just inside the gate, those huge letters looming

ominously over us, spotlit for the employees who wouldn't be coming to work tonight. Which really worked out for the best.

I climbed out, belted on my scabbard. Checked that it was secure enough to allow for an easy draw. And damn if Bloodletter wasn't excited.

Alexei, Lulu, and Dan jumped out of a second vehicle. Both shifters were in a wolf form.

"I hope they let you drive," I told Lulu.

"He drove," she said, gesturing at Alexei. "Human form but naked the entire way."

Yeah. That checked out.

"Thanks for coming," I said, and gave him a scratch between the ears.

Gwen trotted over.

"Kieran?" Connor asked, and some of the earlier chill had fallen from his eyes.

"Alive," she said, voice flat. Connor wasn't the only one now in business mode. "But he's not looking good. That silver does a number on shifters."

"We need to get him out of there as soon as possible," Connor said.

I nodded. "He's your priority. Lulu's going to break through that magic. Dan, Alexei, and you are going to get him to safety." And since they couldn't actually touch the chains, a group of CPD uniforms would assist.

"And who will prioritize you?" Connor asked.

"We will," said Gwen as Petra joined her.

"My girls will," I said, adrenaline moving now. "Let's toast this asshole."

I went in first, since I was the one Black wanted. I walked slowly toward the building where Kieran had been bound. There was magic in the air, some of it demonic, but all of it Black's. I sensed no other demons; they were probably smart enough to avoid him now.

Kieran was chained; he wore shorts and a T-shirt in the evening chill. All of his visible skin was bruised, but I didn't know if that was from Black's treatment or the chains.

Black stood nearby, watched me approach. He wore a suit again today, but as I moved closer, I could see his clothes were dirty and rumpled. We knew from the continued surveillance that he hadn't been home; apparently, he didn't have another hideout.

The obsidian streaks that marked his skin had lengthened overnight and now stretched above his jawline like claws reaching up. The rest of his skin looked paler than usual, and there were shadows beneath his eyes.

I considered my approach. He wouldn't buy "damsel in distress" from me. But he might buy "This will get my boyfriend in trouble."

"Spread a little love," I quietly told monster. And got a tap in reply.

"Let him go," I told Black, striding toward him. "This has nothing to do with the Pack."

Black stepped forward and crossed his arms. "So, you acknowledge it has to do with us?"

"I acknowledge you wish it did," I said. "Let him go."

"Not until I get what I want."

"Did you think Sorcha would have left something for you?" I asked. "Is that why you went looking for her, hoping she left you a balm to fix your magic?"

"So you can do research," he said blandly.

The blast caught me unaware; I hadn't even seen him flinch. The bolt of Black's lightning hit me in the chest, shoved me backward like a fist. It took a light pole to stop me, and the force of my impact had metal groaning.

I hit the ground, bounced. And felt a trickle of blood on my lip, a little pain in my ribs from the contact. But otherwise, I felt okay. Good Sullivan genetics, I thought. No longer hidden by monster.

But ever the actress, I coughed and made a show of slowly climbing to my feet. "I guess that's a sore spot," I said, holding my ribs as I walked closer.

Brat, came Connor's voice.

I'm fine, I said, not entirely sure if this connection worked both ways. *Acting*.

"Let him go," I said again. "Or you die. The CPD is here, and the shifters are eager to get their hands on you."

Black's grin was feral. I didn't know how much of that was his own self-involvement and how much was madness caused by the vast volume of magic he'd absorbed. He flung his head back toward Swift, and black flame burst from the silver chains. The shifter reared back and screamed in obvious agony.

The sound cut through me like a sword. I rushed toward him, but Black turned, grabbed me. His fingers were ice-cold on my arm. I jerked to get away, but didn't put my full strength behind the movement. And that took effort. The corpselike temperature of his fingers was upsetting.

"He is immaterial," Black said. "He's only insurance. They take one step toward me, and he dies."

It was going to have to be the magic, then.

"You can't kill him," I said, and worked a little panic into my voice. "He's the nephew of the Apex of the Western Pack, next in line for the throne, and if he dies—"

"They'll take it out on your boyfriend?" Black leaned closer, the demonic stink burning the air. "That's what you get for lying with dogs."

"What do you want?"

"Sorcha's magic."

"Why do you get it? She didn't give it to you."

Apparently tired of our discussion, brief as it had been, he gripped both my arms now and shoved magic into me.

The violation was profound. Worse than what he'd tried the last time, because his magic was corrupted now, splintered with rot and decay. The magic stabbed through my brain, and this time my scream was real. He pulled, tried to yank the magic from my body. I went limp, and that wasn't acting—there was only my magic. Continuing to breathe through the pain was the only thing on my mind.

Black didn't care about my health. He let go of one of my arms and allowed me slip to the ground. But he kept contact with the other one, and apparently that was enough to transmit his magic.

"Stop," I managed, my head screaming.

And then the pain stopped. Not because *he'd* stopped, but because the Bell–Carmichael spell had kicked in. It wasn't fighting Black's magic, but easing it. Giving it something else to hold on to.

I wanted to lie there in that sudden bubble of bliss, pretend his magic had sent me into a stupor. But to make this believable, I still had pretending to do.

"Please," I said, my wrist encircled by his fingers. "Let me go."

"Not until I get . . . ," he said, then made a sound of pleasure that had me grimacing.

I risked a glance up. The sorcerers must have added some kind of mood enhancer to make Black feel like he was getting exactly what he deserved. His eyes rolled back as magic, bright and golden, floated above him, black wisps of smoke rising through it. The spell was working; he was losing the extra power.

But he jerked, and I risked another glance. He was staring at me—no, not at me, but at the magic.

I screamed again, put my free hand on my head. "Please, don't take it! Please. I need it. Please!" I conjured up tears, looked at him through them. "Please."

Black looked at me for another moment, and then he jerked again, stumbled backward, ripping his hand away in the process—and severing the spell's connection.

Damn it, I thought. And hoped he'd been drained enough.

"What are you doing?" he asked.

"What?" I asked innocently, and reached out for his aura. But before I could tell how much magic he'd lost, he felt the inquiry and slapped me back with magic. Then he lashed out at Swift, tightening the man's chains until blood seeped from his arms.

"You think you can trick me?" Black said, voice echoing through the buildings and the cargo containers. "You think you are better and stronger?"

Ugh. I was sick of pretending.

I stood up, shook off the remainder of the spell. Then I tossed back my hair, unsheathed Bloodletter, and let my eyes silver. "No, you selfish asshole. I *know* I am."

Monster did a little jump, sending a sound like the peal of a bell across the port and cleaning out the residual echo of Black's voice.

"It's all swim!" I called out. "Everybody in the pool!"

Engines roared and footsteps thundered as cops, Ombuds, and shifters—an entire fleet of them on bikes—circled us. Lulu ran to help Swift. Petra took a position between those helping Swift and me facing Black.

For a moment, Black looked stunned and confused. Then that bled away, leaving only hatred. He turned sideways, gathered a ball of black smoke in his hand.

And the game was on.

We both attacked, me with a two-handed upward slice, him with mist. We both mostly dodged what came at us; I cut a stripe into his arm and reveled in the scent of his blood in the air. But the edge of his fireball grazed my shoulder. I sucked in a breath as the fire burned through my jacket, making my skin blister immediately.

I bared my fangs at Black.

I whipped forward, giving him no time to rest or regroup, and slashed up, then down. I caught his chest, the edge of his jaw—and some of those creeping obsidian streaks. They emerged as mist, dissipated. He grunted, but threw out an elbow that had me staggering sideways. I stayed on my feet, but Bloodletter's tip scraped the asphalt, sending up a shower of red sparks.

"Sorry," I told it, righting myself again.

Black looked at me, then at the sword. And lust flared in his eyes.

"You want it?" I asked. "Catch."

Trusting Bloodletter, I threw it like a spear. Black instinctively reached out a hand. The blade sliced a line through his palm. To his credit, he spun and caught it with his other hand, dark blood plunking onto the asphalt. And then he screamed and released the sword.

I dived, caught the sword, came up again.

"It burned me!" he shouted, staring now at his hands.

"Nicely done!" I told it earnestly, and enjoyed the warm purr.

Black lifted his gaze, fury fueling him now, and groaned as he gathered magic in his wounded hands. Then the black fireballs were moving. I dodged the first, but the second caught me in the hip, and the pain of shattering bone sucked the breath from my lungs.

I hobbled, trying to balance on one leg with a sword in my hand and tears in my eyes. I willed the bone to knit faster.

Teeth bared in anger and pain, Black rushed forward. I blocked, but he used magic to shove the sword aside. He grabbed my free hand, wrenched it, and put me on my knees.

"Can't fight a woman on her feet?" I asked.

"You talk too much. You have too much. You *are* too much. It's done."

"Is it?" I asked blandly.

Black threw out his hand for another volley. But other than blood dripping, nothing happened.

"You may not have noticed," I said, "but all that demon magic you collected has been evaporating above your head since you tried to rip the magic out of me. I guess I didn't mention we planted a virus."

He let go of my hand, then put his own atop his head as if to feel the seeping magic.

I rose. I was unsteady but on my feet, blood still trickling down my face. I raised my sword, struggling to keep my balance.

"I may talk too much," I said. "I may have more than I deserve. But I am just right. And I am done. I run you in, or you take a knee. You have three seconds to decide."

Hatred boiled off him.

"Two."

His lip curled.

"One," I said, and let the tip draw blood.

A coward at heart, he dropped to his knees.

And then he grunted and keeled over.

"Sorry!" Behind him, Lulu looked totally unrepentant about the blue smoke rising from his back. "Must've slipped."

Gwen walked closer, nudged him with a foot. "Is he dead?"

"No," Lulu said. "Just napping, and he'll have one hell of a headache when he wakes up." Her grin was feral. "Whoopsy."

"Love to see it," Gwen said, then whistled for the roundup team. "Box him up!"

I let them handle that, ran to where Swift was now on the ground. The chains were a pile of smoking metal a few yards away.

"I didn't know silver could smoke," I said to Petra.

She grinned. "You put enough power into it, pretty much anything will."

"Good job."

A hand grabbed mine, and I turned to find Connor. He looked worn down—that silver again—but alive.

"You were magnificent," he said, and kissed me lavishly, hungrily, greedily as if he wanted nothing else for the rest of his life.

And though we were surrounded by cops and sups and shifters and sorcerers, I let him.

The sun rose, and the cleanup began. Invasive trees and shrubs that the rewilding ley lines had added to the city were cleared away. Repairs began in earnest on roads and buildings. The port was reopened. And slowly, over the coming days, humans began to file back in. And many of them paused to snap photos at the new plaques that marked the outer edges of the demon ward. Uncle Catcher thought that was a security risk; he didn't want anyone else to grok the bubble's precise dimensions. But the mayor overrode him, thinking the city's residents needed to understand what had gone on in their absence.

If Chicago's remaining demons stayed under the radar, hurt no one, they wouldn't be targeted. If they chose violence, we had salt and swords and sigils.

When Kieran was well enough to travel, we met at NAC headquarters to see him off.

"I can't thank you enough for what you did for me," he said.

"We got you into it," I said. "Only fair that we got you out."

He smiled. "I figured you'd say that, because you don't just talk the talk." He shifted his gaze to Connor. "Same goes for you. I wasn't sure what I'd find here. Maybe a coward. Maybe a man bewitched by a vampire. But I found a shifter who loves his people, his family, his woman. And will risk it all to save someone he barely knows."

Connor shook his head. "You're wrong that we're strangers. We fought together. Chewed demons together. That makes you Pack. And I don't put Elisa on the line." He looked at me. "She's just that brave. And she's Pack, too."

Kieran smiled. "You're lucky to have her. And I look forward to seeing you named Apex of the NAC. I'll be making sure the Western Pack is on board."

Connor watched him for a moment, nodded. Then he held out a hand, and they shook.

Kieran put on his helmet, climbed onto his bike, and rode into the darkness.

"Brave, huh?" I asked.

"Too brave," he said, and slid an arm around my waist. "But mine."

EPILOGUE

The sky was banded in pink and purple as twilight fell away. An arbor of graceful vines stood in a meadow that glowed from the light of hundreds of candles; the scent of night-blooming jasmine filled the air. Cicadas hummed in the trees.

A new fall was coming, and it would bring longer nights and chillier air. Winter would follow, with its rest and release before spring's new growth. The world would turn, and the sun would rise and sink, and the stars would shine through darkness as they had for millennia, lighting the way for anyone wise enough to look.

And love would persist.

Love would endure.

It was in the smile of the parents who held hands at the edge of the field.

It was in the grins of the new couples, their eyes full of promise as they waited for the ritual to begin.

It was in the tired but exhilarated faces of new parents, for whom their young children were new kinds of miracles.

It was in the excitement of friends and family and coworkers who'd traveled from across Chicago, or from across the country, and waited for the vows that would unite two families at long last.

First came the maid of honor and the best man. Her in a short dress of midnight blue; him in a tuxedo he swore he'd never wear. And in her arms, atop a silken pillow, was the demon cat who ruled them all.

And then came the groom—tall, with dark hair, the waves tamed back for the occasion, except for the curl that rebelled across his forehead. The tuxedo fit his strong body perfectly, but it was the thrill in his eyes that everyone noticed. The anticipation.

And when he saw her at the edge of the gathering, her hand on her father's arm, her hair a spill of golden curls below her shoulders, there was pride and love and victory.

She wore a crown of jasmine and a delicate dress of silk and lace that whispered as she moved.

Her father escorted her closer to the arbor; there was pride in his bearing, but it was joined there by loss. While he wasn't giving away his daughter, he was releasing her into a new night and a new adventure.

The bride reached the groom, and they stood together beneath the arbor the groom had built with his own hands. For her. For them.

Elisa Sullivan. The only vampire ever born.

Connor Keene. The wicked prince.

Elisa, seeing Connor resplendent in his tuxedo, smiled up at him. "You look beautiful."

That had his grin widening—becoming puppyish and wild at the edges.

"You look beautiful," he said in return, and his eyes didn't leave her face.

He vowed, then and there, in a silent promise to the glorious world that surrounded them, that he would look at her as often and as long as possible until his life was through. He would spend every moment cherishing her, supporting her, worshipping her.

For he knew in his bones, the way these things always seemed to be known, that he was hers and had been from the beginning.

He would love her, he vowed aloud, until the world stopped turning. And beyond, if he could.

She would love him, she vowed aloud, until there was no more night and no more her.

Love was a tricky thing, with its mix of blessing and curse, choice and fate. But it would be easier to bear—good and bad—because they were united. Because they protected each other.

When the ritual was done, Elisa's mother found her, embraced her tightly. "Someday," she whispered, "you'll tell me your entire story."

"Someday," Elisa said, brushing a tear from her mother's cheek. "But I think my story is just beginning."

Keep reading for an excerpt from the first
Captain Kit Brightling Novel,

THE BRIGHT AND BREAKING SEA

There was a ribbon pinned to her coat, and a dagger in her hand. And as Captain Kit Brightling stared down at the little wooden box, there was a gleam in her gray eyes.

Two months of searching between the Saxon Isles and the Continent. Two months of sailing, of storms and sun, of crazed activity and mind-dulling monotony.

They hadn't been sure what they'd find when the *Diana* set sail from New London—the seat of the Isles' crown, named for the city rebuilt after the Great Fire's destruction—only that they'd almost certainly find something. It had been nearly a year since the Gallic emperor Gerard Rousseau was exiled to Montgraf, since the end of the war that had spread death across the Continent like a dark plague. Gerard had finally been beaten back, his surrender and abdication just outside the Gallic capital city, Saint-Denis. The island nation of Montgraf, off the coast of Gallia, was now his prison, and a king had been installed in Gallia again.

There were reports of Gerard's growing boredom and irritation with his exile, with the inadequacies of the island he'd been exiled to, with the failures of his replacement. There were rumors of plans, of the gathering of ships and soldiers, of missives sent across the water. Queen Charlotte had bid Kit, the only captain in the Queen's Own Guards, to find those missives.

They'd patrolled the Narrow Sea that separated the Isles from the Continent, visiting grungy ports and gleaming cities, trading for information, or spreading coin through portside taverns when tipple loosened more tongues. Then they'd found the grimy little packet ship twenty miles off the coast, not far from Pencester. And in the captain's stingy quarters, in a drawer cleverly concealed in his bunk, they'd found the lovely little box.

She couldn't fault its design. Honey-colored wood, carefully hewn iron, and brass corners that gleamed even in the pale light of dawn. It was intended to hold secrets. And given its lock—a rather lovely contraption of copper and iron gears—hadn't yet been triggered, it still did.

Secrets, Kit thought ruefully, were the currency of both war and peace.

"You can't touch that."

That declaration came from the sailor in the corner.

"I believe I can," Kit said, sliding the dagger into her belt and lifting the box from the drawer. She placed it on the desk that folded down from the worm-holed bulkhead, then glanced up. "It now belongs to Queen Charlotte."

"It already did," sneered the man, his teeth the same yellowed shade as his grimy shirt. His trousers were darker; the cap, which narrowed to a point that flopped over one eye, was the sickly green of week-old bread. "I'm from the Isles, same as you, and I'm to deliver that to her. You saw the flag."

"The flag was false," said the lanky man's captor. Jin Takamura was tall and elegantly built, with a sweep of long dark hair pulled back at the crown. His skin was tan, his eyes dark as obsidian in an oval face marked by his narrow nose and rounded cheekbones. And his gleaming sabre was drawn and currently at the neck of the grungy sailor.

Kit thought Jin, second in command of the *Diana*, complemented her perfectly—his patience and canny contemplation, matched against her desire to go, to see, to do. There was no one she trusted more.

"You've no papers, no letters of marque," Jin said, looking over the sailor's dingy clothes. "And certainly no uniforms."

"You aren't from the Isles," Kit concluded, "any more than this box is." She walked toward the pair, smelling the sweat and fish and unwashed body emanating from the smuggler three feet away. Baffling, since water, salty or not, was readily available.

Kit was slender and pale-skinned, with dark hair chopped to skim the edge of her chin. Her eyes were wide and gray, her nose straight, her lips full. She clasped her hands behind her back when she reached the two men, and cocked her head. "Would you like to tell us from whom you obtained it, and to whom it will be delivered?"

"It's for the queen," he said again. "A private gift of some . . . unmentionables. A fine lady like you shouldn't have to deal with that sort of thing."

Kit's brows lifted, and she glanced at Jin. "The queen's unmentionables, he says. And me a fine lady."

"Maybe we should let him return to his business," Jin said, gaze falling to the box, heavy and full of secrets. "And avoid the impropriety."

"Best you do," the sailor said with a confident bob of his chin. "Don't want no impro—whatever here."

"Unfortunately," Kit said, "we're well aware that's nonsense. You're smugglers, running the very nice Gallic brandy in your hold, not to mention this very pretty box. But because I'm a pleasant sort, I'm going to give you one last opportunity to tell us the truth. Where did you get the box?"

"Unmentionables," he said again. "And you don't scare me. Trussed up in fancy duds or not, you're still a girl."

At four-and-twenty years, Kit was more woman than girl, but she was still one of the youngest captains in the Crown Command—the Saxon Isles' military—and there were plenty who'd thought her too young or too female to hold her position. But she'd earned her rank on the water. At San Miguel, by finding deep magic, and reaching for the current just long enough to give her ship the gauge against a larger squadron of Frisian ships—and capture gold and munitions that Queen Charlotte was very pleased to add to her own armory. At Pointe Grise, she'd helped her captain avoid an attack by a larger Gallic privateer, and they'd captured the privateer's ship and the coded dispatches it was carrying to Saint-Denis. At Faulkney, as a young commander, she'd found a disturbance in the current of magic, and led her own squadron to a trio of Gallic ships led by an Aligned captain that had made it through the Isles' blockade and was racing toward Pencester to attack. Kit's ship successfully turned back the invasion.

"Am I a trussed-up girl or fine lady?" Kit asked. "You can't seem to make up your mind." She glanced down at the trim navy jacket with its gold braid and long tails, the gleaming black boots that rose to her knees over buff trousers. "Personally, I enjoy the uniform. I find it affords a certain . . . authority." She glanced at Jin, who nodded, his features drawn into utter seriousness.

"Oh, absolutely, Captain," said Jin, whose uniform was in the same style. "Should I just slit his neck here, or haul him up with the others? August said the dragons are swarming again. Sampson is strong enough to throw him over."

Sampson, another of Kit's crew, nearly filled the doorway with muscles and strength. He smiled, nodded.

That was enough to prompt a response. "I've got information," the smuggler said, words tumbling out.

"About what?" Kit asked. "Because I don't want to hear any further details about the queen's unmentionables."

"Gods save the queen," Jin said with a smile.

"Gods save the queen," Kit agreed, then lifted her brows at the smuggler. "Well?"

"I've information about . . ." His eyes wheeled between them. "About smuggling?"

That he'd made it a question suggested to Kit he really was as oblivious as he pretended to be.

She sighed, made it as haggard as she could. "You know, while Commander Takamura is quite skilled with that sabre, and the dragons probably are swarming—it's that time of year," she added, and Jin nodded his agreement. "Those aren't the things you should be really and truly worried about."

The smuggler swallowed hard. "What do you mean?"

Kit leaned forward, until she was close enough that he could see the sincerity in her eyes. "You should be afraid of the water. It's so dark, and it's so cold. And sea dragons are hardly the only monsters that hunt in its depths." She straightened up again, walked a few paces away, and pretended to look over the other furniture in the room. "Being eaten quickly—devoured by a sea dragon—would be a mercy. Because if you survive, and you sink, you'll go into the darkness."

She looked back at him. "I'm Aligned, you know. I can feel the sea, the rise and fall, like an echo of my heartbeat. I hear a tune just for you, ready to call you home." She took a step closer. "Would you like to be called home?"

She wasn't normally so poetic, or so full of nonsense, but she found getting into character useful in times like this. And it had the man swallowing hard. But he still wasn't talking.

She glanced up at Jin, got his nod. And then he braced an arm against the hull. Behind him, Sampson did the same. They knew what was coming. Knew what she was capable of.

She had to be careful; there was a line that couldn't be crossed, a threshold that couldn't be breached. But before that border, there was power. Potential.

Using her magic, Kit reached out for the current, for the heat and energy, for the ley line that shimmered below them in the waters. She touched it—as carefully as a violinist pressing a string—and the *Amelie* shuddered around them, oak creaking in the wake.

Her trick wasn't familiar to the prisoner. "Gods preserve us," he said, stumbling forward, face gone pale. Jin caught him by the collar, kept him upright, and when he gained his footing again, his eyes had gone huge.

"More?" Kit asked pleasantly.

"I don't know where it came from," the man blurted out, "and that's the gods' truth. I'm in the—I only make the deliveries."

"You're a smuggler," Kit said again, tone flat.

"If we're not being fine about it, yes. I pick up the goods in Fort de la Mer, and I get a fee for delivering them. I don't ask what's in the cargo."

Fort de la Mer was a Gallic village perched on the edge of the Narrow Sea in the thin strait that ran between the Isles and Gallia. It was a busy port for merchants and smugglers alike.

"Delivered to whom?"

"I don't know."

Kit cast her glance to the window, to the ocean that swelled outside.

"All right, all right. There's a pub in Pencester," he sputtered. "The Cork and Barrel. I'm to drop it there."

Pencester was directly across the sea and strait from Fort de la Mer. "To whom?" Kit asked again.

"Not to somebody," he said. "To something. I mean, there's a spot I'm to leave it. A table in the back. I'm to leave the box beneath the bench. That's all I know," he added as Kit lifted a dubious brow. "I deliver, and that's all."

Kit watched him for a moment, debated the likelihood he'd told the entire truth. And decided the Crown Command could wring any remaining information out of him in New London.

"Sampson, put him with the others."

The smuggler blustered as he was led away, muttering about prisoners' rights.

She glanced back, found Jin looking at her with amusement. "'*I hear a tune just for you,*'" he intoned, voice high and musical, "'*ready to call you home.*' That's a new one. And very effective."

"Total nonsense," Kit admitted with a grin. "Sailors like him don't care much for the sea. There's no love, no appreciation. Only fear. One might as well make use of it." She gestured toward the box. "Do you think you can manage the lock?"

Jin just snorted, pulled a thin metal tool from his pocket, crouched in front of the box, and began to work the complicated arrangement of gears and cylinders. He closed his eyes, face utterly serene as, Kit imagined, he focused on the feel of the metal beneath his long and slender fingers.

He'd been a thief once, and very accomplished. But war had made patriots of many, including Jin, who'd used his spoils to purchase a commission. She'd met him at a pub in Portsdon, a lieutenant who'd just lifted from an arrogant dragoon the coins the dragoon had refused to pay for his dinner. The pub owner was paid, and the dragoon was none the wiser. But Kit had seen the snatch, was impressed by the method and the kindness. And was pleased to discover he'd been assigned to the ship on which she served as commander. That wasn't the last time his skills had come in handy.

"There's no ship that's floating but has a thief aboard," she murmured, repeating the adage.

Jin smiled as he tucked away his tool. "We are useful."

He flipped open the latch and lifted the lid, the hinges creaking slightly against humidity-swollen wood. And then he reached in . . . and pulled out a thick packet of folded paper. He offered it to Kit, and it weighed heavy in her hand.

The papers were bound with thin twine and a seal of thick poppy-red wax. But no symbol had been pressed into the wax, and there was no other mark of the sender on the exterior. No indication the packet was from anyone official. Except that it had been sealed into this very nice box with the very nice lock, and hidden away in the captain's quarters, such as they were.

She slipped her dagger beneath the wax, unfolded the papers. And her heart beat faster as she saw what was written there. Nonsense, or so it appeared. Letters and numbers made up words that were incomprehensible in Islish or the little Gallic she could speak.

The message had been encoded. That alone would have been enough to confirm to Kit it was important, even though it wasn't signed. But she knew the hand, as well—the letters thin and tall and slanting, here in ink the color of rust. She'd seen it. Studied it. Had captured more than one such message before the Treaty of Saint-Denis.

Gerard had penned this message.

She wasn't surprised; this had, after all, been the purpose of her mission. But that didn't douse her growing anger—not just that Gerard was sending coded dispatches in clear violation of the terms of his exile, but that conditions of his exile were comfortable enough to afford him the opportunity. He'd been an emperor, the monarchs had said, stripped of his crown and his glory. He would have known better than to try again. But ego and ambition were rarely so rational.

"Captain," Jin quietly prompted, and she handed the packet to him, watched his face as he reviewed, and saw the light when he reached the same conclusion.

He looked up, dark eyes shining. "It needs decoding, but the handwriting . . ."

"Gerard's," Kit finished, and they looked at each other, nodded. They'd found something. They'd have to wait for the message to be deciphered, but they'd fulfilled their mission.

It was one more mark in her favor, added to the column of miles and missions and nights beneath lightning-crossed skies. One more chance to earn some part of the life she'd been given.

Kit was a foundling who'd been left outside the palace by parents who couldn't care for her—or simply didn't wish to do so. The ribbon now pinned to her uniform—silk and well-worn—had been tied to the basket in which she'd been found. It was the only tangible memory she had of her childhood, and it had become her talisman, her reminder.

She'd been taken in by Hetta Brightling, a widow who intended to use her wealth and connections to house and feed girls who had nowhere else to go. Kit had been fed, educated, and brought up to believe in her own skills and the importance of self-sufficiency. And to Kit's mind, each victory for queen and country helped balance those scales.

But for every victory, there was a matching loss.

"This was bound for Pencester," Jin said darkly.

Kit knew from his tone their thoughts were aligned. Someone inside the Isles was the intended recipient of this missive. Someone inside the Isles was receiving correspondence from Gerard.

At least one of her countrymen was a traitor.

Jin folded the papers, handed them back to her. Kit slipped the packet into her jacket and centered herself, reached down through wood and wave to the waters below, to the bright current of power and let its presence—powerful and inexorable—comfort her.

And when she was steady again, opened her eyes. She had a crew to congratulate.

Chloe Neill is the *New York Times* and *USA Today* bestselling author of the Captain Kit Brightling, Heirs of Chicagoland, Chicagoland Vampires, Devil's Isle, and Dark Elite novels. She was born and raised in the South but now makes her home in the Midwest, where she lives with her gamer husband and their canine boss, Baxter. Chloe is a voracious reader and obsessive Maker of Things; the crafting rotation currently involves baking and quilting. She believes she is very witty; her husband has been known to disagree.

VISIT CHLOE NEILL ONLINE

ChloeNeill.com
AuthorChloeNeill
ChloeNeill

Ready to find
your next great read?

Let us help.

Visit prh.com/nextread

Penguin
Random
House